GEORGIA
ON MY MIND
AND OTHER PLACES

Tor Books by Charles Sheffield

Cold as Ice
Georgia on My Mind and Other Places
Godspeed
One Man's Universe

CHARLES SHEFFIELD

GEORGIA
ON MY MIND
AND OTHER PLACES

A TOM DOHERTY ASSOCIATES BOOK
NEW YORK

This is a work of fiction. All the characters and events portrayed in this book are fictitious, and any resemblance to real people or events is purely coincidental.

GEORGIA ON MY MIND AND OTHER PLACES

A Tor Book
Published by Tom Doherty Associates, Inc.
175 Fifth Avenue
New York, N.Y. 10010

Tor® is a registered trademark of Tom Doherty Associates, Inc.

Design by Lynn Newmark

Library of Congress Cataloging-in-Publication Data

Sheffield, Charles.
    Georgia on my mind, and other places / Charles Sheffield.
        p.   cm.
    "A Tom Doherty Associates book."
    ISBN 0-312-85663-6
    1. Science fiction, American.   I. Title.
    PS3569.H39253G46   1995
    813'.54—dc20   94-41077
                                                                  CIP

First edition: March 1995

Printed in the United States of America

0 9 8 7 6 5 4 3 2 1

Copyright Acknowledgments

For Diane

CONTENTS

INTRODUCTION

This book contains fourteen stories written over the past nine years. They range in length from short offerings of little more than a page ("Millennium," "That Strain Again . . .") to long novelettes ("Georgia on My Mind"). They also range in mood from silly to personal and serious.

If you have read any of my previous collections of short stories you will not be expecting much more than this by way of introduction. I see little point in talking about stories before you read them, because no matter what I say each one has to stand or fall on its merits. Introductory words, by me or anyone else, can't change that.

However, I do think that it is nice to give each story its own short afterword, saying how it came to be written and what I was trying to do in it. Then you can judge if I succeeded or failed.

I have one other comment, addressed to any reader worried about the repackaging of old material under a new title: I have published five other collections of short stories, *Dancing with Myself, One Man's Universe* (which, to avoid confusion, I will point out is an expanded version of *The McAndrew Chronicles*), *Erasmus Magister, Vectors,* and *Hidden Variables*. None of these stories has ever appeared before in collected form other than in Best-of-the-Year anthologies, and there is no overlap of material between this book and my other five story collections.

GEORGIA
ON MY MIND
AND OTHER PLACES

THE FEYNMAN SALTATION

THE WORM IN the apple; the crab in the walnut . . . Colin Trantham was
adding fine black bristles to the crab's jointed legs when the nurse called
him into the office.

He glanced at his watch as he entered. "An hour and a quarter the
first time. Forty minutes the second. Now he sees me in nine minutes.
Are you trying to tell me something?"

The nurse did not reply, and Dr. James Wollaston, a pudgy fifty-
year-old with a small mouth and the face of a petulant baby, did not
smile. He gestured to a chair, and waited until Trantham was seated on
the other side of his desk.

"Let me dispose of the main point, then we can chat." Wollaston
was totally lacking in bedside manner, which was one of the reasons that
Colin Trantham liked him. "We have one more test result to come, but
there's little doubt as to what it will show. You have a tumor in your left
occipital lobe. That's the bad news. The good news is that it's quite operable."

"Quite?"

"Sorry. *Completely* operable. We should get the whole thing." He
stared at Trantham. "You don't seem surprised by this."

Colin pushed the drawing across the table: the beautifully detailed
little crab, sitting in one end of the shelled walnut. "I'm not an idiot.
I've been reading and thinking cancer for weeks. I suppose it's too much
to hope it might be benign?"

"I'm afraid not. It is malignant. But it appears to be a primary site.
There are no other signs of tumors anywhere in your body."

"Wonderful. So I only have cancer *once.*" Trantham folded the drawing and tucked it away in his jacket breast pocket. "Am I supposed to be pleased?"

Wollaston did not answer. He was consulting a desk calendar and comparing it with a typed sheet. "Friday is the twenty-third. I would like you in the night before, so we can operate early."

"I was supposed to go to Toronto this weekend. I have to sign a contract for a set of interior murals."

"Postpone it."

"Good. I was afraid you'd say cancel."

"Postpone it for four weeks." Wollaston was pulling another folder from the side drawer of his desk. "I propose to get you Hugo Hemsley. He and I have already talked. He's the best surgeon east of the Rockies, but he has his little ways. He'll want to know every symptom you've had from day one before he'll pick up a scalpel. How's the headache?"

The neurologist's calm was damping Colin's internal hysteria. "About the same. Worst in the morning."

"That is typical. Your first symptom was colored lights across your field of vision, sixty-three days ago. Describe that to me. . . ."

The muffled thump on the door was perfunctory, a relic of the days when Colin Trantham had a live-in girlfriend. Julia Trantham entered with a case in one hand and a loaded paper bag held to her chest with the other, pushing the door open with her foot and backing through.

"Grab this before I drop it." She turned and nodded down at the bag. "Bought it before I thought to ask. You allowed to drink?"

"I didn't ask, either." Colin examined the label on the bottle. "Moving up in the world. You don't get a *Grands Echézeaux* of this vintage for less than sixty bucks."

"Seventy-two plus tax. When did you memorize the wine catalog?"

"I'm feeling bright these days. When a man knows he is to be hanged in a fortnight, it concentrates his mind wonderfully."

"No points for that. Everybody quotes Johnson." Julia Trantham pulled the cork and sniffed it, while her brother was reaching up into the cabinet for two eight-ounce glasses.

"You're late." Colin Trantham placed the thin-stemmed goblets on the table and watched as Julia poured, a thin stream of dark red wine. His sister's face was calm, but the tremor in her hand was not. "The plane was on time. You went to see Wollaston, didn't you, before you came here?"

"You're too smart for your own good. I did."

"What did you find out?"

Julia Trantham took a deep breath. Colin had always been able to see through her lies, it would be a mistake to try one now. "It's a glioblastoma. A neuroglial cell tumor. And it's Type Four. Which means—"

"I know what it means. As malignant as you can get." Colin Trantham picked up his glass, emptied it in four gulps, and walked over to stand at the sink and stare out of the kitchen window. "Christ. You still have the knack of getting the truth out of people, don't you? I had my little interview with Dr. Hemsley, but he didn't get as honest as that. He talked *procedure.* Day after tomorrow he saws open my skull, digs in between the hemispheres, and cuts out a lump of my brain as big as a tennis ball. Local anesthetic—he wants me conscious while he operates."

"Probably wants you to hold tools for him. Like helping to change a car tire. Sounds minor."

"Minor for *him.* He gets five thousand bucks for a morning's work. And it's not *his* brain."

"Minor operation equals operation on somebody else."

"One point for that. Wish it weren't *my* brain, either. It's my second favorite organ."

"No points—that's Woody Allen in *Sleeper.* You're all quotes today."

Colin Trantham sat down slowly at the kitchen table. "I'm trying, Julia. It's just not . . . easy."

The casual brother-sister jousting shattered and fell away from between them like a brittle screen. Julia Trantham dropped into the seat opposite. "I know, Colin. It's not easy. It's awful. My fault. I'm not handling this well."

"Not your fault. Everybody's. Mine too, same problem. You go through life, build your social responses. Then you get a situation they just don't cover. Who wants to talk about *dying,* for Christ's sake?" There was a long silence, but the tension was gone. Colin Trantham stared at his older sister's familiar face, unseen for half a year. "I'm scared, Julie. I lie awake at night, and I think, I won't make old bones."

Little brother, hurt and crying. We're grown-ups now. We haven't hugged in twenty years. "Social responses. I'm supposed to say, don't be scared,

Col, you'll be fine. But while I say it I'm thinking, you're *scared*, no shit? Of course you're scared. Me, I'd be petrified. I *am* petrified."

"Will you stay until the operation's over?"

"I was planning to. If it's all right with you, I'll hang around until you're out of the hospital. Write up a paper on extinct invertebrates that I've had in the mill for a while." She poured again into both glasses, emptying the bottle. "Any girlfriend that I need to know about, before I embarrass her by my drying panty hose?"

"Rachel. Just a now-and-again thing." Colin Trantham picked up the empty bottle and stared at the layer of sediment left in the bottom, divining his future. "Should we have decanted it? I hardly tasted that first glass. I'll try to sip it this time with due reverence." The raw emotion was fading, the fence of casual responses moving back into position. "No problem with Rachel. If she finds you here with me I'll just pretend you're my sister."

The waiting room was empty. Julia dithered on the threshold, possessed by conflicting desires. She wanted news, as soon as it was available. She also wanted a cigarette, more than she had ever wanted one, but smoking was forbidden anywhere in the hospital.

Dr. Wollaston solved her problem before she could. He approached along the corridor behind her and spoke at once: "Good news. It went as well as it possibly could go."

The nicotine urge was blotted out by a rush of relief.

"Minimum time in the operating room," the neurologist went on. "No complications." He actually summoned a smile. "Sedated now, but he wanted you to see this. He said that you would know exactly what it means."

He held out a piece of paper about five inches square. At its center, in blue ink, a little figure of a hedgehog leered out at Julia, cheeks bulging. She could feel her own cheeks burning. "That's me—according to Colin. Private family joke."

"Drawn right *after* the operation, when Hemsley was testing motor skills. Astonishing, I thought."

"Can I see him?"

"If you wish, although he might not recognize you at the moment. He should be sleeping. Also"—a second of hesitation, picking words carefully—"I would appreciate a few minutes of your time. Perhaps a glass of wine, after what I know has been a trying day for you. This is"—Julia sensed another infinitesimal pause—"primarily medical matters. I need to talk to you about your brother."

How could she refuse? Walking to the wine bar, Julia realized that he had talked her out of seeing Colin, without seeming to do so. Typical James Wollaston, according to Colin. Gruff, sometimes grumpy; but smart.

His eyes were on her as they settled in on the cushioned round stools across a fake hogshead table, and she took out and lit a cigarette.

"How many of those a day?"

"Five or six." Julia took one puff and laid down the burning cigarette in the ashtray. "Except I'm like every other person who smokes five—a pack lasts me a day and a half."

"You're going to regret it. It's murder on your skin. Another ten years and you'll look like a prune."

"Skin? I thought you were going to tell me about my heart and lungs."

"For maximum effect, you have to hit where it's least expected. You ought to give it up."

"I was going to. I really was. But you know what happened? Since Mother died, Colin and I have called each other every week."

"Sunday midday."

"That's right. How'd you know?"

"I know a lot about you and Colin."

"Then you know Colin's not one for overstatement. He hadn't said a word about . . . all this. When the evidence was in, he hit me with it all at once. It floored me. I'd got up that morning determined that I was through, that was *it* for cigarettes. I'd just thrown a near-full pack away." She laughed shakily. "Looks like I picked a hell of a day to quit smoking."

"That's from *Airplane*. No points, I think your brother would say."

"My God. You really do know a lot about us."

"When it was clear to me that Colin might have a serious problem, I put him through my biggest battery of tests, checking his memory and his reflexes and his logical processes. We also went over all his background. As a result I know a great deal about you, too, your background, what you do." He paused. "I even understood about the hedgehog, though it didn't seem the best time and place to mention it. Anyway, how's the paleontology business?"

"Just scratching out a living. Sorry. Programmed response. In a very interesting state. You see, every few years there's a major upheaval—facts, or theories. New radioactive dating, punctuated equilibrium, Cretaceous extinctions, mitochondrial DNA tracking, the reinterpretation of the Burgess Shale. Well, it seems we're in for another one. A biggie."

"So I have heard."

"You have? Well, not from Colin, that's for sure."

"True. I read it."

"Fossils bore him stiff. He says that Megatherium was an Irish woman mathematician."

A moment's thought. "Meg O'Theorem?"

"That's her. He was all set to be a mathematician or a physicist himself, 'til the drawing and painting bug took hold. He's the talented one, you know—I'm just the one who wrote papers and stayed in college forever. Anyway, first he started to paint in the evenings, and then—" She stopped, drew breath, and shook her head. "Sorry, doctor. I'm babbling. Nerves. You wanted to talk."

"I do. But I like to listen, too—unless you're in a big hurry?"

"Nothing in the world to do but sit here and listen."

Wollaston nodded. The wine had arrived and he was frowning at the label. "I hope this isn't too lowbrow. It's certainly not the *Grands Crus* that you and your brother like to sample. It's a naive domestic burgundy without any breeding, but I think you'll be amused—"

"—by its presumption. No points. But I get one for finishing the line."

"I need practice, or I'll never be a match for the two of you." He poured the first splash of wine, and in that instant seemed to become a younger and more vulnerable person. "A successful operation. That was the first stage. It is now behind us. Did your brother discuss with you what might happen next?"

Julia shook her head. Colin had not raised the subject, nor had she. Somehow it had not seemed significant before the operation. "Chemotherapy?"

"Not with the conventional antimetabolites. They have difficulty crossing the blood-brain barrier. The normal next step would be radiation. But a glioblastoma is fiercely malignant. Bad odds. I want to try something that I hope will be a lot better. However, I wanted to obtain your reaction before I discussed it with Colin." Another pause, words chosen carefully. Julia nodded her internal approval. A good, cautious doctor. "I'd like to put him onto an experimental protocol," continued Wollaston. "An implanted drug-release device inside the brain itself, with a completely new drug, a variable delivery rate, and an internal monitor sensitive enough to respond to selected ambient neurotransmitter levels. It's tiny, and there will be no need to reopen the skull to install it."

He was not looking at her. Why not? "Price isn't an issue, Dr. Wollaston, unless it's out of this world. We have insurance and money. What are the side effects?"

"No consistent patterns. This is too new. And the implant would be done free, since your brother would be part of a controlled experiment. But"—the kicker, here it came, he was finally looking into her eyes—"Colin would have to fly to Europe to get it. You see, it's not yet FDA approved."

"He'd have to *stay there?*"

His surprise was comical. "Stay there? Of course not. He could fly over one night, have the implant performed the next day, and as soon as the surgeon there approved his release he'd turn right around and come back. But I'm not sure how Colin will react to the idea. What do you think? It's doesn't have FDA approval, you see, so—"

"I don't think. I *know.* Colin doesn't give a tinker's damn about the FDA. He'll do it." Julia stubbed out her cigarette, burned its whole length unnoticed in the ashtray. "Of course he'll do it. Colin wants to live."

She took a first sip of wine, then two big gulps. "What next?"

"On medical matters? Nothing. I'm done. More wine. Relax. Your turn to talk." He was smiling again. "I hope you don't have to run off right away." Julia was staring all around her. His smile vanished. "Do you?"

Julia was still scanning the wine bar. "Where are all the waiters? You know, I didn't eat one thing all day. I'm absolutely famished. How do you order food in this place?"

Walking back to Colin's apartment through the mellow April evening, Julia Trantham was filled with guilt. Ten hours ago a malignant tumor the size and shape of a Bartlett pear had been removed from the brain of her brother. He was lying unconscious, gravely ill. While she . . .

For the past three hours she had managed to forget Colin's condition—and in the company of James Wollaston she had enjoyed herself hugely.

Concorde, Heathrow to Dulles; seventy thousand feet, supersonic over open ocean.

Colin Trantham sat brooding in a left-side window seat, staring out at blue-black sky and sunlit cloud tops. The plane was half-empty, with no one between him and the aisle. Occasional curious looks from flight attendants and other passengers did not bother him. He was beyond that, accepting their stares as normal, just as he accepted the head bandages and bristly sprouting hair. If his appearance were enough to stir curiosity, what would people say if they knew what sat *inside* his head?

Maybe they would be as unimpressed as he had been. Colin had been shown the device before its insertion, and seen nothing to suggest its powers: a swollen iridescent disk no bigger than his fingernail, surrounded by the hollow legs of sensors and drug delivery system. Superbeetle. An unlikely candidate to be his savior. He felt nothing, but according to the London doctors it had set to work at once. The battle was going on now. Deep within his skull, bloated with slow poison, the scarab was stinging the crab's microstases in silent conflict.

And the chance that it would succeed? No one would give him odds. Bad sign.

"Make a note of thoughts that strike you as unusual." Wollaston, on their last meeting before Colin flew to England, had maintained his imperturbability. "We can watch your stomach at work, or your gall bladder. But you're the only one who knows how normally your brain is functioning. Record your dreams."

"My *dreams?* Doctor Wollaston, even before I got sick, my dreams never made much sense."

"They don't have to. Remember what Havelock Ellis said: 'Dreams are real while they last; can we say more of life?' I want to know about them."

Colin was beginning to agree. Dreams and life, life and dreams; he had felt like telling Wollaston that his whole life had become one waking dream, on that morning when a headache came and grew and would not go. Since then nothing had been real. The pain had gone with the operation, but in its place was a continuous foreboding. *Never glad confident morning again.* He did not recall a real dream of any kind since the operation. And he did not want to write notes on his condition; he wanted it never to have happened.

The flight attendant had paused by Colin's row of seats and was staring at him questioningly. He did not want to talk to her; to avoid it he stared again out of the window. The sun was visible in the dark sky, farther toward the rear of the plane. At Mach Two they were outpacing it. Time was running backward. *Call back yesterday, bid time return.*

Colin shivered at a slow stir of movement, deep within his brain. Something there was waking from long sleep. He stared straight at the sun. His pupils contracted, his hands relaxed. Fully awake, he began to dream.

I was standing on a flat shore, watching the sea. Or maybe I was sitting, I can't tell because I had no sense of feeling of legs and arms. I just knew I was there. Enjoying the sunshine on my bare back, feeling good. More than good, absolutely terrific. Cold, perfect day, I could feel the blood running in my veins. Something must have died a mile or so offshore, or maybe it was a school of fish, because thousands of flying things were swooping and turning and settling. I decided I would swim out there and see for myself. . . .

Julia Trantham looked up from the third sheet. "Does it just go on like this for all the rest? Because if it does, I can't help. It's not specific enough."

"I know." Wollaston nodded. "It would have been nice if you could have said, hey, that's where we spent my fourteenth summer. But I didn't expect it would ring any particular bells. Keep reading, if you would—I want you to have the context for something else."

"And I thought you asked me here for dinner."

He did not reply. She went on in silence until she reached the last page, then looked up with raised eyebrows. "So?"

He took four pages of 20″×14″ unlined paper from a folder and slid them across the table. "Colin found what he had written as unsatisfactory as you do. He says he's an artist, not a writer. Pictures, not words. What do you make of these?"

The drawings were sepia ink on white background. Julia glanced for a few seconds at the first couple of sheets and put them aside, but the other two occupied her for a long time. James Wollaston watched her closely but did not speak or move.

"If you tell me these are all Colin's, I'll have to accept that they are."

She tapped the first two pages, spread out on the table of Wollaston's dining room. "But these ones sure don't look like it."

"Why not?"

"Not detailed enough." She picked up one of the sheets. "When you ask Colin to draw something, he draws it *exactly*. It's not that he lacks imagination, but he never cheats. Once he's seen it, he can draw it. And he sees more than you or I."

"He didn't see these. He dreamed them."

"You're the one who's been telling me that dreams are as real as anything else. Anyway, compare the first two pages with the others. These must be birds, because they're flying. But they're cartoon birds, vague wings and bodies and heads, almost as though Colin didn't care what they looked like. And now look at these other two, the tidal shell-fish and crabs and worms. Precise. Every joint and every hair drawn in. See this? It's *Pecten jacobaeus*—a scallop. Look at the eyes on the fringed mantle. You could use it as a textbook illustration. That's Colin's trade-mark. Same with the two lugworms. You can tell they're different spe-cies. But those first two pages are just *wrong."* She paused. "You don't see it, do you?"

"I can't argue with you." Wollaston stared at the pages as though he were seeing them for the first time. He had taken off his tie and draped it over a chair back, and now he picked it up and rolled it around his fore-fingers.

"But you don't like it," said Julia, "what I said about the first two sheets?"

"I do not."

"It's a bad sign?"

"I don't know. I know it's not a *good* sign. In Colin's situation the best change in behavior is no change."

"Do you think it's coming back?"

"I'd love to say, no, of course not. But I don't know. God, I hate to keep saying it to you. I don't know, I don't know. But it's the truth." He came closer, half a step nearer than convention permitted. "Julia, I wish I *could* say something more definite. It could be the treatment—new drug, new protocol, new delivery system."

"But you don't think it is."

"I think these drawings may be the effects of the treatment." He slid the sheets back into the folder. "But they're not the whole story. I go more by look and sound and sense. My gut feel says it's something more than side effects. I think Colin has problems. How long are you staying?"

"I've been wondering. I could stay the whole summer. It's late to do it, but if I moved fast I could even make part of next year a sabbatical. Should I?"

She was tense, hearing the question behind the question, not sure she wanted to hear the answer.

"I think you should." James Wollaston looked more miserable than an objective physician had a right to look. "I think you should stay, until—well, stay as long as you can."

The northern bedroom of the ground floor apartment had been converted to a studio, its bare expanse of window looking out onto a paved courtyard where weeds pushed up between cracked stones. The studio lay at the end of a corridor, far from the entrance to the apartment. Julia stood and listened as she came through the front door.

Total silence. That was odd. For the past three months her arrival had always produced a call of "Hi!" and a quick appearance in the kitchen to discuss dinner plans. He must be really deep into his work.

She slipped off her shoes and stole along the corridor.

Colin was in the studio, standing at the easel with his back half-turned to her. He was working in acrylics, and she saw a vivid flash of colors on the big board. She studied him as she came in. The hair on the back of his head had regrown completely, it must be two inches long now; but he was terribly thin, just gaunt bones, and the skin on his temple had a pale, translucent look. She saw that the food on the tray table beyond the easel was untouched. He must have eaten nothing since she left, over ten hours ago.

"Col?"

He did not seem to hear. He was painting furiously, brush strokes as rapid and sure as they had ever been. She came to his shoulder to examine the picture, but before she reached the easel she glanced up at his face. His gray eyes were unnaturally bright, and there was a smile of exquisite pleasure on his gaunt face. But it was not for Julia. He did not know that she was there. He was smiling away into some private space.

"Colin!" She touched his arm, suddenly frightened. The brush strokes faltered, the moving hand slowed. He blinked, frowned, and turned toward her. "Julie—" he said. "I'm through one barrier. It's wonderful, but now there's another. Bigger. I can't see a way past it yet." His hand jerked up and down, a quick chopping movement with the paint brush. "Like a wall. If I can just get through this one . . ."

The expression of ecstasy was replaced by surprise. He swayed and groaned, his lips drawing back from his teeth. Julia saw his gums, pale and bloodless, and the veinless white of his eyes. The brush fell to the floor. She grabbed for his arm, but before she could catch him he had crumpled forward, pawing at the painting and easel before falling heavily on top of them.

"I don't care *what* you tell Colin. I want your prognosis, no matter how bad it looks."

It was long after working hours. Julia Trantham was sitting at one end of the uncomfortable vinyl-covered couch in the doctor's reception room. Her face was as pale as her brother's had been, twenty-four hours earlier.

"At the moment Colin doesn't want to hear anything. Doesn't seem to care. That's not as unusual as you might think." Wollaston had been standing, but now he came to sit next to her. "People hide from bad news."

"And it *is* bad news. Isn't it?"

"It's very bad. And it's not a surprise." He sighed and leaned his head on the smooth yellow seat back. At dinner he had switched to martinis instead of the usual wine. Julia could see the difference. He was more talkative than usual, and he needed her to be an audience.

"I wonder what it will be like a hundred years from now," he went on. "The physicians will look back and think we were like medieval barbers, trying to practice medicine without the tools. All the cancer treatments except surgery are based on the same principle: do something that kills the patient, and hope it kills the cancer a bit faster. The antimetabolite drugs—like the ones in Colin's implant—kill cancer cells when the cells divide. But a few resistant ones survive, and they go on and multiply. I've seen it a thousand times. You start chemotherapy, and at first the patient does well, wonderfully well. Then over the months . . . the slip back starts."

"That's what's happened to Colin—even with this new experimental treatment?"

He was nodding, eyes closed and the back of his head still against the couch. "Experimental treatments are like lotteries. You have to play to win. But you don't win very often." He reached out blind and groped for her hand. "I'm sorry, Julia. We're not winning. It's back. Growing *fast*. I can't believe the change since the last CAT scan."

"How long, Jim?"

"I don't know. Pretty quick. Colin can come out of the hospital if he wants to, keeping him in won't help. A hospice might be better. A day or two, a few weeks, a month. Nobody knows."

"And there's no other treatment you can try?"

He said nothing. Julia stared across at the wall, where Wollaston had hung one of Colin's postoperative drawings, a lightning sketch of half a dozen lines that was clearly a picture of some kind of bird feeding her chick, the beak inside the little one's gaping bill and halfway down its throat.

"When did Colin draw the picture on the wall there?"

"About two weeks ago." Wollaston stirred. "It's wonderful, isn't it? Have you seen all the others—the ones he's done since the operation?"

"I haven't seen any. It's a habit we got into years ago. I wouldn't look at Colin's work when he was getting ready for a show or a delivery until the end, then I'd give him my opinion of the whole thing. He didn't like me in his studio."

"Maybe it's just as well. Some of the recent ones have been . . . strange."

"You mean he's losing his technique? God, to Colin that would be worse than dying."

"No. The *technique* is terrific. But the animals don't look right. For instance, he drew a pair of seals. But their flippers were too *developed*, too much like real legs. And there was one of a zebra, except it wasn't quite a zebra, more like a funny okapi. I wondered at first if the pictures could tell me something about what's going on in Colin's head, but they haven't. I'd say he's feeling strange, so he's drawing strange." He patted her hand. "I know, Julia, 'Colin draws just what he sees,' don't say it."

"Real legs, you say? And there's *wing claws* on that bird, that's what's odd. But it's not a baby hoatzin."

The hand was pulled from his. There was a rapid movement of the couch next to him. Wollaston opened his eyes. "Julia?"

But she was no longer by his side. She was over at the wall, gazing with total concentration at Colin's drawing. When she turned, her mouth was an open O of confusion and surmise.

"There they are." Julia Trantham patted a stack of papers, boards, and canvases. They were in Wollaston's office, with the big wooden desk swept clear and the table lamp on its highest setting. "Every one we could find. But instead of grouping according to medium and size, the way you usually would, I've rearranged them to chronological order. There are eighty-nine pictures here, all signed and dated. The top one is the first drawing that Colin made when he was flying back from England. The last one is the painting he was working on in his studio when he passed out. I want you to look through the whole stack before you say anything."

"If you say so." James Wollaston was humoring her, knowing she had been under terrible stress for months. It was close to midnight, and they had spent the last hour collecting Colin Trantham's pictures, pulling them from medical records and apartment and studio. Julia would not tell him what game she was playing, but he could see that to her it was far more than a game. He started carefully through the heap; pen and ink drawings, charcoal sketches, oils and acrylics and pencils.

"Well?" Julia was too impatient to wait for him to finish. She was staring at him expectantly although he was on only the tenth picture.

"Did he always draw nothing but nature scenes?" said Wollaston. "Just plants and animals?" He was staring at sheet after sheet.

"Mostly. Colin is a top biological illustrator. Why?"

"You insist he drew from life, from what he had seen. But in these pictures that doesn't seem to be true."

"Why not?" Julia pounced on him with the question.

"Well, I recognize the first drawings, and they're terrific. But this—" he held out the board he was examining "—it looks wrong."

"It's not wrong. That's a member of *Castoroidinae*—a rodent, a sort of beaver. Keep going. What's that one?"

"Damned if I know. Like a cross between a horse and a dog—as though Colin started by drawing a horse's head, then when he got to the body and legs he changed his mind."

"You were right about the horse. That's *Hyracotherium*. To the life. *Keep going.*"

But Wollaston had paused. "Are you sure? It looks strange to me, and I have a pretty good grounding in comparative anatomy."

"I'm sure you do." Julia took a painting from the stack. They were less than halfway through the heap. Her hands were trembling. *"Current* anatomy, Jim. But I specialize in *paleo*anatomy. Colin has been drawing real plants and animals. The only thing is, some of them are *extinct.* The *Castoroidinae* were giant beavers, big as a bear. They were around during the Pleistocene. *Hyracotherium's* a forerunner of the horse, it flourished during the Lower Eocene, forty or fifty million years ago. These pictures are consistent with our best understanding of their anatomy based on the fossil record."

She was shaking, but Wollaston did not share her excitement. "I'll take your word for it, Julia. But I want to point out that none of this is too surprising, given your own interests and the work you do."

"That's not true!" Julia fumbled out a cigarette, lit it, and inhaled hard enough to shrivel the bottom of her lungs. "It's more than surprising, it's *astonishing.* I told you the first time we had a drink together, what I do bores Colin stiff. He doesn't know beans about it and he doesn't care. There's *no way* he got these drawings from me. And do you realize that these pictures are in *reverse chronological order?* Fossil dating is a tricky business, I'm the first to admit that; but in this set, the more recently Colin did them, the older the forms represented."

"What are you *saying,* Julia?" The concern in Wollaston's voice was for sister more than brother. "If you're suggesting . . . what it sounds like you're suggesting, then it's nonsense. And there's a perfectly rational explanation."

"Like what?"

He reached forward, removed the cigarette from her fingers, and stubbed it out. "Julia, the longer you study the human brain, the more astonishing it seems. You say that what you do bores Colin. Probably true. But do you think that means he didn't even hear you, when you talked and talked paleontology all these years? Do you think he never picked up one of your books? They're scattered all over the apartment, I've seen them there myself. It's no wonder you recognize what Colin has been painting—because you put all those ideas into his head *yourself."*

"I didn't, Jim. I know I didn't. And here's why." She was turning the stack, moving down toward the bottom. "Now we're beyond the K-T barrier—the time of the late Cretaceous extinction. See this?"

The painting was in subdued oils, browns and ochers and dark greens, crowded with detail. The viewpoint was low to the ground, peering up through a screen of ferns. In the clearing beyond the leafy cover crouched three scaly animals, staring at a group of four others advancing from the left. The sun was low, casting long shadows to the right, and there was a hint of morning ground mist still present to soften outlines.

"Saurischians. Coelurosaurs, I'd say, and not very big ones." Julia pointed to the three animals in the foreground. "The pictures we were looking at before were all Tertiary or later. But everything beyond that is Cretaceous or *earlier*. I'd place this one as middle Jurassic, a hundred and sixty million years ago. No birds, no flowering plants. I know those three animals—but the four behind them are completely new to me. I've never seen anything like them. If I had to guess I'd say they're a form of small hadrosaur, some unknown midget relative of *Orthomerus*. That flat hulk, way over in the background, is probably a crocodile. But look at the detail on the coelurosaurs, Jim. I couldn't have told Colin all that—I couldn't even have *imagined* it. Look at the scales and wrinkles and pleats in the mouth pouch, look at the eyes and the saw-toothed brow ridges— I've never seen those on any illustration, anywhere. The vegetation fits, too, all gymnosperms, cycads, ginkgoes, and conifers."

James Wollaston laughed, but there was no suggestion from his face that he found anything funny. He was sure that Julia Trantham was practicing her own form of denial, of reality avoidance. "Julia, if you came in to see me as a patient and said all that, I'd refer you for immediate testing. Listen to yourself!"

But she had moved to the final drawing, smeared where Colin Trantham had fallen on top of it before it was dry. "And this is earlier yet." She was talking quietly, and not to Wollaston. He stared at her hopelessly.

"Something like *Rutiodon*, one of the phytosaurs. But a different jaw. And there on the left is *Desmatosuchus*, one of the aëtosaurs. I don't recognize that other one, but it has mammalian characteristics." She looked up. "My God, we must be back near the beginning of the Triassic. Over two hundred million years. These are thecodonts, the original dinosaur root stock. He's jumping farther and farther! Jim, I'm scared."

He reached out for her, and she clung to him and buried her face in his jacket. But her words were perfectly clear: "First thing in the morning, I've got to see Colin."

What James Wollaston had heard with incredulity, Colin Trantham listened to with a remote and dreamy interest. Julia had taken one look at him, and known that no matter what the neurologist might say, Colin would never be leaving the hospital. It was not the IVs, or the bluish pallor of his face. It was something else, an impalpable smell in the air of the room that made her look at her brother and see the skull beneath the skin.

Whatever it was, he seemed oblivious to it. He was grinning, staring at her and beyond her, his face filled with the same ecstasy that she had seen in the studio. His conversation faded in and out, at one moment perfectly rational, the next jumping off in some wild direction.

"Very interesting. The implant and the drugs, of course, that's what's doing it. Has to be." From his tone he might have been talking of a treatment applied to some casual acquaintance. "Did you know, Julia, if I were a bird I'd be in much better shape than I am now? Good old Hemsley operated on me, and he got most of it. But he must have missed a little bit—a bit too much for the implant to handle. Poor little scarab, can't beat the crab. But if I'd been a *bird,* they could have cut away the whole of both cerebral hemispheres, and I'd be as good as ever. Or nearly as good. Wouldn't know how to build a nest, of course, but who needs that?"

And then suddenly he was laughing, a gasping laugh that racked his chest and shook the tubes leading into his fleshless arms.

"Colin!" The fear that curiosity had held at bay came flooding back, and Julia was terrified. "I'll get the nurse."

"I'm fine." He stopped the strained laughter as quickly as he had started it and his face went calm. "Better than fine. But I'm a robot now. I, Robot."

She stared at him in horror, convinced that the final disintegration of mind was at hand.

"You know what I mean, Julie." Now he sounded rational but impatient. "Don't go stupid on me. Remember what Feynman said, in physics you can look on any positron as an electron that's traveling backward in time. You tell me I've been jumping backward—"

"Jim says that's nonsense. He says I'm talking through my hat."

"Jim?"

"Dr. Wollaston."

"So it's *Jim,* is it. And how long has that been going on?" He narrowed his eyes and peered up at her slyly. "Well, you tell *Jim* that I agree with you. I'm going backward, and I can prove it. And according to

Feynman that means the electrons in my brain are positrons. I've got a *positronic brain*. Get it?" He laughed again, slapping his skinny hands on the bedsheets. "Positronic brain. I'm a robot!"

"Colin, I'm getting the nurse. Right now." Julia had already pressed the button, but no one had appeared.

"In a minute. And you know *how* I can prove it? I can prove it because I feel absolutely wonderful."

His face had filled again with that strange bliss. He reached out and held her hand. "Remember how it felt when you were four years old, and you woke up in the morning, and you knew it was your birthday? That's how it used to be, all the time for all of us. But ontogeny recapitulates phylogeny: immature forms pass through the evolutionary stages of their ancestors. And that applies to *feelings* as well as bodies. Little kids feel the way all the animals *used* to feel, a long time ago. That's the way I am when I'm there. Fantastic, marvelous. And the farther I go, the better it gets. You looked at my pictures. If I've been going back, how far did I get?"

Julia hesitated. She was torn. Half of her wanted to believe her brother, to see more of those marvelously detailed drawings and to analyze them. The other half told her she was dealing with a mind already hopelessly twisted by disease.

"Your last picture shows the period of the earliest dinosaurs. They're all thecodonts, nothing that most people would recognize. The fossil record is very spotty there. We don't know nearly as much about them as we'd like to."

"And what would be next—going backward, I mean?"

"The Permian. No dinosaurs. And at this end of the Permian, over ninety percent of all the lifeforms on earth died off. We don't know why."

He was nodding. "The barrier. I can feel it, you know, when I'm trying to jump. I went through one, when all the dinosaurs died off. This one is bigger. I've been trying to fight my way through. I'm nearly there, but it's taking every bit of energy I have."

"Col, anything that tires you or upsets you is *bad*. You need rest. Why are you climbing imaginary walls?"

"You don't know the feeling. If I could jump all the way back, right to the first spark of life, I bet the intensity of life force and joy would be just about too much to stand. I'm going there, Julie. Across the barrier, into the Permian, all the way to the beginning. And I'm never coming back. *Never.*"

As though on cue, the thin body arched up from the bed, arms flailing. The mouth widened to a rictus of infernal torment and breath came hoarse and loud. Julia cried out, just as the nurse appeared. Wollaston was right behind her.

"*Grand mal.*" He was bending over Colin, grabbing at a rubber spatula and pushing it into the mouth just as the teeth clenched down. "Hold this, nurse, we don't want him swallowing his tongue."

But the spasm ended as quickly as it had started. Colin Trantham lay totally at ease, his breath slow and easy. His face smoothed, and the fixed grin faded. In its place came a look of infinite calm and blissful peace.

"Dr. Wollaston!" The nurse was watching the monitors, her hand on Colin's pulse. "Dr. Wollaston, we have arrhythmia. Becoming fainter."

Wollaston had the hypodermic with its six-inch needle in his hand, the syringe already filled. It was poised above Colin Trantham's chest when he caught Julia's eye.

She shook her head. "No, Jim. Please. Not for one month more pain."

He hesitated, finally nodded, and stepped away from the bed.

"Dr. Wollaston." The nurse looked up, sensing that she had missed something important but not sure what. She was still holding Colin Trantham's wrist. "I can't help him. He's going, doctor. He's going."

Julia Trantham moved to grip her brother's other hand in both of hers.

"He is," she said. "He's going." She leaned forward, to stare down into open eyes that still sparkled with a surprised joy. "He's going. And I'd give anything to know where."

Afterword to "The Feynman Saltation"

Anthony Trollope said, "A genius must wait for inspiration. I am not a genius, so I write every day."

I am not a genius, and I don't write every day, either, but there is one guaranteed way to get a story from me. You *ask* me for one, on some specialized subject, and my brain juices start to flow at once.

This story began with a letter from Robert Silverberg, asking if I had a dinosaur story for a new book he was editing. I didn't, and at the time I was not writing anything because I was busy reading deeply about parasitic diseases and cancer treatment. I also know nothing about dinosaurs.

Naturally, I wrote back at once and said yes; I gave him my proposed title, "The Feynman Saltation," and I started to write. But I could not get my mind far away from the morbid fascinations of glioblastomas and chemotherapy and antimetabolite drugs. If this tale seems to be more about cancer than dinosaurs, you now know why.

THE BEE'S KISS

The moth's kiss, first!
Kiss me as if you made believe
You were not sure, this eve,
How my face, your flower, had pursed
Its petals up; so, here and there
You brush it, till I grow aware
Who wants me, and wide ope I burst.

"YOUR GUILT IS not in question. Nor, given the outrage of your offense against the Mentor, is your punishment. Yet the past few days have provided anomalies for which a curious mind still asks an explanation. Will you tell?"

The room where Gilden sat was huge, low-ceilinged, dim-lit, and smoky. The face of the Teller seemed to float on the dead air in front of him, pale and thoughtful, and the questioning voice, as always, was gentle and reasonable.

Gilden shook his head the fraction of an inch that the metal brace permitted. *The past few days.* He grasped that phrase and kept his mind focused on it. He could have been sitting in this chair for months or years, drifting in and out of consciousness as the drugs ebbed and surged within his body. But here was a data point.

Or was the Teller lying, for her own inquisitorial purposes? Perhaps it had been a year, five years, ten years since the arrest. Perhaps his location had been changed a score of times. Perhaps, even, he was no longer on Earth, but transported to one of the Linkworlds within the Mentor's domain.

"You are a clever man." The Teller, patient to infinity, had waited a full two minutes before speaking again. "You think, so long as you have information of value to the Mentor, or interesting to me, so long will your punishment be delayed. But that is a false conclusion. Permit me to demonstrate."

Gilden's forearms were clamped to the arms of the chair. The Teller leaned forward and pressed a blunt cylinder to the upward-facing palm of Gilden's right hand. The flat disk at its end glowed white-hot. Flesh sizzled and sputtered, black smoke swirled. The stench of charring flesh filled the room.

Gilden screamed and writhed. The pain was unendurable, beyond description or comprehension. Somehow he remained conscious as the disk burned through to the bare bones of his hand. Then, at last, the Teller lifted the cylinder.

"One taste of torment. But observe." She nodded, to where Gilden's palm was renewing itself. New flesh pooled eerily into the blackened cavity, new skin crept in to cover it. "We are of course in derived reality. Your body is unmarked. But before you take comfort from that, let me point out the implications. Your condign punishment can continue—and will continue—for many, many years, at the level of pain that you experienced for only a few moments. For although your specific offense is unprecedented, the nature of your punishment is not. Do you recall the name of Ruth el Fiori Skandell, Bloody Ruth, who sabotaged one of the Mentor's aircars and thereby assassinated two of his lesser sons?"

Gilden grunted, deep in his throat. The Teller took it as a sign of assent, and went on.

"Skandell holds a melancholy record within the Linkworlds. After her sentencing she lived on for sixty-three years, enduring at every moment an agony at least as bad as yours. Virtual punishment is no boon, when pain exceeds reality. Someday, some unfortunate will break Skandell's record. It could be you, Arrin Gilden. Behold, one more time, the reenactment of your crime."

The room darkened further. The Teller's pallid face vanished. Only her persistent voice remained, moving closer to whisper intimately into Gilden's ear.

"*When,* I know already. *How,* you have been wise enough to describe to me. Now I must know *why.* Why would the world's leading electronics designer and miniaturist throw away career, bright future, and life itself? What compulsion would lead him to work night and day for a full year, at a level of ingenuity marveled at by all who have studied the process, with a level of risk great enough to intimidate the boldest, to attain such a momentary and apparently trivial gratification? Look again. And tell me *why.*"

The scene began as the ant-sized voyeur threaded its way toward the

Mentor Presumptive's bedchamber. It crept along precomputed hair-thin curves, following a path where the monitors' sensing fields did not quite overlap. To learn the position of those curves, Gilden had thwarted a dozen elaborate and ingenious computer security systems. (And now he was not alone in paying for his skill. Twenty guards, if the Teller could be believed, had been sentenced to a lifetime of labor in the ice-world quarries of Decantil, for their failure to detect the voyeur as it insinuated itself into the Mentor Presumptive's sanctum.)

The Presumptive's new bride had been drugged during surgery and the elaborate preparations that followed, but before leading her into the bedchamber the physicians had followed instructions. All drugs and sedatives were sluiced from her body. She lay now, dark-skinned, naked, and slightly trembling, on a great circular bed sheeted with blue satin. The Presumptive stood by the bedside. He was humming softly to him-self as he removed a belted robe of dark crimson. Beneath it he was naked. The sensors of the voyeur zoomed to take in the Presumptive's facial expression as he moved rampant onto the bed and gripped the woman's quivering thighs. There was a long moment, a pause for savor-ing and anticipation. At the moment of entry the voyeur expanded its field of view to include the woman's face.

This time the surgeons had done a good job. The afferent nerves linking sex organs and hindbrain had been channeled and enhanced, but not too much. The bride's ecstasy during lovemaking took her close to the point of death, but after the Mentor Presumptive's climax she was still alive.

The display changed, turning to show continuing muscle spasms in the bride's inner thighs. The view moved slowly up her body, to pause at a slack-lipped mouth and at eyes where only a sliver of iris showed be-tween whites and upper lids. At last the display moved again, halting at the Presumptive's flaring nostrils and full lips.

"You and I have watched this many, many times." The calm voice of the Teller cut into the recorded sound of the Mentor's heavy breathing. "Your resting pulse rate is fifty-seven beats a minute. Your current pulse rate is one hundred and sixteen. Would you like to tell me why?"

"I explained."

"You explained indeed. In response to my stimuli you explained too much. First it was your stated intention to sell copies of this, the record-ing of a most secret and sacred element of the Mentor Presumptive's life.

But while you have dozens of other illegal recordings in your quarters, there is no evidence that you have ever attempted to sell any one of them—or indeed that you would know how to undertake this or any other illegal enterprise. I reject that explanation. Next you explain that you intended to use the recording to blackmail the Mentor Presumptive, or even the Mentor himself. A preposterous suggestion indeed, since the first hint that such a recording had been made would lead to your arrest and death—as indeed it did and will. You then explained to me that you considered this a final test of technique for your new sensor. If it could penetrate this innermost and highly protected sanctum, it could penetrate anywhere. True, perhaps, but a dangerous notion indeed for anyone who wishes to live. The Empyrium must be able to keep its secrets.

"So I am forced to my own conclusion. You have *explained,* Prisoner Gilden, and explained again and again. But you have not *told.* Tell me now. Why did you do this, and throw away a life most valuable to the Mentor?"

Arrin Gilden stared into darkness. He moved his weary head forward to rest it against the cool metal of the brace.

"Could we have some light?"

"I see no reason why not."

As the room brightened the Teller's face slowly appeared a few feet from Gilden's chair. If this was derived reality, the illusion was perfect. Gilden recognized a dreadful irony. The technology that would doom him to an endless lifetime of torture was the twin of the one that had caught him. No one in the Mentor's entourage had discovered his tiny voyeur device, or even dreamed of its existence. It was Gilden himself, unable to leave the looped reality offered by the voyeur, who had been discovered. And even that might not have been fatal. Many people suffered from illusion lock. But the equipment in Gilden's apartment had also been running its external display. Everyone on Earth knew the face of the Mentor Presumptive.

"You have asked me many questions." Gilden tried for the hundredth time to fathom the unreadable, the expression on the Teller's face.

"That is my function."

"I would like to ask you one."

"That is your privilege."

"Why are you a Teller? You seem a sincere woman, and a friendly one. Why do you pursue a profession that forces you to inflict torture and death?"

The silence in the room lasted less than a second for Gilden. He knew that for the Teller, with total control over her time rate and his, the interval might be minutes or hours—long enough to consider the answer in detail, and match it to the Telling process.

She was shaking her head. "I have no answer to that question. I do what I do."

"And I did what I did. I cannot explain, but I can tell." Arrin Gilden's eyes fixed on the Teller as he tried to see within himself. "I do not know why. I know that I had no choice. I could not help myself. I was *compelled* to observe, to find a way to observe. I believe I was good at it."

"From everything that I have been able to discover, you are the best. Certainly the best in the records of the Empyrium." The lights brightened and yellowed. The chair with its wrist and ankle cuffs became a soft couch. The brace at Gilden's head vanished.

"Real reality." The Teller's voice dropped half an octave. Gilden found himself facing a dark-haired, smooth-faced woman not much older than his own twenty-five years.

"When you stop explaining, and just tell, it makes things so much easier."

"How do you know when I am telling?"

"I cannot force truth. But I can detect lies. Perhaps that is why I am a Teller." She came across to sit next to Gilden on the couch. "And sometimes—very rarely—I can offer an alternative to eternal agony. This is such a time. You must leave Earth, and go to Lucidar."

She gazed at him with calm blue eyes. Gilden found himself unable to remember their color as it had been in that other reality.

She smiled. The Teller had even white teeth, a mouth slightly asymmetrical, the left side higher than the right. "I am sure that I am not the first person to suggest that you are a mental cripple, a person who might have been helped in his youth but who is now incorrigible. Your role as voyeur is the most important thing in your life. That is a statement, not a question."

"It is not a statement. It is an understatement." Gilden breathed deep and again looked inward. "Voyeurism is the *only* important thing in my life."

"Even so, you should have treatment. But not until your return to Earth—assuming, of course, that you do return."

"Treatment? Not torment?"

"Perhaps. You will go to Lucidar on official business of the Mentor. If you succeed at that, you will be pardoned upon your return. A man of your outstanding skills, suitably channeled and monitored, has much to offer the Empyrium. If you fail, you will serve your original sentence, strong agony until your final breath. The Mentor offers inducement to succeed."

"I don't understand what I am being asked to do."

"Of course. It has not been explained, and it is not my position to do that. I am merely empowered to make the offer. Let me say only this: it is a difficult task, but one for which I believe you are supremely well suited. From your point of view, events far from Earth have provided a happy accident of timing. Your unique services are required on the rebel world of Lucidar."

"I have no decision to make. It is either leave here for an unknown purpose, or suffer torture until I die."

"Bravo, Gilden! At last you comprehend, and state things exactly. We are agreed then, you are going?"

"Yes."

"Good. Then I have but one more official duty." The Teller reached out. Again she was holding a stubby cylinder with a flat end. When she pressed it against Gilden's upper arm the grooved disk flared white-hot. Gilden roared with pain and jerked away.

"No derived reality this time. Look at that brand often, Gilden, as a reminder for you to do your best. That pain was a pale shadow of what awaits you on your return if you fail. And the next time you will not be able to pull yourself away."

Gilden rocked to and fro with tears in his eyes. The skin had been seared off his arm in a circle as big as the palm of his hand. His nostrils were full of the stink of burnt flesh and hair. But he had seen the rapturous look on the Teller's face as she pressed that fiery circle into his tender skin.

He knew, even if she did not, why she would never give up her position as Teller.

The Mentor was absolute ruler of Earth. The idea that there were places on the Linkworlds where intelligent beings lived beyond the Mentor's control, that many of those creatures were not human in any way—it was a revelation to Arrin Gilden. He wondered if this was just another derived reality.

For surely this was not the real world. Surely he would emerge to something more plausible. He was supposed to be in space, but there was no sign of the familiar stars of Earth. Instead a bubbling lava, dull-red and chaotic and flecked with orange sparks, stood outside every port of the sealed ship. A faint churning and trembling inside Gilden matched the seething exterior. Two more days of flight through this fiery maelstrom of nonspace, and according to his shipboard companions they would emerge in the Lucidar system. He would meet the representatives of the alien Sigil. And his work would begin.

Or was it all a dream? The woman across the table from him, the only female on the ship, seemed absolutely real and solid. But was she? Or was he still in the interrogation chamber, awaiting the Teller's next question?

Derli Margrave was fair-haired, small-boned, and delicately built. Her eyes seemed too pale and piercing for an Earth native. She sought Gilden's company, as much as her partner (husband? mate? brother?) Valmar Krieg seemed to avoid it. The first few meetings with her had made Gilden profoundly uneasy. His adult intimate encounters with women had numbered in the hundreds but they had been one-sided. A voyeur was not required to endure scrutiny as well as observing, to make conversation as well as listening. A voyeur did not have to worry about his own appearance, about the impression that he was making on another.

By his fifth meeting with Derli, his feelings had changed. She was deliberately seeking his company. Her appearance at his side whenever he happened to enter the communal recreation area was too unfailing to be an accident. But when she was with him she made no demands. If he gave any hint that he did not choose to talk, she remained quiet. If he wanted to speak, she listened to his every word. She groomed her hair and face in his presence unself-consciously, aware of but not displeased by his close attention. And she did not, like the women of his childhood and youth, dismiss, dominate, scorn, or command him. The one tender incident of infancy, when as he watched unnoticed a woman had given birth and held the tiny baby to her naked breast, was more dream than memory. But that woman had been like Derli, small, fair, and gentle.

She was talking now, answering his questions at the same time as she braided her long amber hair.

"You think you don't know much about the Sigil, but actually you know almost as much as anyone. Their exploration ship appeared in orbit around Lucidar only two months ago, and they landed a few days later. Just two of them. That's apparently the way they prefer to travel. The world of the Sigil, wherever it is, seems to be far off toward the center of the Galaxy. This couple are way outside the usual Sigil territory."

"Then why are we so interested in them?"

Derli paused, peering quizzically into the mirror at Gilden past a thick twisted lock of fair hair. "Define 'we.' I am a biologist, naturally I'd like to know the Sigil physiology—something that so far has been completely denied to us. They keep to themselves, stay in their ship most of the time, avoid all direct physical contact."

"What about Valmar? Is he a biologist, too?"

"He is, but that's not why he's here. Lucidar is a rebel world, close to breaking point with Earth. Valmar is one of the Mentor's most trusted advisers. The Mentor wants to know if there is anything else going on with the Sigil—are they what they claim to be, simple explorers? Or are they something else, part of a subversion that the Mentor needs to worry about? Valmar is convinced that they are hiding something."

"From what you say they seem to be hiding everything."

Derli was applying a smooth coat of cream to an area below her right cheekbone. Gilden noticed a slight discoloration.

"It's nothing." Somehow she still had one eye on him. "It will be gone in a day or two. You're right, though, the Sigil do seem to hide everything now. They were not like that when they first made contact. But that's where you come in. It should be a real challenge."

"They never leave their ship?"

"Briefly, for special occasions. But they have to wear suits. No one has been able to obtain a tissue sample—not even a flake of skin. And naturally their ship remains totally sealed all the time, to hold its atmosphere." She inspected herself in the all-around mirror, then to Gilden's disappointment stood up. "I have to go. Valmar will be waiting for me."

Gilden stood up too, on the brink of a question: Is Valmar Krieg your husband, or your lover? He did not ask it, but waited until she was gone and the last trace of the perfume that she wore had been sucked away by the room's air purifiers.

Then he went to his own quarters. Most of his specialized voyeur equipment was stowed away, inaccessible until the arrival on Lucidar. But what he carried with him in his personal luggage should suffice for such a simple job.

Gilden told himself that it was necessary work. In another two days his skills would be taxed to their limit. He could not afford to be out of practice.

Valmar Krieg was long-limbed and powerful, with a jutting red beard and golden-red hair over his whole body. He proved to be aggressively sexual, a brutal stallion of a lover who obviously hurt Derli and took no notice of her discomfort. She endured the violence of his passion without a murmur. When he was finished she stroked his body, fondling him and holding him in her arms, seemingly taking her own pleasure from his sated stillness. Only after he was asleep and quietly snoring did she ease away from him to examine the bruises on her neck, arms, and tender thighs.

Gilden watched everything in total absorption. And misery. For the first time in his life he had observed a sexual encounter in which he knew and *liked* the woman. It changed everything. He had experienced no vicarious thrill. Instead he had shared the pain felt by Derli. His only pleasure had come in observing her afterward, when she explored and tended to herself. And then it had been an impossible transference, Gilden's virginal self becoming explorer and gentle nurse of Derli's abused body.

He felt that he could not bear to meet her again, nor to act as voyeur for her lovemaking. But the urge to do so grew on him steadily for the next day and a half. He was almost relieved when it was Valmar Krieg rather than Derli who sought him out.

"Been enjoying yourself?" Krieg's self-confidence matched his physical presence. He sat down at the table opposite Gilden. "Come on, man, don't act innocent. You've been watching Derli and me."

Denial was the immediate reaction. But it was overridden by another concern.

"How did you detect the presence of the voyeur? No one else has ever managed to do that."

"Relax. I didn't. One of my jobs is to keep an eye on you. I reviewed all your records back on Earth, and I've seen you ogling Derli. You have no work to do until we get to Lucidar. Put all those together, you had to be watching us. I don't mind."

"Derli—"

"Doesn't know. And doesn't care right now. She's sick." Krieg laughed at Gilden's expression. "Oh, nothing to get excited about. Space doesn't agree with her, makes her want to throw up. But I didn't come here to talk about her. I came to talk about you."

"You saw my records. You know all about me."

"I do. But I don't think you do. I don't think you understand what you are."

"You think my records are wrong?"

"Not at all." Valmar Krieg leaned back and hooked his hands over one knee. "The records are fine. But everyone has missed their significance. Did you know that your pulse went from below sixty to way over a hundred when you invaded the Mentor Presumptive's bedchamber?"

"The Teller informed me of that."

"Ah, but did she mention that the peak value, one hundred and thirty-eight, was attained *before the voyeur was in position?* By the time you were able to see the Presumptive and his bride, and the actual sex act began, your pulse rate was already dropping."

"I did not know that."

"I thought so. And the Teller could not interpret it. But I can." Valmar Krieg laughed again, with the dominant self-confidence that Arrin Gilden could never feel. "You see, man, you're no different from me. You're as big a stud as I am. It's just that you operate in a different area. Show you a protected, forbidden zone, like the Presumptive's bedchamber, and it has all the challenge of a reluctant virgin. You can't rest until you've eased your way in past the barriers, broken down all her defenses, and she lies wide open and helpless before you. *That's* the exciting part. It's the penetration of *defenses* that gives you your kicks—not when she says yes, and the screwing starts."

Krieg stood up. "And you know what? You've got the time of your life waiting for you on Lucidar. Because according to what I'm hearing, the Sigil ship is hermetically sealed and totally impenetrable. The ultimate virgin." He slapped Gilden on the shoulder. "Rest up, swordsman, and conserve your testosterone. You're going to need it in another couple of days."

Derli had been wrong. Gilden's first meeting with the humans on Lucidar convinced him of that. They knew far more about the Sigil than anyone from Earth, and they had their own theories.

"Something changed." The man responsible for briefing the new arrivals had an unpronounceable Lucidar name, glottal stops and deep throat consonants spoken through a mouthful of gravel. "Something we told them, or maybe they told us. After the first two weeks we had a translation program that made sense most of the time. So we started to exchange information. We were doing fine, talking physics and linguistics and getting into biology and social structure and philosophy. Then one evening the two of them went off to their ship. Next morning they didn't come out. They've emerged only for short intervals ever since. And they will no longer swap information with us."

Gilden was nodding agreement, but he was having trouble absorbing information. Even without the alien Sigil, Lucidar provided an overload of strangeness. Gravity, sun, air, exotic flora and fauna. People. The gravel-voiced Bravtz'ig—the nearest that Gilden could come to his name—was tall and broad enough to have qualified as a giant on Earth, but here he didn't draw a second glance. It was tiny Derli and Gilden himself who would make the Lucidar freak show.

Alien world, alien thoughts. He stared out of the window of the spaceport tower, to where the Sigil ship was visible as a far-off speck of pearly white.

To penetrate its shields, of unknown nature and number, without leaving evidence of your presence. To plumb the impermeable hull's deepest secrets . . .

He forced his attention back to the conversation. Bravtz'ig was still talking. What had he just missed? Derli, sitting at his side, had a recorder. Was it running? He would need to review this meeting later.

She gave him a private smile and a raised eyebrow. She knew! Knew he had been observing her with the voyeurs. He was convinced of it. Valmar must have told her. And she didn't *mind*. He had a sudden voyeur flashback, a memory of Derli sitting naked and straight-legged on the bed. She was arching her back to reveal delicate pink-nippled breasts, then bending far over to massage overtaxed thigh muscles. Long amber tresses tumbled forward to hide her flat belly and pubic thatch. Had she done that deliberately, knowing he was watching?

Once again he had to fight his way back into the present. What was happening to him? It must be pure travel fatigue. For the past day and a half he had found himself unable to sleep, his head pulsing with thoughts of Valmar Krieg's prophecy about the challenge of the Sigil.

While he had been daydreaming, another of the Lucidar group had produced surround-videos of the Sigil couple, made not long after their original landing. Now their display was beginning.

Any single element of data about the aliens might be the crucial one. Gilden had seen videos of the two Sigil, but these were much more revealing. He studied them closely, knowing as he did so that he would review them again many, many times. The suits worn by the aliens concealed everything but broad general features. He could see that both Sigil were similar in morphology, bipedal and with bilateral symmetry. The legs were attached close to the middle of the forward-curving torso, and not far above them two long arms emerged at right angles to the body. The dark, hairless head formed a broad cone above a thin neck and ended at the front in a prominent black muzzle.

There were certainly differences between them, but the main surprise was the disparity of sizes. One Sigil towered high over its smaller companion and was at least three times the bulk. Gilden assumed that the huge Sigil must be the female, because of the loving deference and exaggerated care with which it was treated by its diminutive partner. Then he thought of gentle Derli, and Valmar Krieg's indifferent brutality, and wondered if he had things exactly backward.

"Sexual dimorphism." Derli spoke softly, more to her recorder than to Gilden or anyone else. "A substantial size difference between the sexes. Common among certain arthropods and mammals with harems. However, analogy with existing Terran forms is more likely to be misleading than helpful. The presence of just one of each of the Sigils argues against multiple mates."

Bravtz'ig was speaking again. "The Sigil told us—when they were still telling us anything—that a ship always carries one of each. By the way, although they can both apparently talk the big one never does. All we've been told about them comes from the little one."

"What do you mean, when they were telling you anything?" Valmar had seemed half asleep. Now he was alert. "I thought they were still talking? If you have concealed information from the Mentor . . ."

"Relax, Master Krieg." Bravtz'ig laughed, and his expression was more aggressive than respectful. "We've not concealed a thing. Don't get wrapped around the bureaucracy."

Gilden had another revelation, one that again turned his world upside down. The Mentor was nominal ruler here, but Bravtz'ig clearly had no fear of him. No one on Lucidar was worried about being carried off for arbitrary Teller inquisition and eternal torment. And yet the Teller had seemed absolutely confident that Gilden, whether he succeeded or failed in his task with the Sigil, would return to Earth. How could she be sure?

The answer was obvious: red-bearded Valmar Krieg, trusted adviser to the Mentor, was Gilden's unstated guardian. He would be responsible for Gilden's return.

Bravtz'ig was continuing, and Gilden had to postpone his own worries: "The Sigil still talk to us, but there's been an enormous change since the first days of communication. We found out how their civilization is organized, and how their ship works, and that this is their first contact with our section of the Spiral Arm. But the real information stopped coming on the day they went into seclusion in their ship. They still come out now and again, but we get what my boss calls party chat—they tell us trivia."

"Maybe they received instructions from their home world." Valmar Krieg had taken the Terran lead, even though Gilden was the one who was supposed to solve the problem of the Sigil.

"If they did, they must be far beyond us in communications technology. We've been monitoring their ship with everything we've got. No sign of an outgoing signal."

"Any theories for what happened?"

"Bunches. But they all boil down to one of two ideas: either they learned something about us that they didn't like, or they're afraid we'll learn something about *them* that they don't want us to know."

"So why didn't they just up and leave?"

"We've been afraid they will. We've deliberately kept dribbling them useful information, bit by bit—a lot more than they've given us recently. But we soon realized we needed expert help." Bravtz'ig nodded to Gilden. "If you can get an observation instrument into their ship, you'll be a Lucidar hero no matter what you did on Earth."

"I'll need help, too." It was close to noon, and Lucidar shimmered with heat haze. The speck of white pearl danced tantalizingly on the horizon. A matching tingle of anticipation shivered within Gilden. "First, I'll need everything you have about their ship."

"You'll get that. But I don't think you'll be happy. They're closed tight. We measure zero material exchange with our atmosphere, no transparent materials, and no emergent radiation." Bravtz'ig glanced at Derli. "What about you? What do you need?"

"I'll be as dependent on Gilden as you are. I can determine a little biology from external appearance, but with an alien species it's not very reliable. Their suits are a problem. I need X rays, sonograms, tissue samples." She turned from Bravtz'ig to Gilden. "Unless you can get me those, Arrin, I can't really begin."

The easy things had to be done first. Even if there was only one chance in a million that they might succeed, Gilden could not afford to overlook the obvious. He also could not assume that Bravtz'ig's team was as painfully thorough as he had to be.

The Sigil ship sat on six splayed legs in the middle of the open plain of the landing field. It was, as Bravtz'ig had warned him, sealed against matter gain or loss. Not a molecule from Lucidar went into the rounded hull, and none escaped. That eliminated the use of every material voyeur device in Gilden's arsenal.

Which left only radiation, in its various forms. It was not the first time that he had faced such a problem. Gilden, from the mobile experiment station provided by Bravtz'ig, set out to observe the Sigil ship using every wavelength from hard gamma to long radio.

Nothing.

He took a more active step and bathed the ship with monochromatic radiation generated from his own sources. The return signals at every frequency were quite featureless. No radiation penetrated more than a millimeter into the shining surface. Not in the ultraviolet, not in the visible, not in the reflective or emissive infrared. He went doggedly on, creeping through the spectrum from shortest to longest wavelengths.

Again, nothing.

At last, when the sun was setting, Gilden abandoned his experiments in favor of pure thought. Sometimes, a negative result could be as significant as a positive one. One fact nagged at him: there was no anomalous thermal signature, no elevation of ship hull temperature above ambient. How could that be? If the Sigil ship was in exact temperature balance with the atmosphere, where did the heat go that was generated in the interior?

He was not able to answer that question, but it was an important one. Surely the Sigil, no matter how advanced their science, could not evade the laws of thermodynamics. Even if all power devices were turned off inside the hull, any living organism had to eat. Eating implied energy conversion from one form to another. Heat production was an inevitable by-product.

Gilden's neck ached, and his closed eyes saw nothing but the red afterimages of dials and monitors. His head was suddenly buzzing with a swirl of speculation and unanswered questions. He filed his observations and went back to the living quarters that Bravtz'ig had assigned to the visitors.

On the way in he stopped at the bathhouse to bathe his weary eyes. Derli was there, leaning against a washbasin. He nodded to her, but only after he had laved his face and dried it on a hand towel did he notice her stooped posture.

"What's wrong."

"Nothing." Her smile was forced, her lips pale.

"There is." He stepped closer. "You look awful."

"I'm just a bit sick, still."

"I thought that was space nausea, and you were over it."

"I thought so, too." She leaned forward to rest her forehead against the cool gray metal of the washbasin. "Guess a new planet can do it just as well. Unfamiliar air, food, gravity."

"I'm sorry. I'm working as fast as I can, but it's slow going. The ship's really impenetrable. Maybe you should return to Earth and come back here when I find some information you can use."

"No!" Derli straightened her back. "Leaving is the last thing I want to do. I don't feel good, but I love this place. I'll stay on Lucidar until I'm forced to leave." She took a deep breath, and reached up to touch Gilden's cheek. "But thanks for the thoughtfulness. I'm not used to that. Maybe we can talk later, when I feel better."

She walked unsteadily out, leaving Arrin Gilden with something new to ponder. *Until I'm forced to leave.* He had assumed that as Valmar Krieg's partner, Derli Margrave was one of those who made the rules. But it seemed she was no more free to choose than Gilden himself. Derli's domination extended beyond sexual possession.

Gilden touched his cheek, and admitted for the first time his full resentment—hatred?—of Valmar Krieg.

Gilden stayed in his quarters for the whole evening, his thoughts sliding uneasily from one subject to another. The Sigil, Valmar, the Teller, Derli. She did not come, although his voyeurs told him that she was alone. Valmar Krieg was far away, meeting with Bravtz'ig. The Sigil were locked tight within their ship.

Finally Gilden took the unprecedented step, walking the twenty paces from his rooms to Derli's.

She was looking better, leaning back on a broad divan covered with a beige cloth that complemented the color of her hair. Gilden realized that his voyeurs needed to be slightly recalibrated. On their imagers the hair and divan had not quite matched.

"I wondered if you would come. I was going to give you another half hour." She patted the seat beside her. "I thought you might be afraid of Valmar."

I was going to give you another half-hour. And then what?

"I am." Gilden remained standing. "I mean, I am afraid of him."

"You came anyway."

"He's miles away."

"I see." Derli gave a little shrug. "I guess you would know, Arrin, if anyone would. No point in taking a risk, is there?"

The tone was a criticism, far more than the words. Gilden sat down at her side. "I told you earlier that I was making slow progress. But that's not true anymore. I think I know a way into the Sigil ship—not with an actual voyeur, nothing as direct as that. But a way to send in a probe signal."

"You told me earlier that the ship was impenetrable."

"The hull is. But I realized that there had to be some way to get rid of generated internal heat. It's going out through the ship's support legs, diffused deep into the surface of Lucidar itself."

"And you can get a probe in the same way?"

"Nothing material. But I can send in my own signals that way, use high-frequency modulated phonons—ultrasonic packets—if I have to."

"It sounds difficult."

"I've done it before. Give me a few days."

"I'm a patient woman." She turned to face him. "You came here to tell me that?"

"Yes." It was a lie. The Teller would have picked it up at once. "And to ask you something."

"Ah!" Derli leaned far back on the divan. "That's more like it. Ask me, Arrin. I'm waiting."

"You say that you love Lucidar, and hate the idea of leaving it. But you are not a condemned criminal, like me. What's to stop you staying here after the work on the Sigil is over?"

"You don't know?" She abandoned her languorous pose and sat straight up. "You really don't?"

"If I knew, I would not ask."

"Lean toward me, and give me your hand."

Gilden did so, and allowed her to guide his hand to a place on her head just behind where the thick amber hair was parted.

"Feel that?" She set his index finger on a spot where the skin of the skull was slightly rough. "That's scar tissue, over the implant. Valmar knows the code. If I refuse to return to Earth or do something disloyal to the Mentor, he will activate it."

Gilden was still touching her head, feeling the delicate bones of the skull. "What would it do?"

"I don't know. I'm not supposed to know. Uncertainty is part of the control. Maybe the top of my head would be blown off. Maybe I'd be in permanent agony. Maybe I'd just become a drooling idiot or a nympho-maniac for the rest of my life. I've seen all those and worse." She took Gilden's hand in hers, and again guided it. This time to a place on his own skull. "You, too, Arrin. Anyone gets it who leaves Earth and works directly for the Mentor."

"Even Valmar?" Gilden fingered with awful fascination the unno-ticed small patch of scar tissue on his own head.

"Of course. Lucidar might subvert him, too. The difference is, Val-mar controls you and me, but some other person controls him."

"He *owns* us!"

"Not all of us, Arrin. Some of our actions are our own." Derli was pulling him toward her, at the same time as she sank back on the divan. Gilden struggled free of her arms, stood up, and stared down at her. He was trembling.

"You don't want me?" A smile would have made it intolerable. But Derli looked hurt and sorrowful, like an abandoned child. Gilden groaned, turned, and blundered out of the room and the building, out into the evening gusts of Lucidar's spring. He walked blindly and ran-domly, hardly aware of time or direction until increasing cold drove him home.

Back in his own quarters, he activated a voyeur. Derli was still sitting on the divan. Somehow she knew. She stared right at the minute observation instrument and raised her hand in a wave.

This time she was smiling, but Gilden saw no reproach or scorn on her face; only an understanding that for him some things were still impossible.

He waved back, knowing that she could not see him. And then he settled down to work. He had an additional task now, as difficult in its way as the problem of the Sigil—and far more dangerous. There was one place where no sane voyeur would ever dare to look. In this case, Gilden had no choice.

He worked until close to dawn at a level of intensity that approached a trance. When he finally collapsed into bed the new problem ran on inside his head, distorted and paradoxical. And when Valmar Krieg marched into his bedroom early the next morning, Gilden saw his arrival as part of another cloudy dream sequence.

"Derli says you've cracked it." Valmar sat down uninvited on the end of the bed.

The words sent Gilden's heart into a mad race. Then he realized that the other man couldn't possibly know what he had worked on through the night. Because Derli herself didn't know. Krieg had to be talking about the Sigil and their ship.

"I haven't cracked it. But I do have ideas."

"Tell me." Krieg held up his hand. "Don't get the wrong impression. It's not that I feel I can't trust you, but I have to file my own status reports. I must know what you're doing, at least in outline. How will you get your voyeurs into the Sigil ship?"

"I won't. It's utterly impenetrable for solid objects without alerting the Sigil." Thinking about technical questions calmed Gilden at once.

"So how can you learn what's inside?"

"That's a different problem. We can be fairly sure that the Sigil ship has its own internal monitoring system, probably with imaging components just the way that our ships do. So I don't need to get my own voyeurs inside—I just have to control the Sigils' own monitors. Then I have to get that information out."

"It sounds impossible."

"I've done it half a dozen times, back on Earth. The trick is to find an access point. That's what I think I have. The Sigil ship is getting rid of excess heat down into the planetary surface. So I have an avenue. I can send pulses in by the same route and read their returns. After that it means lots of data analysis, none of it automatic. But I'm comfortable with that. The part I'm less sure of is my interaction with the Sigil ship's computer systems. I have to plant my own code in there, hidden in a way that won't be noticed, before I can control the ship's monitors."

Krieg was thoughtfully stroking his red beard. "That doesn't sound so hard. Logic is logic, universal."

"Maybe suspicion is, too. If the Sigils have enough triggers built in against interference they'll spot me before I'm hardly started."

"So the sooner we know that, the better. Out of bed, and get to work. You weren't brought all this way for a vacation." But Valmar Krieg's nod was one of satisfaction as he strode out.

More sleep would be impossible anyway. Gilden, muzzy-headed, forced himself to take a hot and cold shower, and then to eat a full breakfast before he set to work.

He had oversimplified the problem for Valmar Krieg to the point of imbecility, and at the same time deliberately made its solution sound more difficult. Gilden didn't want anyone, most especially Krieg, aware of the sophistication of the tools he had developed over the past ten years. And no one must suspect that during the following days of intense dawn-to-midnight effort Gilden would be feeling his way through not one mental maze, but two.

Derli found him on the afternoon of the tenth day, asleep in the dining area. His head rested on the hard table, he was snoring, and in front of him sat a cold and untouched plate of food.

She took a seat cushion and eased it under his gaunt cheek. She did it as gently as possible but the disturbance awoke him. He stared at her, bleary-eyed.

"Mmph. What time is it?"

"Four hours after noon. You look terrible. Why don't you go to bed and get some real sleep?"

"I was going to. As soon as I'd eaten. I was coming to see you. To show you." He was mumbling, still hardly awake, working his jaw from side to side and turning his head to ease the muscles of his stiffened neck. "I don't have all you need Look for more as soon as I'm rested. But I have something."

"You're inside the Sigil ship?"

"Five days ago. Not too hard. Difficult part is time-sharing the monitors. So our observations won't be noticed. And then getting information out." Gilden stood up, leaning against Derli for balance. "Come on, if you want to see it. Krieg, too."

"He's not here. He flew to Montmorin for a meeting with a Lucidar group. I think there's a big fight brewing with Earth. He'll be back tomorrow."

"Mm." Gilden hardly seemed interested, leading the way into his own living quarters. "Doesn't matter. Unless you need him."

"For my work? I don't. Valmar started out as a biologist, but he hasn't done any real research or analysis for years. I don't need him."

Gilden grunted. He was already at work, setting up a linked series of displays. "Take a look at this first. It's just a summary, an overview of what we've got. When you see what's here and what's missing, you can tell me where I should concentrate my efforts tomorrow." He stood up and gestured to his seat.

"What about you?" But Derli sat down. The temptation was too great. A first image was already forming on the screen, of what could be an interior chamber of the Sigil ship.

"I'm going to take a shower while you do a run-through. You don't need me for that—probably manage better without me."

She said nothing. Gilden knew why. He had developed the displays slowly and painfully, over days of frustrating effort, but even that had been fascinating. For Derli the impact would be a thousand times as great.

He stood staring at her in silence for a couple of minutes. Then he retreated quietly to the bathhouse. Derli did not even notice his departure.

Progress was slow, but finally overwhelming. For the first couple of minutes of display Derli saw only blurry green outlines of two Sigil, moving jerkily from place to place. Frequent incomprehensible breaks or swirls of random color provided a maddening distraction, as did passing glimpses of what seemed to be chamber ceilings and floors.

But then, as Gilden's mastery of the interaction technique had slowly deepened, the recorded images improved in focus, depth, color, and detail. Derli could discern odd features of the Sigil ship interior. The chamber walls had a convoluted, organic look to them, unlike anything constructed by humans. Even the control banks lacked clean, hard, functional outlines. She waited, impatient but understanding. Her interest was in the biology of the Sigil but she was not the only customer for Gilden's magic. Others cared to know about the ship, not its occupants.

Finally, as though responding to Derli's impatience, the display settled down to show the Sigil themselves. Derli leaned forward. They were not wearing the suits that had cloaked every record in the Lucidar data banks. She confirmed overall structure. Both Sigil were certainly bipedal, with bilateral symmetry. Now that she could see their external colors, she learned that the legs and arms springing from the forward-curving torso were a bright orange-red. The trunk was banded, in crimson and white for the smaller Sigil and in darker red and white for the other. Only the head of each was dark. The prominent muzzles, almost black, were ciliated with delicate silver tendrils like the feelers on a catfish.

Derli watched the display through to its last incomplete image. Then she backed up to the beginning, longing for more: more detail of the mouth, especially its inside; more and higher-resolution images of the lower part of the trunk where the reproductive and excretory organs were logically housed; X rays, to reveal internal structure; most of all, tissue samples.

She began to make a list, even though she knew that the last two elements would almost certainly be denied to her regardless of Gilden's skill. Ship monitoring systems used X rays routinely for status reports on the drive and X rays also served a purpose with living organisms. But that was in diagnosis of abnormal conditions, not during routine survey of the ship's interior.

As for tissue samples, Gilden had already assured her that he could return no material object, however small, from the inside of the ship. But he had performed other miracles. As the record progressed from beginning to end the Sigil became smoothly moving solid objects rather than flat, jerky cartoons.

Derli stopped wishing for what she did not have, and concentrated her attention on the similarities and differences between the two Sigil. She moved to the appropriate part of the file.

She knew from the original records provided by Bravtz'ig that the smaller alien was about one and a half meters tall, the big one maybe three meters. Such a large size imposed structural limitations on any form evolved on a planet with gravity comparable with Earth or Lucidar. Gilden's new data confirmed it. The larger Sigil was bigger in every way, thicker, clumsier, slower moving. The small one danced anxiously around it, bringing food and drink, adjusting cushions, apparently catering to its partner's every demand. Structurally, both of them possessed a generally similar body pattern except for variations of the lower trunk. That suggested the varying genital configurations appropriate to male and female. The color differences of the torso were also presumably sex-linked, brighter crimson bands fitting the display pattern of the smaller male.

It was all plausible and consistent. But something, somewhere, did not quite fit.

What?

She leaned back in her seat, placed interlocked hands on the back of her head, and pondered.

Derli had frozen the display at a certain point, concentrating on a smooth boss at the base of the male Sigil's torso, when she heard a noise behind her. It was Gilden, his hair dark and wet and slicked down across his forehead. He was paler than ever, but far more alert.

"Is this everything?" Derli nodded to the display.

"Everything I thought you'd need to see. I have hours and hours of other records, about the ship itself and its computer system."

"I think I should see them all. Just in case." She pointed to her own notes. "And here's my wish list. Without cell samples I'm reduced to guessing on things as basic as sex. Maybe you can work out some way to provide me with a substitute for that information."

"I can try." Gilden stared at the display. "You're still in the middle sequence after all this time. Or did you go all the way through?"

"Twice." She frowned up at him, then glanced across to the general display board. "Phew. I've been sitting here over three hours. Unbelievable. I thought you were just going for a shower."

"I was. I took a nap first." He hesitated. "Want to eat? I don't remember when I last had a full meal." And, when she seemed slow to answer, "We can talk about the rest of the data you need. Don't know if I'll be able to get it. But I'll try. Just tell me what you want."

He was too nervous. His jittery movements reminded Derli of the anxious male Sigil (if it was the male) hovering over its hulking partner.

She stood up. "All right. I'm hungry, too. And we don't have to discuss my problem. We can talk about anything you like." She took Gilden by the arm.

A mistake. He flinched away from her touch. He would not look at her as they walked together to the dining area, and he stared up at the ceiling while Derli made food selections for both of them.

It was a chance too good to miss. She glanced at Gilden's tormented, too-pale face, and quietly added a mixture of tranquilizers and stimulants to the drinks that she was ordering. He did not notice, even when they sat down and he took the first sip. He was staring at her when the food was served, but never into her eyes. He was studying her mouth, nose, and ears, as intently as a portrait artist.

The drugs were slow to take effect. They ate a full three-course meal, while Derli discussed Sigil physiology in as much detail as she was able, including her need for high-resolution body images, and Gilden remained silent. But at last, when the plates were cleared and a third drink had been served and drunk, he met her eyes and said: "You like it here. You don't have to go back to Earth if you don't want to."

"I told you, Valmar knows the code of my implant as well as yours. He can make us do what he likes. Kill us both, if he has the codes set that way."

"He might kill me, but surely he won't kill you. He wouldn't set your implant that way. You are his lover."

"More than that. And less than that." Derli laughed and reached out to stroke Gilden's hand where it sat palm-down on the table, realizing as she did so that the drugs were affecting her as much as him. "He loves me, he loves me not. Arrin, I don't know what Valmar would do if I said I was staying on Lucidar. But I know I dare not take *that* risk. Other risks, I want to take."

All the initiatives had to come from her. She had known it would be that way. He said nothing as they stood up from the table and she led him slowly back to her bedroom. He knew exactly how to undress her and touch her, as though he had done it before a thousand times. Yet at the same time he was clumsy and breathless, a boy fumbling his way toward a first encounter.

Derli understood. When the time came she moved on top of him and took the final initiative. And when he was too nervous and sudden, finished before she was even close, she understood that, too. She was part of the problem, unable to respond in full despite the drugs' assistance. In any case, there was more than one form of satisfaction.

When it was over he drifted off into sleep without a word. She lay beside him, studying the tight mouth and hollow cheeks. She leaned over and kissed the fading red circle of scar tissue on his muscular right arm. Physical union had changed everything. She had realized that it would—even counted on it. Now she had to tell him.

She patted his shoulder and his chest, not roughly but hard enough to bring him back to wakefulness. When his eyes opened she waited patiently until at last he turned to look at her.

"That was wonderful." But he did not look happy.

"Yes."

"But not for you."

"That was my fault." There was no point in her putting it off. "I couldn't get into the right mood, because of what I kept thinking."

"About the Sigil?"

"*No.* Damn the Sigil." The residual effect of the drugs made her want to giggle when there was nothing funny. "I kept thinking about you, and about Valmar. And my condition."

It was as bad as she had feared. He was staring at her in mystification. She would have to spell out everything for him.

"You knew I was throwing up on the ship coming here. And you knew I was sick when I got here. Wasn't it obvious to you that I was pregnant? Pregnant with Valmar's child."

He gazed at her with no expression that she could read. "He forced himself on you, made you do whatever he wanted?"

So easy, to agree to that lie. Derli sighed. "No. I was quite willing. I can say now that I wish I hadn't done it, but I did."

He sat up and laid his hand gently on her bare belly. "Are you telling me that you are pregnant now? That there's a baby in here?"

"Yes. I'm at nearly two and a half months. I hope the morning sickness is all finished."

"Good."

He turned toward her, and she saw the last thing that she had expected. He was physically aroused.

All the tension in her body melted away. She lay back and closed her eyes. "The second time will be much better, Arrin, I promise you—for both of us."

* * *

The first lovemaking with Derli had been agony for Gilden of an unusual and terrible kind. He liked her, more than he had ever liked any woman; but when she moved above him and took control of his body she became all the Harpies of childhood, playing with him, mocking him, tormenting him, using him for their own ends without any regard for his needs or wants.

His body had brought him rapidly to a climax, divorced from his anguish, and he had pretended to a satisfaction he did not feel. As he drifted toward sleep he was convinced that this was the only form of physical sexual experience he could ever know.

But then Derli had spoken of her pregnancy. That both soothed and excited him. His mind pictured her again with Valmar; and he had an answer.

He distanced himself mentally from their new union, even as he moved on top of her and entered her waiting body. Once again he became the voyeur, the involved but remote participant. The difference was that he functioned now as both observer and player, embarked on a dizzying self-referential exercise that sent him spinning down an endless regression of sexual congress. He was watcher and actor. He knew the right moves, he had seen them a thousand times over. And when his climax arrived, moments after hers, his dual selves coalesced with a force as painful as torture. His shudders were both physical and mental; this time they signaled a pleasure almost too much to bear.

It was Derli who drifted off to sleep, while Gilden lay wide awake and tried to understand what had just happened. In the dim overhead lights he studied her body. She lay flat, legs still spread wide. She was breathing slowly and her mouth was slightly open. She would probably not wake until morning.

It occurred to him that he might never have a better opportunity. He also realized that his workload had just increased again.

He had to create yet another voyeur, of unmatched sensitivity and operating lifetime.

She did not move as he leaned over to plant a delicate moth's kiss on her navel, dressed in silence, and left the bedroom.

Derli had said what information she needed. She had not suggested any way to obtain it. As soon as Valmar Krieg returned from Montmorin,

Gilden moved his base of operations into the mobile experiment station next to the Sigil ship and went into round-the-clock surveillance.

He was trying to be cautious, but he suspected that he was pushing the limit. It would require minimal effort by one of the Sigil to learn that their privacy had been violated and the computer system subverted.

He began to confine his intrusion into the ship to microscopic time slices, just enough for a spot check of events. It was during one of these flashes, occurring close to the middle of the Lucidar night, that the crucial event began.

Gilden came fully awake. The ship's monitors were showing him the Sigil sleeping area. He had caught a glimpse of the big one crouched on the floor. Above it hovered the small one, clinging on to its partner's body with all its limbs.

If there was ever a time to take risks, this was it. Gilden set the ship's computer to provide and export to him continuous observations.

The massive body of the lower Sigil was wriggling uneasily as though she was not satisfied with her position. The smaller one clung on resolutely. A long, tapered member was emerging slowly from the rounded boss on the front lower part of its body. The new organ was pale yellow, glistening, and slightly corrugated along its upper side, as though another ribbed tube ran along it. After a preliminary probing the member's pointed tip stabbed into an invisible entry point in the rounded bulk of the other's lower back. The restless movement of the female ceased at once. The Sigil pair became motionless except for a steady pulsing within the thin pipe that coupled them. Waves of contraction passed along it, running in ripples from male to female.

The act went on for nearly forty minutes, until a shudder racked the whole body of the upper Sigil. As soon as the long spasm was over the creature began to withdraw and loosen its hold. The lower partner did not react to the decoupling. Its splayed body remained immobile, apparently asleep on the floor of the chamber.

Gilden had been lost in the scene that came to him through the monitors. He was dismayed when he finally thought to glance at the time. He had obtained exactly what Derli had asked for—but at a price. It was hard to believe that an intrusion of such duration and intensity would not raise alarms within the ship's security systems. Now that he checked he saw that for the past fifteen minutes there had been a flurry of activity on the ship's computer. Introspection routines that he had never before encountered were coming into operation.

An unfamiliar signal sounded through the ship's interior. The smaller Sigil, all its lethargy gone, came scuttling across to inspect the contoured control bank.

Gilden cut off interaction with the ship, made extra copies of the new records, and hurried with them toward Derli's apartment. Even though it was the middle of the night she would want to see what he had found.

He entered her bedroom reluctantly, afraid that he would find Valmar Krieg with her. But she was sleeping alone, covered to the neck by a thin sheet. When he woke her she sat up, sighed, and put her arms around him.

"No." Gilden resisted as she tried to draw him down beside her. "It's not that. Please."

She released him at once and pulled the sheet up to cover her body. "You've been avoiding me. Hiding from me."

"Not true. I've been working, all the time—to get you this." Gilden held out a copy of the new data record.

"What is it?" She dropped the sheet and reached out for the little box, ignoring, as Gilden could not, the bare shoulders and breasts that were revealed.

"The Sigil. Mating. The images show everything, with more body detail than anything I've given you earlier."

"Ooh! At last." She cupped her hands around the data block and held it to her chest. "Arrin, I must see this. Right now."

She scrambled out of bed and into shirt and shorts. Gilden fancied that he could see a slight additional swell in her belly.

He looked away. "I hope this gives you what you need. I went much too far to get it. I think the Sigil realize that we have been observing inside their ship."

Derli was hardly listening. Although she reached out to give him a token squeeze as she passed by, her attention was on the data block. She went to the waiting computer and inserted the new record. Gilden watched over her shoulder until the first frames of data appeared, showing the smaller Sigil clinging to the back of its partner. Then he went in search of Valmar Krieg.

He found the red-bearded guardian where he was supposed to be, in his assigned living quarters and bedroom. Krieg was not alone. Asleep at his side lay a huge Lucidar woman, blond, big-bosomed, and thick-limbed. Gilden thought at once of the Sigil, with its far larger partner.

"This had better be important." Either Krieg had been awake or he slept so lightly that he awoke at Gilden's first touch. "It's the middle of the goddamn night."

"I have new information about the Sigil. I passed a copy on to Derli Margrave."

"So what?" Valmar Krieg was sitting up while the woman at his side snored on. "Derli doesn't need me to help her analyze it. I can find out what it tells tomorrow."

"I suspect I went beyond prudence in obtaining the new information. The Sigil are aware that I have tapped their ship's monitors."

"That's another matter—and bad news for you if it's true." Krieg swung out of bed and moved toward the door, ignoring the sleeping woman. "You were supposed to operate *invisibly,* for God's sake. Not blunder around and announce your presence."

He went to the upper floor and stared out of the window. The Sigil ship was visible, sitting at the center of a permanent circle of lights.

Krieg grunted. "All quiet so far." But even as he spoke the ship began to lift, drifting upward from the smooth spaceport surface. As it rose higher its six support legs retracted into the pearly white body. A few moments later the personal monitor at Krieg's belt called for attention.

"Emergency!" It was Bravtz'ig, by the sound of his gravel voice still three-quarters asleep. "You there, Krieg? We just received a Sigil departure flight alert. Their ship is moving out."

"This is Krieg. I'm watching it happen. What can we do about it?"

"Not a damn thing—unless you want to tell me to try and stop it."

"How would you do that?"

"Good question. Destroy the ship, that's the only way I know. And I can tell you now, our space command would refuse to do that even if you ordered it."

"So I won't waste time trying. Can you follow their path?"

"Until they go to subspace. Then we've lost them. You know that as well as I do." Bravtz'ig's face appeared on the tiny screen, squinting and suspicious. "Did you *cause* this, Krieg, you and your cock-up Earth friends?"

"How could we? Follow their ship as far as you can. If we lose it we're all in trouble."

"You're in trouble anyway. Get off the line, Krieg, so I can talk to someone useful."

Bravtz'ig vanished. A moment later the unit went dead. Krieg turned to Gilden.

"I suggested we didn't cause this. But you *did* cause this, didn't you? You stupid asshole. It was the same on Earth. Your damned voyeur urges, you couldn't let go watching until it was too late. Now I have to go back and tell the Mentor that instead of learning more about the Sigil it was our party that drove them away from Lucidar. Come on." Krieg grabbed Gilden roughly by the arm and dragged him back down the stairs.

"Where are we going?"

"To collect Derli. With the Sigil gone our value on Lucidar is less than zero. We have to get out before this place blows up. Better be ready for pain, Gilden. The two of you will spend the next fifty years in purgatory."

"Derli had nothing to do with this."

"Don't kid yourself. You were screwing her, or more likely she was screwing you. Don't bother to deny it. She pushed you to get the data she wanted. Well, I hope she thinks it was worth it when she finds out what's coming to her."

"You can't hurt her." They were at the entrance to Derli's apartment. "She's pregnant—with your baby."

"I've got a hundred kids." Krieg did not even slow down. "All my women have 'em, I make sure of that. Wise up, Gilden, that's what they're for. One kid more or less means nothing."

The door was unlocked. Derli was still at the display. She turned when they entered but she hardly seemed to see them. The screen showed an enlarged view of the glistening yellow organ that coupled the small Sigil to its great partner.

"Arrin! Did you realize what you were seeing when you made this recording? We had it wrong, everything wrong."

"That doesn't matter now." Krieg released his hold on Gilden and went over to Derli Margrave. He switched off the computer and left a static display. "You can stop screwing around with all that. You and Gilden fucked up big-time. The Sigil left, and now we're leaving. We're going to Earth."

Still it seemed as though Derli was not listening. The screen held her attention. Gilden came to stand between her and Krieg.

"She doesn't want to go back to Earth, can't you see that? She loves it here on Lucidar."

"She's going. So are you, dead or alive. Get out of my way."

"What happened on the Sigil ship was my fault." Gilden moved to put his arms around Derli. "You don't have to take her. Just take me."

"I'll do whatever I like. I'm taking both of you." Krieg was reaching for his belt. "Hands off her."

Derli at last noticed what Krieg was doing. She cried out in horror and tried to pull free of Gilden's hold. "Do what he says, Arrin—whatever he says."

"Take her advice, Gilden." Krieg's fingers were poised above his belt. "Do what I tell you. Last warning. Move!"

"I won't." Gilden tightened his embrace, holding Derli to him. "Try and make me. But I wouldn't if I were you."

"You bloody fool." Krieg's face was red with fury. "I've warned you, three times. You can't say you didn't ask for it."

He pressed a sequence of buttons along his belt.

There was a moment of total stillness, followed by an inhuman groan. It came from Valmar Krieg. He stood, unable to move. All the muscles of his body were contracting at once, tighter and tighter. Sinews and tendons snapped and popped, bones burst from their joints, arms and legs became shapeless bags of blood as veins and arteries ruptured. As he toppled forward the moan of expelled air from the tormented rictus of his mouth continued. But he was dead before his face smashed into the floor.

Gilden moved to stand by the body. "That's one question answered. I wondered what you had in store for me. Sorry, Krieg. I have to say you deserved it."

"You did that to him?" Derli Margrave had collapsed to her knees and was staring at Arrin Gilden's impassive face and Valmar Krieg's body with equal horror.

"I guess I did. He ought to have known better. Dammit, Derli, I'm a *voyeur,* and I'm the best there is. Krieg should have had more sense than to mess with me. Once you told me that coded sequences would activate implants in our skulls I had no choice. There's easy access through the nose and mouth. I sent voyeurs in to discover and erase the sequence from my implant. Yours, too."

"But what happened to Krieg?"

"I changed his coding to match the sequence that used to be in my implant." Gilden gestured to the shapeless hulk at his feet. "That would have been me, Derli. That's what he intended me to be. You, too, maybe."

He went across and lifted her to a standing position. "We're free now. Both of us. We can go where we like, do what we like."

Her eyes were empty. He was not getting through to her.

"Derli!" He shook her. "Snap out of it. If you want to stay on Lucidar without getting arrested we'll have to explain what happened to Krieg." And, when that warning produced no effect, "What's wrong with you? You were like this when we came in, before Krieg ever started in on you. What did you mean, we have everything wrong?"

The question broke her trance where shaking had failed. She began a shallow nod, almost fast enough to be a tremble.

"We did. We misunderstood everything. Now I know why the Sigil cut off contact with people here. I think I know why they left Lucidar— and if we send the right message, I think maybe they'll come back. I have to reach Bravtz'ig."

She started for the communication line, but Gilden stopped her.

"Bravtz'ig won't talk to us. Better if we go over there."

He led the way. Derli was talking nonstop behind him.

"I got off on the wrong foot during the very first meeting with Bravtz'ig. Sexual dimorphism, I said, to explain the size difference between the sexes. I also said that analogy with Earth forms could be misleading and dangerous, but I didn't listen to my own warning. When the records came in from their ship I found myself having trouble whenever I looked at the big Sigil and the small Sigil. To me, they *both* resembled females. But they weren't."

"Of course they weren't." Gilden had to pause to take his bearings. He had never been to Bravtz'ig's work area before in the dark. He turned slightly to the left and set off walking again. "We saw them mating."

"No, we didn't."

"You may not have—but I did. Their coupling is on the data block I just gave you!"

"I know. But you didn't see them mating. For one excellent reason: *the Sigil do not use sexual reproduction.* They are asexual animals. I suspect that they had never encountered sex in any form before they landed on Lucidar. That's what terrified them when they began to learn our biology. Sexual reproduction is such a terrific way of performing genetic variations, anything without it seems at a terrific evolutionary disadvantage. They're *scared* of our biology."

Gilden had to stop, even though it was only another forty or fifty yards to Bravtz'ig's office. "You don't understand, Derli. I don't know what was wrong with the data block that I gave you, but I *saw* them mating. In real time."

"No, you didn't. You just thought you did. There is a valid Earth analogy, but it's not the one that we've both been using. Did you ever hear of a Sphex wasp?"

"What have wasps to do—"

"Everything to do with this. A Sphex wasp is one species of the order of parasitic wasps. Its larvae eat grasshoppers. But the larvae don't catch them. The parent wasp does. She stings the grasshopper, enough to paralyze but not to kill. Then she lays her eggs inside it. They hatch and consume the host grasshopper from within. Some of the other parasitic wasps, ones that lay their eggs in caterpillars, are even trickier. The caterpillar is stung, but it doesn't stay paralyzed. It recovers and goes on feeding. The wasp larva inside feeds on it, eating the caterpillar's organs in ascending order of importance so that the host stays alive as long as possible.

"*That's* the analogy for the Sigil. We are observing two different, asexual species. They look pretty much the same to us, but a grasshopper and a wasp probably look the same to aliens. The little one has evolved to prey on the larger—and carries it on long journeys, so that the smaller one's young will have food. The yellow organ you saw isn't for transfer of sperm. It's a combined sting and ovipositor, to paralyze the big one and then lay eggs inside it."

Gilden recalled the wriggling Sigil, suddenly becoming still as the tapered member pierced its body. "But the big one is *intelligent*. It must realize very well what's being done to it."

"It surely does. But we can't begin to guess how it *feels*. Maybe it even believes itself privileged, to carry the offspring of a superior being. Like the old stories of mortals who bore the children of the gods."

Any horror that Derli might feel was overwhelmed by professional satisfaction. She seemed to experience none of Gilden's revulsion as she moved ahead, leading the way to Bravtz'ig's offices. "But we can go into details on this later," she said over her shoulder. "What we have to do right now is send a message after the Sigil ship, pointing out how asexual animals survive on Earth and Lucidar and compete very well with sexual forms. Of course, that message won't be necessary if the Sigil has simply gone off for solitude during the larval growth period. That's what lots of Earth creatures do. Then the ship may be back anyway in a month or two."

Gilden trailed after her. He was not listening. To experience as the climax of life's experience, not love but the exquisite pain of a wasp's sting. To be protected and cherished not as a companion, but as a living larder. To be consumed slowly and agonizingly from within. And above all else, to *know* your fate and comprehend exactly what was being done to you.

Somehow, the old torments threatened by the Teller seemed feeble and halfhearted.

The Sigil ship had not returned three weeks later when Gilden appeared one evening in Derli's living quarters. She was still hard at work. As Lucidar's expert on both the psychology of the Mentor and the biology of the Sigil, her services were constantly in demand.

She nodded to him. "Dinner? Sit down, Arrin. Ten minutes more and I'll stop."

"You don't need to stop." Gilden did not sit down, but began to pace back and forward behind her. "I didn't come to suggest dinner. I came to say I'm leaving."

"You have to go to Montmorin again?" She was focused on the screen in front of her.

"No. I'm leaving Lucidar."

"Didn't I tell you? We don't have to. Bravtz'ig says the Mentor daren't try a military move, and Lucidar would never agree to our extradition. We're quite safe here."

"It's not that. I came to say *goodbye*."

She froze, still staring at the screen. "You mean—you're leaving me?"

"Yes."

"I thought you . . . cared for me." She swung around. "No. I thought you *loved* me. That's what you've been telling me for the past few weeks."

"It was true. It *is* true."

"I see." Derli stared down, to her swelling belly. "I *see*. I've been a fool. I started a relationship with you when I had another man's child growing inside me. That was crazy. You can't put up with that, no man could."

He said nothing, and at last she went on, "It's the baby, isn't it? You can't stand the idea that I'm carrying Valmar Krieg's baby. But it's *my* baby, too. And you want me to get rid of it. You think, I could just go and have an abortion—"

"Stop it. Right there." Gilden halted in front of her. "I could agree with you, tell you that it's the baby. That's an easy out. But it wouldn't be true."

"Then what is it?" Derli could not hide her misery and confusion. "I know I've not had enough time for you, I've been so busy the past couple of weeks."

"It's not that I'm feeling neglected, either. I've been busy, too. And it's certainly not the baby. It's *me.* You tell me I'm cured, that everything is fine now. That I'm sexually normal—"

"More than normal. You are a wonderful lover."

"So you say. But Derli, inside my head I'm a *mess.* I dare not tell you what I think about when the two of us make love. I have to go away and try to sort myself out."

"But you'll come back?"

"I hope so."

"When?"

"I don't know."

"Might you come back when the baby is born? I mean, you say it's not the baby. . . ."

"One more time: *it's not the baby.*"

"Because I haven't said anything to you, but I've been really worried. I came through a subspace trip when I was pregnant, which you're not supposed to do. Then when we got here there were the changes of air and food and gravity, and no one seems to know what effect that might have. Maybe it's going to be abnormal, maybe it will be deformed. . . ." She paused. "I don't see anything funny in this!"

Because Gilden was smiling. "Derli, you don't give me credit for anything, do you? Not for caring about you, not for worrying about you, not for watching over you. Not even for competence in the one field where I'm supposed to be better than anyone in the Empyrium."

He leaned forward and touched his fingertips to her abdomen.

"Don't worry about the baby. Take my word for it: she's doing just fine."

> *The bee's kiss, now!*
> *Kiss me as if you entered gay*
> *My heart at some noonday,*
> *A bud that dares not disallow*
> *The claim, so all is rendered up,*
> *And passively its shattered cup*
> *Over your head to sleep I bow.*

—Robert Browning, from "In a Gondola"

Afterword to "The Bee's Kiss"

I usually tell people that I don't write horror stories, but if this isn't one then I don't know what is. The horror for me lies not in the fiction, which is a homey tale of human obsession, domination, cruelty, torture, and death. No. The horror is all in the factual statements about parasitic wasps that occur late in the story.

I have seen the event for myself, and it's much worse than I described. The biggest Sphex wasp (*Sphecius speciosus,* a monster up to two inches long) captures cicadas and takes them underground to feed its young. However, it is big and strong enough to grab its prey *in flight.* The cicadas make a loud squealing noise when they are caught, which they keep up until the wasp stings and paralyzes them. There is no way that they can know what is going to happen to them, but they certainly sound as though they do and the result is truly awful to hear.

If you see this happening and are tempted to interfere on behalf of the cicada I suggest that you think again. This species of wasp is said to have the most painful sting of any insect—and that refers to its effect on a human, a hundred pounds or more in weight. What it must feel like to a tiny cicada is beyond our power to imagine.

But I couldn't help trying.

Millennium

Portents are tricky things. You have to know how to look for them.

I saw the last one as soon as I came out of my house after morning prayers. I went across to where my neighbor, Newberry, was digging his fool garden.

"See that?"

He peered in the wrong direction.

"Nope."

"Not there. *There.* The sun—it has a ring around it. Take a look."

"Without sunglasses? You crazy?" But he stared anyway, shielding his eyes with his hand. He shook his head. "Can't see a thing. Should I?"

"You should. This is the last day of December, 1999. The last day of the last week of the last year before Judgment Day. Are you ready for *that*, Newberry?"

He didn't answer. Just shook his head and went back to digging up parsnips, or whatever them white carrot things are. He was a gardening maniac.

At least his hobby was an innocent one. Newberry and I were bachelors, and he might go to Heaven. But the woman in the house the other side of his wouldn't. She was married. Her husband worked weekends. There was a delivery truck in Maggie Milner's drive, and no doubt what was being delivered. It was the same every Saturday. One more day, though, and Maggie would be roasting in Hell with a white-hot you-know-what.

Serve her right.

And Joe Sotter on the other side of her. He was out in his yard, too, waiting for his dog to sniff its way all along the fence. Joe must have tipped the scale at over five-fifty. He had a triple-decker sandwich in one hand, his chins were covered with grease, and his jaws never stopped moving. It would take a year of rendering on Lucifer's griddle just to bring him to normal size.

I went back indoors. The thing that I couldn't understand was that last Sunday they'd all been in church—the same church as me. But not one of them seemed to realize that if they didn't shape up quick, in another week the Millennium would arrive and it would be too late. Then they'd all be writhing and wriggling for eternity on the tines of the Devil's Fork.

And serve them right. I went to my basement and set to work again. I was almost finished.

What I was doing was a bit different, but I'd checked and checked and it wasn't forbidden by any Scripture. A man couldn't *survive* Judgment Day, but there was nothing to say he couldn't last just long enough to take a peek around after the final trump sounded. And Charbonneau, the little faggy Frenchman at the factory, swore that Neutrite, the material he had made in his lab, could stand *anything:* heat and pressures that were out of this world.

Well, I was going to put *that* statement to the test—not that he would be around to know the result. No doubt where *he* was going, with his earring and perfume and curled hair. Serve him right.

It took the rest of the day to put the finishing touches on the big coffin I had built from the Neutrite smuggled home from the factory. Finally . . .

Eleven o'clock. One hour to go to the Millennium. I climb in the coffin and fix the seal. Against all the odds, I fall into a sound sleep.

Morning. Judgment Day. And the world is still here.

Or some of it. I climb up out of the basement, and my house is sheared off at the foundations. So is Newberry's, next door, and Maggie Milner's, and Joe Sotter's, and on down the row. Gone, all of them. Sotter's dog is still there, though, sniffing around the flat, fenceless yard.

And along the empty street, ten doors down as it used to be, one house still stands complete and untouched.

My legs don't want to move, but I manage to walk to it. Unbelievably, I see a man standing in the open doorway.

But I am the last man in the world. He can't exist.

"What are you doing here?" I wonder if I am addressing an angel.

He gives me that polite-but-insolent look you get from foreigners.

"Excuse me?" he says. His eyes stray back down the street. Now I can see that other isolated houses are still standing. "Excuse me, sir," he says again, "but can you please explain to me what has happened?"

Arab, from his voice. I had been right.

"The end of the world, boy, that's what's happened. Exactly as I expected. Yesterday was the last day. Judgment Day. The final day, in the final month, in the final year of the millennium. December 31st, 1999."

He shakes his head. "With all respect, sir, that is not so."

"Huh? What's not so?"

"This is not the millennium."

"It sure is."

"No, sir. Not for me. Like all good Moslems, I date events from the flight of Mohammed from Mecca. According to your calendar, that took place in your year 622. So according to *my* calendar, we are now in the year 1378."

1378! I take another glance down the street. Now I can identify the few houses that still stand. There's where that fat Chinese lived, the one who ran the fast food store. There's the Jew's house, the one who worked at the bank. And that's the home of the skinny little Indian from the dry cleaner's.

They are coming out of their scattered houses, one by one, staring up and down the near-empty road. And they are coming this way, godless heathens all who measure the passage of the years with their nonsensical non-Christian calendars.

The *Christian* Millennium.

Left behind, Chinese, Egyptians, Japanese, Algerians, Burmese, Pakistanis, Indians, Jews. Millions and billions of them, crawling all over the world.

And me.

It is going to be a bad day. A bad year, a bad forever.

What a fool to think I might postpone Judgment Day. This is Hell, and I am in it.

Afterword to "Millennium"

According to Sheffield's Law, stories of less than 2,000 words are excused Afterwords.

FIFTEEN-LOVE ON THE DEAD MAN'S CHEST

"EVERYTHING," WALDO SAID morosely, "is *relative.*"

He slumped low in his office chair, a man bearing the weight of the whole world.

I nodded in mute sympathy. He was right, and there was little that I could do to console him.

"It's ridiculous," he added. "I mean, it's not as though I was *dead.*"

I could only nod again and reflect, not for the first time, that there ought to be a collective noun to describe the group of relatives who, unseen and unheard from since early childhood, rush in after a family death to attend the reading of the will and to fight over the best bits of furniture. A *concupiscence* of *nephews?* A *grab* of *grandsons?* A *covet* of *cousins?*

Except that in Waldo's case, none of these applied. He was merely the victim of circumstance. As he rightly remarked, he was not dead, and nothing but pure coincidence had decreed that, in the same month of the same year, a major tennis tournament and the solar system's largest morticians' convention would be held in Luna City. And long before that, nothing but blind fate had persuaded his maternal aunts, Ruth and Ruby, to choose for their soulmates a wealthy tennis fanatic, Pharaoh Potter, and a leading undertaker, Mortimer C. Wilberforce.

The four had moved far away, to Mars in the case of Pharaoh and Ruth, to the Venus Domes for Mortimer and Ruby. But now they were back. Pharaoh, after many years of talking about winning a tennis tournament, had actually entered as a player in the Luna Senior Doubles; and

Mortimer C., still obliged to work for a living, was enrolled in a Do-It-Yourself embalming course on the other side of the city, while also taking in the convention, plus the occasional funeral, for entertainment.

Simple pleasures, you might say. The bad news was that both wives and husbands were staying with Waldo; and by their attitude the four members of the Potter and Wilberforce party were making him most unhappy. As he complained to me, they pushed him around all the time. He didn't know how to argue with them.

It's a baffling thing. You have one man who spends his whole life hitting a little ball so some other half-wit can hit it back to him, and another who paints up dead bodies so they'll look nice and healthy when they're burned or buried. You have their two wives, who do nothing at all. Yet *all* of them look down on Waldo, because he is a lawyer.

And it's not as though Waldo had plenty of time to entertain his odious relatives. Quite the opposite. He and I, after several slow months, had just become busy with what could well be the biggest case of our careers.

It had begun with no more than a rumor. There are certain words that will start one, anytime or anywhere that they are whispered or even breathed.

Try this word: *immortality.*

But to Waldo and me it had been no more than a rumor. In Luna City rumors are as common as cockroaches, and about as fast-moving.

All that had changed, though, with the late night arrival of Imre Munsen at the offices of Burmeister and Carver, Attorneys-at-Law.

Imre Munsen, Special Investigator for the United Space Federation; Imre Munsen, my nemesis, convinced despite much evidence to the contrary that I was, like him, a starry-eyed, patriotic hero with nerves of steel. Imre Munsen, with the authority to force anyone to do anything that he asked.

Imre Munsen, idiot. I never wanted to see him again. But there he was, sitting in Waldo's favorite chair and shaking his rugged-jawed head at us.

"Perhaps not a mere rumor, gentlemen. There may be a lot more to it than that. Here's what we know, for certain sure. Carlo Moolman flew to Luna last week, from Oberon. He claimed, and he wasn't bashful about it, that an inventor out there had discovered an 'immortality serum.' Moolman said he actually had a sample with him, a little phial of liquid. He didn't claim it would let a person live forever, but he did insist that it would increase your life expectancy to a thousand years. He wanted to sell shares in its development and marketing. What does that suggest to you?"

Waldo and I exchanged glances.

"A confidence trickster," Waldo said firmly. "Looking for suckers. Everybody knows there's no capital available on Oberon."

"True." Munsen leaned forward, and gave us his patented steely-eyed glare. "And Carlo Moolman does happen to have a criminal record. But suppose this time it's different. *Suppose this time he's telling the truth?*"

"I wouldn't put any money on it if I were you," I said.

"Maybe not. But the USF *has* to take the possibility seriously. Can you imagine what an immortality serum would do to the solar system?"

Waldo suddenly took on a mournful air. I think he was imagining Ruth, Ruby, Pharaoh, and Mortimer staying with him forever.

"I don't understand this," I said. "Carlo Moolman came to Luna, and presumably, since you didn't say he left, he's still here. Why not take him in for direct questioning? If it comes to that, why not go to Oberon and question the inventor of the serum?"

"Excellent thinking, Mr. Carver." Munsen favored me with a flash of white teeth. "We can't do that, for two very good reasons. The inventor is dead; and so is Carlo Moolman."

It was not difficult to spot a certain weakness in Imre's argument. "Two men with an immortality serum," I began, "and both are dead—"

"But not of natural causes, Mr. Carver. I don't know about the fellow back on Oberon, but I saw Moolman's body. Somebody blew a hole in his belly, big enough to put your whole head through."

A less appealing course of action was difficult to imagine. I suggested as much.

"And of course," Munsen went on, as though he had not heard me, "there was no sign of the immortality serum on his body."

"Might he have drunk it himself, or hidden it somewhere on or in his body?"

"Not according to the autopsy. No." Munsen stood up and began to pace around the office. "I think that if it existed at all, he hid it. But where? There must be a clue, somewhere. We're looking, you can be sure of that. Meanwhile, his funeral is the day after tomorrow. And of course, his enemies may attend—the people who killed him. They're as keen to get their hands on the serum as we are. It's important for us to know what they are up to."

"So you and your men will be there," I said slowly. I didn't know what was doing it, but I felt an uneasy creepy sensation up my back, as though a Hidalgan centipede was ascending under my shirt.

"Me and my crew can't do that." Munsen shook his head firmly. "We're too well known; we'd be recognized in a minute. Anyway, we'd have to more or less force our way in. What we need is someone who can be invited to the funeral in a natural way. Someone like Mr. Burmeister—whose uncle, as I understand it, is a big wheel in mortician circles and could get him invited into almost anything connected with funerals."

I felt a giddy sense of relief. The Angel of Death, dive-bombing in on me, had suddenly veered aside and picked the next man in line.

"Of course," I said.

"Of course not," said Waldo.

"Actually, Mr. Burmeister is correct," Munsen agreed. "He won't quite do. He is—with all due respect, Mr. Burmeister—rather too conspicuous because of his size. We need someone less noticeable, someone who can keep a low profile, blend into the background. Someone like—"

"I don't know Uncle Mortimer. I'd never get invited to the funeral."

"Mr. Burmeister could invite you to dinner at his home."

"I don't have the right clothes for a funeral."

"They will be provided. Black top hat, dark cutaway coat, black polished shoes, everything."

"And if you just let Uncle Mort talk corpses to you for an hour or so, Henry," Waldo said cheerfully, "he'll be so tickled he'll get you invited to any funeral on the Moon. He's been trying to drag me to one for days. What a pity, as Mr. Munsen says, that I'm too conspicuous." Waldo stared down happily at his ample belly, and hugged his fat to him like a protective shield.

I wondered, in a hopeless sort of way, how much fat a human being could put on in a couple of days. Not enough, I felt sure, to save me.

Waldo had described the family dinners to me, but I had discounted much of what he said. Having seen Waldo's own prowess with a knife and fork, I deemed it remotely improbable that anyone at a meal table could deprive him of his rightful share of sustenance.

That, of course, was before I met the Potter and Wilberforce wives.

I arrived a few minutes late. Waldo was busy in the kitchen, and at my first sight of his living room when I entered, it seemed totally filled with aunts. A second look revealed just one massive pair, trampling and trumpeting like angry mastodons over the mangled ruins of trays of hors d'oeuvres.

Ruth and Ruby were a year apart in age, and perhaps two kilos apart in bulk. There was less difference between them than the mass of any one of their many chins.

I used to blame Waldo for being fat, but after I saw his aunts I vowed never to accuse him again. With such genes, he didn't stand a chance. In fact, it was a tribute to the size of Ruby and Ruth that Pharaoh Potter was not himself a noticeable landmark. He was a big-framed man, well run to seed now but still possessing plenty of muscle on arms like a gorilla. He shook my hand, in a grip that mashed my bones together.

"Play any tennis?" he said.

"Haven't for a while. I used to." It seemed the safest answer: express interest, but don't let yourself get dragged into any possibility of playing. I did not know it at the time, but my reply exhibited an uncanny prescience. "I never was much good," I added.

"Because you're little and weedy," Pharaoh replied. "A person needs some *weight* to make decent tennis shots." He went off to sit in the corner with his head bowed. He was a man apparently in the grip of some great sorrow.

I turned to Mortimer C. Wilberforce, just as Waldo called us through for dinner. Mort was the odd man out in the group, a function I suppose of his job. It's probably a sort of professional requirement among morticians, that if you can't actually *be* a corpse, you ought to look as much like one as you can. Mortimer did his best. If he had been the right height for his weight, he would have been about four-foot-two. As it was he was six-five, and pale as a well-blanched stalk of celery.

I suppose he ate, but in this he was rather like a government official working. No matter how long and hard you looked, you would never see it happen.

From my point of view, his behavior at the dinner table had one great disadvantage. I wanted to talk to him, but like a mute at a funeral he had no conversation and no apparent interest in anything. He seemed half-asleep. It was left to the others, and Pharaoh in particular, to make the running in the talk department.

Which he certainly did. According to Waldo the dinner table conversation usually consisted of a catalog of deficiencies, Waldo's personal ones and that of the free food that he was providing. Tonight, however, another concern predominated.

Pharaoh Potter's tennis partner had become disabled, and would be unable to play the next day. Pharaoh seemed to regard this as an Act of God, although he admitted that the other's injury had occurred when Pharaoh knocked him flat and ran right over him.

"It was actually his own fault," Pharaoh explained. "He was poaching. The ball was clearly in my territory on the court. He should never have been there at all."

"But now, my love," said Aunt Ruth, "you have a problem. You need a partner."

"Yeah. I know." Pharaoh glanced along the table. I could see him dismissing me.

'Little and weedy.' Well, better that than a great fat lout.

Mortimer, as the closest living relative of the stick insect, received an even lower approval rating. Ruth and Ruby were clearly A-1 in the weight department, but they had the great disadvantage, for a men's doubles, of being females.

That left . . .

I saw Pharaoh's eye rest on Waldo, who was fighting the good fight for his share of the victuals.

I watched the wheels turn. Adequate weight, certainly. Apparently in good health, as anyone must be who could hold his own with Ruth and Ruby in the struggle to be at the top of the food chain. Available tomorrow, since lawyers never did any useful work.

"Waldo!"

My business partner, distracted in his tug-of-war with Aunt Ruth over a dish of sliced green beans, turned to face Pharaoh.

"What?"

"You. You can be my tennis partner tomorrow."

"I cannot!" Waldo, in an excess of emotion, lost his grip on the plate of food.

"Of course you can, Waldo," Aunt Ruby said firmly. "You know how to play. I've seen you."

"When I was a child!"

"It's like riding a bicycle. You never forget."

"I have to work tomorrow."

"Nonsense. You can take a day off." Aunt Ruth turned to me. "Can't he, Mr. Carver? You can spare him, can't you?"

It was time to come to the aid of my old friend and colleague. But I could not forget that I was supposed to attend a funeral tomorrow, where more than likely people would be trying to kill me. Compared with that, a tennis tournament was nothing. And Waldo had been more than happy to throw me to the wolves who had murdered Carlo Moolman, so long as he didn't have to face them himself.

I nodded. "I can spare him."

"I don't have a tennis outfit." Waldo was grasping at straws.

"As it happens, I have one in the next room." Pharaoh stood up. "I bought it for my old partner, but for some reason he refused to wear it. He's just about your size, too."

He was back in half a minute. In his hand he held a tennis outfit. Waldo gave it one appalled glance.

"You can't expect me to wear that! Look at the color."

"What's wrong with it? A nice, warm brown."

I realized at this point that Pharaoh Potter must be color-blind. What he was holding was the most hideous shade of hot pink I had ever seen. If Waldo wore that, he ought to be arrested for multiple offenses against society.

Waldo thought so, too. "It's hideous," he said. "Isn't it, Henry?"

"It is. But you can have it dyed."

"Mmph?" Mortimer jerked into life at my side. "Who died?"

He was awake at last. I had found the magic word. Leaving Waldo to fight on alone, I seized my chance, and threw at Mort a snappy series of questions on the theory and practice of embalming.

In five minutes, as Waldo's weakening howls of protest rose from the other end of the table, I knew I had Mortimer C. Wilberforce eating out of my hand. Certainly he knew the right funeral home directors. Surely I would be welcomed at the final rites for my friend Carlo Moolman. He would arrange it. What a pleasure it was to meet a man with a proper interest in funerals. All he asked was that I not embarrass him by wearing inappropriate dress.

I was able to reassure him. On that sort of detail, Imre Munsen was infinitely reliable. I promised that I would actually arrange for the outfit to be delivered to Waldo's home tomorrow, so that Mortimer could review it personally if he so chose. He didn't seem to think that would be necessary. When I described the promised clothing to him, he nodded approval of every last stitch.

For his part, Mortimer assured me, if he was not present himself when I arrived to change into my funeral garb, he would make sure that directions to get to the funeral home—one of Luna City's biggest and most prestigious—would be written on a little yellow card and left on the hall table.

Dinner was over, the evening's work was done. I made an earlier than usual departure. Waldo was still fighting a rear-guard action, but I knew already that he had lost his argument. He would be Pharaoh Potter's tennis partner tomorrow. It served him right for abandoning me to Imre Munsen. Still, I had to leave. It gave me no pleasure to see a grown man's misery.

I thought that I had allowed plenty of time to get dressed after I arrived at Waldo's home the next day. But there must be a special technique for getting into funeral clothes, one that I didn't have, and Uncle Mort was not around to help. I struggled with the shirt, with the tight collar of the shirt, with the studs of the shirt, with the tie, with the shoes, with the laces on the shoes. When I finally had the shoes on and tied, I had to take them off and start again, because I couldn't get into the trousers unless I was barefoot.

I was already late when I ran downstairs, grabbed Uncle Mort's little yellow card from the hall table, and hurried out. Then it was bad luck again. It was ten more minutes before I could flag a groundcar cab to take me through the complex multiple domes of Luna City toward my destination. I had never heard of the address of the funeral home, but that was no surprise. Luna City just grew and grew, bigger and more difficult to navigate around every year.

Traffic was hell, and half the time we didn't seem to be moving at all. When I at last paid off the cab, I glanced at my watch. I should have been here twenty minutes ago. Did funerals run on schedule? As I hurried inside and along a dimly lit and seemingly endless tunnel, I wondered if funeral reporters had a special word to describe people like me, who did not arrive on time for the ceremony. "The late Henry Carver" would be too confusing.

The tunnel made a final right-angle turn, and abruptly ended. I dashed the last ten yards and emerged into a large open space.

Suddenly I had trouble breathing.

Perhaps it was the tightness of my collar, cutting off the blood supply to my brain. Perhaps it was the light, far brighter than I had expected.

Or perhaps it was the fact that everyone standing close to me was dressed in tennis clothes, while all around me a crowd of maybe two thousand people roared with delight at my appearance.

In my surrealist daze, I saw one familiar face: Pharaoh Potter. I went to him.

"There's been a mix-up," I said. "I got the wrong address card. I'm going now. I'm supposed to be at a funeral."

I started to edge away, but Potter grabbed my arm.

"Are you trying to tell me that Waldo's not coming?"

"I guess not."

"But he's my partner!"

"I'm sorry about that. I have to go." I tried to pull away again.

But Pharaoh still held my arm. He stuck his red face close to mine. "I didn't travel fifty million miles, and get this far in the tournament, not to play. You stay. You're going to be my partner. You said that you know how to play tennis."

"That was twenty years ago! I've forgotten."

"Then you'd better learn again, real quick." He raised his racket, and his muscles bulged. "Unless you want to leave here with a couple of broken arms and a concussion, and your liver tied in knots."

Pharaoh certainly had a way with words. Five minutes later I had been equipped with a racket and stood waiting to receive service.

It had not been an easy few minutes. The crowd, pleased already by my initial appearance, was ecstatic to learn that I would stay to play. The wits among them went to town.

"Five to two against Gravedigger Jim and Fat Jack Sprat!"

"Done! They're bound to win once their reinforcements get here— you know pallbearers always come in sixes."

"Ashes to ashes and deuce to deuce."

"Hey, Mister Undertaker, don't ask me to stay for *your* service."

Our opponents also did not escape the notice of the masses. They were Mason and Mulligan Coot, two shiningly bald-headed and bow-legged brothers of like age and physique, once presumably athletic, but now only slightly less creaking and musclebound than Pharaoh Potter. They seemed to blame me for the unwanted attention, and they seethed at us across the net while the crowd gave them their moment of glory.

"New balls, umpire. Those two have lost all their fuzz."

"Come on, the bandy-Coots. Show a bow leg there."

"What did Gravedigger Jim say to the Cootie brothers? 'Who'll inherit your money, when you've got no hair apparent?' "

Even bad things must come to an end.

"Play," called the umpire. Mulligan lifted his racket. One second later, a head-high serve that I only just saw went like a bullet past my right ear and on into the crowd without touching the ground.

"Out," called a line judge.

"Well left!" cried Pharaoh Potter.

"Second service," said the umpire.

Mulligan raised his racket again.

I saw this one coming clearly enough, but I failed to hit it.

"Out!" shouted Pharaoh optimistically.

"Got to move faster, Gravedigger Jim!" cried someone in the crowd. "Stop imitating your clientele."

"Fifteen-love," the umpire said. "Quiet, please." But he spoke without much hope in his voice.

Things did not improve as the match went on. I had dispensed with my top hat at the outset. After a couple of minutes of running about in stiff black leather shoes, I was forced to take those off, too, or blister my feet beyond bearing. Soon after that, the heat of battle led me to remove my jacket and tie, and to open my shirt all the way down my chest.

At that point the coarser elements of the crowd, for whatever reason, changed their line of attack. They now affected the conceit that I was neither a tennis player nor a pallbearer, but a male stripper.

"Let's see them flowered undies!" they called. And "Don't be shy, sweetheart, give us a peep at your wedding tackle," and "Take 'em off, take 'em all off!"

With such distractions, it is not easy to play one's best. It is, in fact, not even easy to play one's worst. Pharaoh Potter and I began disastrously, four games without a single point, and we would surely have continued that way had not I, in the middle of the fifth game, stuck my racket in the way of a speeding topspin forehand, mishit it, and accidentally popped the ball way up into the air for an easy midcourt smash.

Mason was standing waiting, in a perfect position.

"Mine!" he shouted to his partner watching at the net.

"Hit it ha-a-a-a-rd," Mulligan roared.

Mason did. Stepping back a couple of paces, he drove the ball with supernatural force and accuracy straight into Mulligan Coot's open mouth.

The line judges pried it out all right, with a little bit of effort; but after that the Mason/Mulligan combination was never the same.

Mulligan, you see, was convinced that brother Mason had done it on purpose. The next time Mason was up at the net, Mulligan took careful aim and sent his rocket first serve smack into the back of his partner's bald head. The ball rose about a hundred feet in the air before it came down—on our side of the court and in play, oddly enough, but of course the point was already over.

Their game went rather downhill from there. With neither of them willing to approach the net for fear of flesh wounds, and each trying to make sure that he stood at all times safely behind the other, anything of ours that managed to creep over the net to their side of the court became a near-automatic winner.

Even so, it was far from a rout. They still had power, and when they could not aim at each other their shots came screaming across the net like artillery shells. On our side, we swung and sweated and cringed and sliced and hacked. Pharaoh lashed out in a ferocious half volley at one ball right at his feet, then had to take a break to pry his mutilated left big toe from between the strings of his racket.

I was not without my own problems of timing. I flailed at one of Mulligan's whizzing forehands and missed it completely. The ball flashed past my questing racket and vanished inside my open shirt. No one—partner, opponents, umpire, or onlookers—had any idea where it had gone. It was not until I wriggled and squirmed, and the ball to the crowd's delight appeared from the bottom of my black trousers, that the point was decided.

Even that infuriated Pharaoh Potter. "You should have kept it hid," he growled at me. "They hit it last. It would have been called out."

Pharaoh wanted to win in the worst way. As we went on, I realized that might be exactly the way we would do it. On the other side of the net, Mulligan and Mason cursed and hollered at each other, ran backward far more than they ran forward, and tried to return the ball only when their brother and preferred target was nowhere in the field of view.

We lost the first set but we won the second one easily.

The third and final set, however, was something else. Pharaoh Potter was too fat for sustained running and I, while trim, had the muscles and stamina of one whose daily exercise seldom went beyond lifting a restraining order.

Mulligan and Mason had started in better shape, but since the fifth game they had been continuously running to get behind each other, and shouting brotherly oaths and accusations as they did so. They were also peppered with round pink impact marks, and they sat at courtside longer and longer between games.

The match in its third set went the way that I rather imagine the heat-death of the universe will go, entropy increasing to a maximum and everything gradually running down.

Pharaoh and the Coot brothers were built for short sprints, not for endurance events. Rocket serves became light zephyrs that drifted over the net. Returns, if they happened at all, floated through the air like summer thistledown. Protests at line calls became increasingly feeble.

As the pace slowed, the crowd quieted. Only our anguished sighs and despairing groans punctuated the gentle ping of ball on racket.

It went on for an endless age, and I knew it would go on forever. So it was a great shock to look up at last at the scoreboard, and find that Pharaoh and I were leading by five games to four, with my serve to come next. I was in a position to win the match.

At that point, the crowd became totally silent. I think they realized that they were witnessing something unique in tennis history. After all, how many other final games of a tournament match have been played with three of the four contestants sitting down?

It had been hard on all of us, but the other three were carrying twice my weight. For the final game, Mason Coot sat in the middle of the court. His brother slumped a few feet in front of him, all fear of violence from behind long since past. On my side Pharaoh was close to the net, lying facedown on the center line.

All I had to do was serve to the right part of the court and we would win, because no one else would move no matter where the ball went. It gives some idea of the quality of my play when I confess that the game went to deuce seven times, before the umpire could at last proclaim, "Game, set, and match to Potter and Carver."

The crowd swept onto the court and carried us off. They had to. The victory ceremony was conducted with all parties lying down.

Pharaoh and I not only won our match, we won another prize, too. It was a special award, given for the contest that in the opinion of the crowd was the most enthralling of the day. No one else, I gather, came even close.

I thought that Pharaoh Potter might be offended about that, once he had somewhat recovered. But not at all; to him, a tennis trophy was a tennis trophy, however won. He was thrilled, and when he could again stand up he insisted on taking us to the pavilion and buying me and the Coot brothers, our good buddies now, as many drinks as we chose to take in.

In our depleted condition, that turned out to be rather a lot. It was maybe four hours later that I was buttoning my shirt, seeking my shoes, and reflecting to myself that it had been, despite a bad beginning, a perfect day for me as well as Pharaoh. I had never before, in my whole life, won anything in an athletic event. It is strange what such an experience can do to a man's mind.

A perfect day, I thought.

I wrinkled my brow.

Perfect?

That didn't seem quite right. Shouldn't it be *almost* perfect?

Something started to drift back into my muddled consciousness. Hadn't I been supposed to go to a funeral?

I had. Carlo Moolman's funeral. What about that, and what about the immortality serum? If I had come to a tennis match instead of a funeral, then was it possible that . . .

For the first time in many hours, I wondered what had happened to Waldo.

Waldo had been late for his appointment, too, but for quite different reasons. The bleach had worked reasonably well on his tennis outfit, enough to mute shocking hot pink to a pale, fleshy tone. However, the washing process had produced an unforeseen side effect.

The tennis outfit had shrunk. A lot. Waldo managed to squeeze his bulk into it, but only with enormous effort. It was like a second skin. When he caught a glimpse of himself in a full-length mirror, the combination of tight fit and fleshy tones produced the momentary illusion that he was staring at a stark naked Waldo Burmeister.

He shuddered, but there was no time to change. Not that he was sure he could; getting those clothes off promised to be even harder than putting them on.

He glanced at a clock. He was *late,* late as he could be. Uncle Pharaoh would kill him.

He grabbed socks and tennis shoes, picked up the little yellow card that Pharaoh Potter had left on the hall table giving directions how to reach the tournament, rushed barefoot out into the street, and hailed the first cab that he could find.

He held out the card. "This address, fast as you can get there."

The cabby, Waldo insists, was struck dumb by his appearance. This, if true, does much to support Waldo's claim of looking something well beyond the mundane, since Luna City cabbies are not easily silenced. However, the cab made excellent speed, and when Waldo was dropped off in front of a huge circular building he gave the driver a big tip. It was only as the taxi vanished from view that he realized that he had left his socks, tennis shoes, and wallet on the cab seat.

No time to pursue them—Pharaoh Potter would be chomping at the bit. Anyway, Waldo could borrow shoes and socks before the match. He hurried into the building's entrance foyer, which struck him as unusually somber, silent, and formal for a sports pavilion.

There was just one person to be seen, a wizened individual standing at the other side of the room and apparently guarding the players' entrance.

Waldo padded to him across cold marble tiles. "I'm a beginner at this sort of event," he said.

The man, who according to Waldo had the air of someone wearing a previously owned body, stared at Waldo's attire. "I can see that."

"So I wondered if there's a special warm-up area, for people who don't do this sort of thing regularly."

It was a natural enough question, but the man was more than unresponsive. He was eyeing Waldo with odd suspicion.

"No," he said. "Everybody has to go the same way. Right in there, and follow the line. Slowly now. No rushing about once you're inside."

It was an odd injunction. How did you ever win a tennis match, if you didn't do a certain amount of rushing about?

Waldo went through the door and found himself facing an altogether excessive abundance of flowering plants. There were floral arrangements everywhere. The tennis courts, he decided, must be on just the other side of all the shrubbery.

He pushed aside a great mass of greenery. He blundered through. As he emerged into subdued lighting and soft music, it crossed his mind for the first time that perhaps things were not quite what they seemed.

Where was the net, where was the court? Where were all the other players?

Not, he was fairly sure, anywhere near here. He was standing in the middle of a group of maybe twenty people. But it was difficult to accept them as participants in a tennis tournament, since every man was clad in a customary suit of solemn black, while the women were all hatted and veiled. The whole line was moving slowly toward a dais, on which stood an elaborately carved casket. Waldo, willy-nilly, moved with them.

His present attire had made his flesh crawl, even in the privacy of his own bedroom. Now he realized what an overreaction that had been. All crawling of the flesh should have been saved for this moment, when every eye was on him and the moving line bore him irresistibly toward the dais. Soon he was approaching the coffin, wondering what to do next.

Waldo is given to exaggeration. It may well have been, as he said, an open-casket ceremony. It is not, I am sure, true that the corpse of Carlo Moolman rolled its eyes in horror at Waldo as he walked to stand by the coffin.

Carlo had been arranged to look his best for his final appearance. He was wearing a white shirt, a well-cut suit of subdued gray with a dark red pinstripe, and a maroon bow tie. Waldo stared down at those conservative clothes, and he coveted them. He was already dreading the return journey home, penniless, on public transportation. Just give him ten minutes alone with that corpse. . . .

It was pure wishful thinking. Already the line was moving on, past the open casket. And it was then that Waldo became aware of something else. Everyone was staring, but they were not all looking at him the same way. Two men, standing on the other side of Carlo Moolman's open coffin, had in their eyes a strange and speculative gleam as he moved past them.

Big men. Hard-eyed, tough-looking men. The sort of men who would cheerfully blow a large hole through Carlo Moolman, then attend his funeral in the hope of learning the whereabouts of the missing immortality serum.

Waldo hadn't listened to much of what Imre Munsen said, because the words seemed at the time to have little relevance to him. But he remembered this comment: "Of course, his enemies will attend—the people who killed him. They're as keen to get their hands on the serum as we are."

It occurred to Waldo, with the force of revelation, that he and he alone knew exactly who those enemies were. They still didn't have the serum, but it must be somewhere close by. Somewhere, probably, within this very funeral home.

Then came what Waldo described as his finest moment; or possibly, depending on your point of view, his act of supreme folly. Inadequately briefed—in both senses of the phrase—he decided that he must pursue the investigation.

Once the viewing line was past the coffin, it lost all cohesion and focus. Some people headed straight out of the door, back toward the entrance foyer. Others in the line broke into little groups, chatting together in low voices. Waldo waited for one of the rare moments when everyone did not seem to be staring at him. Then instead of going toward the exit he went on, through an unmarked door that led deeper into the funeral home.

He at once found himself in what might be termed the business district. The walls were cement, the floor uncarpeted. Lights were unshaded and harsh, and no flowers were anywhere in sight. What Waldo did see were a number of metal tables, and a variety of most unpleasant-looking surgical implements. Needles and stout thread on one of the tables, plus elaborate makeup kits, did nothing to make him feel more comfortable.

He hurried on, to still another door. As he passed through it, he heard the door through which he had come in beginning to open. Heavy footsteps sounded at the entrance.

Waldo pushed the door shut behind him and stared around in panic. It was another room, severe, chilly, and dimly lit, with only a couple more doors and no cupboards or closets within which he might hide. The furnishings were just a half-dozen metal tables. Most of them bore suspicious-looking long lumpy objects, each covered with a white sheet.

The footsteps in the other room were louder. Waldo could hear voices. He shuddered, climbed onto the one unoccupied table, and pulled a white sheet over himself. It was a little too short. He was able to cover his head, but then his bare feet remained uncovered.

The door was opening.

"Not here," said a gruff voice, just the sort of voice Waldo expected a ruthless murderer to have. "It's a bunch of stiffs."

"He must have come through here, though." That was the other man. "Nowhere else he could have gone. You head back and tell the boys what's happening. I'll keep going."

Heavy feet clumped, closer and closer. Waldo tried to stop his heart beating. If they pulled back the sheet, and got one look at his face . . .

Another door opened and closed. Before the echo died away, Waldo was off the table. They would be back, no doubt about it. Shivering, he scurried across to the only other door and hustled through.

At least this little room was *warm,* for a change. And there was more. All along one wall was a broad shelf, about three feet wide. On it stood a dozen blue boxes, each one labeled with the notation, HOLD FOR PICK-UP. Below that, each one bore a person's name.

Personal possessions, they had to be. Things that happened to be on a body when it was brought to the funeral home. Waldo moved along the line of boxes. Near the end he saw, to his excitement, the name that he was looking for: CARLO MOOLMAN.

The blue box held a miscellany of objects: articles of clothing, cleaned and pressed; shoes; watch, wallet, keys, checkbook, pens, coins, comb. And then, the jackpot: a small phial, no bigger than Waldo's thumb.

Waldo picked it up. Three-quarters filled with a pale green liquid. This was the serum, it had to be. All he had to do now was find a way of getting out of the funeral home in one piece, and delivering the phial to Imre Munsen.

Unfortunately, that could be a problem. The room he was in had only two doors. The one through which he had entered would not be safe to use. And the other one . . .

Waldo went across, opened it, and recoiled. It led to the crematorium. A few feet beyond the sliding door lay the flames of hell. No wonder this room was pleasantly warm.

He gripped the phial tighter and ran back to the other door. And again he heard the sound of footsteps and voices. Many footsteps. Coming closer.

He was trapped. No matter how much he protested his innocence and insisted that he had just got lost inside the funeral home, they would not believe him. Not when he was carrying a phial of immortality serum.

Waldo came to a desperate decision. He uncapped the phial and raised it to his lips. It did not taste like an immortality serum—quite the reverse, as a matter of fact—but he gulped down every disgusting drop. Then he took the phial and tossed it into the consuming flames of the crematorium.

The fatal evidence was gone. Now it would be up to Imre Munsen and the United Space Federation to determine from an examination of Waldo just what the immortality serum contained. With luck, they would have a thousand years to do it.

The door was opening. Waldo crossed his arms and stood defiant, prepared if necessary to sell his life dearly.

The two hard-eyed uglies entered. "There he is!" one of them exclaimed. "I told you he had to be here. Come on in, chief, and take a look at him."

They stepped aside. Through the open door strode Imre Munsen. "Oh, he's all right," he said. And then, to Waldo, "Hello, Mr. Burmeister. I didn't expect you'd be coming here, so the undercover boys didn't have your description."

"Moolman's k-k-killers!" The fluid that Waldo had drunk was puckering his mouth and throat, so that he could hardly talk.

"No sign of them, I'm afraid. And the funeral's over. I'm beginning to agree with you, the whole thing was a scam, just an attempt by Moolman to get money."

"No." Waldo pointed to his mouth, then to the crematorium. "The phial was here. I found it. I swallowed what was in it, and I threw the empty container in there."

"You *found it!* Where, for heaven's sake?"

"In the blue box there. With Carlo Moolman's personal effects."

"But we went through all those, as soon as he was killed. We didn't find a thing. Can you describe what you found?"

"Certainly." Waldo's stomach gave a premonitory rumble. "A little plastic tube, about this long. It was nearly full of green liquid. Tasted horrible."

"Oh, that." Imre Munsen gave a casual laugh. "Sorry, Mr. Burmeister, but we already took a good look at that when we were going through his things. We put it back. It's certainly not an immortality serum."

"Then what is it?" A terrible thought struck Waldo. "Is it poison?"

"No, no. It's medication. You see, when Carlo Moolman arrived here on the Moon, he developed an upset stomach. Change of food, change of water, the usual thing, it gave him awful diarrhea. So he went to a doctor and got something for it. He took a dose every morning, and he had no more problem."

"A *dose*. How big is a dose?"

"Three drops a day of the green fluid. Four, for a really bad case. Mr. Burmeister, are you feeling all right? You're looking a bit pale."

Well, all that was nine days ago. There has still been no sign of Carlo Moolman's immortality serum. The Luna City rumor mill has shifted to another Elvis sighting, and this morning Imre Munsen called to thank me and Waldo, and tell us that he is going to change the Carlo Moolman case description to simple murder.

The other good news is that Waldo's relatives have gone. The bad news is that Waldo himself has not, despite the employment of a whole arsenal of powerful purgatives.

He lives in hope. He says it could happen any day now. I am encouraging him to work at home.

Afterword to "Fifteen-Love on the Dead Man's Chest"

In the late 1970s when I was just starting to write fiction, my young children (young back then, grown-ups now) ordered me to produce stories about every funny or disgusting thing in the world. They made the list for me. It had on it items of comic low appeal to them—sewage, visits to the dentist, mushrooms, fat aunts, opera singers, flatulence (I think they used a different word), comic Germans and Italians, fad diets, pigs, morticians, and head lice.

Not an easy assignment, but I did my best. Over the years I have published ten politically incorrect stories tackling one or more of the listed topics. For the avid collector, I will mention that the stories are, in order of publication: "Marconi, *Mattin,* Maxwell"; "The Deimos Plague"; "Perfectly Safe, Nothing to Worry About"; "Dinsdale Dissents"; "A Certain Place in History"; "The Dalmatian of Faust"; "Parasites Lost"; "Space Opera"; "The Decline of Hyperion"; and "Fifteen-Love on the Dead Man's Chest." Together they form what I think of as my "sewage" series. They feature my two favorite lawyers, Henry Carver and Waldo Burmeister, and they are depressingly easy to write.

Purists have argued that this tale makes tennis on the Moon sound just like tennis on the Earth, and that is implausible. I reply by asking them if that is the most implausible feature of the story.

Deep Safari

TRADITION CALLS FOR a celebration on the evening that the hunt is concluded.

The hunters will be tired, some will be hurting, some may even have died. There will be a party anyway, and it will go on for most of the night. Tradition is the younger sister of ritual. Rituals are better if they do not make sense.

I do not like to attend the parties. I have seen too many. The theory is that the hunters should be permitted to overindulge in food, in drink, in sex, in everything, but particularly in talk, because on hunt night they want to relive the glorious excitement of the chase, the shared danger, the deeds of valor, the climactic event of the kill.

Sounds wonderful. But for every hero or heroine flushed with quiet or noisy pride there will be three or four others, drinking and talking as loud as any but glancing again and again at their companions, wondering if anyone else noticed how at the moment of crisis and danger they flinched and failed.

I notice. Of course. I couldn't afford not to notice. My job is to orchestrate everything from first contact to *coup de grâce,* and to do that I have to know where everyone is and just what he or she is doing. That is much harder work than it sounds, so when a hunt is over all I want is sleep. But that relief is denied to me by my obligatory attendance at the posthunt party.

The morning that Everett Halston called, the hunt celebration the previous night had been even harder to take than usual. The group had consisted of a dozen rich merchants, neophytes to hunting but in spite of that—because of that?—determined to show their nerve by tackling one of the animal kingdom's most efficient and terrifying predators.

I had warned them, and been overruled. When we finally met the quarry, all but two of my group had frozen. They were too overwhelmed by fear to advance or even to flee. Three of us stepped forward, stood our ground, and made a difficult kill. A *very* difficult kill. Without a little luck the roles of hunter and prey could easily have been reversed.

Perhaps because of that near-disaster the hunt party had been even noisier and wilder than usual. My group of twelve participants was augmented by an equal number of male and female partners, none of them the least tired and every one ready to dance 'til dawn.

About four-thirty I managed to slip away and collapse into bed. And there I found not the calm and peaceful sleep that I had looked forward to for twelve hours, but a dream-reprise of the hunt finale as it might have been.

I had managed to move the whole group to the bottom of the pit in good order, because they had not so far had a sight of the living prey. I anticipated trouble as soon as that happened. Before we entered Adestis *mode we had studied the structure and actions of the spider, but I knew from previous experience that wouldn't mean a damn during live combat. It's one thing to peer at an animal that's no bigger across the carapace than the nail on your index finger, to study its minute jaws and poison glands and four delicate tubelike spinnerets, and plan where you will place your shots for maximum effect; it's another matter when you are linked into your* Adestis *simulacrum, and the spider that you are supposed to hunt and kill is towering ten paces away from you like a gigantic armored tank, its invincible back three times as high as the top of your head.*

Before I had the group organized to my satisfaction, our quarry took the initiative. The spider came from its hiding place in the side of the pit and in that first rush it came fast. *I saw a dark brown body with eight pearly eyes patterning its massive back. The juggernaut drove forward on the powerful thrust of four pairs of seven-jointed legs. Those legs had seemed as thin and fragile as flower stamens in our studies, but now they were bristly trunks, each as thick as a simulacrum's body. The* chelicerae, *the pointed crushing appendages at the front of the spider's maw, were massive black pincers big enough to bite your body in two.*

Without taking the time to see how my group was reacting, I did what I had explicitly warned them not to do. I lifted my weapon and sprayed projectiles at the three eyes that I could see. I think I got one of them, but the carapace itself was far too tough to be penetrated. Ricocheting projectiles flew everywhere. The spider was not seriously injured—I knew it would not be. But maybe it wondered if we were really its first choice for dinner, because it halted in its forward sweep. That gave me a little breathing space.

I scanned my group. Not reassuring. For ten of them the sight of the advancing spider had been more than they could take. Their personal simulacra stood motionless, weapons pointed uselessly at the ground.

These Adestis units were not furnished with sound generation or receiving equipment. Everything had to be signaled by our actions. We had rehearsed often enough, but unfortunately this was nothing like rehearsal. I ran forward waving at my group to lift their weapons and follow me, but only two of them did. They moved to stand on either side and just behind me.

I glanced at their two helmet IDs as I turned to urge the rest to advance and deploy in a half-circle as we had planned. Even though I would never reveal the information to anyone, I liked to know who the cool ones were—they might play Adestis again some day. None of the others moved, but a second later the weapon of the simulacrum on my right was lifting into position, while his other arm reached to tap my body in warning.

I spun around. Forget the half-circle. The spider was coming forward again, in a scuttling rush that covered the space between us at terrifying speed.

Before I could fire the predator had reached us. I saw the maw above me, the dark serrated edge of the carapace, the colonies of mite and tick parasites clinging to the coarse body bristles. Then I was knocked flat by the casual swat of one powerful leg.

I sprawled under the housewide body and saw the chelicerae *reach down, seize one of my companions at midriff, and crush until his simulacrum fell apart into two pieces.*

He writhed but he did not scream—here.

(I knew that his real body, coupled by its telemetry headset to control his simulacrum and receive its sensory inputs, would be writhing and screaming in genuine agony.

It didn't have to be that way. I would have been quite happy to do without pain signals altogether, useful as they might be as a warning for simulacrum injury. But any proposal to eliminate pain was consistently vetoed by the paying customers for Adestis. They wanted referred pain when their simulacrum was injured. It was part of the macho *(male and female) view of the game. The Adestis hunt had to feel real, as real as it could be; occasional deaths, from the heart failure that can accompany terror and intense agony, were an important part of what they were paying for.)*

And at the moment my own body, the gigantic form that somewhere infinitely far above us sat motionless in the Adestis control theater, was within a split second of its own writhing, screaming agony. The spider knew I was underneath it—knew it not from sight, which was a sense it did not much rely on, but from touch. The legs, in spite of their power, were enormously sensitive to feel and to vibration patterns. The spider was backing up, questing. It wanted me. I was shaking with fear, my hands trembling and my belly so filled with icy terror that the muscles of my whole midsection were locked rigid.

And then came the single precious touch of good luck, the accident of position that saved me and the rest of our group. As the spider moved over me I saw the pedicel; there it was, the thin neck between cephalothorax and abdomen, the most vulnerable point of the whole organism. It was directly above my head, impossible to miss. I lifted my weapon. Fired. And blew the spider into two clean halves that toppled like falling mountains on either side of me.

But not this time. In my dream, the pedicel moved out of view before I could squeeze off a shot. I was staring up at the hard underside of the cephalothorax—at the head section—at the doomsday jaws and glistening poison glands as they lowered toward me. They would engulf me, swallow me whole, to leave me struggling and hopeless within the dark interior cavern of the spider's body.

I knew, at some level of my mind, that spiders do not swallow their prey. They inject enzymes, predigest their victims, and suck them dry. But we select our own personal nightmares. I would die slowly, in the night of the spider's body cavity.

I braced myself for the unendurable.

And came to shuddering wakefulness at the loud, insistent ring of my bedside telephone. I realized where I was and groped for the handset, almost too relieved to breathe.

"Fletcher?" The voice in my ear was familiar. It ought to have suggested a face and a name, but in my dazed condition it was just a voice.

"Uh-uh." I squinted at the clock. Seven-fifteen. Two and three-quarter hours of sleep. Although I had eaten little and drunk nothing last night, I felt hung over and a hundred years old. Seven-fifteen P.M. was what I'd had in mind as a decent wake-up time.

"*Clancy* Fletcher?" insisted the voice.

"Uh-uh." I cleared my throat. "Yes. That's me. I'm Clancy Fletcher."

"Don't sound like him. This is Everett Halston. I need to talk to you. You awake enough to take anything in?"

"Yes." I'd found the face, and the name, even before he gave it. He sounded older.

Palpitations and inability to breathe came back, worse than when I woke. *Everett Halston.* He really was old. The Pearce family's professional aide and confidant for three generations. And Miriam's personal lawyer.

"Did Miriam—" I began.

"Listen first, Mr. Fletcher, then you can ask questions." The brisk, salty voice was oddly reassuring. Its next words were not. "Dr. Miriam Pearce left a tape with me, some time ago, and gave me specific instructions. I was to play that tape only if, in my judgment, she was in very serious trouble and unable to act on her own behalf.

"Late last night I played the tape. I played it because Miriam is unconscious, and no one seems able to tell me when or if she is likely to awaken."

"Where is she?"

"I'll get to that. You were always a good listener. Listen now. Miriam is at New Hanover Hospital, on the fifth floor. *Don't hang up, Mr. Fletcher. I know you want to.* Wait until I am finished. She was moved to an intensive care unit two days ago, from her own research facility, a few hours after she was discovered unconscious. Her vital signs are stable and she is being fed intravenously. However, the attendant physicians are much concerned about her condition. They state—insofar as one can persuade a physician to make any firm statement whatsoever—that they have ruled out all forms of stroke, tumor, and subdural hemorrhage. CAT and PET scan show no abnormalities, although they plan to repeat those today.

"I am now going to play you Miriam's tape, or at least the portion of it that concerns you. Wait a few moments."

I waited, suspended from life. It was three years since I had seen Miriam Pearce, more than two since I had spoken to her.

"If there is a strictly legal decision to be made, Everett, and I am for any reason unable to participate, I want you to use your own best judgment." Miriam's delivery had not altered at all. Slightly uneven in rhythm, as though she constantly changed her mind about how the sentence ought to end. Confident, jaunty, and a little short-tongued, so that "r" was always a trifle breathier than normal.

"However, other situations may arise. I could be in danger, or encounter a problem where conventional solutions cannot be applied. It may even be that you do not know what has happened to me, or where I am. In such a case, I want you to contact Clancy Fletcher. Ask him to help me. And commit to him all the financial or other resources that you control in my name."

The message ended, or was more likely cut off by Halston. There was a dead silence, while my head spun with questions. The financial resources of Miriam, and of the whole Pearce family, were huge. They could buy the absolute best of anything including medical care. Danger I might have been able to handle. But what could I possibly do for her if she was sick?

"Mr. Halston, I'm not a doctor."

"I am aware of that."

"I can't help Miriam."

"If you do not try, you certainly cannot. However, I think you are wrong. Let me suggest that you should not prejudge your potential usefulness. If you intend to proceed to New Hanover Hospital, your point of contact there is Dr. Thomas Abernathy."

Halston paused, I am sure for my benefit. He felt that I would need time to recover from the shock. Halston knew that Tom Abernathy was Miriam's close colleague and probably her sexual partner, as surely as he knew that I was Miriam Pearce's sometime collaborator and lover. He also, by the sound of it, suspected or knew something that he was not going to reveal to me.

"I have told Thomas Abernathy of Miriam's instructions to me," he went on. "I have also informed him that those instructions will be supported by me and by the full weight of the Pearce estate."

"He must have loved that."

"Let us say that he did not offer an argument, once he had listened to Miriam's tape."

Of course not. Tom Abernathy was far, far smarter than Clancy Fletcher. Abernathy knew instinctively what I had only learned the hard way: You should not try to argue with fifteen billion dollars. That much money creates winds like a hurricane, all around it. A wise man allows himself to be swept along with the gale, but he does not fight it. Because he cannot win.

"Could I hear the tape again?"

"Certainly."

We both listened in silence. Miriam's voice was so infinitely familiar. *Too* familiar. I had heard her on a nanodoc television broadcast less than a year ago, a couple of months after a minor operation on her larynx. Her voice was slightly affected then. I had assumed that the change would be permanent.

"Mr. Halston, *when* did Miriam make that tape?"

There was a click as though some recording device had been turned off, followed by a dry chuckle at the other end of the line. "Mr. Fletcher, you are as perceptive as ever. This tape has been in my possession for over three years."

Three years. Before Miriam hated me.

"I suspect that Miriam Pearce forgot about it," he went on, "or did not get around to changing it. However I will argue, in a court of law if necessary, that no action of Miriam has ever led me to suspect that the recording reflects anything other than her current wishes. Now. Will you be going to New Hanover Hospital?"

"As soon as we get through."

"Then I will say only three more things. First, I will make sure that you are expected at the hospital. Second, Thomas Abernathy will probably not be your friend."

"I know that. What's the other one?"

"Just good luck, Clancy. Good luck for you; and good luck for Miriam."

The New Hanover Hospital was a nine-story spire of glass and carved stone, a whited sepulchre jutting from well-tended lawns.

In one sense it *was* a memorial, a testament to Pearce money. The entrance hall bore a message inlaid into its marble mosaic floor, informing the world that the construction of the edifice had been made possible by Pearce munificence. The fifth floor, where Miriam lay unconscious, was known as the Meredith Franklin Pearce ward.

I did not get to see Miriam at once, much as I wanted to. When the elevator door opened Thomas Abernathy was there, lying in wait for me.

We had never met, although I had studied his career from afar. But still I did not *know* him. As he came forward with outstretched hand I watched his face closely, as a Druid might have peered from the misted woods at an arriving Christian. What *was* the newcomer who had taken my place?

Just as important, what had she told him of me? Had there been long afternoons of naked revelation, luxurious nights when Tom Abernathy heard all about poor, despised Clancy? Miriam babbled after love-making, in a dreamy stream of consciousness at odds with her usual controlled speech.

We all give to ourselves an importance that is seldom justified. Dr. Thomas Abernathy did stare at me when we shook hands, but it was with perplexity rather than knowing amusement. He did not seem to know who or what I was. But he himself looked a real smoothie, tall and fair and elegant, with a just-right handshake and a physician's perfect bedside manner.

One that he was not willing to waste too much on me.

"I do have the right person, don't I?" he said after a few moments of critical inspection. "When Everett Halston said Clancy Fletcher, I thought, if that's the toy man . . ."

"The Small Game Hunter. That's right. That's me." It was the way that the present owners of *Adestis* ran their television advertisements, a business over which I had no control. *Did you think that the Big Game Hunt became impossible when the largest carnivores became extinct? (Television shots of a rearing grizzly, a leaping tiger). Not so! The world's most deadly game has always been at smaller scale. (Three shots, in rapid sequence, of a praying mantis, a dragonfly, and a trapdoor spider, enlarged to the scale that would be seen by a simulacrum). These prey are available to hunt today, in unlimited numbers. Join an* Adestis *safari, and go on a* Small Game Hunt—*where the line between hunter and hunted can never be drawn. (A final shot of a writhing figure, totally human in appearance as a true simulacrum never was, being dismembered by a quartet of furious soldier ants).*

It was one way to make a living.

"I'd like to see Miriam Pearce. I assume that she is still unconscious?"

"I'm afraid so."

Abernathy hesitated. It was easy to see his problem. Someone had been dumped in his lap who presumably knew nothing about medicine, someone who made his living in a trivial way from what Thomas Abernathy must regard as toys designed for adults with more money than sense. And poor Doctor Tom, who was surely a god in his own domain, had to *humor* this clown. Because the clown had unfortunately been given the keys to the Pearce treasure chest, and if Clancy Fletcher felt like it he could throw Abernathy out of his own hospital, at least until Miriam Pearce awoke.

The terrible thing was my own feelings. I hated Abernathy from deep inside me. If I was to help Miriam, I had to control myself.

The other terrible thing, of course, was my conviction that I was inadequate to help Miriam in any way.

"Do you have any idea what happened to her?" I had to start Abernathy talking, or that conviction was bound to prove correct.

"I have—a theory." He was finally moving, leading me along the corridor away from the elevator. "You know, I assume, that Dr. Miriam Pearce is one of the world's pioneers in the field of microsurgery?"

"Yes. I know that."

"Well, what is not so well-known is that she has over the years been operating at smaller and smaller scales. When she began, ten years ago, her first generation of remotely guided instruments for microsurgery were huge by today's standards. Each one was as big as your fingertip. They were also primitive in their remote-control capability. The human operator could use them to perform only limited surgical functions. However, about three years ago Dr. Pearce learned how to produce a line of much more sophisticated instruments, smaller and more versatile."

I knew all about that, too, far more than Thomas Abernathy would ever know. But my attention was elsewhere. As we were talking we had moved along the corridor and at last entered a private room. Miriam lay on a bed near the window, eyes not quite closed. I stepped nearer and saw a thin slit of pale blue iris. Her color was good, her expression calm. She was still beautiful, not at all like a person unconscious because of accident or disease. She seemed only asleep. But in her arm were the IVs and next to her stood a great bank of electronic equipment.

I lifted her hand and pressed it gently. She did not stir. I squeezed harder. No response. I leaned over and spoke into her ear. "Miriam!"

"Naturally, we have tried all the usual and safe stimulants." Tom Abernathy's expression said that he disapproved of my crude experiments. "Chemical, aural, and mechanical. The responses have been limited and puzzling."

*Chemical, aural, mechanical. Drugs, noises, jabs. They won't wake Sleeping
Beauty. Did you try a kiss?*

I wanted to. Instead I straightened up and said, "You say you have a
theory for what's happening?"

"I do. Dr. Pearce next produced a line of smaller microsurgery instruments, each one no bigger than a pea, and each capable of much finer
control by the human operator. They were a huge success, and they have
transformed surgical technique.

"But they were still too big for certain operations, particularly for
fine work within the brain. A few months ago Dr. Pearce took the next
step. Nanosurgery, with dozens of multiple, mobile, remote-controlled
tools far smaller than a gnat, and all under the control of a single operator."

He glanced at me for a reaction. I nodded to show that I was impressed. If he hoped to amaze me, he had a long way to go. There were
Adestis games in which the player's simulacrum was small enough to
fight one-on-one with hungry single-celled amoebas, and there were
other games in which one human controlled dozens or even hundreds of
simulacra. But I was beginning to see why old Everett Halston believed
I might have a role to play in solving Miriam's problem. I didn't know
medicine or surgery, but I knew *Adestis* technology better than anyone
on earth.

"We tested the nanodocs on animals," went on Abernathy, "and
they seemed to work fine. So after we had the permits we performed our
first work on human subjects. That was just five days ago. In my opinion
those operational experiments succeeded perfectly. But Miriam—Dr.
Pearce—had her reservations. She believed that although the operations
had given satisfactory results, our level of control of the nanodocs was an
order of magnitude more crude than the design ought to permit. Her
theory was that we were making tools so small that their performance
was being adversely affected by quantum effects. I tended to agree with
her.

"That was where we were three days ago, when I left for a conference
in Rochester. I returned a day later, and learned that Miriam had been
found unconscious in the lab.

"She had been in perfect health when I left, but naturally we assumed at first that it was some conventional medical problem. It was
only when the routine tests showed normal results that I went back to

see what Miriam had been doing while I was away. Yesterday I found that a set of the new nanodocs was missing—and the monitors insisted that they had been placed under Miriam's control. According to the monitors, they are *still* under her control, even though she is unconscious."

"But where are they?" I was afraid that I knew the answer. Miriam had her own ideas as to how medical tests ought to be conducted.

Thomas Abernathy nodded to the body on the bed. "I feel sure they are inside her, a couple of hundred of them. I can't prove that idea—or let's say, I dare not try. The only way to be sure would be to break the telemetry contact between Dr. Pearce and the nanodocs. If they *are* inside her, then letting them run out of control might kill her. Because in view of her condition it is natural to assume that they are lodged somewhere within her brain."

I took another look at the silent beauty on the bed. If hundreds of nanodocs were running wild inside Miriam, it did not show.

"What do you plan to do about it, Dr. Abernathy?"

He stared at me, uncertain for the first time since we had met. "I do not know what to do, Mr. Fletcher. Several of my colleagues are urging exploratory surgery—" (*Saw the top off Miriam's head. Slice open the protective membranes of her brain. Dive in, poke around, and see what you can find.* I shivered.) "—but I regard that as a last resort. I would rather wait, watch, and pray for a change in her condition."

Which was also a last resort. Strange. Abernathy had analyzed the problem to the point where it was obvious what had to be done. But he could not or would not take that next step.

"Are there more of the nanodocs—the same size as the ones that are missing?"

"There are several sets of them, in all important respects identical."

"That's good. Is there a staff cafeteria in the building?"

"What?"

"I must have something to eat, because I don't know how long this might take. And then I'll need to practice with your nanodocs for a few hours, to make sure I have the feel for these particular models. Then I'm going into Dr. Pearce."

I took a last look at Miriam, willing her to wake as I started for the door. Given a choice, I certainly didn't *want* to have to go in. I wanted to go home, and go to bed. Preferably with Miriam.

"You can't do that!" Abernathy had lost his smooth self-control. "You are not a physician. You are an *Adestis* employee. Just because you have a bit of experience with your stupid little toys doesn't mean you can handle nanodocs! This is very specialized equipment, very complex. It takes months to learn."

"I've had months. In fact, I've had years." I tried to keep the bitterness out of my voice as I walked from the room. I'm sure I failed. "While I'm gone, Dr. Abernathy, I suggest that you check the name of the patent holder for the first microsurgery developments. The name of the *original* holder, I mean—the idiot who had all the patents, until the Pearce family broke them and acquired the rights for themselves. And while you're at it, check who was the creator, founder, and hundred percent owner of *Adestis,* before it was bankrupted and taken over."

Whatever I had done to Miriam, her family had paid back in full.

The food in the cafeteria was ridiculously overpriced at seven dollars. I know it cost that, because I had left home without money or any form of credit, and I had to sign what amounted to a personal IOU with the manager for the contents of my tray.

But that's all I do know about the food, or the cafeteria. I must have eaten, but I don't remember it.

I was almost finished when Thomas Abernathy marched in and sat down opposite me. He had with him an attractive, dark-haired woman in her early twenties, who gave me a tentative smile as she sat down.

Abernathy took the document that he was holding and pushed it across the table toward me.

"This is a hospital, Mr. Fletcher, not a carnival." He was struggling to be polite, but hardly succeeding. "It isn't 'anything goes' here. We have strict rules, which every one of us has to obey."

I glanced at the paper. I had an idea what it might say.

"All right. So I'm not 'authorized personnel' for the use of the nanodoc equipment. Who is?"

"I have some experience. Dr. Pearce, of course. And Miss Lee, who is a specialist in nanodoc operations." He nodded his head at the woman sitting next to him.

She held out her hand but glanced at Tom Abernathy for approval before she spoke. "Belinda Lee. When Dr. Abernathy said you were here,

I told him that I'd just love to meet you. You don't know it, but you and *Adestis* are putting me through medical school."

I let that opening pass. She was being as sociable as she knew how, but we didn't have time for it.

"You could *make* me authorized personnel if you wanted to, Dr. Abernathy. It is under your jurisdiction."

"There's no reason for me to do so. I now agree with you, Mr. Fletcher, interior exploration of Dr. Pearce by nanodocs is a logical and urgent step. Miss Lee and I will make that exploration. I also admit your experience with remotely controlled microsurgical equipment"—so he had checked on me, at least a little. What else had he found out?—"but we do not need you. Also, we cannot afford the time needed to train you."

"I have to disagree. You need me, even if you don't *want* me. You'll be making use of hospital equipment. This whole place runs on Pearce support. If I call Everett Halston he'll contact the Board of Trustees. You'll have an injunction slapped on you against using nanodoc equipment, one that will take weeks to break."

The last trace of bedside manner vanished. "You idiot, are you trying to *kill* Miriam? *You* are the one who suggested we have to go in and find out what happened to the nanodoc units inside her."

"We must do that. We *can* do that. As a team. You, I, and if you like Miss Lee. If you authorize me to use the equipment, I'll bless the exercise at once with Everett Halston."

He grabbed the paper, stood up, and rushed out of the cafeteria without another word. Belinda Lee gave me an unhappy and puzzled look before she followed him. Why was I being so unreasonable?

I carried on with the meal. I was unreasonable because I sensed possible dangers that Abernathy could not. He lacked the right experience. He would agree to my participation—he had no choice—but it was not an auspicious beginning to a safari when team members were so divided and suspicious at the outset. Teams were supposed to cooperate totally.

On the other hand, I had been on an expedition where the team members had started out as close and loving and trusting as humans could get, and that one had ended in bitterness, disappointment, and heartbreak.

Maybe this time the process would work the other way round.

* * *

Belinda Lee was my instructor for the nanodoc units. Perhaps Tom Abernathy would not spend more time with me than he was obliged to; but to be more charitable, he also had two important tasks to perform.

First, a set of nanodocs had to be tuned to Miriam's individual body chemistry. Otherwise her immune system would be triggered at our entry and we would be attacked by every leukocyte that we encountered. Although they couldn't damage the nanodocs, they could certainly impede them.

As a second and trickier assignment, Tom Abernathy had to decide our access route into Miriam's brain. He and the neurological specialists had already decided our destination. Although the sleep state of humans and animals is controlled by an area at the rear of the brain known as the reticular formation, Miriam's responses to stimuli had them convinced that her troubles did not lie there. The problem was in the cerebral hemispheres. But to the tiny nanodocs, those hemispheres were like buildings a mile on each side. Where *specifically* should we be heading?

I was glad I did not have that responsibility. My own worries were quite enough.

Two hours had been allocated by the hospital for my training session, but it was clear in the first five minutes that they had been far too generous. True, two hours was less than half the training time that I insisted on before anyone could take part in *Adestis,* and in that case the simulacra were far more human in appearance than the hospital nanodocs. But for most team members the training session was a first exposure to microoperation. Familiarity with the shape of their remote analogues was reassuring to them.

In fact, the proportions of a human are quite wrong for optimum performance of anything less than half an inch tall. Holding to the human shape in some ways makes things harder. As the size of an organism decreases, the importance of gravity as a controlling force becomes less and less, while wind and vibration and terrain roughness are increasingly dominant. Six legs become much better than two. At the smallest scale, the Brownian motion forces of individual molecular collisions have to be taken into account. Learning to gauge and allow for those changes is far more important than worrying about actual body shape.

On the other hand, as soon as I had seen the latest nanodocs I could not agree with Miriam and Thomas Abernathy that quantum effects might be important. Wispy and evanescent as the tiny currents might be that control the simulacra, they were still orders of magnitude too big to be affected by quantum fluctuations.

There was certainly an unanticipated problem with the new nano-docs. I certainly had no idea what it might be. But it was not what Miriam and Tom Abernathy suspected.

As soon as Belinda Lee had watched me work a team of nanodocs for a few minutes—each one a little bloated disk a few tens of micrometers long, with half a dozen legs/scrapers/knives along each side—she took off her telemetry coupler and leaned back in her seat. She waited patiently until I emerged from remote-control mode.

"You ought to be teaching *me,* you know." She was a different person when Tom Abernathy was not around. "How on earth did you make them zip *backward* so fast, and still know where they were going? I'm supposed to be our expert, and I can't do that. The optical sensors won't turn up and over the back."

"No. They will turn *downward,* though, and scan underneath the body. You don't have enough experience looking between your legs and running backward."

She offered me an owlish look. Belinda Lee thought I was poking fun at her. I was and I wasn't. I had never done what I suggested in my own body, but I had done it a hundred times with *Adestis* simulacra of all shapes and sizes. As I said, the hunter simulacra are all humanoid; but I had been both hunter and hunted, because we run hunts with remote-controlled simulated prey as well as with the real thing.

"So how is *Adestis* putting you through medical school?"

Belinda Lee seemed really nice, and I didn't want to upset her. I needed at least one friend at the New Hanover Hospital.

She laughed, the sort of full-throated laugh I had once heard from Miriam. "I was convinced you didn't want to hear. I was crushed in the cafeteria when you didn't ask."

"Sorry. I had other things on my mind. What did you have to do with *Adestis?* I'm sure you've never been involved in a hunt. I would have remembered you."

She took it for the compliment it was, and dipped her head toward me in acknowledgement. "I had problems when I was a teenager. My parents wanted me to be a doctor, but I'd heard of *Adestis* and I was fascinated by it. My life's ambition was to be team leader on an *Adestis* underwater safari. You know, the Larval Hunt."

"I sure do. Scary stuff. They wouldn't sign off?" You need written parental permission to enter *Adestis* mode before age twenty-one.

"Not in a million years, they said. So I did the dutiful daughter bit, went off to college and majored in biology. But I never stopped thinking about *Adestis*. For my senior thesis I wondered about the possible uses of that sort of technology in medical work. I wrote and asked, and some sweetheart at *Adestis* headquarters sent me a bale of terrific information. I used it to write probably the longest undergraduate thesis in the college's history. Of course I had no idea that Dr. Pearce was years and years ahead of me. But my prof knew, and he sent my finished project to her. She called a couple of days later. And here I am."

That sounded like Miriam. She recognized the real thing when she saw it. Her first exposure to *Adestis* had come through a friend at the hospital, a woman who had been on a hunt and regarded it all as a lark. But Miriam didn't. Before the end of the first training session she was asking me if I knew any way that *Adestis* control technology could take her clumsy microsurgery tools down in size and up in handling precision.

That had been the beginning of the patents. And the *Adestis* expeditions with Miriam. And all the rest.

I used to think I knew the real thing, too. I recalled that highly detailed and imaginative student inquiry, even if I had not remembered Belinda's name.

At the same time, I began to worry. If Belinda Lee had begun to work with *Adestis* technology only after she graduated, she couldn't have more than a couple of years experience with simulacra. Also she had never been on a hunt, and therefore probably never been exposed to a dangerous situation. Yet Tom Abernathy had described her as a *specialist* in nanodoc operation—a specialist, presumably, compared with him. In agreeing that the three of us would go into Miriam, I had burdened myself with two team members lacking the right sort of experience.

Or was I being paranoid? What made me think that a safari into Miriam might be *dangerous?* Tom Abernathy and Belinda Lee certainly didn't think so.

Maybe that was one reason.

The other reason was more complex. For this safari, I too would lack the right experience. I had never, in all my years with *Adestis,* been ex-

posed to a situation where the environment within which my simulacrum would operate was more precious to me than my own survival.

Our entry into Miriam began with an argument. I wanted to go in with
a single nanodoc simulacrum each. Tom Abernathy argued for many
more.

"There are several *hundred* in Dr. Pearce's brain. Three simulacra
won't be able to remove them, even if we find them."

"I know. Once we understand what's happening, though, we can
introduce more."

"But think of the *time* it will take."

He seemed to forget the full day that he had wasted before I came
along to force a decision.

And yet he was right. His way would be quicker. So why wouldn't I
go along with it?

That was a difficult question. In the end it all came down to instinct.
A single simulacrum was easier to control than a group of them, even
though a group had more firepower. But firepower against *what?* The
nanodocs were not armed, the way that *Adestis* hunters had to be armed.
Why should they be? I was too used to thinking in terms of a prey, and
that didn't apply in this case.

Yet I stuck to my position, and overruled Abernathy. We would go
with single simulacra, one per person.

But I also, illogically, wished that my nanodoc unit was equipped
with something more powerful than the tiny scalpels and drug injection
stings built into its eight legs.

Destination: Brain.

We had adopted remote-control mode outside Miriam's body, as
soon as the nanodocs were inside the syringe. We remained there for
fifteen minutes, long enough to become completely comfortable with
our host simulacra.

By the end of that time I knew my partners much better. Tom Abernathy was confident but clumsy. He might understand the theory, but
no matter what he *thought* he knew about nanodoc control he didn't have
good reflexes or practical experience.

Belinda Lee was far better, a little nervous but quite at ease in her
assumed body. If she ever dropped out of medical school there would be

a place for her on the *Adestis* underwater safaris. (And I'd be more than glad to give up my own involvement in those. The larval animal life of streams and ponds is fierce enough to make a mature insect or arachnid look like nature's pacifist. Maybe Belinda would change her mind when she saw at firsthand Nature red in mandible and proboscis.)

We were injected into Miriam's left carotid artery at neck level, our three nanodoc units at my insistence holding tightly to each other. I did not want us separated until we were well within her brain. Otherwise I at least might never get there.

As we ascended Miriam's bloodstream toward the three meninges, the membranes that surround and protect the brain, it occurred to me that my two partners would soon know my own weaknesses. I could handle my nanodoc better than Belinda and far better than Tom, but I was missing something they both had: a good working knowledge of human anatomy or microstructure. Abernathy had given me a lightning briefing, of which I remembered only a fraction. I peered around us. The minute compound eyes of the nanodocs couldn't see much at all. They delivered a blurry, red-tinged view of surroundings illuminated by the nanodoc's own pulsed light sources, enough so that I could see that we were being carried along a wide tunnel whose sides were barely visible. All around swam a flotsam of red blood cells, not much smaller than we were, interspersed with the occasional diminutive platelets. Through that swirl a white cell would occasionally come close, extend a testing pseudopod, and then retreat. Tom Abernathy's preliminary work on the nanodocs was satisfactory. The prowling leukocytes had no great interest in us.

I knew that the blood also carried an unseen flux of chemical messengers, taking status information from one part of the body to all the rest. Tom Abernathy could probably have explained all that to me, if our nanodocs had been capable of better communication. They were better than most *Adestis* units, because they did possess a primitive vocal interface; but it was at a bit transfer rate so low that Abernathy, Lee, and I were practically restricted to single word exchanges. We would mostly convey our meaning by stylized gestures.

Our progress through the internal carotid artery was far slower than I had expected. As we drifted from side to side and occasionally touched a spongy wall, I had time to explore every function of my nanodoc. And to reflect on its present owners.

Three years ago I was convinced that the Pearce family had acted in direct reprisal for what I had done to Miriam. It took a long time to realize that nothing *personal* was involved, that anger at the family made no more sense than rage at the gravid Sphex wasp who takes and paralyzes a live grasshopper as feeding ground for its hatching larva.

I doubt if Miriam herself was aware of what had happened. Through her the Pearces had been alerted to the existence of a highly valuable tidbit, in the form of the *Adestis* patents. Miriam wanted and needed those for her own medical work, but that was irrelevant. It was the desire to increase assets that controlled group action, and to the family there was nothing more natural than the use of wealth to acquire my patents. They had simply turned on an existing machinery of scientists, lawyers, lobbyists, and political influence. I doubt if any one of them ever suspected that the owner of the patents also happened to be the man who had hurt Miriam. For if she had never talked of me to her present lover, would she have spoken to her family?

I liked to think that she would not.

The nanodoc hooked tightly to my four left legs started to tug gently at them. I turned and saw Tom Abernathy's gesturing digit.

"Cir-cle—of—Will-is," said a thin, distorted voice.

We had reached Checkpoint One. After passing along the internal carotid artery we were through the protective membranes of the *dura mater* and *pia mater* and were now at the *circulus arteriosus,* the "Circle of Willis," a vascular formation at the base of the brain where all the major feed arteries meet. Abernathy was steering us into the anterior cerebral artery, which would take us into the cerebral cortex.

From this point on it would be up to me. Abernathy had made it clear that he could guide us no farther.

I had not told him that I too had little idea where we would go once we were within the cerebral hemispheres. He had worries enough.

And I was not quite ready to mention, to Tom Abernathy or to Belinda Lee, that something seemed to be slightly wrong with my simulacrum.

The change was so subtle that I doubted if Belinda, and still less Tom, could notice it. Only someone who had developed the original *Adestis* circuits and lived with them, through every good or bad variation, would sense the difference. The motor response was a tiny shade off what it had been when we were outside Miriam's body.

"Ex-peri-ment." I released my hold on the other two, then deliberately reduced motor inputs within my simulacrum to absolute zero.

I should now be floating like a dead leaf in the arterial tide, carried wherever the blood flow wanted to take me. But I was not. Not quite. There was a tiny added vector to my motion, produced by faint body impulses that I was not creating. I was angling over to the left, away from the broad mainstream of blood flow. When the artery divided, as it would shortly do, I would be channeled into the left branch.

Tom Abernathy and Belinda Lee were following, not knowing what else to do. I restored motor control to my simulacrum, and noted again the difference between my directive and the unit's response. Slight, but not so slight as before.

"Mov-ing," said Belinda's faltering and attenuated voice. She was noticing it too, and she was frightened. That was good. I did not want on my hunts anyone who was not scared by the inexplicable. The force did not feel external, either. It was arising from *within,* a phantom hand affecting our control over the simulacra.

"Stay." I halted, and laboriously sent my instruction. "I—go—on. You wait—for me." I believed we were surely heading for the missing nanodocs, and just as surely it might be dangerous for all to travel together. If I did not return, Abernathy and Lee could find their way to the left or right jugular vein exit points. Equipment was waiting there to sense, capture, and remove from Miriam's body any returning nanodoc units.

I again reduced motor inputs and allowed myself to drift with the arterial flow. Soon the channel branched and branched again, into ever-finer blood vessels. I had no idea where I was, or where I was going, but I had no doubt about my ability to return to the safe highway of the jugular veins. Every road led there. All I had to do was follow the arrow of the blood, down into the finest capillary level, then on to the fine veins that merged and coupled to carry their oxygen-depleted flow back toward heart and lungs.

And while I was filled with that comforting thought, I noticed that the motion of my simulacrum was changing. Without input from me the left and right sets of legs were twitching in an asynchronous pattern. Their movement added a crablike sideways component to my forward progress. Soon my nanodoc was squeezing against the wall of the blood vessel. It pressed harder, and finally broke through into a narrow chamber filled with clear cerebrospinal fluid.

I thought that might signal the end of the disturbance, but after a few seconds it began again. Every thresh of the side limbs made the anomaly more obvious. I restored motor control and willed the leg movements to stop. They slowed, but they went on. My simulacrum was turning round and round, carried along in the colorless liquid of the new aqueduct until suddenly it was discharged into a larger space. After a moment of linear motion we started to spin around the vortex of an invisible whirlpool.

I had arrived in one of the larger cerebral *sulci,* the fissures that run along and through the human brain. Tom Abernathy could undoubtedly have told me which one. For the moment, though, I did not care. I had found the missing nanodocs.

They extended along the fissure, visible in the watery fluid as far as my crude optical sensors could see. Each one appeared to be intact. And each was obsessively turning on its own individual carousel, always moving yet never leaving the main chamber of the *sulcus.*

It took thirty seconds of experiment to discover that I too was trapped. I could think commands as well as ever. The simulacrum would start to respond. And before the movement was completed another component would reinforce my instruction. The result was like an intention tremor, a sequence of overcorrections that swung me into more and more violent and uncontrolled motion.

I dared not allow that to continue—I was deep in the delicate fabric of Miriam's brain, where even light contact could cause damage. The only way I could stop the spinning in random directions was to inhibit the motor control of my nanodoc unit. Then we returned to a smooth but useless cyclic motion around an invisible axis.

There was no way to signal the other nanodocs except through gestures. Designed to be worked as a group by a single operator, they were of a more primitive design than the unit I inhabited. I tried to make physical contact with one, but I was balked by its movement. Each unit remained locked in its own strange orbit, endlessly rotating but never advancing within the fissure's great Sargasso Sea of cerebrospinal fluid.

I was ready to try something new when I experienced my worst moment so far. In among the hundreds of nanodoc units I saw one different from the rest. But it was identical to my own; therefore it must belong to Tom Abernathy or Belinda Lee. A few seconds later I saw the other.

Somehow they had been unable to follow my instructions. Like me they had been carried willy-nilly to this dark interior sea. Like me, they would be trying to assert control. And failing.

I knew how they must feel. The whole success of *Adestis* depends on the power of the mental link. When you are in *Adestis* mode you do not *control* a simulacrum, you *are* the simulacrum. Its limbs and body and environment become your own. Its dangers are yours, its pain is your pain. If it is poisoned by a prey, it dies—and you experience all the agony.

Without that total transfer, *Adestis* would be nothing but a trivial diversion. No one would pay large sums to go on a Small Game Hunt.

That same total immersion of self had been carried over, by design, into the nanodocs. I knew how helpless Tom Abernathy and Belinda Lee would be feeling now. They could not control their spinning simulacra, nor could they escape to or even recall the existence of their own bodies, *outside* the world of the nanodocs.

I knew that all too well; because three years ago Miriam Pearce and I had been in the same situation.

Our quarry was a first-time prey for both us and Adestis. *No one had ever before hunted* Scolopendra. *Although Miriam and I knew it as one of the fastest and most ferocious of the centipedes, we started out in excellent spirits. Why should we not? We had hunted together half a dozen times before, and knew we were an excellent team. Shared danger only seemed to draw us closer.*

And after it was over we planned to hold our own private posthunt party.

Scolopendra *came flickering across the ground toward us, body undulating and the twenty pairs of legs a blur. I took little notice of those. My attention was on the poison claws on each side of the head, the pointed spears designed to seize an unlucky prey and inject their venom. Between the claws I saw the dark slit of a wide mouth. It was big enough to swallow me whole.*

We had agreed on the strategy before we entered Adestis *mode: Divide and conquer. Each of us would concentrate on one side of the centipede. As it turned toward one of us, the other would sever legs and attack the other side of the body. The animal would be forced to swing around or topple over. And the process would be repeated on the other side.*

But why were we hunting at all? Although we found the danger stimulating, neither Miriam nor I had a taste for blood sports for their own sake. As usual on our hunts, we wanted to refine a new piece of Adestis *control technology. When it was perfected it would find a home in the world of the nanodocs.*

The centipede picked me as its first choice of prey. It turned, and Miriam disappeared behind the long, segmented trunk. I caught a glimpse of jointed limbs—each one nearly as long as my body—then the antennae were sweeping down toward me and the poison claws reached out.

Scolopendra *was even faster than we had realized. I heard the crack of Miriam's weapon, but any damage she might inflict would be too late to save me. I could not escape the poison claws by moving backward. All I could do was go closer, jumping in past the claws to the lip of the maw itself.*

It was ready. A pair of maxillae moved forward, to sweep me into the digestive tube.

I had never before hunted a prey able to swallow a victim whole. And I had never until that moment known the strength of my own claustrophobia.

I crouched on the lower lip of the maw, and thought of absorption into the dark interior of the body cavity. I could not bear it.

I threw myself backward and fell to the ground. A suicidal movement, with the poison claws waiting. I did not care. Anything *was better than being swallowed alive.*

The claws approached me. Shuddered. And pulled back. The antenna and the wide head turned.

Miriam's shots were doing their job. I sprawled full-length, peered under the body, and saw half a dozen severed legs in spasm on the ground.

Now it was my turn to shoot. I did it—halfheartedly. I dreaded the broad head swinging back, the mandibles poised to ingest me.

And it was ready to happen. I had shot off two legs. The body was shaking, beginning to turn again in my direction.

I stopped firing. For one second I stood while the centipede hesitated, unable to decide if I or Miriam provided the greater threat. The head turned once more to her side.

Then I was running away, a blind dash across dark and uneven ground. I did not look back.

I left Miriam behind, to die in agony in Scolopendra's *poison claws.*

Three years, three bitter years of remorse and analysis and self-loathing; in three years I had learned something that maybe no other *Adestis* operator had ever known. If I had known it *then*, it might have saved Miriam.

The body of the nanodoc, shell-like back and eight multipurpose legs, was *my* body. I had no other. As I gyrated in the brain *sulcus* along with Tom and Belinda and a couple of hundred other units, I turned off every input sensor.

I *imagined* an alien body, a body nothing like my own. A strange body with a well-defined head and slender neck, with two legs, with two jointed arms that ended in delicate manipulators. When the imagined body image was complete I took those two phantom arms and moved them to the sides of the head, just above a strange pair of external hearing organs.

I grasped. And lifted. And reeled with vertigo, as the whole *Adestis* telemetry headset that maintained my link with the nanodoc ripped away from my skull.

I leaned forward and placed my forehead on the bench in front of me. Of all the warnings that I gave to attendants in *Adestis* control rooms, none was stronger than this: *Never,* in any circumstances, rupture the electronic union between player and simulacrum.

Hospital staff were hurrying across to me. I waved them away. The nausea would pass, and I had work to do. I understood what had happened to Miriam. I knew what had happened to me, and what was happening now to Tom Abernathy and Belinda Lee. Unless I was too slow and stupid, I could end it.

The control system for *Adestis,* and for all its applications such as the nanodocs, has built-in safeguards. I opened the main cabinet, found the right circuits, and inhibited them. I turned the electronic gain for my own unit far past the danger point. Then I went back to my seat.

"Tell the technicians with Dr. Pearce to watch for us coming out," I said. "Maybe fifteen minutes from now."

And cross your fingers.

I took a deep breath, gritted my teeth, and crammed the control headset back on.

The pain and dizziness of returning were even worse than going out. I was again a nanodoc, but the overloaded input circuits were a great discordant shout inside my head. Every move that I wanted to make produced a result ten times as violent as I intended. I allowed myself half a minute of practice, learning a revised protocol. The interference that had kept me helpless before was still there—I could feel a pulling to one side—but now it was a nuisance rather than a danger.

First I steered myself across to Belinda Lee's nanodoc. As I suspected, her loss of control included loss of signals. She could not talk to me, and she probably could not hear me. I simply took her by the legs on one side, and dragged her across to where Tom Abernathy was drifting around in endless circles. I linked the two units together, right four legs to left four legs, and locked them.

After that it was a purely mechanical task. I proceeded steadily along the brain fissure, systematically catching the nanodocs and linking them by four of their legs to the next unit in the train. The final result was itself something like a very long and narrow centipede, with over two hundred body segments. When I was sure that I had captured every nanodoc I positioned myself at the head of the file, attached four legs to Belinda's free limbs, and looked for the way out.

I had seen it as too simple. *Follow the direction of the blood.* But we were in one of the major *sulci,* where in a healthy human there must be no blood. (As I learned later, blood cells in the cerebrospinal fluid is one sign of major problems in the brain.)

Where were the signposts? I pondered that, as our caravan of nanodoc units set out through one of the most complex objects in the universe: the human brain. We went on forever, through regions corresponding to nothing that Tom Abernathy had described to me. Finally I came across the rubbery wall of a major blood vessel.

Artery or vein? The former would merely carry us back into the brain. The latter would mean we were on our way out.

I entered, and pulled the whole train through after me. But still I did not know where we were heading, until the channel in which we rode joined another of rather greater width. Then I could relax. We were descending the tree, all of whose branches would merge into the broad trunk of the jugular.

I knew it when we at last entered that great vein; knew it when we were removed from the body, all at once, in the swirl of suction from a syringe.

The return to our own bodies under technician control was—as it should be—steady and gentle. I blinked awake, and found Tom Abernathy already conscious and staring at me.

I grinned. He looked away.

My hatred of him had dissolved after shared danger. Apparently his disdain for me persisted. I glanced the other way, at Belinda Lee. And found that she, like Tom Abernathy, would not meet my eye.

"We did it," I said. I couldn't stop smiling. "They're all out. I bet Miriam recovers consciousness in just a few minutes."

"*We* didn't do anything," Belinda said. "*You* did it all. I was useless."

I couldn't see it that way. But her reaction seemed too strong to be pure wounded ego.

"I couldn't have done anything without your help," I said. "Hey, without you two I'd never even have found my way *into* the brain."

"You don't understand." Tom Abernathy's face was pale, and his voice was as sour as Belinda's. "I know how she feels, even if you don't. Because I'm the same. We're not like you, with your crazy *Adestis* heroics. I wasn't just useless and helpless in there, I was *scared* when I lost nanodoc control. Too frightened even to follow what you were doing. Too terrified to *try* to help Miriam."

I laughed. Not with humor. The irony of Clancy Fletcher as heroic savior for Miriam Pearce was too much to take.

"It's not courage," I said. "It's only experience."

And then, when they stared at me with no comprehension, it all spilled out. I had bottled it up for too long, and it *hurt* to talk. But I could feel no worse about myself no matter what they knew, and perhaps a knowledge of other cowardice would help them to deal with what they thought of as their own failure.

"But there's a bright side," I said as I concluded. "If I hadn't failed Miriam then, I would never have experimented later with forced interruption of *Adestis* mode. And we'd still be inside Miriam's brain.

"I've never told anyone this before. But now you understand why she won't talk to me after she recovers consciousness."

They had listened to my outpourings in an oddly silent setting. As soon as they were sure that we were all right the nanodoc technicians had hurried off to the next room, where Miriam Pearce was reported to be showing a change of condition. The only sound in the room where we sat was the occasional soft beep of nanodoc monitors, reporting inactive status.

"I'm sorry to hear all that." Tom Abernathy's sincerity was real. Rumpled and sweaty, he was no longer the elegant physician with the polished bedside manner. "Miriam won't talk to you?"

He ought to know that, if anyone did.

"Not for years."

"Strange. Doesn't sound like the Miriam Pearce that I know."

"Nor me," said Belinda. "She's nice to everybody. But when are you going to tell us what was going on in there? I try to pass myself off as somebody who knows nanodocs, and I can't even *understand* what you did, let alone do it myself."

"It was no big deal. It all depends on one simple fact. As soon as you know that, you'll be able to work everything else out for yourself. The key factor is *interference effects.* The electrical currents that control an *Adestis* module—including a nanodoc—"

I was interrupted, by a technician hurrying through from the next room.

"Dr. Abernathy. We think Dr. Pearce is waking up."

I was first through the door. Miriam's condition was clearly different—she was stirring restlessly on the bed—but her eyes were closed. Before I could get to the bedside Tom Abernathy had pushed me aside and was checking the monitors.

"Looks a hell of a lot better." He leaned right over Miriam, and was inches from her face when her eyes flickered open.

"I knew you would." The faint thread of sound would not have been heard, had not everyone in the room frozen to absolute stillness. "I knew you'd come and save me."

Her mouth and eyes were smiling up—at Tom Abernathy. Then the smile faded, she sighed, and her eyes closed again in total weariness.

I blundered out of the room more by feel than sight. Company was the last thing I wanted, but Belinda followed me.

"You can't leave it like that," she said. "What *about* electrical currents?"

She wanted to talk. Well, why not? What did it matter? What did anything matter?

"The electrical currents that are *sent* to an *Adestis* unit are a few milliwatts," I said. "But the ones that are received at the unit, and the magnetic fields they generate, are orders of magnitude smaller than that. They're minute—and almost exactly the size of the fields and currents within the human brain. When Miriam sent nanodocs *into her own brain,* they were subject to two different sets of inputs, one arriving fractionally later than the other. In her case that set up a resonance which left both her brain and the nanodocs incapable of functioning normally. She was trapped. Maybe she even knew that she was trapped.

"In our case it worked differently. Her brain currents *interfered* with our nanodoc operation, so we lost control, but there was no resonance and no loss of consciousness.

"All I did was break out of *Adestis* mode and reset the input currents to the highest level on my unit. When I went back in there was still a disturbance from Miriam, but it was one small enough for me to be able to handle."

Belinda was nodding, but she was beginning to stare at the door to the next room. "You know, Tom has to hear this, too."

"He'll hear it. Just now he has other things on his mind."

I don't know how I sounded, but it was enough to earn Belinda Lee's full attention.

"What *is it* with you and Tom? I thought you hadn't even met until today."

"You really don't know? I'd have expected it to be the talk of the hospital." And then, when she gaped at me, "Miriam Pearce and Tom Abernathy"—he had opened the door and was walking into the room, but it was too late to stop—"are lovers."

"*Tom* and Miriam Pearce." Belinda exploded. "Over my dead body—and over his, if it's ever true."

She rushed to his side and grabbed him possessively by the arm. "He's *mine*. He's *my* lover, and no one else's."

Abernathy must have wondered what he had walked into. Whatever it was, he didn't care for it. "My God, Belinda! You know what we agreed. Shout it out, so the whole hospital hears you." He actually blushed when he looked at me, something I had not seen on a mature male for a long time. And then his expression slowly changed, to an odd mixture of satisfaction and defiant pride.

"It's *his* fault." She was pointing at me. "He told me that you and Miriam Pearce are lovers!"

"Miriam and *me?* No way! Honest, Belinda, there's nothing between us—there never has been."

"I hope not. But I know she doesn't have a man of her own." Belinda was persuaded. Almost. "And she did say to you, 'I knew you'd come and save me.' "

"To *me?* What a joke that'd be! I was as much use inside her head as a dead duck. She wasn't talking to me, she was talking to *him*. She said his name, Clancy, right after you two left. I came out here to get him."

"She *doesn't* have a man—doesn't have a lover?" That was me, not Belinda. Shock slows comprehension.

"Not anymore. She once told me she had some guy, years ago, but he dumped her. Her family did something terrible to him. He wouldn't see her, didn't answer phone calls. In the end she just gave up."

"I thought a Pearce family member could get absolutely anything." That was Belinda, too cynical for her years.

Tom Abernathy patted her arm. With their secret out, his attitude was changing. "Almost anything. Miriam told me that a billionairess can have any man in the world. Except the one she wants."

"Does she want *you?*" Belinda had to be sure. But long-suffering Tom Abernathy was spared the need to offer that reassurance, because again one of the hospital staff came running through from the other room.

"Dr. Abernathy," he said. "She's finally waking up. *Really* waking up this time."

Tom and Belinda hurried away. I followed, more slowly.

Finally waking up. *Really* waking up. If only that had happened years ago, before it was too late.

I walked to the open door. Tom Abernathy was at the bedside. Miriam was sitting up, pale blue eyes wide open and searching. I stood rooted on the threshold. Belinda Lee was coming toward me, suddenly knowing, one hand raised.

I forgot how to breathe.

Sleeping Beauty slept for a whole century, and that still worked out fine.

Perhaps for some things it is never too late.

Afterword to "Deep Safari"

Nature is not cruel. Animals merely do what they have to do to ensure their food supply and the perpetuation of the species. If we *see* them as cruel, it is only because humans are capable of conscious cruelty. We apply our own perspective and imagine that animals, like humans, are able to know of—even perhaps enjoy—the pain that they are inflicting on another living being.

Right. That's the rational side of me taken care of. The irrational side, which rules half my days and all my nights, is convinced that the world of spiders and ants and centipedes is more bloodthirsty and somehow infinitely more *cruel* than the world of humans, elephants, and tigers. It may be no more than word association. Anything smaller than a shrew is going to be a *cold-blooded* animal, and that adjective carries two meanings.

At any rate and for whatever reason, while I can imagine facing a lion or a bear and hoping to survive the encounter, the very idea of tackling a preying mantis or a spider as tall as I am reduces me to a quivering jelly. Which is obviously why I have been led to write about such microcombat in this story and in the novel *The Mind Pool,* where the game of *Adestis* is also played.

One other small point for anyone curious about the name of the game: *Adestis* is simply Latin for *You are present.*

BEYOND THE GOLDEN ROAD

THE WISE MEN in the court of the Great Khan say that Life and Death are the two great arcs of the world. Close to each other at birth, they move apart in middle life, and in old age they converge again and finally meet.

I am too young to be a sage, and I do not question the words of wise men and great philosophers. But when we finally stumbled across the merchant caravan in the wastes of the Tarim Desert, I knew that the arcs of Life and Death for me, a young man, stood no more than a fingernail apart.

We had been walking for six days, the last two without water. According to the soldier Ahmes, the desert should have been no more than four days travel wide. Long since we ought to have emerged from its eastern margin and found the Ghadi oasis. Instead we were dying under a late-October sun.

Ahmes was not a man to understand guilt. He strode on, still strong and erect, still carrying his curved Damascene sword and leather shield. A gray-black layer of dust covered his cheeks and caked around his lips, but his face was as cheerful as ever. He was sucking on a smooth pebble, and now and again he would turn to us and smile his mysterious crinkle-eyed grin of white teeth.

I had carried most of our baggage, and all of the water for as long as we had water. Now I was staggering, close to collapse. Johannes, who *does* feel guilt—much too acutely—knew how near I was to giving up. He had an arm around me, half-carrying me forward, while he whispered encouraging words. "A little farther, Dari," he said, "it cannot be more than another hour or two. We have come too far, you and I, to be stopped now." And then, when I was near weeping with pain and thirst and weariness, "I am sorry I brought you here. But courage, little Dari. This too shall pass."

He liked Ahmes. He had trusted him since we first met in the freezing heights of the Hindu Kush, winding our way east through the high snowy passes and glittering glaciers. Ahmes had led us then on a supposed shortcut, one that left us lost and shivering on a mountainside, in air so thin and clear and cold that the midday sky looked purple-black, and the leaves of the flowering plants were as brittle as dried tea. We had been lucky to survive that day, and had done it only by taking a hair-raising slide down three thousand feet of a blind snow-slope. It could have ended in a precipice. The luck of Ahmes, it ended in soft snow and, just below, a pleasant valley.

Johannes believed him even now, when we had been led so far astray that our lives were again in terrible danger. He could not see past that bluff, cheerful exterior to the bloody, reckless warrior inside. But I knew Ahmes. I had seen men like him all my life, ever since I was a mewling baby.

And now Ahmes was going to be the death of us all.

I leaned my head against Johannes's shoulder. He would always be kind to me, but he would not listen, would not think of me as a man. I was still "little Dari," even though I had grown half a head since we set out from Acre more than a year ago. He had never taken me seriously, and now there could never be a chance for such a thing.

"Eh-hey!" The shout broke into my thoughts. Ahmes had been walking twenty paces ahead, and now he turned to grin at us in triumph. "There we are. Straight ahead."

And there it was. The luck of Ahmes. A rising streak of dust on the next sandy ridge. Within that dust as we topped our own dune I could see the line of camels and ponies, walking nose to tail along the high line of the hard sand. Five minutes later I had my face buried in a juicy section of *hendevane*—watermelon. Nothing had ever tasted so good.

I swallowed cool red pulp, ran the cold, sticky rind across my forehead, and looked up. Ahmes was chattering with half a dozen of the merchants while Johannes, less fluent, did his best to follow the babble. I had been coaching him for a year, but his ear was blind and he did not have my gift for languages. As Ahmes talked now of the desert crossing, just as though we had planned everything this way, Johannes was nodding. Was it worth pointing out to him, one more time, that the advice of Ahmes had been hopelessly wrong, that we had found no oasis where he promised, and that the encounter with this caravan was nothing but the act of a kind Fate?

Useless. Johannes thought and spoke nothing but good of anyone. Except himself.

I did not want to hear the lies and boasting of Ahmes. I finished the slice of melon and began to wander back along the broken line of the halted caravan. And there, in the middle of a group of soldiers who each looked even bigger and stronger than Ahmes, I had my first sight of her.

The witch-woman.

At the time she seemed no more than a girl, sitting on the most beautiful little pony that I had ever seen. Can I confess it, that my interest was drawn first to that darling horse, dappled dark-brown and black, with a flowing white mane? I coveted that pony.

She sat upright on its back, muffled in a dark blue cloak from feet to eyes. Those eyes were wide, with irises the color of honey, and eyebrows thick and black above them. From her bearing I took her for a fully mature woman, perhaps the senior wife of one of the merchants. Only when I looked closer could I see that she was not so old. Fifteen or so, and my senior by only two years.

She urged her pony forward along the line toward the head of the caravan. When she arrived there she stood staring at Johannes, and ignoring Ahmes. That was unusual. Ahmes was tall and broad and loud, the dominant figure in most groups.

"Who is that?" I spoke to one of the foot soldiers, a man wearing fronded leather leggings, and pointed to the woman. I had spoken in Turkic, but I was ready to try with Pushtu and Persian and Arabic if that did not work.

He understood me all right, and so did his companions. They all roared with laughter.

"Eyes off her, little warrior," the man said. "She is forbidden fruit. Kings-meat, reserved for the Emperor himself. Anyone who touches her will find he's two balls short. You don't want to lose 'em, do you, before you've had a chance to use 'em?"

He was burly and bearded, but his eyes were good-humored and they took the roughness from his words. And he had told me something of supreme importance. If the woman were intended as a bride or concubine of the Emperor, then the caravan must be bound for Karakorum itself and the court of the Great Khan. That was many days travel away, but by staying with them, we would reach our own destination. We were luckier than we had realized.

It was late afternoon, and our arrival had provided a sufficient reason for the traveling merchants to stop for the day. The girl came riding slowly back along the line, and the soldier next to me saw my look.

"All right, little warrior, go and talk to her if you want to. Talk is certainly permitted." He laughed, but he was not laughing at me. "We are here to protect her, but not from talk. And we will protect you, too, if you need it. Go."

I did not need to approach her. She was heading straight for me. When the pony and I were nose to nose she stopped and pulled the veil of the *chador* from the lower half of her face. I saw a straight nose with flared nostrils, a lower lip full enough to be new-stung by a honeybee from the thyme fields of the Elburz Mountains, and a skin as pale and clear as their first-fallen snow. Kings-meat, indeed.

"Dar-i," she said, and it was the first sign that she was a witch-woman. How did she know my name? "Dari, the caravan is stopping now. When we eat the evening meal, I want to talk to you."

Her accent was strange, her voice deep, and I could only just understand her. She was not from this part of the world, but we had enough common language to talk freely. Before I did more than nod she had swung around and was heading down the line. I was left looking at the pony's swaying haunches. And then Johannes was calling me from the head of the line, needing help to converse with the merchants.

I sighed. How would he have managed without me, if I had died out there in the desert? How *had* he managed, in his many years before we ever met?

Nataree, her name was. She came from the mountains north of Kabul, far to the west of this eastern desert, and because of her great beauty she had been picked out by the local khan from all the girls of his region, and sent to be a bride for the Great Khan; or to be whatever the Great Khan, in his wisdom, wanted her to be.

She smiled when she said that last piece, as though it was a joke. I nodded, just as though I understood, and wondered why we were talking at all. I wanted to get back to Johannes, he was not safe without me.

"Your own journey," she said at last. "It is also to visit the court of the Great Khan?"

"That is correct."

She was silent for a long time, those honey eyes staring into the distant firelight. We were sitting apart from the other groups, off in the cold and dark that fills the world twenty paces or more from the fires. She ate daintily and little, as though food was nothing to her. At last: "But you have no gifts for the Khan, no wives, no jewels, no new inventions?"

And now it was my turn to be silent. Our mission was certainly no secret, but it was perhaps better explained to people by Johannes, not by me. But he could not explain to her!—not until he learned to speak her language. And even then, there were things that he might not want said, about his own reasons for being here. On the other hand, what harm could there be in my telling Nataree of the questions we sought to answer? We would look for information from anyone.

"We are here to learn certain things of the court of the Great Khan," I said at last. "And we do bring gifts. Gifts of learning."

Her eyes glowed with interest. I began to speak, and as I did so I reflected that this at least was not misleading. We brought learning, and no one could doubt Johannes's fittingness as an ambassador of knowledge and wisdom. I had known it the first time we met, at the house of my master, di Piacenza, the papal legate in Acre.

I had been there for two years as a house servant, sold from Bactria via Bokhara. When Johannes appeared at the house he was ushered in at once to see the legate. I was there, as usual, to run errands or to bring tea and sweetmeats. I sat at my master's feet. As Johannes came in I saw this ancient, bent-shouldered man. Then he lifted his head, and something strange and wonderful was revealed. A young man and an old man were living together in one face, with wisdom, knowledge, and love shining from pale blue eyes. I had never seen such abstract intelligence in a human countenance, coupled with such naivety for worldly affairs.

"Welcome, Johannes of Magdeburg," said my master. He spoke of course in Latin, and I had reached the point in my knowledge of that language where I could understand everything that was said. But I had not revealed my progress to M. di Piacenza, not mainly in truth because

I sought to deceive him, but because I was thus allowed to be present in many cases where I would otherwise have been excluded. "A good journey from Venice, I trust?" added my master.

Johannes nodded. So far as he and my master the papal legate were concerned, the proprieties had now been observed and they could get down to business. I never ceased to marvel at the abruptness—the crudity—of the leaders of the Church of Jesus. In my homeland, even relative strangers would chat for a few minutes and drink tea or wine together before they began any work of negotiation. Here, it was hello, hello, now let's talk business.

"We have made a list," said my master, "in cooperation with His Holiness and the advisers in Rome. We have seven reports—rumors, let us call them, pending some confirmation—of strange inventions and discoveries in the regions ruled by the Great Khan, Kublai. We would like to know more about them." He held out a roll of paper, tied with a bright blue ribbon. "Study these at your leisure as you travel, but let me offer you my own opinions in a few words. First, the Philosophers' Stone, which can transmute base metals to noble metals."

Johannes smiled at once and shook his head.

My master nodded. "I know. We have seen it on a hundred lists, and it never reveals anything but fraud and deceit. But it was reported by Father de Plano Carpini, the Franciscan, on his travels for His Holiness among the Mongols, and he is an honest man. It should be checked. Let us move on to others of more interest. The Auromancers, the little worms that spin golden thread, they sound at first impossible. Except that silk cloth is surely no myth, and there is good evidence that it is made by a little worm or caterpillar, far off in Cathay. You must check the Auromancers. Myself, I believe they exist. Possession of that secret would be a path to great wealth, but we do not ask that you seek to buy or steal an Auromancer. Only seek the knowledge of truth or falsehood of the story.

"Now, I am more skeptical of the Templars, next on our list. I might perhaps believe a centipede three feet long, with a sting fatal to humans—though all such wondrous beasts have a habit of shrinking, you know, the closer you get to their home territory. I find it harder to accept such a centipede as a Templar, a temple guardian intelligent enough to know the difference between worshipers and robbers. And when we are told that such creatures are *themselves* worshipers in the temple, we tread on strange ground indeed: the notion of a soul in the body of a beast. That is a clear heresy. But you, Johannes, will separate truth from falsehood."

(I sat quiet at the feet of M. di Piacenza and hugged myself with excitement. Johannes of Magdeburg was heading off beyond the rising sun, to Cathay or farther, on a journey of magical discovery, and I would give my right hand to go with him. How could I persuade my master to give me permission?)

"I will group together and pass over the questions of birds as big as elephants, or of two-headed, fire-breathing lizards, or of peacocks that eat only rocks and shit pure opals," went on my master. "You will surely ask about them. But whether they exist or whether they are no more than myth and legend will make little difference to the Holy Church. Neither property nor belief is at issue, merely human curiosity. However, this last item is another matter." He tapped the yellow paper. "Ants, says Father Carpini. He heard of ants the size of men, Quarry Ants who operate the diamond mines of the Great Khan. Ants that speak in human tongues, ants who have learned the use of fire, ants who worship a divine creator. You know what that would do to the roots of our beliefs."

Johannes nodded. He knew, but of course I did not—not then. Later, he explained to me that they were concerned because in his religion God made Man in his own image, and so creatures other than those in the shape of Man could not worship or have souls. They would have to be Satanic creations, inventions of the Devil.

"Now," concluded my master. "Here is the letter from His Holiness, for delivery to the Great Khan, Kublai. According to Father Carpini, the Great Khan lives in such splendor that material gifts are useless, although almost everyone offers them. We hope that your own scientific and mathematical powers will interest the Khan more than anything else. Do you have any new suggestions for this?"

While my master was still speaking, Johannes reached into his battered brown bag of calf's leather and pulled out a little book, bound in red. "This is not new, but I think it may be new to the court of the Great Khan. It is the *Liber Abaci* of Leonardo of Pisa, known as Fibonacci. I have studied it closely, and I believe it to be of overwhelming importance for science."

"Indeed." My master looked at the book, and to tell the truth there was a skepticism in his voice that only someone who knew him well would recognize. "This little volume here?"

"Yes. It introduces a quantity, the *sifr*, or *cifra*, and a new way of writing numbers based upon it. I agree with Fibonacci, this will transform every aspect of calculation, from astronomy to the sale of goods. With your permission, and the permission of His Holiness, I propose to instruct the philosophers at the court of the Great Khan in the mathematical techniques of the *Liber Abaci*."

"Oh certainly, certainly, do that if you wish."

But it was clear that my master thought this of little consequence compared with Auromancers and Templars and Quarry Ants.

By contrast, Nataree seemed indifferent when I spoke of animals with near-magical powers, and flamed with curiosity when I mentioned the little book that Johannes carried with him everywhere.

She had huddled inside her cloak as she listened to me talk of Johannes and our mission, with only her eyes showing. Now she suddenly stirred and said, "Tell me more about the book. Tell me what it allows you to do."

I tried to explain; and of course, I could not. I had heard Johannes talk a hundred times of the new methods, and seen him do calculations so fast that some scholars swore he must be in league with the Devil; but nothing of Johannes's techniques had ever made sense to me.

Nataree listened to me for a while, then pushed back her cowl and stood up. "Dari, you do not make sense. It is not your fault. I will talk about this to Johannes myself."

And then she was moving, heading for the line of campfires. As she walked away, I was tempted to shout after her, "Talk all you want, you silly girl. Johannes does not speak your language, and you do not speak his." Then I shivered, and remained silent. I realized that in the hour or less that we had been talking together, Nataree had somehow caught much of my vocabulary and accent, and was already speaking closer to my own choice of tongue. I am quick with languages; most people would say, incredibly quick. Could anyone, ever, learn another's language in a few hours or a few days? Only, I would say it again, if she were a witch-woman.

I was cold, not fully recovered from our ordeal in the desert, and again feeling hungry; but I did not go back at once to the cooking pots and the warmth of the fires. I felt strangely disloyal and ashamed. In thinking to acquire information, I had learned nothing, and perhaps I had told too much.

It was good that Nataree had left when she did. Otherwise the force of those pale, piercing eyes might have sucked out of me the rest of the story of my first meeting with Johannes; and that was something that he surely wanted no one to know about—not even me.

My master, when the official business was over, had drawn a chair up close to Johannes, and his voice changed to a solemn tone I had never heard him use before. I froze at his feet.

"My son," he said, and Johannes bowed his head. "Do not look on this journey as a punishment, or even as a penance."

"Father di Piacenza, Your Holiness, I try not to not think of it that way. I try to see it as an opportunity."

"It is, indeed. An opportunity to give service to God, and a chance to renew your faith. If you would like to tell me what happened to you . . ."

Johannes had sighed like an old, old man. "That is part of the problem. Nothing happened. There was no event, no moment of temptation, no sight of Satan high on a church spire trumpeting at me like a thousand elephants to bring me to sin. But the more I studied, the more I asked questions, the more I tried to understand—the less became my certainty. I waited and prayed and hoped. Six months ago I at last went to Monsignor Alienti and asked for advice. He suggested some kind of pilgrimage, and thought that with my interests and background in the sciences, one of unusual type might serve better both me and the Holy Church. And so here I am."

There was a great simplicity and honesty to Johannes, no one could mistake that. And although what he said made no sense at all to me, apparently it did to my master. "If the result of this mission is that you are helped," he said, "then even if nothing else is accomplished, it will not be a failure. A soul is quite beyond price. Nothing is more important than your return to full conviction."

Johannes's eyes were turned down, but I could see them from where I was sitting. Instead of the clear certainty they held when he spoke about mathematics and the *Liber Abaci,* now they were tormented and filled with misery.

"You have questions," my master went on. "The Church has no objection to questions. It welcomes debate and logical thought, it even thrives on paradox. But logic must ultimately be subordinated to Faith. We begin with Faith, and end with Faith, and Faith conquers all. If in your studies there was a failure to understand God's plans for the world down to the level of the smallest logical detail, that is proof only of human fallibility. It adds to the glory of God, if understanding Him is not simple. You are making a grave error if you say, 'because I cannot understand everything, God is lacking'! Remember again, the soul of a human is priceless."

I listened closely—and still I had little idea what he was talking about! It was more of the cold tangle of Christ that I heard so often in the palace. All words and no warmth. But this time I felt something new: the pain in Johannes. I was so drawn to him, so taken with him, I could not dismiss this dialogue as unimportant.

"Perhaps," Johannes said after a few moments of silence, "I will convert the Great Khan himself, to make him become a follower of Christ."

His voice was wistful. My master blew that sorrow away with a great gust of laughter.

"Ah, my Johannes, would that you could! But no, we are not so ambitious as that. Go east, and bring back a little new knowledge, and your faith made whole, and that will be all we can ask." He finally noticed me, staring up at him, and switched at once to speak in Persian. "Now then, Dari, why are you still here? Off, and bring *chai* for our honored guest."

I would never have a better chance.

"Master," I said, and bowed low. "The honored guest has come a great distance, and I think he must travel farther. I heard you talk of the court of the Great Khan. That is far, far away. If the guest does not know the language you are using now, or those of the tribes still farther to the east, he will find travel very difficult. I have some gift for languages. I would be honored to serve him, and speak to others on his behalf."

My master stared at me as though he had never seen me before in his whole life. I shivered, and waited. At last he smiled. "This desire to serve does you credit, Dari. But there is one problem. How can you help the holy Johannes, when you cannot even speak *his* language. What would you be able to say to him, or on his behalf, if you cannot understand him?"

"I would say"—and now I turned to face Johannes himself, and changed to Latin; not very good Latin, on purpose, since I did not want to upset my master with my earlier eavesdropping—"*Domine,* I want to serve you. My Lord, I will go with you wherever you go, and speak on your behalf, and make your goals my only goals."

M. di Piacenza's mouth hung open. "Such cheek! You'll do no such thing. Be off with you, little Dari, get out of here and bring hot tea. Johannes and I have much to talk about."

I went, and my feet bore me along the carpeted corridor like the wings of eagles. My master might fool Johannes with the severity of his manner, but he did not fool me. When he was angry he called me Daryush, when he was pleased with me, it was Dari; when he was *really* pleased, it was little Dari.

I was going, I was going, I was going, I was going.

Johannes of Magdeburg and I, we would travel east and east and farther east. We would walk the shining world, go together beyond the eye of the rising sun, to travel the Great Silk Road—the Dragon Road, the Smoke Road, the Snowy Road, the Golden Road, the magic road that would lead to the court of the Great Khan himself.

I hugged myself. I was going!

When I lived in Bactria, before I was sold to M. di Piacenza, I slept always with the horses and the camels. My master told me at once when I reached Acre that he did not want me stinking of animals in his house, and he made me bathe often and sleep in an inside chamber; but I have never lost my fondness for the warmth and comforting smell of the great beasts.

In desert country, now, where there is no hope of forage, all the animals of the caravan are herded together for the night in the middle of the circle of campfires. It is smelly and intimate there, and the finest place in the world in freezing weather. When I at last came in from the darkness, chilled to the bone, I headed inside the circle for old time's sake, and also for a late-night look at Nataree's beautiful dappled pony.

To my surprise, Johannes was at the first campfire I came to—and he was sitting with Ahmes and Nataree.

I watched for a few moments before I joined them. Johannes had his beloved *Liber Abaci* held out in front of him, and he was doing most of the talking. Nataree was listening very closely, and asking occasional questions in a slow and correct Persian. My teaching for the past year had been enough to allow Johannes to follow her, and to reply to her.

"So this mark," she was saying. "The *sifr*. It does not mean that *hichi*—nothing—is there. It says that there is something specific there; that in this space there are no tens in this particular number. So it serves to mark the place where numbers of tens are written. This number, 308, has none of the tens. Three tens of tens in this place, here. No tens, in this place here. And eight units, here."

"Exactly right!" Johannes leaned forward and gripped the hand that touched the book, something which he definitely should not have done. I looked around at once to see if her guards had seen, but they were arguing and dozing by the next fire. "And the *sifr* can mark the position of any sort of number—it could show, for instance, that there are no hundreds in a number which has some thousands and some tens. It makes calculation easy, almost trivial."

Nataree was nodding, while Ahmes was yawning. I can't say that I blame him. I'd heard Johannes and his "sifr position notation" far too often, myself. But Ahmes was by no means asleep. His eyes were on Nataree, and the expression they held was one that I had seen a hundred times. I am perhaps a little skinny, but I am fair-skinned and graceful in movement, and many men have found me attractive. I have never given myself to one, but I recognize that red-eyed glaze of blind lust easily enough; and Ahmes had it now. If he was not careful, he would get himself into worse trouble than any he had seen so far.

"Teach me more!" said Nataree suddenly. "Let us do another calculation!"

"Give me a problem!" Johannes was as excited as she, like a child showing off a toy. "Any numbers that you choose."

"My age, added to your age, added to his age, added to his age." She pointed at me and Ahmes.

"Too simple—once I know the ages." Johannes made a column of numbers. "Twenty-eight, that is me. Thirteen, that is Dari. Ahmes, how old are you?"

"Twenty-three years." The soldier shrugged. "And what good will your answer be when you get it?"

"And I am fifteen," said Nataree. But as Johannes made his column of numbers, and did odd things with it, I saw through her game. She wanted to know how old Johannes was. And she had found out, without asking.

But why did she want to know? To cast horoscopes, perhaps? To set a spell on him? Nothing made sense. She was destined to be a bride of the Great Khan, that was her future, and the future of Johannes was irrelevant to her.

I was suspicious. I disliked Nataree anyway, without needing more reason. She was a witch-woman, and I had already given her too much information about me and about Johannes.

The whole desert was wider than Ahmes had said—far wider. If we had not met the caravan, the three of us would have ended as sun-dried corpses, days short of any supply of water; and we had been only in the Little Desert, the western end of the Great Desert.

Even with the experienced merchants of the caravan to guide us, the journey across that Great Desert was not easy. The most foolhardy traveler would not plunge on into the heart of the *Takla Makan Shamo* itself, the place that we had been heading for, in our sublime ignorance. The caravan turned north on the Great Desert's western margin, to find and follow the southern edge of the *Tien Shan,* the Celestial Mountains, where we could take our water from their snowmelt.

It was four weeks before we reached the plain that we would follow north-east toward Karakorum itself. The weather turned colder and colder. We would find Karakorum, home of the Great Khan, a snow-girt city with (according to false legend) walls of gold and towers of diamond.

Not that at all, said the merchants, many of whom had made this journey before. But a place of incredible wealth, nonetheless. And what, pray, did we hope to trade there?

They were polite, but it was a politeness reserved for madmen. I could tell what they thought of us, but Johannes could not. He did not speak Turkic. He knew what he knew only through my translations, and I was not about to translate the "Ah!" 's and the "Oh, yes?" and "Indeed?" 's that greeted discussions of new science and strange mathematics.

After the first week with the caravan I began to be aware of other things. The caravan itself was by no means a single unit, as it had seemed when we first encountered it. It comprised three groups in addition to us: first, the true merchants, devoted only to the acquisition and sale of trade goods. They were easy to understand, because the nature of a trader is the same in Samarkand or Karakorum as it is in Acre or Persepolis. Unless they were dead, they would haggle endlessly and price everything they saw. If they could have done it, they would have set a value for my master on Johannes's immortal soul, something he had said was impossible!

Then there was the party from Kabul, including Nataree and her guardian soldiers. She would arrive at Karakorum a virgin, they told me, or they would all die. According to Khosro, my soldier friend in the leather leggings, a girl-gift for the Great Khan had once arrived in Karakorum from the local khan not only seduced, but visibly pregnant! The local khan's ambassador in Karakorum had ordered that the whole group of guards be flayed alive. The Great Khan, in his compassion, had given instructions that the men be strangled first, before their skins were removed and sent back to Kabul. There was no love, according to my friend, between the Great Khan and the lesser khan of Kabul. The homage offered to Karakorum was a grudging and reluctant one, provided only because of fear of the Great Khan's long arm of power.

With that threat of slow death hanging over them, it was amazing to me that the guards of Nataree took their duties so lightly. That they would allow me to talk to her freely and even wander outside the camp with her was not perhaps so surprising, since my voice was not yet a man's voice. But she wandered the whole caravan, with apparently little control or even surveillance of her actions. I understood that better after a few days. The man who could seduce or rape Nataree would be an unusual one. The fire and ice in her eye frightened most people away (though not Ahmes—he still had that look). She spent her time as she chose, almost all of it talking endlessly to Johannes about things that no sensible person was interested in. He was delighted! For the first time, someone cared about science and mathematics and understood his precious *Liber Abaci* as fully as he did.

And beyond that, Nataree learned Persian—and Latin from long sessions with Johannes—so fast it surprised even me. However, not even the guards were worried about Johannes. They saw him as a holy man, a man whose life was consumed with learning, one whose pure soul shone from his clear eyes.

What fools we were, all of us! We could not see Johannes as she saw him.

Well, with Johannes talking and talking to Nataree and not wanting an interpreter at the moment, I had plenty of time on my own hands. The third group in the caravan was that of the drovers, the men who looked after the horses and the camels. Since I had been raised among drovers, it was natural for me to seek them out. Within a few days I was a dung-boy, an honorary member of the group. We trailed last in the caravan, and carefully collected all the dung and dried it. Each morning we did the same thing within the camp. In the desert it was our main fuel, the difference between raw, unpleasant food and delicious cooked food.

A dung-boy is like a fly, present everywhere and totally invisible. No one noticed me with my flat pan and shovel. And as we were emerging from the foothills of the Celestial Mountains I saw something I was not supposed to see.

One of the soldiers sent to guard Nataree was an odd man out. His name was Maseed, and he was a skeletal, long-limbed man with a huge nose and a walleye. But it was his actions, not his appearance, that made him noteworthy. While the others sat around the fires, drinking or dozing, he would be off by himself, wandering the perimeter. He would set a cup on top of a rock, move three or four paces away, and then throw a small round pellet toward it. I say he threw, but actually the pellet was propelled with an almost imperceptible flick of the middle fingertip from the thumb, and flew so fast and so invisibly that I knew of its motion only by the rattle of its arrival in the cup. His accuracy was astonishing. I counted, and he missed only one or two times in a hundred. Even when I looked for it, I could not follow the pellet's flight.

He did the same thing over and over, day after day; flicked and flicked, while I watched and wondered. (Pointlessly? Perhaps. M. di Piacenza back in Acre always told me that my nosiness would be the death of me).

What was he doing? I was tempted to ask Nataree about it, to see if it was a game or custom of her country, but I never did. I would not accept the idea of her doing me any favors.

No less odd, late one night I went to watch Maseed . . . and found Ahmes with him. They were away from the others by their own little campfire, heads close together.

"One simple act," Maseed was saying, "and that one with no risk. A moment's diversion. After that, wealth will be yours."

"And the other?" asked Ahmes. "The fair one was promised."

"The promise will be kept. Her body will be yours, to do as you like with. But you must make the move exactly when I tell you, precisely as I direct. Then there will be no danger at all."

I had often wondered what Ahmes was doing on this journey. I had suspected the oldest motives in the world: blood and gold. Now I had proof of that, and I was ready to add lust to the list. Ahmes was a mercenary, pure and simple, and he could be bought by anyone who could afford him. But as to *what* he and Maseed were doing . . .

I waited and watched, a lesson I had learned almost before I could walk.

Meanwhile, we steadily drew nearer to the city of Karakorum, the home of the Great Khan. From twenty miles away it was finally visible across the snowy plain, a great rising tower of blue smoke above the horizon. When we camped for the last night, we sent our runners on ahead to make sure that the Great Khan knew we were arriving. An unnecessary gesture, the merchants said, since Kublai Khan's own intelligence service had made him aware of our approach for at least the past five days; however, notification of arrival was diplomatically necessary.

On that final cold evening, I sat close to the campfire and listened while Johannes and Nataree talked together. Not on the speculation of any sane person, as to the sights and sounds to be found in the court of the Great Khan. By no means. It was as bad as being back in Acre, listening to Johannes and my master.

"You do not understand," he was saying. "Faith is the most important thing in the whole world, since it leads not only to happiness on earth but to life eternal. And faith is what I lost. I have lost it still."

"No," she said. "It is you, Johannes, who understands nothing." She was speaking Latin, and it jolted me to realize that her knowledge of that language now seemed to match my own. "You say you have lost faith. All that you lost is simpleminded certainty. There are many faiths in this world, dozens of them, hundreds of them. Who is to say that your church's Trinity is truer than this man's demons, or that man's different beliefs? Your prophet, Christ, you say he is the son of God, and he was taken to the top of a high mountain and tempted with all the treasures of the world. Very well. I am the daughter of God, or at least one of God's daughters. If you would allow me, I could take you to another peak, just as real, and tempt you with a whole other world, just as sacred."

It sounded as though she was offering her body—and yet just as clearly that was not what she meant at all, for she went on, "You tell me yourself, your geometry and your calculations are eternal, pure logic that will exist forever. The proof of the parabola theorem that you showed me today, what could ever be more beautiful than that? Surely *these,* and not some fixed group of wordy ideas, are your *veritates aeternae,* your eternal verities."

"You don't understand me," said Johannes. He sounded anguished, and yet at the same time enthralled. He loved this sort of pointless talk. "What I mean is this . . ."

And off he went, on another camel ride across a desert of theories and proofs. He was the most handsome and wonderful man I had ever known, and he was never anything but patient and thoughtful. But he was also the world's most obstinate and persistent man when it came to his ideas, and the hardest man to understand when he talked about them. But perhaps she did understand him, very well. For although they had talked like this many times, endlessly, hour after hour, neither ever seemed to tire of it.

I left, and became a dung-boy again. No one saw me, wandering along with my flat pan and shovel. And near the end of the camp, where few people went because the food and water was far off at the front, I again saw Ahmes and Maseed. They were saying little, but Ahmes was holding a beautiful little shield of polished brass. Maseed had placed a metal cup on a rock, and was standing four paces from it. In the twilight, I saw him lift his left hand to touch his ear, and at that moment Ahmes dropped the shield. It fell clanging to the ground, and a second later Maseed flicked his finger. There was a rattle of a round pellet into the cup.

"Very good," he said, and he laughed, but there was no humor in his voice. "One more time, and that will be the last time."

It was something bad. Maseed was a bad man. I knew that, as surely as I knew that Johannes of Magdeburg was a good man. But what were they doing? I sought Johannes, to ask his advice, but he was no longer by the fire, nor was he with Nataree. She was with her guards, settled in for the night.

I wandered around the whole camp, and finally went into the beasts' circle and lay down for comfort next to the dappled pony. Tomorrow that pony would carry Nataree into Karakorum itself. And then perhaps Johannes would stop talking and begin his search for the knowledge that we came for. It would be nice to know we had succeeded, and could begin to think whenever we chose about the journey home.

Karakorum certainly had walls, but they were not of gold, nor were its towers of diamond. According to Johannes, it was less of a city than other places he had been, Paris and Rome and Athens. However, it was a wonderland by my standards, and it was undeniably the home of the Great Khan, ruler over an empire that stretched across more than half the world.

We came to it across a long, cleared plain, and from miles away we could see the great palace within the walls. It was huge, a hundred paces long and seventy wide, towering up on its sixty-four wooden columns on their granite bases. Inside the city itself most of the buildings were of brick, including Shamanist shrines, mosques, and temples to Buddha.

"And perhaps one day," said Johannes, "a Church of Christ." But he did not sound very confident.

I had finally found out where he went the previous evening. He had wandered off by himself, alone into the night, something he was apt to do when he wanted to work hard on his beloved calculations. No one else in the world had his power of concentration on a single problem. I had known him stay in one place for twenty-four hours, totally lost in thought.

Today he was pale and moody, rubbing the palm of his hand along his forehead and his unshaven chin. I told him what had happened last night with Ahmes and Maseed, and asked him what he thought was going on. He heard me all right, I know he did, but instead of replying he stared at me as though I were a passing cloud. Then he reached out, and touched me gently on the shoulder.

I said he was never anything but loving and patient, and that is true. But when the philosophical fit was on him, he could be unreachable.

We were entering Karakorum, the whole unwieldy procession of us, and soon we learned that our audience with Kublai Khan would not happen for another day. Fortunately, most people in the caravan were not seeking to pay their respects to the Great Khan. The merchants went their way, the drovers another, and a group of about a dozen of us, including Nataree and her guards, were left to hang around near the entrance to the palace, and haggle with the local merchants for an evening meal at inflated prices. I did our haggling. Johannes was not good at that sort of thing, he would believe whatever the storekeepers told him.

After dinner I once more sought him out. As always, he was talking to Nataree, their incomprehensible babble of circles and lines and squares. I interrupted them. I told Johannes again what I had seen with Massed, and at last I asked Nataree if she, as Maseed's countrywoman, knew the meaning of his ritual. She listened closely, and so did Johannes, but then they both shook their heads. They did not disbelieve me, but the mystery remained.

Our audience with the Great Khan had been set for early the next day. Soon after dawn Nataree's soldiers were up and busy polishing their brass. They all wore new tunics and their best headgear.

I wished I could have done the same. I was supposed to be the interpreter for Johannes, and although in the desert a little dirt didn't show, now I was aware of the whiff of horse and camel dung that came from my clothes. Brushing at the dirt just made it worse.

All the groups who would be presented to the Khan entered the palace at the same time. Naturally, all weapons, and anything that might conceivably be used as a weapon, were left outside with the palace guards. It would hardly be a necessary precaution, since the person of the Great Khan was always surrounded by his trained guards.

First into the palace was a group of rich merchant princes from India. They were seeking trade agreements, and to increase their chances they brought lavish gifts of ivory, jade, and sapphires. Next was the Nataree party, with smarmy Maseed in front and Ahmes, bearing the little ornamental shield on a velvet cushion, just behind. It was clear that it was to be a gift for Kublai Khan. Nataree, beautifully dressed in a long gown of purple and white, walked demurely after them. She looked no more impressed by the court of the Great Khan than she did by anything else.

We came last, after Nataree, with Johannes clutching his copy of the *Liber Abaci*. It seemed pathetic, and I wondered what sort of reception we were likely to get. Ivory and jewels as gifts, then a beautiful new wife, and then us, a dung-smelling servant and a man carrying one battered book with the world's most boring information inside it.

The greeting hall itself was enough to unnerve me. It was over forty paces long, and the floor and walls were covered with the most beautiful tapestries and carpets I ever saw. Each one depicted some aspect of the life of the Great Khan—hunting, hawking, receiving royal guests, bestowing honors, or sitting in judgment on cases of noble wrongdoing. The rugs of the greeting hall were so thick that our advance across them was almost silent.

At the far end of the hall the Great Khan was already present. He was sitting on a carved wood and ivory throne, painted in gold and brown, and as we all came in he did a surprising thing. He stood up, and then to my amazement he walked past the Indian merchant princes, past

Ahmes and Maseed and Nataree, and right up to Johannes. He stared at us without speaking. His robes were fine gold cloth, woven perhaps from the thread of the Auromancers that we had come so far to study, and he carried a long golden staff.

"Great Emperor," I said, and my voice cracked on the first word. "It is an honor to be here at this great court. We bring no material gifts, but our respect is not less for that. We hope we bring something more precious than rubies or gold. We bring knowledge."

His face was stern and terrible, with a long, straggly mustache across a thin upper lip. But then he smiled, just a little. "A king can have enough gems and jewels," he said. "But no man can ever have enough knowledge. And I receive wives on many days, but strangers from so far away are a rarity. Welcome."

Johannes was smiling also, not understanding a word. My knees were wobbling. All I could say—croak, that's a better word, for my voice had chosen the worst possible moment to begin breaking to a man's tones—the one word I could utter was, "Thankyou."

Fortunately it did not matter, because the Great Khan had taken the *Liber Abaci* from Johannes's hands and was already turning to the other groups. Our audience was not over, but to avoid a slight to anyone, all would be greeted formally before longer discussions began.

The group accompanying Nataree presented to the Great Khan a set of gorgeous goblets of finely chased gold, and equally fine plates on which they were seated. He took them, made a little speech of formal thanks, and called at once for wine. A servant hurried forward with a glass flask and filled the cups, passing one each to half a dozen of the surrounding nobles.

One of Nataree's party offered a toast, to the long life and prosperity of the Great Khan, and lifted his cup. Kublai smiled, but instead of drinking he passed his own goblet to a dark-skinned servant standing next to him. The black man sniffed cautiously at the wine and poured a few drops into a little beaker that he held. We waited. When nothing happened after a few seconds, the man sipped a little wine and finally nodded. He handed the goblet back to Kublai Khan.

While this had been happening, the whole assembly was frozen— until the Great Khan moved, no one could move. When he finally took the goblet, and lifted it in front of him, everyone relaxed and lifted his own glass.

Out of the corner of my eye, I saw Maseed reach up to scratch his left ear. Inevitably, I looked across at Ahmes, and at that very moment he dropped the brass shield from its velvet cushion. It made a hollow, brazen boom as it hit the thick carpet. Everyone turned to see what was causing the noise.

Everyone except me. I knew what would happen next, and already I had turned to look at Maseed. The flick of the finger against the thumb was a tiny movement in the direction of the Great Khan. I waited for the familiar rattle that signified the arrival of a pellet within a cup. When it did not come I thought for a moment that he must have missed his target; and then I realized that a full goblet of wine would silence the sound completely.

One of Nataree's guards had bent over to pick up the dropped ornamental shield, while another was giving Ahmes a vicious cut across the shoulders with a whip.

The Great Khan, after the few moments of distraction, ignored what was happening to Ahmes. He offered a brief and formal statement of thanks and a welcome to Karakorum, and again raised the goblet to his lips. As he did so I leaned close to Johannes and whispered, "He did it, same as I told you. Threw something—into the Great Khan's cup."

I spoke in Latin, probably with some brainless idea that my insolence in speaking in front of the Great Khan would somehow be less in a foreign language.

Johannes had no such inhibitions, and for once he was not off in his clouds of calculation. He looked at me for one split second. Then he jumped forward, pointed at the Khan's goblet, and cried out what I knew but dared not think: "Don't drink that cup! It's poisoned."

He was lucky he wasn't run through on the spot. Not knowing the language, he had shouted in Persian. Half the Khan's guards had no idea what he was saying. But then Nataree took an instant cue from Johannes, and she shouted out, too, in Turkic: "Don't drink. Poison!"

There was a tremendous hubbub. The Khan had the gold goblet at his lips. Now he jerked it away. The soldiers around him drew their swords, but of course they didn't know what to do next. They had seen nothing, and had no idea who to attack.

Maseed, standing four paces away, tried to look innocent, but I recovered my voice, pointed at him, and cried, "That one! He threw a pellet into the cup, when you were all looking at the dropped shield."

Well, Maseed was too wily to run, but it did him no good. After five minutes questioning of me and, through me, Johannes, Kublai Khan had learned all that we knew and surmised. He ordered that Maseed and Ahmes be taken away and forced to drink from the same goblet. Maseed began to scream and beg for mercy. But as the Great Khan said, if the goblet were not poisoned, then no harm would come to them.

It showed us that he was a merciful Khan. Whatever happened to Maseed and Ahmes, it would be better than a death by slow torture.

They were dragged away. Kublai Khan turned again to me and Johannes.

"Tell your master this," he said to me, as calmly as though assassination attempts happened every day. "I owe him my life. Tell him to ask any favor, and if it is in my power I swear that it will be granted."

Well, this was the moment when I knew that Johannes and I would succeed brilliantly in our mission. The Great Khan was promising it. Auromancers, Templars, Quarry Ants, we would learn all there was to know about every one of them.

Johannes was silent for a long time when I told him the Great Khan's promise. The whole court waited. At last he turned away and looked at Nataree. She nodded, with one slow movement of her head, and closed her eyes as though in prayer.

Johannes looked back at the Great Khan. "I would like," he said. He paused, and his voice straightened. "I would like to take this woman, Nataree. I ask that you allow us to travel freely, she and I, through your territories, toward the rising sun and beyond, on to the end of the world to seek true knowledge."

Everyone was silent, waiting for a translation. My heart was a lump of stone. I had to pass on those words, but it was too much for me. I stood, tongue-tied, until at last one of the merchants chimed in to translate what Johannes had said.

Then the Great Khan frowned. "Nataree?" he said. He looked at Johannes in incomprehension.

An old adviser came forward and whispered something in his ear. Kublai Khan nodded, but he looked no less astonished. He stepped closer to Johannes.

"Honored guest, you have saved my life. For far less than you have done, a hundred women would be yours. That gift is not sufficient. The woman Nataree is nothing to me—why should she be, when I never saw her before today? Ask again, and ask more, much more, or you will shame me as the Great Khan of the Tartars."

Again the merchant translated for Johannes, and at last he nodded. This was it, surely, the moment when he would ask for the answers to all our questions. But he did not. Instead, he moved to Nataree's side, put his arm around her—and turned to point at me!

"That young man" (a man at last! But how bitter the feeling) "is Dari. He is as dear to me as my own life. He has no parents, no family. Would you take him, Great Khan, and give him a home and an education here, in Karakorum?"

The Great Khan stared at me while the request was translated, and I felt a shiver from top to toe.

"Come here," he said at last. "Come close."

I walked forward, and began to kneel before him. He caught my arm in a grip that could have broken it, and would not allow me to sink to the floor. Before I knew what was happening, he pulled me close and kissed me on the forehead, then on both cheeks. He looked around him.

"Dari belongs here," he said. "From this day he is not Dari, he is *Dari Mangu,* and he is a member of my own family." And then he went on—the thing that made the whole court gasp aloud: "Dari Mangu is my son, as much as any of my sons. Like them, he is in the line of succession to become the Emperor, next ruler of Karakorum, the Great Khan of the Tartars. Come, all of you, and offer loyalty and obeisance."

Man after man came forward.

I stood there quaking, the smell of dung still strong upon me, while promises of love and servitude poured into my ears. After half a minute, I began to weep.

That was one year ago. The snows have come again to Karakorum, but Johannes and Nataree have not returned. They went off to the east, to the great sea and beyond.

I think about them always. Did Johannes find a faith, I wonder, somewhere in the breathing world, to replace what he lost long ago in Magdeburg? Did Nataree show him, as she promised, all the kingdoms of the earth?

I do not know.

I thought that Nataree was a witch-woman when first I met her, and I think she is a witch-woman still. But now I suspect that every woman is a witch-woman, casting their spells on men.

I do not hate Nataree, but I resent her greater freedom. Even as a gift-girl to the Great Khan, she could do what I could not. When she held those long, intense conversations with Johannes as we traveled from the Great Desert to Karakorum, she surely fell in love with him. That was easy to do. But having fallen, she could then speak her love. Whereas I . . .

I could not, because he would not allow it. The Holy Church of Johannes told him that love from me was anathema, a mortal sin, a love so forbidden that it was wrong even to say its name.

I was trapped. I loved, as much as she, perhaps more than she, but I could not speak without making him feel revulsion.

And so I live on, in the court of the Great Khan. I have power, I have luxury, I have influence. Perhaps one day I will in truth become the Great Khan, Emperor, Lord of the Tartars, ruler of Karakorum and of half the known world.

Power, glory, honor, possessions. Those are all mine. They feel like nothing. Nothing but waiting, waiting, until the convergence of the Great Arcs at last brings its own peace.

It was right for Johannes to leave his old Church, with its cold Christ, its stern laws, its bleak Heaven. There was nothing there for him, nothing for anyone who loves.

But if he had to leave that church, why could he not have left it for me?

Afterword to "Beyond the Golden Road"

Susan Shwartz, the editor of the book in which this story first appeared, shares with me an interest (better call it an obsession) in the Taklamakan Desert of western China. When she was putting *Arabesques* together she asked me to write something using that general part of the world, creating a romantic tale somewhere between Persia and Mongolia.

I protested, "But I just sold a story like that, "The Courts of Xanadu," to Gardner Dozois at *Asimov's* magazine!"

She said, "So that proves you can do it."

I, recognizing superior guile, retreated and wrote "Beyond the Golden Road."

Reviewers of *Arabesques* did not know what to make of my story. The rest of the book was populated by djinni, houris, demons, phoenixes, rocs, viziers, caravanserai, and all the other mainstays of the Arabian Nights. The other stories were clearly high fantasy. On the other hand, "Beyond the Golden Road" is pure science fiction. I do not know of one word in it that goes beyond what was known or believed about 1250 A.D. For example, the *Liber Abaci* of Leonardo of Pisa, better known as Fibonacci, appeared in 1202 and explained the virtues of the Arabic system of numeration when compared with roman numerals. In the next half century it achieved wide acceptance among the mathematicians of Europe.

In the main, reviewers of the book ignored my story. This rather annoyed me, because for one thing I was very fond of it, and for another I had found it difficult to write. The narrator's character was a hard one to define, plus he had to tell everything he heard while not understanding a good deal of it.

Long after the story was published, a medium-level friend (defined as one I would willingly share lunch or dinner with, but not a hotel room at a convention) read it and said to me, "I didn't know you were gay."

Nor did I. But that remark at last made up for any reviewer neglect. Dari was what I had hoped he would be.

HEALTH CARE SYSTEM

THOMAS MATLOCK DROVE out to the Greenwood estate one foggy morning in late December. Money was the bait, but curiosity was initially a stronger lure.

It was three days after Christmas, and the roads were almost deserted. The limousine wound its way up to the highest point of the Catoctin State Park, then began a cautious descent over roads treacherous with moisture and patches of ground ice. At Matlock's request, the car slowed at an overlook when they were still a mile and a half from the estate. He lowered the window and peered out. The valley below was covered in dense ground mist, but the four wings of the mansion jutted high above it, light gray stone and steep slate roofs. Matlock inspected all that he could see and guessed at the rest. Five hundred acres of land inside the nine-foot fence, maybe another thousand outside it. A hundred-plus rooms to the house. Four gatehouses and guest "cottages," each one bigger than Matlock's own suburban villa.

Matlock breathed deep, inhaling the clear mountain air. At least a million dollars a year in upkeep down there, according to the rumor mills. But that was less than a quarter of the interest, according to those same mills, on Miriam Greenwood's estate. Lifestyles of the rich and reclusive.

He finally nodded. "All right. Anytime."

The car nosed forward, down the long slope and on until it came to heavy steel grilles that swung half-open at an electronic signal from the driver. A uniformed guard walked forward, peered in, checked Thomas

Matlock against something he held in his hand, and signaled to open the gates the rest of the way. The car moved on inside the fence, proceeding toward the main house at a sedate ten miles an hour.

Security procedures were stricter inside. Three guards waited there. Matlock had to produce his hospital ID, and watch while his fingerprints were checked electronically. At last he was allowed in through a second set of doors, saw his TV image matched to a stored template on a color screen, and could finally walk on to inspect Miriam Greenwood's private domain.

The entrance to the mansion had kept its original appearance, oak-paneled walls and polished floors of black-and-white square tiles. Expensive rugs dotted the forty-by-forty expanse. Matlock and his two escorts passed over them, traversed a short, dark corridor, and came to the transition. Decor moved from early twentieth century dry rot to modern sterile; no carpets; walls tiled as well as floors. They walked on. The room that Thomas Matlock was finally ushered into was as antiseptic and lacking in character as any lab at the hospital.

Miriam Greenwood was sitting in an electric wheelchair, behind a desk furnished with a clock, a pad of paper, and a single telephone. She differed from her pictures in only two minor respects: the sparse gray hair was covered with a soft woolen skullcap, and she was not smoking a cigarette. She inclined her head to Matlock, inviting him to sit on the chair opposite.

"Five thousand dollars were deposited in your bank account when you entered the door of this house." Miriam Greenwood's voice was rusty, but still strong. She inclined her head again, this time toward the telephone. "Check, if you wish to do so. Otherwise, we can proceed to business."

"It is not necessary to check."

"I agree. That deposit was designed only to capture your attention." Greenwood sat up straighter. "So watch, and wait."

She pressed a control in the arm of the wheelchair. There was a delay of maybe half a minute, then a door to Matlock's left opened. A woman in a nurse's uniform looked through.

"Yes, ma'am?"

"I would like orange juice. For me, and also my visitor."

"Yes, ma'am." She nodded, and retreated.

Miriam Greenwood gestured at the clock. "Twenty-nine seconds.

Adequate. Two seconds better than usual. On the other hand, this is the day shift. Response is slower at night."

Thomas Matlock kept his face expressionless. "I've done timing comparisons at the hospital. The mean time between a call and a nurse's response to it is eighteen minutes. Twenty-three minutes at night."

"But your patients are not promised fast, exclusive, twenty-four hour, continuous care. That's what I'm paying for." A thin hand lifted and stabbed a finger at Matlock. "And I'm not getting it! Twenty-nine seconds. A person could die in that much time. I've had two heart attacks already. Who knows when there might be another one?"

She paused and checked the desk clock again, when the nurse reappeared and placed full glasses and a pitcher of orange juice on the desk. As the nurse was leaving, Greenwood gestured to the two men behind Thomas Matlock. "I'll signal you if I need you. Stay close."

She picked up a glass, took one tiny sip, and waited until the others were out of the room. "Forty-four seconds, from the order for orange juice until its appearance. More than a minute from the time I first called. Do you think the response would have been any quicker if I were seriously ill? I can answer that for you. It wouldn't."

Miriam Greenwood leaned forward. The lines on each side of her mouth deepened. "Dr. Matlock, I'm eighty-nine years old. I'm fragile. I'm going to die someday. You know that, I know that, and I don't expect miracles. But I'm going to fight like hell for every second. There's no way I'll die sooner than I have to. And I've studied the statistics. Get to a trauma patient soon enough, and their survival chances go up dramatically."

"They do. But I've never heard of a health care system with a mean service time of less than a minute. What you have is incredibly good."

"It may be. It's the best that money can buy. But it's not good enough."

"I don't see how you could get a better one."

"You can build me one." Greenwood's withered lips offered a faint smile. "Ah, you don't think you can, eh? But listen to me." She paused for a long, shallow breath. "Give me five minutes of your time."

"You bought four hours of it."

"I want to buy more than that. Hear me out." She touched one of the controls on her wheelchair, and the back moved to a deeper reclining angle. "One nice thing about having a bit of money, people come to you, instead of you having to go to them. Now, you might think that must be to my advantage, but funnily enough, it's not. Not always. One month ago, the director of your hospital called, to tell me that the new wing I'd financed was going to be opened, and would I like to be there for the ceremony. I hadn't left this building for over a year, because my doctors were advising against it. But I decided I was going. I didn't know why. I think my subconscious did. All my life I've played hunches. I said I was going, and I told Ronson—my head doctor—to shut up. If I dropped dead while I was out, that would be my own dumb fault. So they wheeled me out, and they propped me up in the limo, and took me down to Georgetown." She sighed, the weak, chesty sigh of a sixty-year smoker. "I saw the new wing, but I saw more than that. I saw the equipment in the wing. And I saw OPEC—the On-line Patient Experimental Clinic. Your own lab. Telemetry feeds, direct from patient to computer. Feedback within ten milliseconds."

Greenwood lifted her head, and chuckled at the expression on Matlock's face. "That's it. Finally know why you're here, don't you? If you could do it for them, you could do it for me."

But Thomas Matlock was shaking his head. "You only saw the director's demonstration project. It's based on my lab, but it's bogus."

Miriam Greenwood creaked upright. "Bogus?" Her voice was no more than a thin whisper. "Are you saying Livingstone set out to fool me? If he did . . ."

"No, no. Not the way you think." Thomas Matlock saw a vision of wealth appear and disappear. He didn't want that. "The telemetry feeds from the patient to the computer are near-instantaneous, just the way you said, and the computer analysis of patient condition takes only a few milliseconds. But a physician always approves the treatment before it's given. The director cut that step out of the demo to make it go faster and used cases where approval for treatment had already been given. So it wasn't so much *bogus*—I shouldn't have used that word—it was oversimplified."

"Ah." Miriam Greenwood was relaxing again in her chair, eyes closed. "I see. But it wouldn't have to work that way."

"Really, it would."

"You said the computer does the analysis, the computer decides the treatment. So cut out the physician, and the computer could start a treatment in a couple of heartbeats. Ronson's a pretty good doctor, but he'll never compete with a computer for speed. Use on-line feedback of medication. You know how to do it, build an expert system that incorporates the best medical knowledge in the world into the computer code. And you can hook up all your sensors directly to me—permanently, if you have to. Hell, I *live* in this damned chair. The catheters and sensors could be built right into the seat and arms."

"No." Matlock hesitated. "We couldn't do that," he said at last. "You see, a physician *has* to be there—physically present—to give approval before treatment begins. It's illegal any other way."

"Ah. Illegal." Miriam Greenwood sighed, and her dark eyes blinked open. "Is that all? I thought for a horrible moment you were going to tell me it wasn't *feasible.*"

Thomas Matlock rolled down his car window and waited patiently as the ID checks were performed. Even though the guards all knew exactly who he was, and why he was here, it made no difference. They went through the whole nine yards with him each time.

"Thanks, Jack. Be back in a few hours." He grinned at the guard as he was finally waved through. The man wasn't to blame. He was reflecting Miriam Greenwood's personal paranoia. Matlock drove his Lamborghini up to the circular driveway, parked, and submitted cheerfully to the second set of identification checks before he was allowed in.

To an outside observer, the changes in the past year had been negligible. Miriam Greenwood sat in the same chair, in the same study. A compact box, located under the wheelchair seat in the same place as the batteries, was the only visible addition. Greenwood herself was a little thinner, a little frailer. She nodded at Matlock as he moved to sit across from her.

"You said I'd reach the point where I wouldn't even notice it happening, and I think we're almost there."

"Let's take a look." Matlock whipped his hand toward her eyes, stopping a couple of inches short. She flinched, then nodded. "There it is. I don't feel a thing, but if you listen hard you can hear the pump starting. It's balancing the adrenaline now. The whole thing is perfect."

Matlock nodded and waited. By now he knew Miriam Greenwood.

"Or *nearly* perfect," she went on. "I was talking yesterday on the telephone to Livingstone, over at Georgetown, and he mentioned there's a new drug, xanthyl, being used as a beta-blocker. I queried the computer here"—a minute nod downward to the base of the wheelchair—"and there's no mention of it. Ronson had never heard of it, either."

"There's a good reason for that." Matlock shrugged. "Xanthyl is being used in European tests, but it's not yet FDA-approved. Most on-line databases don't have it in them, because it might be dangerous."

"Or it might be a lifesaver."

"I can't take that sort of risk."

"What risk? I haven't asked you to do anything yet."

"You will."

"Tom, it's a very simple request. I want two things, and you can't possibly object to the first one. I'd like the on-line patient care computer in my wheelchair hooked up to the main household computer. In fact, I'd like to slave the main computer to this one, so that I have an override from here if I ever need it. Would you do that for me?"

"That doesn't sound too bad. What's the second one?"

"Tom, you're getting paranoid. How old are you, thirty-seven? You shouldn't be suspecting everybody for another forty years."

"What's the second one?"

"Nothing terrible. I don't want to die before my time, that's all. You gave me an expert system, but it's not expert enough. It uses the best existing know-how, but it lags behind the real edge. I don't want that. If any new treatments are coming down the pike, I have to know about them—soon. I want my household computer hooked direct into the big centers and information systems—the Mayo, and Sloan-Kettering, and the Medline system at the National Institutes of Health. Not shared modems, either, I want dedicated lines. Then we'll have a *decent* system. And anytime I want to browse through and look at new treatments or experimental drugs, I can do it here without bothering anybody."

Matlock stood up and stared down at the frail figure in the wheelchair. "Do you realize what that would take? This house would have to be defined as a full-fledged medical research facility. There would have to be a validation process, certification of staff, data-handling procedures, drug-handling procedures . . ."

He paused. Miriam Greenwood had moved her chair forward and skimmed an envelope across the desk.

"Open it, Tom, before you tell me it's impossible." She was wheezing, a rare sign of emotion. "My life is my life. My money is only my money. I'll trade one for the other. That check is all for you. Take it, and tell me how much more it takes to deal with anyone else we need."

*　*　*

The rule had been established in the first few weeks: Miriam Greenwood did not want to talk to Matlock over the telephone. If he needed to communicate with her, he would come to the estate.

He broke that rule once, early in the second year. It took ten impatient minutes of hard talk and threats to push the house staff into putting him through to her, and when the connection was at last made he insisted on a video channel. He wanted to see Greenwood, see how she reacted.

"You lied to me," he said, as soon as the TV was active.

"Did I?" Her lined face was calm. It seemed his call was no surprise.

"You know you did." He shook his finger furiously at the camera. "When I arranged for your computer to be hooked into the information systems, our agreement was completely clear."

"Quite true. It was."

"Your medical facilities would be defined as a full research center, but you would get only information. No supplies. No screened labs— and no experimental drugs!"

"That is correct. Are you resigning?"

The cool question was like a splash of ice water. Matlock paused.

"Because if you are," went on the quiet voice, "I certainly can't stop you. But I want to remind you what that will mean. Nine-tenths of your income. The home on St. Kitts. The ownership interest in the casino. Sylvia, too, unless my judgment is badly in error—yes, of course I know all about her and the apartment, just as I know how much you have in each of your bank accounts. Would you like to know what *her* background is? I suppose not—you're too obsessed with her. But it's not at all what she told you, Tom."

He shook his head in an abrupt shivering motion. "Experimental drugs, from all over the world. My signature splashed all over the applications, certifying their uses. If anything were to happen at the house, I'd be ruined. Totally ruined."

"It won't happen." The thin figure in the wheelchair sat up straighter, and her voice strenghtened. "Now, Tommy Matlock, get all this in perspective. We spent a lot of time and money, you and I, making sure I have access to the latest information. Fine. But what good would that be, if the drugs I needed—urgently—were half a world away? We could get data in a fraction of a second, but I might have to wait days for drugs. That's the exact opposite of an efficient health care system. I realized that we needed the drugs on hand *here.* Maybe we would never use them, but maybe they would save my life. Wasn't that the purpose of everything we've been doing?"

"They're experimental drugs—dangerous drugs, with God knows what side effects. If Ronson were to start playing around with them—"

"Which he won't do." As Miriam Greenwood leaned back, Matlock could see new catheters trailing from her lower body. How long was it since she had left that wheelchair, for any reason? Now that he looked closer, he saw the recent changes. Her arms were just bony sticks, and her head was supported by a padded brace. Her mouth was lipless, drawn back over prominent dentures.

"Ronson won't do anything wild," she went on, "for the best possible reason. Today he has a large income—a very large income. But the hour that I die, so does the money supply. His contract is clear. He's cut off that same minute, and out the door looking for another job. If anything can keep me alive, our good Doctor Ronson will do it."

She paused, then nodded her head as though listening to something. "In fact, Tommy, don't you think it would be a good idea if you worked with me on the same basis? You're not going to resign, are you?"

The vacation home, the casino, Sylvia . . . Matlock did not speak.

"So that's all settled, then." Miriam Greenwood smiled. "You'll get more money, naturally . . . as long as I'm alive. We all want that, don't we, more than anything. Let's work on it, Tom. I'm nearly ninety-one now. Let's try for a century, then we'll worry how we go on to a hundred and five."

"It was a shock, Tommy, a nasty shock. And you know as well as I do, shocks could be very bad for me."

The toothless mouth was moving, but the harsh, metallic voice came from the synthesizer and voice enhancer on the back of the wheelchair. Matlock stared at Miriam Greenwood in annoyance. He had installed that system four months ago for emergency use, but now she employed it all the time in preference to normal speech.

"I quite agree, we don't want any sort of shock. But I still don't know what happened. Your message didn't give any details." Matlock hid his irritation. He had dropped everything and headed for the house, the moment the urgent call reached the hospital. He had risked police pursuit and his own skin, pushing the Lamborghini up over a hundred and twenty on quiet parts of the road. And after all that—nothing! Miriam Greenwood appeared to be perfectly normal.

"Of course I didn't give details. It's too important a problem to talk about over the telephone." The frail figure was covered to the neck by a white sheet, but Greenwood's hands were moving beneath it, fingering the controls in the arms of the wheelchair. She came rolling around the desk and stopped right by Matlock's chair. "I thought we had taken care of everything, Tommy, I really did. And now I find there's a terrible weakness in what we've done. Not your fault." A clawlike hand emerged from the sheet, patted his arm in a conciliatory way, and retreated. "It's my fault. I need your help."

"What happened?"

"This afternoon, a little after one o'clock, I noticed one of the television screens had a problem with its colors." The skeletal head nodded upward, to the array of monitors set along the interior wall. "I rang for one of the nurses on duty. There are always two of them, twenty-four hours a day, and they know the rule as well as we do: they must be here in the room with me, in less than thirty seconds. I waited—two whole minutes. Then I rang again. And still no one came, not for another five minutes. I could have been dying. I could have been dead!"

"I'll check into it at once."

"No need for that. I found out what happened from Ronson. The two nurses on duty were a man and a woman, and they were having an affair. When they should have been on duty they had sneaked off to bed together, away where they couldn't hear or see my signal."

"They should be fired." There was real anger in Matlock's voice. If Miriam Greenwood should die now, when his own cash flow needs were at a maximum . . . "I'll talk to Dr. Ronson."

"I took care of it. They were gone hours ago. I can do most anything when I set my mind to it, and I've dismissed hundreds of servants in the past fifty years. Surely you didn't imagine I'd drag you here for something I can do perfectly well myself? No, Tommy, I said I had a real problem, and I meant it."

She rolled the chair back around to the other side of the desk, to face him again. The old eyes and mouth were like cracks in a parchment face. It was another minute before she spoke again. Matlock had time to reflect on the fact that he was a servant, too, one who would be dismissed as casually as the nurses if he were no longer useful.

"Your on-line patient care system," went on Miriam Greenwood at last. "It takes care of anything that I need in the way of medication, and that's fine. But it's only one part of health care. Suppose something happens where I need help from a human? Cardiac arrest, or choking, or a fall? The best computer and telemetry in the world won't do a thing for me. I'm right back where I started, totally dependent on help from nurses and doctors. We proved today that they're as unreliable as ever. Seven minutes, before anyone came!"

Matlock's stomach rumbled. He had spent the whole lunch hour at the apartment, arguing with Sylvia. He was sure she was being unfaithful to him, but he had no proof. Now it was four-thirty, and he had not eaten since breakfast. "I agree, it's unforgivable," he said hurriedly. "But I don't see how you can do anything about it. People are people. Even with the best staff in the world, there will be delays sometimes."

"Why?"

As usual, Greenwood could floor him with a simple question. He stared at her.

"If you're paid to be here without delay," she went on, "and paid handsomely, with that as your top priority, why should there be delays?"

"It's human nature. Someone may be in the middle of doing something else, and they think it's important. So . . ." He shrugged.

"I'm glad you agree with me." The fingers were busy beneath the white sheet. "If we just let things slide along, it may happen again. Once I had that thought, I remembered something I found last week in a database search. It's an extremely interesting line of research being carried out in Guangzhou, in southern China. Behind you."

Matlock swung around, to see a research abstract scrolling onto one of the display screens.

"Do you know the work, Tommy?" said the metallic voice behind him.

"Well enough to tell you it's forbidden."

"In this country."

"Anywhere, outside China. Do you understand what it's reporting?"

"I think so. It's telling how to control a human's primary response, through a computer and a programmable implant. When the person takes the action approved by the computer, the implant provides a stimulus to the pleasure centers of the brain."

"In other words, a form of mind control. The Chinese have apparently been trying it in infantry training. Successfully, if this can be believed. It's hard to imagine a more powerful stimulus to obey a command."

"Well?"

Matlock swung back to face Miriam Greenwood. The ancient face was staring at him with strange intensity. "Well, what?"

"Don't you see, Tommy? It's exactly what we need. We have the computer, right here. I control it. If the medical staff here at the house were all equipped with the right implants . . ."

"That's the craziest—" Matlock paused. "Mrs. Greenwood. I've learned a lot in these past two years, and I respect your brains more than you think. But don't you see, you'd never in a million years get any of the staff members to agree to your putting a microcomputer in their heads. And as for—"

"Save your breath." The face carried a look of sly triumph. "Tommy, you just don't understand money and people. I can explain it in very simple terms. First, I wouldn't even attempt to affect anyone's actions, unless those actions conflicted directly with care of my health. I have no interest otherwise in what they choose to do. Second, it's for a limited time. I want to buy that sort of service for one year from the staff, at forty thousand dollars per person per month. At the end of that time, they can either sign up again—their choice, no pushing from me—or they'd be free to have the implant removed and leave."

"You'd never get anyone to agree. It would mean an illegal operation, with no—"

"I already asked. Ronson agreed, and so did nine others. That's more than enough volunteers to make it work . . . provided you will help. We don't have the facilities or the skills to perform the operation. You have both."

"Absolutely not. I don't even want to discuss it. Don't you understand, we're not talking medical hand-slapping now—we're talking jail sentences."

"No one who worked for me would ever go to jail. I may not know medicine, but I do know law."

"I don't care. The answer is still no."

"Maybe it is, but don't say it now. Drive back home, take your time, and then come and see me in a couple of days. Remember, my life might depend on prompt service, and nothing is more important to me. I'd hate to have to fire you. And if you help, naturally it would mean more money. A lot more."

Matlock shook his head and stood up. He was heading for the door when the final words came.

"—and of course, there could be other benefits. Wouldn't it be nice to put an implant in Sylvia, with just your finger on her pleasure button? I don't think you'd find that difficult to arrange . . . with my help. Think about it, Tommy. Just think. . . ."

There was no reason for Sylvia's trip to the big house, unless it was to show off his handiwork to Miriam Greenwood.

As the Lamborghini approached the barred metal gates, Matlock noticed something new. Instead of a uniformed guard, a gray metal cabinet stood beside the fence. A camera turned to track the car's progress, then a synthesized voice requested that both passengers advance to the machine and provide identification.

He turned to Sylvia. "Don't worry, it's just Mrs. Greenwood. She's been reducing the number of staff to make things more automated."

She reached out to touch his arm. The implant was programmable, with Sylvia's default values set to produce pleasure when she looked at him, rather more when she touched him. The most powerful joys had been reserved for other situations, and Matlock could vary the overall level, from thrilling pleasure to a sensation which apparently made Sylvia unable to think or speak. In some ways, Matlock envied her. Nothing in his own life provided that much joy. Maybe someday, an implant of his own, under his own control . . .

The inside of the house had changed also in the past three months. With a staff reduced from forty to ten, most routine functions had been delegated to the household computer. Identification checks were automatic, and a small mobile robot glided before them as they headed for Miriam Greenwood's study. It ignored Matlock's protest that he knew the way perfectly well.

She was there, as always, in the wheelchair. Matlock had become so used to her that Sylvia's gasp of dismay came as a surprise to him. For the first time in a year, he looked at Miriam Greenwood with an objective eye.

She never bothered now with the gray woolen cap, and her skull showed veined and delicate, its few thin strands of white hair falling forward onto the lined forehead. With the regular use of the synthesizer, she no longer wore dentures. Her lower face had collapsed inward, wizened, hollow cheeks framing a pursed, sunken mouth. Fortunately, the white sheet covering her from neck to feet hid the worst features, along with IV's and catheters and waste bags.

Matlock took Sylvia's hand in his, and turned up the pleasure level a notch. She sighed, and moved to stand close to him.

"So this is Sylvia." The voice box spoke softly, thoughtfully. "Welcome, my dear. You look very well."

"I feel well." Sylvia sounded happy, but a little puzzled. "I feel wonderful."

"That is good to hear." The frail head turned slowly from the woman to the man. "A handsome couple. Ah, Tommy, you won't believe it, but I once possessed such soft charms myself."

"How is everything else going?" The question was perfunctory. Matlock was vaguely uneasy. He could increase Sylvia's pleasure level, if he had to, until she was oblivious to Miriam Greenwood's appearance or indeed to any of her surroundings, but he didn't want to do so. That would spoil his own plans for systematic pleasure-probing with Sylvia, at another time and place.

"I believe things are going extremely well." The death's-head smiled. "I would almost say, perfectly, but I know you do not like to hear that word."

Matlock came to full attention. "Problems?"

"Not for anything that we have done so far. In a few minutes time, I would like to run a small experiment, so that you can see for yourself. But there is one other matter. Raw materials."

"We already took care of that. Ronson has every damned drug in the book, new and old."

"Drugs, yes. That is one form of raw material. But suppose that we had a different problem. Suppose that I suffered some organic failure. Suppose that we urgently needed a transplant, and nothing that closely matches my tissue type was available fast, and locally. That would be a real problem. I've already had Ronson do tissue-typing for me, and no one here at the house is even close to me." A white hand crept out from under the sheet, and a finger moved up to rub the sunken temple. The forearm was festooned with sensors and IVs. "A bank, Tommy, that's what we need. An organ bank, and a tissue bank."

Matlock thrust his hand into his pocket, and turned the setting of Sylvia's unit up a random three or four notches. She shivered and gasped as the telemetered signal went to her implant, and sat down suddenly on the floor. But at least she was no longer listening.

"For God's sake, we shouldn't talk about that now." He stared around the room. "I'll do it, you know I will, but it will take a while. We'll have to set up an acquisition program, search the area for donors—"

"The country. We want tissue types as close to me as possible. Unfortunately, I have no close living relatives."

"Then we'll have to set up the facilities here—they're very special, controlled low-temperature. But we can't talk about it now. Not with—" He gestured to the floor. Sylvia lay panting on her stomach, her mouth gaping and her eyes rolled up so that only the whites showed.

Greenwood gazed down at her calmly. "A pretty creature, isn't she? Lucky Tommy. However, I must point out that it was your choice to show her off to me, not my request that you bring her. I would suggest a little less stimulation, then you can leave her here with me while you check the rest of the system. And before you leave, we must of course discuss the financial needs of the tissue and organ bank. Now, to work. You go ahead, and I'll give the signal in one minute. Low level, so they won't do anything dangerous getting to me."

Matlock walked quickly toward the back of the house until he came to the kitchens. Two of the household staff were there, preparing food and talking quietly to each other. They nodded to him, but did not stop work. He was a familiar figure to them.

He examined the two men closely. They looked and sounded completely normal. The programmable implants were hollow cylinders, less than a millimeter wide and three millimeters long. The operation to install them took a precise brain mapping using a PET scanner, followed by a five-minute procedure in which a hollow needle was driven through the skull and meninges to its destination deep beneath the *pia mater*. The implant was then passed inside the needle, along with its hair-thin antenna, and the needle itself was withdrawn. No inflammation, no postoperative recovery period. Matlock had observed the process most closely in Sylvia's case. She had been anesthetized early one evening in her apartment, carried to the hospital, received the implant, and been taken home again within three hours. She knew nothing of what had happened to her. So far as she was concerned, she had drowsed off after lovemaking and woken at midnight with Matlock still at her side. He had observed no aftereffects, not even a complaint of an itch at the installation site or a headache from the anesthetic.

As Matlock watched, the two men suddenly straightened. They placed the utensils they were holding neatly on a counter, and one of them switched off the oven. Then they turned in unison and headed for the door, pushing past him without a word of comment. They marched off side by side along the corridor that led to Miriam Greenwood's quarters, making good speed but with no great urgency. Each man had a contented smile on his face.

Matlock followed slowly. It was a low-level test, true enough, but the men's response was surely too leisurely to satisfy Greenwood. Probably a signal loss in the circuits that connected the wheelchair to the household's main computer. If he had some time at the weekend, he might return and give the system a bit of fine tuning.

But the next weekend, Matlock was in Bermuda. The sudden decision to leave felt like random impulse, caused by cold, snowy weather at home and a desire to explore his new relationship with Sylvia. But sitting on a beach in warm sunshine, a planter's punch in his hand, Sylvia adoring by his side, he also reached a new insight.

He wanted to break away from Miriam Greenwood—desperately. And he could not.

In the past two years, he had made more money than he had ever dreamed of. There ought to be four million dollars in his bank account. Instead he was broke, with new bills coming in every day. The casino was an endless maw, its opening date still six months away, and the vacation home was far from paid for. Back taxes loomed larger and larger. He did the calculations over and over. If Greenwood survived for another year and a half, and he remained in her employ, he could be home free. If she died before that, he was on the rocks.

He rose to change for dinner filled with a new resolve. Since Greenwood wanted to live, desperately, he would throw all his efforts into helping her. If necessary he would ask for a leave of absence from the hospital—it produced only five percent of his income now—and devote himself to the care of Miriam Greenwood. He would become her slave, as Sylvia was now his slave.

The decision helped a lot. He was at last able to enjoy his meal, and notice the envious glances of the men around him. Here was a young, stunning, sexy woman, with no eyes for anyone except the man who sat opposite. Whenever there was an opportunity to do so, she was touching his hand, reaching out under the table to rub his calf with her stockinged foot, or nudging her knee against his. And the most curious thing about it was the secret looks that he was receiving from the women. They seemed even more interested than the men, particularly a pouting brunette who sat two tables away. Twice she had caught Matlock's eye, and held it regardless of the irritated looks from her companion, a bald-headed man in his late fifties.

New vistas were opening. Sylvia was healthy and obviously happy, with no harmful physical effects from the implant. She had remembered nothing of the episode with Miriam Greenwood, and other experiments suggested that times spent with the pleasure impulse at its maximum were lost at once from memory. She would do anything to please him now, anything to touch and hold him. But she was not the only woman in the world—already he found it hard to recall his own desperate obsession of just a few weeks earlier.

Why not that brunette? Why not two women with programmable implants, or a dozen of them? He could make them all dote on him alone, all ready to do whatever he wanted them to do. It would take only a little more money and help from Miriam Greenwood. One more reason to stay in her service . . .

Matlock returned from his holiday mentally relaxed, pleasantly sated physically, and resolved to make his patient live indefinitely. He landed at BWI Airport in the beginning of a new snowstorm, dropped Sylvia off at the apartment, and drove by the hospital for a routine check for messages.

He felt a twinge of guilt as he approached his office. Two years ago he had promised to leave notice of his whereabouts, so that Miriam Greenwood could always reach him if she wanted to; but in his urge to get away from everything he had told no one at the hospital where he was going.

At the threshold he stopped and stared. He had left the modem in his office computer switched on, and now the whole floor was covered with paper from the printer in the corner. The machine was chattering even as he walked across to it.

COME AT ONCE, NEED YOU URGENTLY.

Thirty seconds later, the printer was at work again.

COME AT ONCE, NEED YOU URGENTLY.

Was that all? He knew the message could have come from only one place, but surely Ronson and Miriam Greenwood would have sent more than just those few words.

Matlock sank to his knees and began to look for the beginning of the paper scroll. His heart was pumping a hundred beats a minute. If she had died while he was away, without even a day of notice, he was a ruined man.

He scrabbled at the folded and twisted sheets. It was there, the beginning of the whole message sequence—and it was from Ronson.

Miriam Greenwood had suffered a major stroke in the left occipital lobe of her brain. Substantial hemorrhaging. She was alive, but there were other problems. Ronson was too busy to describe them. Matlock was to come to the house at once, then he and Ronson—

The message broke off in midsentence.

Come at once. Matlock's eyes went to the top of the first sheet and he cursed aloud. 09:02:33—88/1/3. That meant nine A.M. on January 3rd. Three days and four hours ago, while he had been lounging on a sunny beach. And since then?

He ran the scrolled paper through his hands, sheet after sheet. Nothing more from Ronson, but at 9:05 on January 3rd, just three minutes after that first message, a single command appeared and went on and on.

COME AT ONCE, NEED YOU URGENTLY.

COME AT ONCE, NEED YOU URGENTLY.

No signature, no other word anywhere on the page.

Matlock left the room at a run. He was inside his car and out of the parking lot within thirty seconds. It was still snowing. Midafternoon traffic was light. He was able to reach 270 North in fifteen minutes. The road had been well-plowed, but other drivers were nervous and hindered his progress. He tailgated, passed as soon as he could, and still averaged no more than fifty.

Stroke, in the occipital lobe. Sight would be affected, almost certainly. Hemorrhaging. But how much hemorrhaging, and where was the blood flow? Was there significant clotting? God, after three days there could be just about anything. The one good sign was that repeated message. It came from the household computer, and that was under Miriam Greenwood's direct control. She was still alive.

"Hang in there, old woman. Don't die on me now." He muttered it to himself under his breath. Ronson was a fair doctor, but he didn't have Matlock's skills and knowledge. The only hope was Miriam Greenwood's own will to live. If there were any way to cling to life until Matlock arrived to help, that tough old mind would find it.

Conditions worsened when he hit Route 15. The snow fell more heavily, the Lamborghini's heater and defroster were inadequate, and the road narrowed to a two-lane highway. Overtaking was impossible. He became part of a procession, moving with the speed of the slowest and most nervous. By the time he reached the road that led through the park, struggled over its highest part, and was at last descending toward the Greenwood estate, it was nearly dark. He forced himself to slow down. If he slid the car off the road now he would never get out of the drifts.

Another ten minutes. The fence and the metal gates were finally visible through the swirling snowflakes. Matlock hunched over the wheel, his shoulders and neck tight with tension, and stared at their dark outlines.

Something was wrong. As he came closer he realized what it was. The gates. They were not tightly closed. Instead they were moving through a jerky cycle, like the wings of some great maimed bird. While his car crept closer the barred gates came to maximum aperture, held for a second, then swung quickly in to clash shut.

He drove to within ten feet of the gates, left the engine running, and stepped out of the car. No other vehicle tracks were visible, entering or leaving the estate. The metal sentry box was in its usual position, covered with driven snow. He walked to stand shivering in front of it. Instead of the usual request for identification he heard a sinister mechanical growling, its volume changing in a cadence that matched the moving gates.

Within a few seconds his feet, already chilled from the journey, were freezing. He hurried back to the Lamborghini, held his hands for a second in front of the heater, backed the car up thirty feet, and waited. After a few seconds the gates began to open again. He eased the car forward in second gear, careful to avoid spinning the wheels on the untouched snow. By the time he reached the wide-open gates he was traveling at maybe twenty miles an hour. He went safely through before they again began to close.

He drove the rest of the way to the house, parked, and ran to the main door. It was not locked, and like the main gates it was opening and closing in an irregular rhythm. No time to worry about guards. He waited for his moment and darted inside. In the entrance, the level of the lights flickered and fluctuated, in that same strange cycle. He dashed across the stone floor and headed straight along the corridor to Miriam Greenwood's study.

It was deserted. Silent and empty. For the first time in his experience, the wheelchair with its familiar, fragile occupant was not there.

Matlock wiped melted snow from his forehead, walked across to warm his hands on the hot-water radiators on the other side of the room, and stood frowning up at the TV monitors. They had never before been turned off, and now they were dark and silent.

A flicker of movement at the door caught his attention. Someone had hurried past along the corridor.

"Hey!" He ran across to the door. "Hey, you."

The man did not pause or turn around. He was wearing the white uniform of a nurse and carrying a shiny metal tray. His pace did not change. If he heard Matlock, he did not acknowledge it.

Matlock swore and started out after him. They were heading for the back of the house—toward the main medical area and surgery! Naturally. Matlock felt an enormous relief. If Miriam Greenwood needed an operation, that was exactly where Ronson should have taken her.

"Hey, wait for me." He called out again, and increased his pace. Still the man in front did not respond. He was moving in through the wide-open doors of the main treatment center and operating room. Half a dozen other white-clad figures were visible inside, and Matlock recognized Ronson's flaming red hair and broad back.

"How is she?" He started to ask questions before he was even in the room. "I was wondering on the way here about intracranial pressure. How much edema did you see? And how did the CAT scan look?"

She was there, as he had hoped and expected. Matlock pushed past the others and moved to her side.

They had not tried to take her out of her wheelchair. Instead they had moved the setting to full reclining position, raising it to form a bed and, when necessary, an operating table. Her clothes had been cut away. The telemetry sensors, computer leads, catheters, and IVs of blood and antibiotics still hung from the chalk-white, skinny body and attached to the bare, delicate skull. Her eyes were closed and the whole upper rear of her braincase had been opened up. Matlock could see the pinky-gray cerebral cortex, partly obscured by a darker stain of venous blood.

But was she alive? Matlock leaned closer. He could see her chest rising and falling with a now-familiar irregular rhythm. She ought to have died—days ago. But she had not. The will to live was in every harsh, shallow breath.

"How is she?" He repeated the question, realizing how foolish it was and suddenly aware that no one else had spoken since he came in. He stared around him for the first time.

Beyond Miriam Greenwood was a standard operating table, and on it stood a container of blood and a frightful jumble of organs and body parts. The organ bank?—except that Matlock had not yet begun to create it. What he was looking at had once been a man.

He turned and started to move away, but Ronson was right behind him. His white coat was filthy and blood-streaked, and a long yellow stain of urine ran down his left trouser leg. The red hair, always carefully styled and brushed, hung down in greasy locks across his forehead. Ronson's eyes were sunken and bloodshot, and there was a smear of blood on his unshaven left cheek.

"Test tissue type." The whispering came from all around, from every audio outlet. "Need a better match."

The white-clad figures in the room moved with the drunken gait of men who had been given no moment of rest for three days and nights, but they moved with perfect coordination. Suddenly there was a tight ring of people around Matlock, closing in on him.

He backed away, shrinking from the touch of bloody hands. Soon he could go no farther. The wheelchair dug into his back.

He spun around in a frenzy. "Die." He screamed at Miriam Greenwood's unconscious body. "You monster. Die, damn you. Let them go."

Strong fingers were on his shoulders. His own hands grabbed at a cluster of IVs and jerked them out of the wasted arm. The hands that held him shivered and released their grip. All the lights in the room went out for a second, then flickered back to half-power.

"Die, die, DIE." He was roaring at the top of his voice, but all the audio outlets in the room were screaming back in fury: *"Live, live, LIVE."*

He had his fingers at Miriam Greenwood's open skull, driving them toward the spongy brain tissue. He was pulled away. A dozen hands lifted him, carried him across to the operating table.

He dropped into a soggy welter of still-warm organs. He was held by his arms and legs so that he could not move. Above him the flickering lights of the room reflected from a gleaming scalpel. As the knife moved toward his throat, Matlock lifted his head. Six men were holding him, the seventh about to cut.

"No, no, stop." He jerked and writhed. "For God's sake, stop."

The blade moved in. And all around the table the faces smiled down at him, with the serene ecstasy of a mother holding her firstborn.

Afterword to "Health Care System"

I'm reasonably conscientious regarding my health and continued existence. By this I mean that I do not smoke cigarettes, I do not drink to excess, I do not sky-dive or race cars for a hobby, and given the choice I will walk rather than ride. On the other hand, I am not *unreasonably* conscientious about my health. I'm about fifteen pounds overweight, I smoke a cigar maybe once a month, I keep irregular hours, I do not exercise every day, and I do not follow a low fat or a low cholesterol diet.

In other words, although I enjoy life and certainly do not want to die, I am not willing to go to extreme measures to remain alive. When I realized that truth about myself a few years ago, I found myself asking the obvious question: Suppose that a person would go to any lengths to prolong his life. What would he do, if living as long as possible was the only thing that mattered?

This story provides an answer. And an unpleasant one it is. I think my mother has a much better answer. She will be ninety-two years old in December. She has no idea of her blood pressure or her cholesterol level, and her diet is high in fat, sugar, caffeine, and salt. She does not smoke cigarettes, having given them up when she was eighty-three, but she still enjoys alcohol. She attributes her longevity to living one day at a time and avoiding doctors. She must be the despair of the health care profession.

One other thing. It should be obvious from the publication date, but I want to point out that this story was written long *before* health care systems became one of our national obsessions.

HUMANITY TEST

"IN THE PAST few days we have heard a great deal of talk about the *origins* of the Shimmies. It has been stated—several times—that Jakob Schimmerhann's actions were completely illegal; that we all know this to be the case; and that he richly deserves punishment.

"Very well. Suppose that we admit it. His actions were certainly illegal. The use of human DNA in genetic experiments was and is strictly forbidden. Some form of punishment is surely not inappropriate.

"But now let us go on, and admit that the origin of the Shimmies has no bearing at all on the findings of this tribunal! Whether or not the Shimmies *should* exist is quite irrelevant. They *do* exist! When we ask what rights a child has, do we ask who its parents were, or how it came into the world? Of course not. Once a baby is here, we insist on its fair and humane treatment. Origins and rights have little to do with each other.

"*Prove* the Shimmies are human, says counsel for the defendant. But no one has ever devised a foolproof humanity test. Genetically speaking, we are told, a Shimmy is closer to a chimpanzee than he is to a human, since Jakob Schimmerhann used less than one tenth of one percent of human DNA sequences in creating the Shimmy form. The defendant therefore suggests that a Shimmy is only one thousandth part human. But what is left unmentioned is that we—humans and chimpanzees—share ninety-nine percent of our DNA sequences! Humans and chimpanzees are close cousins. The Shimmies are closer to us yet. So when the Attarian Corporation claims, in their use of Shimmies as slave laborers—"

"Objection. Your Honor, the term 'slave laborers' is an inappropriate one to describe working animals, which the Schimmerhann chimpanzees in our contention are."

"Objection sustained."

"I withdraw the term. I will say that the differences between humans and Shimmies are mainly the superficial ones of appearance, but in all real respects we are astonishingly close.

"But reject all those arguments about DNA, if you will, and say that they are no more than scientific mumbo jumbo. Look instead at the bald, undisputed facts, and our case still holds. As Professor Miraband pointed out earlier this week, an adult Shimmy can speak, and speak better than a human child at three years old. What difference does it make if that speech must be done through sign language? Would my honored colleagues suggest that a human person without a larynx, who must also communicate through sign language, ought to be stripped of his or her human rights for that reason? Or that a human child of three, who happens to be sick, may be put down for convenience? It is just as wrong to murder a Shimmy—"

"Objection. The term 'murder' is not appropriate to describe the death of an animal."

"Objection sustained. Counsel, please employ a terminology that bears less semantic loading. I am sure you are able to do so."

"Yes, your Honor. I repeat, would a human child who was sick, or a human unable to communicate by speech, be mistreated, or killed? Of course not. Even the suggestion is ludicrous.

"And when it comes to manual skills, or the ability to follow direction, or—let us be quite explicit—the ability to *think,* our last witness made it very clear: an adult Shimmy surpasses the average human child of four years! Would you agree that a four-year old has no human rights? If there happened to be an excess of four-year olds, how do you react to the idea that their numbers be reduced? And yet that is exactly what could happen to any Shimmies, until their rights are established and protected.

"I say in conclusion, we are asking for full rights. But we are not talking animal rights here, we are talking *people* rights. Those rights for the Shimmies are not merely due, they are long overdue. It is immoral and it should be illegal to treat them as animals. They must be treated as *people.* They *are* people. Our case rests."

Leon Karst was smiling as he nodded to the trio on the tribunal—

one woman, two men—and resumed his seat. But Sally Polk could see that he was sweating. Karst had told Sally that the first week was crucial: "We make our case on direct testimony, not on cross-examination. By the end of the week we need to have the tribunal persuaded, and make sure the other side is staggering."

If he were right—and Sally had seldom found him wrong—then this case was by now won or lost. Sally glanced around the packed courtroom, then looked up at the tribunal, leaning back in their seats after nearly thirty hours of testimony. As a new junior it was her first time in court. She tried to read their expressions. Dean Williams, the retired judge, was inscrutable. He wore a polite, remote expression, as though his mind was somewhere else. But the precision of his questions proved that was far from true. It was merely that his face gave nothing away. The man and woman flanking him were perhaps easier. Richard Kanter was a shrewd, dark-haired, out-of-condition lawyer from the Midwest, and he was nodding slowly, clearly approving of Leon Karst's summation for the plaintiff. Laurel Garver, youngest of the three, and sitting to Judge Williams' right, was leaning across to speak earnestly in his ear. Through the whole week she had seemed sympathetic to the case that Karst was making on behalf of the Shimmies.

Judge Williams listened carefully to Laurel Garver, nodded, and leaned back in his chair. "We'll have to resolve that later," he said. Then, to Leon Karst and his counterpart on the other side, "Unless you have procedural matters to take care of, the tribunal is adjourned until nine o'clock on Monday morning. Do you have anything?"

Sally stared at the lawyers for the other side. All of them had been no more than names and reputations on Monday morning. Now she had a strong feel for each of them. Deirdre Walsh—the famous Deirdre Walsh, chief counsel for the defendant—was shaking her head in reply to Judge Williams's question. From her record and Leon Karst's comments, she had to be tough, smart, and ruthless. She showed no sign at all that she was ready to give up on the case, but Sally would never have known of her toughness from her manner in court. Deirdre Walsh was conservatively dressed in a trim blue-gray business suit, set off by a wisp of blue lace at the throat and a sprig of fresh lavender on her lapel. She seemed friendly and quiet-spoken. ("But wait a bit," Leon Karst had told Sally a couple of evenings ago. "Next week she'll show her teeth." He sounded pleased at the prospect. The press coverage would peak during the second week of the hearings.)

"One small point," Karst was saying now to Judge Williams. "We will need to know the names of Monday's witnesses."

This was an important moment. The tribunal did not meet over the weekend, but no one pretended that it was a time for rest The three tribunal members would be reviewing the evidence presented during the week, then meeting at mealtimes to discuss the theory of the case. Deirdre Walsh and her assistants would be combing the transcripts of the previous week's testimony, looking for any material that helped their case; and Leon Karst, with Sally's help, would be deciding on the line of cross-examination for the first witnesses produced by the defendant. Each afternoon at close of business, the side whose case was being presented finally provided the names of the next day's witnesses; each evening, the other side desperately prepared cross-examination materials.

"We will have only one witness on Monday." Deirdre Walsh sounded casual. "That will be Captain Russell Grenville."

There was a great buzz of conversation through the courtroom. Leon Karst grunted in surprise, while Sally puzzled over what was happening. She knew Grenville's name—everyone did—but it had not been mentioned before during all the preparation for the Shimmy rights' case. Surely that meant he could not be offered as a witness?

Karst was on his feet again, speaking through the din. "Your Honor, no one has previously offered Captain Grenville as a potential witness. He is therefore ineligible."

"Quiet, please." Judge Williams inclined his head toward Deirdre Walsh. "Counsel?"

"Normally, yes," she said. "But let me remind my honored colleague for the plaintiff of the legal code, as established following *Rose v. Watkins.* 'In the event that a potential witness is off-Earth, and the time of the return of such witness cannot be guaranteed in advance, then such witness may appear without prior notification, with cross-examination postponed upon request of counsel for an added twenty-four hours.' That applies exactly to Captain Grenville."

"Is he on Earth now?" asked Laurel Garver. "For the code you cite to be applicable . . ."

"He is not. But he is on the way. I can guarantee that he will be here, in this tribunal, on Monday morning."

"Then the witness is approved. Any more discussion?" Judge Williams glanced around the room, smiling for the first time in a week. "Very well. Court adjourned."

The cross-referenced database yielded masses of information about Captain Russell Grenville. Too much information. Sally Polk had to boil it down to something that could be summarized and used.

Commander of *Sunskimmer,* and first human to lead a landing party on the surface of Mercury. Tsiolkovskii Medal winner. First human to take a ship through the rings of Saturn. Congressional Medal winner. First human to lead a party surviving an encounter with Karkov's Object. Explorers' Club Award for Gallantry. First human to return volcanic samples from Io. Daedalus Award. . . .

The list went on for pages. Nothing to grab on there. Grenville's reputation as a commander and a leader was pure gold.

She keyed to personal data. Unmarried, but apparently heterosexual. *No long-term relationships.* She underlined that mentally, for possible future reference. Religious, high-church Episcopalian, but no evidence of extreme views. From a moderately wealthy family, two brothers, one an army general, one a successful businessman. No evidence of financial problems, or even of much interest in money. Politically conservative, consistent with the family's background (in Sally's experience, only *very* rich families were liberals—*moderately* rich ones ran conservative).

She stopped fiddling with the cursor control, and leaned back in her chair. It was nearly ten o'clock, and still she had nothing useful for Leon. Russell Grenville's personal data matched his public image. Everything in his political, religious, and financial history spoke of a solid, conservative outlook on life, the profile of an upright, rigidly moral man with a strong Calvinist streak—and a tough witness. It would not be surprising if he preferred to think of the Shimmies as animals rather than humans. But there had to be more to it than that. There were billions of people on Earth who shared that opinion. Why would Deirdre Walsh drag Captain Russell Grenville back from wherever he was, back at vast cost from somewhere in the middle of nowhere millions of miles from Earth, unless there was something more?

Sally sighed and went back to the searches. Just where had the defendant's lawyer dragged him from?

The Egyptian Cluster. Thirteen months ago he had set out on an expedition to the region of the Egyptian Cluster, to catalog and assay outlying members.

Sally pulled in a cross-reference. She had been right, it really was the middle of nowhere. The Cluster was an odd little group of asteroids, with orbits different from anything else in the System. "The common plane of their orbits lies at sixty degrees to the ecliptic." What was the *ecliptic?* Another ten minutes went into answering that, but she had no choice. Leon Karst had a rule: "Never ask a witness a question if you don't know what the answer will be. And never bring me a fact you can't explain—because I may have to explain it to a judge and jury." A year with him had taught her he wasn't joking.

She read on. It was time-consuming and very expensive in fuel to visit the Egyptian Cluster. The only sizable colony there was a fifty-person mining outpost on Horus. Had Grenville intended to visit Horus itself? Somewhere in the general databases there ought to be his complete flight plan.

She wriggled her way through the reference banks, hopping from one index to another. In another half hour she found the mission profile. She had intended to inspect the flight plan, but before she did that she took a look at the manifest. What she saw there sent her hurrying off to find Leon Karst.

"It's half the story." Leon Karst went through a vitality dead spot between eight and nine at night, but once clear of that he was ready to work until dawn. Now he had his second wind. "So Grenville had half a dozen Schimmerhann chimps on his ship, as part of his crew. And he objected to their presence."

"I've got Richard digging for an actual copy of that objection."

"Quite right, we have to, for completeness. But I don't have great hopes. It'll be a formal thing. Hell, no matter what he says about the Shimmies, it wouldn't justify dragging Grenville all the way back here on a hyperbolic orbit—don't bother to look it up, I know what it means, it says you have to spend money, lots of it, to get from here to there." He was frowning at the projection screen, where the crew and manifest of Grenville's ship were listed. "I'm telling you, Deirdre Walsh has something else up her sleeve. Something to do with Grenville and the Shimmies on his mission."

Leon Karst was married, with three children. Sally had heard him talk of his family dozens of times, but he never spoke his wife's name with half the intensity that he said "Deirdre Walsh."

"If she didn't have something special," he went on, "she'd have called by now, suggesting a weekend meeting and maybe an out-of-court settlement. I've been watching the judge and the rest of the tribunal, and they're sold on our case. We did really well last week. Deirdre sees the way the river flows as well as I do. She ought to be crawling here on her belly. And since she's not . . ."

"What next?"

"We'd like to find out what happened on Grenville's ship. I already put in a call to Phil Saxby, over in the USF, but there's a blanket silence on anything to do with that mission. We know where they went, and who went, and that's all. I don't have the right level of insider. Did you know that Deirdre Walsh's brother works for the USF, up near the top? No need to guess where *her* information comes from. The only thing I found out for certain is that Grenville won't arrive on Earth until Sunday night. No chance for us to get anyone in to see him before he testifies."

"So you can't find out what's been happening?"

"I'm going to find out, all right. I'm going to find out when Captain Russell Grenville, damn his navy breeches, stands up in court at nine o'clock on Monday morning and tells me and the rest of the universe." Karst glared at Sally. "You thought you saw newsmongers today. Just wait until Monday morning, Sal. We'll be able to paper the walls with press credentials."

Sally thought at first that she was seeing anger. Only later, flopping into bed at nearly four A.M., did she recognize Leon Karst's expression. He was full of a vast, visceral excitement.

By Sunday afternoon even Leon Karst was ready to admit they had done all they could by way of preparation. At Sally's urging he allowed himself to be dragged along to the old Virginia estate, twenty miles west of the city, where the Animal Rights League had their headquarters. It was his second visit, and her twenty-fifth.

To Sally, the hundred-acre wooded lot always felt more like a prison than a nonprofit organization's main facility. There was a tall fence of thick chain-link, a line of electrified wire along its top, and the entrances were guarded by heavy metal gates. The men and woman on duty carried electronic communications devices and stun guns.

Perhaps not a prison, thought Sally, as they passed inspection and were ushered through by the uniformed guard. More like a beleaguered fortress, maybe.

Almost at once they saw the first Shimmies, wandering freely through the woods in the mild October sun. Leon opened the car window and stuck his head out to stare at a group of five walking along the grass verge.

"They look just like chimpanzees, don't they?" he said. "I know they're a little taller and heavier, but you don't notice that from here."

"That's part of the problem," said Sally. "If you don't know Shimmies, and you haven't interacted with them, you can't help thinking of them just as chimps. In fact, for all I know, that group *is* chimps. It's hard for us to tell the difference. That makes people uncomfortable."

"You bet it does. Once we get the Shimmies their rights as humans—and we will, Sal, no matter what Russell Grenville says—then we'll have a new problem. How will the average person know if he's dealing with a Shimmy or a standard chimp? And you know where *that* will take us. Right where the Animal Rights League wants us to go."

"They say that ordinary chimps are smart enough to deserve full rights, too. Did you know that there are chimps on the West Coast with a working vocabulary of four hundred words?"

"Yeah. And gorillas." The car stopped, but Leon stayed in his seat. "*And* orangutans. I'll say this before we get inside, Sally. We're going to do our damnedest to win this case, but the problem with *all* cases like this is that they're never an end. They're always a beginning. We'll have full rights for Shimmies, then it will be human rights for chimps, then rights for baboons, then rights for dogs and cats. These people will never stop. And if you think I'm going to stand up in court, and plead for rights for oysters . . ."

You might, Leon—if Deirdre were your opposition. But Sally said nothing.

The inside of the main building had a strange smell, like a cross between a hospital and a zoo. Leon Karst wrinkled his nose. He had come along to humor Sally, but he did not pretend to be comfortable.

"Intellectual commitment to a client is right, Sally," he had said, when the case began. "In fact, it's absolutely essential, even if it's a *pro bono* case where we don't get paid. But *emotion* for a client's cause is the worst thing you can do for them. It clouds your judgment. That's why I don't think it's a good idea to spend too much time with the Shimmies."

But he had not objected when Sally made regular visits to this facility. She felt that she had to understand for herself just how intelligent a Shimmy might be.

It took a while for her to realize a basic truth: Shimmies were as variable in their intelligence as humans. In a population at the Animal Rights League headquarters of about six hundred, Sally had met Shimmies who could sign for food and water, and little else. But there was also Skeeter, a female Shimmy who knew the name of every human in headquarters, who loved to make jokes and puns in Ameslan, and who seemed to catch on to ideas as fast as any human. And Skeeter was still immature, still developing.

She was waiting for them just inside the door. Sally recognized her, even without the identifying color-coded waistband. The Shimmies saw no point in wearing clothes, but many of them found it convenient to hang a carrying pouch on their belt.

"Hello again," Skeeter signed, slowly, knowing the limits of Sally's mastery of sign language. "Say hello Mr. Karst from me. How case going?"

Skeeter was all chimp, except for the expression in her brown eyes. That expression, to Sally, made her all human.

"It went well last week." She spoke very slowly and clearly, though in Skeeter's case that was hardly necessary. "But tomorrow the other side begins their case. We do not know what they will say."

"Wish I there." She gave the sign for humor. "Be witness."

Sally smiled back, and turned to Leon Karst. "Skeeter says she wishes she could appear in court, too, and be a witness for us."

"Sure. Tell her—" Leon paused and shook his head. He smiled at the Shimmy. "Sorry, Skeeter. I forget that you understand. I wish you could be a witness, too. It is a flaw in our legal system—a bad piece of our system. Until you have human rights, you cannot be used for a witness, even though your testimony is just what we need to guarantee you those rights."

"Say, I understand." Skeeter signed to Sally. "Mr. Karst not comfortable here, right? Tell him, we all thank his work. Know he win for us. Take him now, keep his thinking happy for tomorrow."

And if *that* isn't human (or superhuman) sensitivity, thought Sally, then I don't know what is. "We have to go upstairs first, Skeeter, and talk to general counsel—"

"Who 'General Counsel'?" Skeeter spelled the words out, syllable by syllable.

"General counsel is top lawyer for the Animal Rights League. He'll want to know what to expect tomorrow."

"Me, too. Good luck."

"Thank you." Sally returned the sign for "Good luck"—one of the few dozen she could make with confidence, and led Leon toward the elevator.

And since we don't know what to expect tomorrow, she thought, we need all the luck we can get.

Leon Karst had been right on almost all his predictions. Neither Sally nor anyone else in the office had been able to learn more about Russell Grenville's mission to the Egyptian Cluster, or its outcome. A check at the Wallops Island spaceport on Sunday evening revealed only that Grenville was expected there about midnight, and would be driven to the tribunal in time for the Monday hearings. Deirdre Walsh did not call at any time during the weekend, to propose settlement negotiations or for any other reason.

But on two points, Leon Karst proved dead wrong. First, Captain Russell Grenville did not stand up in court on Monday morning. He could not.

The courtroom was full to capacity by eight-thirty. Judge Williams and the other two tribunal members were in their seats by eight fifty-five. At one minute to nine, the doors to the chambers occupied by representatives of the Attarian Corporation and their legal counsel opened. Two men entered. They were carrying a flat padded table between them. On that table, upright, was Captain Russell Grenville. He was held by a harness at chest and midriff. He was armless and legless.

The broad head and the full beard were unmistakable. But the heavy shoulders no longer supported well-muscled arms, and the long, strong legs had been removed at the hips.

And contrary to Leon Karst's prediction, Russell Grenville did not begin his testimony at nine o'clock. The screams, shouts, and general chaos that erupted at Grenville's entry took fifteen minutes to subside. One woman and one man fainted, and had to be carried out; another three were forcibly ejected, shouting unintelligible slogans. Sally could not tell which side of the case they were on.

In the middle of the confusion, Leon Karst leaned over to her.

"That's the way you do it, if you're Deirdre Walsh." He spoke in a low voice, but he could have shouted without drawing attention. "You see, it doesn't *matter* what Grenville says now. He has the sympathy of everyone in the courtroom, even the tribunal members. They'll try to be objective, but they're human, too. Bang goes our case."

His eyes were gleaming—with admiration, not emotion. (Sally remembered what she had been told when she first came to work. "Leon leaves his emotions outside the courtroom. He has a guiding principle there: 'What counts in legal practice is honesty, decency, and sincerity. As soon as you learn to fake those, you have it made.' ")

"What can we do, Leon?"

He shrugged. "Lie low. Listen, watch, think. But we may be dead in the water. Unless something new comes up, I'm not a big enough fool to cross-examine Grenville."

Sally realized just how carefully Grenville's appearance and testimony were being managed when order was finally restored and it was time to swear in the witness.

Deirdre Walsh turned to the judge and said simply, "Your Honor, Captain Grenville has never told anything other than the truth. I hope that is enough." She left it to the audience (and the tribunal) to realize that the usual practice of the witness raising his right hand for swearing-in was here impossible.

Russell Grenville held his torso upright on the cushions. If what had happened to him had affected his mind, it was impossible to tell that from his face.

"Captain Grenville." Deirdre Walsh began quietly, speaking so softly that the courtroom stilled to hear her. "Let me first ask you to confirm certain details of your personal history."

She began to list his accomplishments, the same ones that Sally had read two nights before. It took many minutes. Russell Grenville said no more than "That's right," or "That is so," as he was asked for confirmation of an event or an award. But at the end, there was not even a whisper in the courtroom.

"Very well," said Deirdre Walsh at last. "Now I would like to ask you certain questions about your most recent expedition. Would you agree, Captain Grenville, that this was not supposed to be a particularly dangerous mission? That perhaps the participants of that mission were rather more worried about possible boredom than about catastrophe?"

"Solar System exploration always has an element of danger." Grenville's voice was calm and rational, and yet its utterance from deep within his chest somehow made the listener more aware of the truncated body around it. "However, I would agree that I did not see peril as the major element of the mission."

"And for the reason, you permitted a group of Schimmerhann chimpanzees to be included in your ship's crew?"

"I did."

"But it would be fair to say, would it not, that you objected to their presence?"

("She's leading him!" whispered Sally.

"She sure is," replied Leon Karst, just as softly. "But there's times you object, and there's times you don't. For the moment, we keep quiet.")

"I objected very much. Orally, and in writing." For the first time, there was an element of feeling in Grenville's voice.

"Would you mind explaining to the court the basis for your objections?"

"I would not mind at all. The ship that I was commanding, the _Poseidon_ of the Hecuba series, calls for eight crew members and a central command computer. That is ample to permit efficient operation of the vessel. There is plenty of space, but ideally that should be reserved for cargo. I was asked to add to the usual complement of crew six Schimmerhann chimpanzees, and to evaluate their possible use in the space environment. I stated, orally and in writing, that it was my task to undertake a serious mission, with serious objectives. I had no interest in managing a spaceborne zoo, whether of Shimmies or anything else."

While the courtroom buzzed with excited reaction, Leon Karst turned to Sally and shook his head. "I know," he said softly. "We could object to the implication that Shimmies belong in a zoo. But this isn't the time for it."

"You allowed the wishes of your superiors to override your better judgment?" went on Deirdre Walsh, as the hubbub died down.

"I am a member of the Space Navy. As such I believe that we are all better served by the obeying of orders, rather than the following of individual whim. Any naval officer who feels otherwise ought to resign his or her commission."

In other words, said Sally to herself, I did it because it was my duty—not because I thought that it was a good idea. The packed court-room was again dead silent.

"Tell us now, if you will, about the trip to the Egyptian Cluster. The six Schimmerhann chimpanzees were with you for over a year. Did you learn to work with them during that time?"

Grenville hesitated for a moment. "Yes, we did. I personally, and several of my crew. But not in the way that we had expected before the trip began. The crew resented the idea that they ought to learn Shimmy sign language. I did not feel it was my task to insist that they should. The Shimmies understood verbal commands—"

"*Simple* verbal commands?"

"Simple verbal commands, exactly." *(That's right, Grenville,* said Leon Karst, just loud enough for Sally to hear. *Stick to the script.)* "Enough to carry out simple shipboard duties. And one of my crew members devised a system using a video camera and the ship's main computer that allowed sign language gestures to be translated into audi-ble form."

Judge Williams leaned forward. "Excuse me, Captain." His voice was friendly, almost deferential. "Do you mean that, by a Shimmy mak-ing gestures into the camera, some sort of dictionary of gestures was stored in the computer and used to generate spoken language equiva-lents?"

"Exactly, your Honor. I should point out that this called for consid-erable changes to the standard Shimmy sign language, in order for the computer translation to work. But there was plenty of time to work on that. By the time that we had been in space for nine months, the system had reached a satisfactory form. I could use it, though I was not our expert."

"And by that time, what were you doing?"

"We had reached the outlying members of the Egyptian Cluster, and we were busy with assay work. A number of the smaller bodies con-tain high-grade deposits of valuable minerals, but they had never been inventoried. We spent the next two months on that work."

"And the Schimmerhann *chimpanzees*"—as always, the counsel for the Attarian Corporation emphasized the last word. She never referred to them as Shimmies—"were they used in this assay work?"

"By no means. That work calls for scientific training. I would en-trust it only to my crew." Grenville hesitated, then added: "However, occasionally one or two of the Schimmerhann chimpanzees would accompany crew members in the pinnace. That is the small free-flying exploration module that was housed in the main ship—"

"But the Schimmerhann chimpanzees had no active role to play, did they?" interrupted Deirdre Walsh. Sally had the feeling that Grenville had been moving onto unrehearsed ground. She made a note for later discussion with Leon Karst.

"Not in the assay operation. Nor in the operation of the pinnace. They were there, if you like, as supercargo."

"Very well. Now, Captain Grenville." Deirdre Walsh dropped her voice a tone. "Now we must come to something that I know will be a very painful memory to you. Would you please describe to this court the final terrible hours aboard your ship, just as you remember them."

"Very well." Grenville cleared his throat. When he continued his voice was perfectly steady, but nonetheless a shiver of anticipation ran through the courtroom.

"We had examined a small fragment co-orbiting with Bast—that's one of the bigger Cluster members, eleven kilometers in mean diameter. We were ready to head for Atmu, and on the way I was proposing to pay a visit to Horus and drop off medical supplies to the mining colony there. It was early in our working day. I and three of my crew members were in the forward part of the ship. The other crew bunked aft. The Schimmerhann chimpanzees were all midships, in a modified cargo compartment. I was initiating the control sequence for an in-space attitude change, ready to direct us on a low-thrust approach path to Horus, and as I was leaning over the control board I was struck a violent blow on the back of the head."

Grenville lifted his face to the ceiling, and rolled his head back and forth from shoulder to shoulder. Sally Polk felt that what Grenville really wanted to do was rub at the back of his skull with one vanished hand.

"I began to turn, but before I could get more than halfway round I was hit again, even harder. That knocked me cold."

"What else do you remember of events inside the ship?"

"Inside the ship? I remember nothing. My next memory is of waking in the emergency medical facility on Horus. Two of my crew were with me. We were all—like this." Grenville turned his head, to look at the empty jacket sleeves.

"Where are those crew members now?"

"They are still on Horus. In due course they ought to be brought to Earth. We will all be fitted with prosthetics. I am told that these days they can do wonderful things with prosthetics."

"The other two are expected to survive?"

"Oh, yes. We will all survive. Unfortunately."

The impact was in his words, not in his calm tone. Sally felt sick. A few weeks ago Russell Grenville had been a complete man, healthy and powerful. Now . . .

"What happened to the other crew members?" said Deirdre Walsh gently. "And to the Schimmerhann chimpanzees?"

"I am not sure. This can be only a conjecture." Grenville nodded at Leon Karst, forestalling any possible objection. "But it is, sir, a conjecture based on good evidence. First, we arrived at Horus in our little pinnace, not in the ship. It's a miracle that we made it at all, because we were down to our last dregs of power. The main ship itself has not been found, although a search is being made for it throughout the Egyptian Cluster."

"So could the other crew members perhaps be alive on that ship?"

"Absolutely not. We each wore life-support beacons, transmitting on selected frequencies and with coded identification signals. They function as long as their wearer is alive, and they have enough power for years of operation. The other crew members are dead."

"And the Schimmerhann chimpanzees. Did they also wear beacons?"

"It was not considered necessary. Or appropriate."

"So the Schimmerhann chimpanzees might still be alive?" Deirdre Walsh glanced across at Leon Karst. "Before my honored colleague can object to that question as leading or conjectural, let me ask Captain Grenville to comment in his own way."

"Thank you, Counsel," said Judge Williams. But the reproof in his tone was mild.

"They might certainly be alive," said Grenville. "But it's my bet they are all dead. One of them certainly is. We had been having some discipline problems with all of them for a week or two. They didn't like some of their assignments, and they were doing a sloppier and sloppier job. I think they became angry when they were chastised, and so they attacked without warning. I feel sure they put my crew out of action and gained the run of the whole ship. They killed some, and then did—what they did—" he drew in a long, controlled breath "—to the rest of us. Then they stuck us in the pinnace, and let us fly off to die. But they were stuck, too, because running the ship was way beyond them. They could be gibbering on their way to Sirius by now, with no idea how to turn off the drive."

"And what would you say, Captain Grenville, if you were asked again to lead a ship with Schimmerhann chimpanzees as part of the crew?"

Grenville smiled wearily, and took plenty of time to look all around the courtroom. "Don't you think that is rather an improbable request, Counsel, given my present condition? But I'll answer you. I would say, no. I would say, definitely no. I would say, never. I would say, not under penalty of court martial, or any other penalty you care to name. I will never again permit myself to be in a situation in which a Schimmerhann chimpanzee is in a position to do me harm."

Deirdre Walsh moved forward to stand directly in front of him. "So based on your experience, you would say that the Schimmerhann chimpanzees are no more than animals—and murderous, unreliable animals at that?" And then, before Leon Karst could voice his objection: "I withdraw that question. Thank you, Captain Grenville. You are a true hero. No further questions, your Honor."

"Thank you, Counsel." Judge Williams consulted his watch. "Captain Grenville, we have several more hours available today. But I know that you arrived recently on Earth, and this recollection of events must have been dreadfully taxing to you. I want to express the appreciation of this court for your testimony. And I want to ask if you need a rest, before we permit cross-examination. I must add that, because of the unusual circumstances of your appearance here, counsel for the plaintiff has the right to defer cross-examination until tomorrow."

"I would prefer to continue now," said Grenville. "If plaintiff's counsel is willing."

Every head in court turned toward Karst. He gave Sally Polk one quick glance out of the corner of his eye (*Screwed—I'm damned if I do and I'm damned if I don't*) and rose to his feet.

"Thank you, Captain. I have just a few questions. And thank you, your Honor, for noting plaintiff's right to hold over some cross-examination for tomorrow."

He moved to stand in front of Grenville, blocking the captain's view of Deirdre Walsh.

"Captain, I was perplexed by one point of your testimony. If I am quoting you correctly, you stated concerning the probable dead state of the Shimmies on board your ship: 'One of them certainly is.' And you mentioned this in connection with discipline problems on board. Am I to infer that a Shimmy was put to death on the ship?"

"Certainly not." Grenville's reply came without hesitation. "I put no Shimmy to death. However, I would certainly claim my right to do so to save a crew member."

"So what was the basis for your comment?"

"One of the Schimmerhann chimpanzees was on the pinnace that reached Horus. No surviving crew member was conscious at the time, but the miners on Horus saw what had been done to us. They formed their own conclusion as to what must have happened on the ship. And they tried and executed that Schimmerhann chimpanzee, within hours of our arrival."

There was a gasp and a stirring in the courtroom, but Leon Karst was pressing on. " 'Trial and execution'—you suggest, Captain, that the miners recognized the Shimmy's humanity."

"I used the wrong term. They had the Shimmy put down."

"Then let me ask another question. You lived closely with a group of Shimmies for over a year. You had a chance to observe them. Did you notice much variability in Shimmy intelligence?"

"Your Honor." Deirdre Walsh moved to stand between Karst and the tribunal. "I hope that this is relevant. We have had testimony *ad nauseam* concerning the intelligence or lack of it of the Schimmerhann chimpanzees. I don't see what can be added at this point."

Judge Williams nodded. "Your comment is noted. Captain Grenville, please answer the question."

But Grenville was hesitating. "Variability of intelligence. You mean from one Shimmy to another, Mr. Karst?"

"I mean exactly that."

"Then, yes. Three of them—Pip, Squeak, and Wilfred, the crew called them—were very dumb. Only able to follow the simplest directives. But one of the others, Skip, he was . . . well . . ."

"He was more intelligent than the others?"

"He was supposedly much more *alert*. I would not use the word intelligent. More . . . If I say that the crew found him more understanding of instructions, I hope I will not be misinterpreted. He was certainly no more responsive, in my opinion, than any well-trained sheepdog."

"Very well. Could you tell us in a little more detail what the functions of the Shimmies were on your ship?"

"They were various. The Schimmerhann chimpanzees all helped in cleaning and general maintenance. Two of them did simple tasks in the galley. One of them was assigned to help the ship's physician. One of them assisted in the preparation of samples for mineral assay." Grenville turned to look at the members of the tribunal. "I want to make it clear that in every case the functions of the Shimmies were controlled and checked by human crew members. I insisted on it."

"Even if it was not necessary?"

"In my opinion, it was always necessary."

"Very well. Captain Grenville, you were unconscious when the pinnace reached Horus. Do you happen to know which of the Shimmies was on that ship?"

"I assume I do. I saw his identification band, after he'd been spaced."

"Spaced?"

"Dumped out of an airlock by the miners. Unless for some reason two of the Shimmies changed IDs, the one that arrived at Horus on the pinnace was Skip."

"The most intelligent of the Shimmies?"

"Objection. Your Honor, Captain Grenville explicitly stated that the word 'intelligent' is inappropriate."

"I withdraw the question. Let me replace it with this. You mentioned that when the pinnace reached Horus, 'it's a miracle that we made it at all, because we were down to our last dregs of power.' Now, isn't it possible that your 'miracle' happened because Skip, the most alert and responsive of the Shimmies, had a hand in *directing* the progress of the pinnace toward Horus?"

Grenville shook his head. "Mr. Karst, almost anything is possible. You ought to ask me if it is *probable.* Then I can assure you that it is most improbable that Skip had any hand in the arrival of the pinnace at Horus."

"But it is not impossible. Captain, one final question. The mutilation and injuries that you have suffered are dreadful, truly horrifying. It is difficult to imagine beings depraved enough to inflict them. Have you ever heard it suggested that Shimmies, anywhere, might be such fiends?"

"No, sir." Grenville gave a slight shrug of his shoulders. "But I am here. And two of my crew are as badly off as I am. A fiend is only known as a fiend when he behaves like one."

"But we do not make such an assessment without direct evidence. Thank you, Captain." Leon Karst nodded to Grenville, turned, and faced the tribunal. "Your Honor, until Friday afternoon we had no idea who the witness would be today. Captain Grenville arrived on Earth just last night. We have no records relevant to his testimony, nor information as to what records even exist. With your permission, I would like to request of the defendant that certain information be made available to me for review. And I would like to defer further cross-examination until nine o'clock tomorrow morning."

Sally Polk couldn't understand what was happening. With their own case drifting out of control and Russell Grenville dominating the courtroom, the atmosphere that night in Leon Karst's offices should have been gloom and despondency. Instead, Karst was crackling with energy and enthusiasm.

He sat facing Sally across a heap of transcripts, tapes, and photographs, a fat Dutch cigar unlit in his mouth. Deirdre Walsh, anticipating Karst's request for information, had delivered a mountain of data at five o'clock, as late as the court permitted, and now they were taking their first skim through it.

"We have to look at all this before tomorrow morning, every bit," said Karst cheerfully. "And we're going to do it. But the index to what they've given us is missing at least one thing I may need. What's the signal travel time to the Horus mining colony?"

"I've no idea."

"Nor have I. Find out. If it's less than a few hours, send a message asking Horus to transmit through a video link anything they have that shows the actual trial and execution of the Shimmy. Sound and picture. We'll pay all costs. I'll notify the tribunal and the defendant that we're making the request, and we'll ask the court's permission to use what we get as evidence."

"What are you going to do with it?"

"Try to get some courtroom sympathy for the Shimmies. In the manifest they're identified only by number, but Grenville's crew helped us a lot by giving them *names.* If we're lucky, the court will witness the death of poor, helpless *Skip,* not some anonymous monkey. And the *other* thing we have to do is somehow cast doubt on Grenville's version of what happened. He's too damned charismatic."

Sally stood up. "Leon, didn't you tell me that the first rule of cross-examination is to ask questions that allow the witness only to give a yes or no answer?"

"I certainly did."

"But today you asked Captain Grenville questions that allowed him to say all sorts of things."

"Sure. Circumstances alter cases. They damn well altered *this* case. On Friday afternoon, we had it won. By noon today, we had lost."

But Leon Karst did not have the look of a man who had just lost a big case.

"So I had to go on a fishing expedition," he went on. "I told you that you win cases on direct testimony, not on cross-examination. But the introduction of Grenville changed the rules—for all of us. Don't think that Deirdre is resting easy tonight. She's sweating her way through this material, as much as we are. A lot of it will have arrived with Grenville on Sunday, and she doesn't know what's in there any more than I do. It's like a game of poker. When one of the players throws in a wild card, everybody starts biting their fingernails."

As Sally went out, she realized something that ought to have been obvious long ago. Leon Karst didn't care about the *Shimmies.* All he cared about was the *case.* He would have worked just as hard for the defendant if his legal firm had been approached by them.

And yet the Shimmies *were* intelligent! Sally was absolutely convinced of it, after her meetings with them. They deserved protection and rights. So what did Leon really mean, when he said he did not want too much exposure to the Shimmies? That he did not want justice—*real* justice—to interfere with his fighting of the case! And Deirdre Walsh, almost certainly, was just the same. They were both obsessed with the legal battle and unconcerned with issues and ethics. Was that "true human" behavior?

Sally wondered how much she really wanted to be a partner in a leading law firm.

* * *

The change in less than twenty-four hours could not be missed. Yesterday the tribunal members had greeted Leon Karst and his team warmly, while remaining just a little cool toward Deirdre Walsh.

Today, Judge Williams was as unreadable as ever; but Laurel Garver, seated as usual on the judge's right, was avoiding even looking in Sally and Leon Karst's direction. Instead, she was smiling at Russell Grenville and Deirdre Walsh. And since the tribunal members would have dined together the previous evening, thought Sally, Garver's attitude surely reflected the tenor of those dinner discussions.

The members of the public did not try to disguise their views. Leon was hissed as he stood up to continue cross-examination. Order was restored quickly enough by Judge Williams, but the overwhelming sympathy felt for Russell Grenville showed on every face.

The captain himself looked different today, pale and tired. His head nodded forward, resting his chin on a torso that now seemed shrunken and pathetic on its cushioned support.

"Good morning, Captain."

Grenville nodded minimally at Karst's greeting, but he scarcely glanced at the smiling lawyer. Like Sally, Leon Karst had slept for less than two hours. Unlike Sally, he seemed to thrive on it. His hair was neatly combed, his white shirt pressed, his modest pearl tie clip exactly centered. He had told Sally his strategy over breakfast. Since the known facts about Grenville's mutilation were so damning to their case, it was time to take a blind leap. Karst's Rule: Conservatism is only right if you're winning.

"Captain Grenville," he began. "I would like to return to something that you told this court yesterday. One of your crew members had developed a method of converting the Shimmy's sign language to sounds. Is that correct?"

"Quite correct."

"And those sounds can then be interpreted?"

"By someone familiar with them. Not by anyone. The sounds are in a short of sonic shorthand."

"You were familiar with them, yourself?"

"Moderately so. Less than two of my other crew members, who are now dead."

Leon took a small recording disk from the table in front of him, and showed it to the judge. "Your Honor, I request that this be admitted to the case as Exhibit 27. It constitutes a copy of a recording disk found on the pinnace carrying Captain Grenville and his crew members when they arrived at Horus."

Sally saw a quick look pass between Deirdre Walsh and her two assistants. Had they been able to review the disk last night with Grenville? Leon was betting that they had not, since the captain had been taken away for medical examinations.

"Captain, do you recognize this disk?"

"All the data disks on the *Poseidon* were identical in appearance. But I certainly recognize its type as one carried on the ship."

"But you have not listened to this disk yourself?"

"How can I say, without knowing its contents?"

"Captain, we are not sure ourselves of the contents of this disk. We would like to play it to you now through earphones. You will be able to activate the on/off switch, simply by moving your head backward. Would you listen, and interpret what you hear?"

"I could certainly try."

Deirdre Walsh half rose from her seat, glanced at the judge, and subsided.

This is it, said Sally to herself. I hope I'm right, but if I'm wrong, then boy, am I wrong! It will be all over.

She had spent five hours during the night, sweating over the disk, trying to convert a strange form of oral shorthand to full meaning. She had finally been able to convince Leon—but was she convinced herself?

"I should explain to you," Leon Karst was saying, to the general audience as much as to the tribunal, "that this disk carries on it the time and date of its own recording. The time will of course be confirmed by independent sources, but I can tell you it was made three and a half days *before* the arrival of the *Poseidon*'s pinnace at Horus—and just three hours *after* the last routine transmission from Captain Grenville's ship."

His voice was matter-of-fact, but Sally could not take her eyes off Russell Grenville's expression. Leon was going to throw the man back into a terrible time, perhaps the very time when his mutilation had occurred. And yet Grenville looked totally stoical. A superhero. When someone had already been through so many shattering experiences in his life, maybe nothing could ever break him.

And perhaps no one could discredit him.

The earphones had been adjusted, while the witness sat there with eyes closed. The sounds he was hearing from the disk were broadcast at low volume through the courtroom, a series of slow, harsh monosyllables. Sally had been forced to write them out, one by one, and then try to string them together to make sense. But he had had a year of practice, he would do it on the fly.

"*Chest hurt,*" said Grenville after a few moments. "*Chest bad.*" (So she had been right, on at least the first item! Sally's flood of relief was so intense that she almost missed the next sentence.)

Grenville's head had jerked back to stop the recording. His eyes flickered open. He turned to give Deirdre Walsh one startled look, then his head moved compulsively forward.

"*Ship die—breaking,*" he said. "*Five man die, three Shimmies die. Three man sleep, three Shimmies wake. Ship dying, breaking.*"

Again the bearded head jerked back. Grenville stared at Leon Karst. "Is this genuine—a recording truly found in the pinnace?" His voice was hoarse.

"According to the counsel for the defendants, it is. They gave it to us." Leon Karst nodded toward Deirdre Walsh and smiled at her. *But you didn't listen to it, did you, sweetheart? And the captain is hearing this for the first time.*

Grenville could not resist. His head was moving forward again, his eyes closing in concentration as the slurred sounds began again.

"*Little ship. Little ship fly. One man yes, two man yes, three man no. But need Shimmy. Three man sleep, three man small, two Shimmy die, one Shimmy fly. Sad, sorry. Only answer.*"

The sounds from the disk continued, but Grenville was opening his eyes. "It goes on, but the message is repeating."

"And did you understand it, Captain?"

"I understood the words, not the meaning. It's gibberish."

"Then would you allow me to offer you an interpretation, and see if you agree with it?"

But Deirdre Walsh was on her feet. "Your Honor, do we have to waste the time of this court on a stream of what is rightly described as gibberish? Captain Grenville has said he does not understand it, and he is the expert. What purpose is served by listening to the plaintiff's imaginings?"

"Mr. Karst?" Judge Williams was staring at Leon with eyebrows raised.

"A most important purpose, your Honor. If you will permit me five minutes, no more, I believe we will be able to cast a new light on Captain Grenville's arrival at Horus."

"Then proceed." The judge held up his open hand. "Five minutes."

"Thank you, your Honor. Captain Grenville, let me ask you one preliminary question. The single most basic fact taught to any Shimmy is that the life of a normal human is sacred—far more so than the Shimmy's own life. Have you heard that?"

"Many times. But that does not make it true."

"We shall see. Let me propose a sequence of events aboard your ship. You were on the way to Horus when some major catastrophe took place. Perhaps it was an internal ship malfunction, perhaps it was an impact with some other body. You were knocked unconscious. Is that possible?"

Grenville gave a dismissive shrug. "If I was unconscious, you can suppose anything."

"You and two other crew members, in the forepart of the ship, were rendered senseless. The rest of the crew were killed outright. Three of the Shimmies were killed also, while the other three—including Skip— were unharmed. But the ship was disintegrating, losing air. 'Chest hurt,' as one Shimmy told us, 'Ship die—breaking. Five man die, three Shimmies die. Three man sleep, three Shimmies wake. Ship dying, breaking.' That is a clear statement of the situation. It was left to the three Shimmies—intelligent or not, we won't argue that point now—to save themselves and the three unconscious humans.

"Skip and the others must have tried, but unfortunately it couldn't be done. The ship was doomed, and although the pinnace was intact— 'Little ship, little ship fly,' as Skip told us—it didn't have enough fuel and power. Not for three men and three Shimmies. It could just carry the mass of two men and no Shimmies, or one man and one Shimmy, and squeak through to Horus. But no more. The Shimmies could have stuffed two humans into the pinnace and stayed behind themselves, but that wouldn't solve anything, because the men were all unconscious and they couldn't fly it. Again, Skip told us the whole thing: 'One man yes, two man yes, three man no. But need Shimmy. Three man sleep, three man small, two Shimmy die, one Shimmy fly. Sad, sorry. Only answer.'

"In other words, the pinnace could carry one Shimmy, to fly it, with three men—but three men small—three unconscious men whose mass had been surgically reduced as far as possible, to the approximate total mass of *one* man. '*Sad, sorry. Only answer,*' said Skip. Not a nice answer, but to the three Shimmies, the *only* answer. They could not bear the thought of killing a human, of allowing a human to die who might somehow be saved. So they performed that awful surgery, on Captain Grenville and the other two crew members. Then two Shimmies stayed behind, to die on the ship. The other Shimmy—Skip, the most able of them all—piloted the pinnace, and just made it to Horus with, to quote the captain, the 'last dregs of power.' The three human passengers survived."

Leon Karst allowed his eyes to roam slowly over the hushed but restive courtroom. "*That,* my friends, is the true story behind the loss of the ship, the mutilation of the crew, and Captain Grenville's improbable survival. The Shimmies were not murderers. They were saviors, who gave their own lives so that three humans—"

"Objection." Deirdre Walsh was on her feet, speaking in a suddenly turbulent court. "Your Honor, this has gone on far too long. This is not evidence. We do not know how those messages originated, or who created them. We have been listening to something that is less than hearsay! It is pure fabrication. I ask that the last speech from the plaintiff's counsel be removed from the record."

Judge Williams acknowledged her with a nod, but his attention was on Grenville. "Captain." He spoke through the noise, not trying to silence it. "If your ship suffered an accident, as Mr. Karst has suggested, what is the chance that it will ever be recovered?"

"Out near the Egyptian Cluster? Very small. Negligible."

"Do you accept the counsel for the plaintiff's reconstruction of events?"

"I—think not." After Karst's analysis, Russell Grenville had become hesitant. His eyes were blinking rapidly. "There—there could be many other scenarios that fit such a message."

Grenville's sober manner carried great moral authority. The judge nodded. "Mr. Karst, based on the captain's comments I am forced to concur with the defendant's counsel. Ingenious as your speculations—"

"Your Honor." Leon Karst was breaking one of the first rules of legal practice; never interrupt a judge. "Before you make that decision, I beg you to consider one more item of evidence. It will take only a moment."

"Has it been introduced as an exhibit in this case?"

"Not yet. It could not be. It arrived only early this morning from

Horus. We have had no time to make it available to the defendant, though of course they will receive a copy."

"Describe its nature."

"It is a recording made by one of the miners, of the execution of Skip—"

"Objection!"

"—of the death of the Shimmy, Skip, on Horus."

Judge Williams glanced to the other two tribunal members, but it was a formality. His own curiosity had been roused. "If it is brief, you may proceed."

"If we could reduce the lighting level . . ." Leon Karst nodded to Sally, who had the recorder ready to run a projection onto the courtroom wall.

She switched on with a shiver. Leon was risking everything on the next sixty seconds, winnowed by Sally out of an hour of recording received from Horus. She had warned him that she found the modified sign language used on Grenville's ship unintelligible, but Leon must feel that this was his last chance to save the case.

The picture had been recorded by an amateur and transmitted over a low-bandwidth channel. Grainy and noisy, it showed a surging group of men in miners' close-fitting black suits. They were floating in the low-gravity enclosure of an outside asteroid chamber. Their faces were angry and pitiless. In their midst hung a Shimmy, his brown fur marked by cuts and patches of blood, and one of his legs bent at a strange angle. They were treating him roughly, forcing him toward an airlock.

"Murdering monkey," said a loud voice from the group. "Get in there, and go straight to hell."

"Captain Grenville." Leon Karst spoke over the noise of the recording and the rising tumult in the courtroom. "Did any of the miners on Horus understand Shimmy sign language?"

"I doubt it. Why should they?" Grenville spoke quietly, nervously.

"Then can you tell us what Skip is saying?"

For the Shimmy, battered and bleeding, was gesturing frantically at the men as he was dragged and pushed closer to the lock entrance. They were taking no notice of his frenzied signals, interrupting them with blows and slaps.

"I think I can," said Grenville. "If I can just get a good look . . . Uh.

I think . . . *Not—kill. Never—kill—man. Save—man. Save man. Skip save man."*

Then the Shimmy was being handled so roughly that he could make no more gestures. He was flung violently into the lock by a dozen miners, bounced off the outer metal wall, and hung alone covering his head with his hands. After a few seconds he turned to face his executioners. In the bare, functional chamber, with vacuum only a few moments away, his expression changed. It became calm and resigned, almost peaceful. And as the door slid closed he made another set of gestures, over and over.

"Captain Grenville?" said Leon Karst. The captain was staring at the screen, white-faced and silent. "Sir? Can you read them?"

But Grenville had lowered his head. Tears were trickling down his cheeks, and he seemed to be speaking only to himself.

The courtroom froze. And as the whispered words reached her, Sally knew that the case was over.

"Skip—forgive you," Russell Grenville was saying. *"You not know— what you do. Skip forgive. Skip forgive. Skip forgive."* He looked up, beyond the tribunal and beyond the courtroom. "Great God in Heaven. Skip, can you forgive us all?"

Afterword to "Humanity Test"

I've heard writers at conventions envying the first generation of science fiction writers. There were all these neat fresh ideas, you see, waiting to be written about *for the very first time.* So it isn't fair for the rest of us who came along later, because we don't have that virgin intellectual forest waiting to be explored.

That thought makes about as much sense as envying Newton or Maxwell because the laws of gravity and electromagnetism were sitting about waiting for somebody to discover them. The creative process was probably *harder* then than now, since many tools that make work easier today had not been developed.

The problem is a real one, though. What does a writer do when someone has already had the basic idea and written the classic story? One answer is, have a different idea and write a different story.

Another answer is to take the same idea, and push it one step forward.

Tom Godwin's "The Cold Equations" is a science fiction classic. A young stowaway on a spaceship must be jettisoned, because the added mass that she gives to the ship will make its mission impossible. The story was chilling; once read, never forgotten.

But was it the only answer? I decided that it was not, and wrote "Humanity Test"—a solution to the insoluble problem set up in Tom Godwin's story.

Poul Anderson's *Tau Zero* is another absolute classic, a story that can be written only once and seems to be the logical end of the line. I tried to go beyond it in *At the Eschaton,* a novella that will be coming out from Tor Books in the next year or so. I'm sure I can't top *Tau Zero,* but it was certainly fun to try.

THAT STRAIN AGAIN . . .

DEAR WERNER,

I see what you meant about Vega IV. After the places I've been posted for the past three years, it's Paradise. An atmosphere you can breathe, and people who seem like humans (only, dare I say it, nicer)— what more could you ask for?

Did you know that their name for themselves translates as "The Ethical People"? It seems to apply a lot better than "The Wise People"— homo sapiens—ever fitted us. Maybe it's the Garden of Eden, *before* the Fall. You know, just a little dull, all the days the same length, and no change in the weather. It takes some getting used to, but I'm adapting.

One other thing. Remember the way that Captain Kirwin described the Vegans' reaction when he first landed here? "They were surprised to see us, and they seemed to be both relieved and rejoicing at our arrival." A lot of people have puzzled over Kirwin's words—and today I found out why he sensed that reaction. The Vegans *were* relieved, and they were surprised when we appeared. You see, they'd made an expedition to Earth themselves, just a few years ago.

Sorrel has been translating the diary of that expedition for us, and he gave it to me today. I'm enclosing part of it here. To make it easier to read, I have translated the times and places into terrestrial terms. Otherwise, it's just as they wrote it.

September 12th. All arrived safely. The transmitter worked perfectly and has deposited us in an unpopulated forest area of the northern hemisphere. We will make no attempt to look for a native civilization until we have settled in. Gathor's warning is being well-heeded. We are watching closely for evidence of infection from alien bacteria and microorganisms. So far, no problem and we are all in good health.

September 23rd. All goes well. A beautiful and fertile planet this, but a strange one. Surface gravity is only five-sixths of ours and we all feel as strong as giants.

This world is tilted on its axis, so days and nights are not all the same length. This has caused some confusion in our sleeping habits, but we are adjusting satisfactorily.

October 8th. Strange things are happening. The trees all around us look less healthy, with a strange blight spreading over their leaves. We thought at first that it was a trick of illumination when the sun is lower in the sky, but now we are sure it is real.

October 20th. We must return to Vega IV. Gathor was right, in an unexpected and terrible way. Alien microorganisms have not harmed us— but we have infected Earth. All around us the great blight spreads. Everywhere we look the Earth is dying. We are contagion and bear guilt for the murder of this world. Tomorrow we must transmit home.

—and they came home, Werner, back to Vega IV. Do you see what I mean about "The Ethical People"? I've looked up the climate records, and I find that fall in Vermont was exceptionally beautiful that year, all glorious reds and browns and yellows. It made me think. Somewhere out there we are going to run into a planet with as big a shock in store for us as our seasons were to the Vegans. I just hope we can come out of it as well as they did. . . .

Afterword to "That Strain Again . . ."

See Afterword to "Millennium."

DESTROYER OF WORLDS

"NEITHER SNOW NOR rain nor heat nor gloom of night stays these couriers from the swift completion of their appointed rounds." Those words were not penned by a dedicated employee of the United States Postal Service. They were written by Herodotus, in about 450 B.C., and he was talking about the postal system of the Persians.

The first postage stamps in the world came long after the first postal service. They were introduced in Great Britain, in 1840. They were the "Penny Black" and the "Twopenny Blue," and the picture on their face was based on the 1837 medal portrait of Queen Victoria engraved by W. Wyon.

A *reprint* is a stamp printed from the original plate after that stamp is no longer valid for use as postage. Its existence tends to depreciate the price to collectors of the original stamps.

Philately, as a term used to describe the collecting of postage stamps, was a word coined in 1865 by a Frenchman, Monsieur Herpin. Before that, stamp collecting was known by the less complimentary term of *timbromania.*

Everyone in the world knows these things. Don't they? That's what Tom Walton seemed to believe when I first met him.

I went to his shop on 15th Street in downtown Washington in early May, on a warm and pleasant midafternoon. A reporter friend of mine had given me his name and the address of his store, and assured me that he knew more about stamps than any ten other people combined. To tell the truth, it was only faith in my friend Jill's opinions that persuaded me to go into that shop. The storefront was a hefty metal grating over dirty glass, and behind it on display in the window I saw nothing but a couple of battered leather books and a metal roller. It was a dump, the sort of shop you walk past without even noticing it's there.

The inside was no better. Narrow and gloomy, with a long wooden counter running across the middle to separate the customer from the shopkeeper. Bare dusty boards formed the floor and one unshaded lightbulb just above the counter served as the only illumination. Cobwebs hung across all the corners of the ceiling. As furniture there was one stool on my side and a tall armchair on the other. In that chair, peering through a jeweller's loupe at a stamp in its little cover of transparent plastic, sat a fat man in his early twenties. At the ring of the shop's doorbell he took the lens away from his eye and gave me a frown of greeting.

"Mr. Walton?" I said.

"Mmph. Yer-yes." A quiet voice, with the hint of a stammer.

"I'm Rachel Banks. I don't want to buy any stamps, or sell any, but I wondered if you could spare me a few minutes of your time. Jill Fahnestock gave me your name."

"Mm. Mmph. Yes."

It occurred to me that I should have asked Jill a few more questions. I hadn't, because there had been a fond tone in her voice that made me think Tom Walton might be an old boyfriend of hers. But seeing him now I felt sure that wasn't the case. Jill was one of the beautiful people, well-groomed and chic and dressed always in the latest fashions. Tom Walton was nice looking in a chubby sort of way, with curly fair hair, a beautiful mouth, and innocent blue eyes. But he hovered right at the indefinable boundary of fatness beyond which I cannot see a man as a physically attractive object. Also he hadn't shaved, his shirt was poorly ironed, and he was wearing a baggy coverall cardigan that was as shapeless as he was. There was even a smudge of oil or something around his left eye that had come from the lens he had been using.

Not Jilly's type. Not at all.

"I have a question," I said. "About a postage stamp. Or what may be a postage stamp. Jill thought you might be able to help me."

"Ah." At least that was a positive sound, a tone approaching interest. But I still had to get the preliminaries out of the way. I'd been in trouble before when I didn't announce at once who I was and what I was doing.

"I'm a private investigator," I said. "Here's my credentials."

He hardly glanced at the card and badge I held out to him. Instead, a faint expression of incredulity crept across his face, while he stared first at my face, then at my purse.

"Hmph," he said. "Hmph."

Those particular "hmph" 's I could read. They meant, you don't look tough enough to be a private eye. Too young, too nervous. And anyway, where's your gun? (Raymond Chandler and Dashiell Hammett—I'd like to bring them back to life long enough to strangle the pair of them. Between them they ruined the image.)

"I'm investigating the disappearance of Jason Lockyer," I said. I *was* nervous, no doubt about it. Eleanor Lockyer had that effect on me.

"Jason Lockyer. Never heard of him."

"No reason you would have. Mind if I sit down?"

I took his silence for assent and perched on the stool. Tall and skinny I may be, but high chairs were made for legs like mine.

"Lockyer is a biologist," I went on. "A specialist in algae and slime molds and a number of other things I'm forced to admit I know nothing about. He's famous in his own field, a man in his early sixties, very distinguished to look at and apparently a first-rate teacher. He's on the faculty over at Johns Hopkins in Baltimore, as a full professor of an endowed chair, and he has an apartment there. But he also keeps an apartment here in Washington. Not to mention an apartment in Coral Gables and half an island that he owns in Maine. As you'll guess from all that, he's loaded."

With some people you can lose it right there. They resent other people's money so much, they can't work around them. Tom Walton showed nothing more than a mild disinterest in Jason Lockyer's diverse homes, and I went on: "He usually spent most of the week over on campus in Baltimore, and his wife is mostly down in Florida. So when he disappeared a couple of weeks ago she didn't even realize it for three or four days. She called me in last Friday."

"Why you? Why not the p-police?"

The question came so quickly and easily that I revised my first impression of Walton. Slob, maybe, but not dumb.

"The police, too. But Eleanor Lockyer doesn't have much faith in them. When she reported that he had disappeared, all they did was file a report."

"Yeah, I know the feeling. Same as they did when my shop was robbed last year."

"She expected more. She thought when she called them they would run off and hunt for him in all directions. As it was they didn't even come to search their apartment."

I was losing him. He was starting to fidget in the armchair and fiddle with the jeweler's loupe on the counter in front of him. It didn't look as though he'd had a customer in days, but I probably had only two more minutes before he made up a reason why he was too busy to listen to me.

I opened my bag and took out a 9″ × 12″ manila envelope. "But I did search the apartments," I said. "All four, the one here in Washington and the one in Baltimore and then the other two. No signs that he left in a hurry, no signs of any problem. A dead loss in fact, except for one oddity. An empty envelope in the Baltimore apartment, addressed to Jason Lockyer—didn't say Professor, didn't say Doctor, just Jason Lockyer—standard IBM Selectric typewriter, but there was a very odd stamp on it. Here."

I took the photograph out of the envelope and slid it across the counter. It was an 8″ × 10″ color print and I was rather proud of it. I had taken it with a high-power magnifying lens, and after half a dozen attempts I had obtained a picture with both good color balance and sharp focus. The image showed the head of a black-faced doll with staring eyes and straight hair sticking up wildly like a stiff black brush. The doll was black and green and red, and an oval red border ran around it. At the bottom of the stamp was a figure "1" and the words, "One Googol."

My satisfaction at the work was not shared by Tom Walton. He was staring at the photo with disdain.

"It's a color enlargement," I said. "Of the postage stamp. And the picture in the middle there—"

"It's a golliwog."

That piece of information had taken me hours to discover.

"How did you know? Until two days ago I had never even *heard* of a golliwog."

"I used to have a doll like this when I was a kid." He was a little embarrassed, but the sight of the picture had brought him to life. "Matter of fact, it was my f-favorite toy."

"I never knew a doll like that existed—I had to ask dozens of people before I found one who knew what it was. It started out as a character in children's books, you know, nearly a hundred years ago. How on earth did you get one to play with?"

"Aw, I guess it was a pretty old doll. Handed down, like."

"I know the feeling—all the clothes I ever saw came from my big sister."

For some reason he looked away awkwardly when I said that. I reached out and touched the photo. "This is a picture of the stamp, the best one I could take of it. I was wondering what you might be able to tell me about where it was made, maybe where it came from."

He hardly glanced at it before shaking his head. "You don't understand," he said. "This is useless. And it's not a stamp intended for use as real postage."

"How do you know?"

"Well, for a start you'll notice that it hasn't been postmarked. It was on an envelope but it was never intended to go through the mails. More important, a googol is ten to the hundredth. Making a stamp that says it has a value of 'one googol' is the sort of joke that the math class would have done back at Princeton."

It had taken me another half hour to discover what a googol was. "You went to Princeton?"

"For a while. I dropped out." His voice was unemotional as he went on: "There are plenty of interesting stamps that were never intended for postage and don't have currency value—Christmas seals, for example, that Holboll introduced in 1903 as part of an antituberculosis campaign. Some people collect those. But what you have given me isn't a stamp at all. It's just a *picture* of a stamp, and that's a whole lot different. For instance, you missed off the most important piece."

"Which is?"

"The edges. You've blown the main picture up big, and that's good, but to get it you've cropped all four edges. I can't see how it's perforated. That's the first problem. Then there's the materials—the dyes and the gum, you can't tell one thing about them from a photograph. And what about the type of paper that was used? And the watermark. Look, you said you found the stamp in Lockyer's apartment. Don't you have it anymore?"

"I do."

"Then why on earth didn't you bring it with you? I've got all sorts of things in the back of my shop just for looking at stamps." He leaned closer across the counter. "If you would let me take a look at it here I'm sure I could squeeze out some information. There are analytical techniques available today that no one dreamed of twenty years ago."

Finally, some enthusiasm—and such enthusiasm! He was itching to get his hands on the golliwog stamp. I wanted to hear more, but whatever miracles he had in the back of the shop were apparently of no interest to my stomach. It chose that moment to give a long, gurgling groan of complaint. I had breakfasted on a cup of black coffee and lunched in midmorning on a dry bagel, and it was now after five. Hunger and nerves. I put my hand on my midriff.

"Pardon me. I think that's trying to tell me something. Look, I'm sorry about not bringing the stamp. It's locked up in my safe. I've grown so used to protecting original materials—if I don't do it, the courts and the lawyers beat me into the ground. But if you'll let me pick your brains some more for the price of dinner . . ." He was going to say no, I knew it, and I hurried on, "—then I'll go get the stamp and bring it here in the morning. And if there's work for you to do—for God's sake don't destroy that stamp, though—I'll tell Mrs. Lockyer that I need you and I'll pay you at the same rate I'm being paid."

"How much?"

"Three hundred and fifty a day, plus expenses."

He didn't seem thrilled by the prospect, though it was hard to believe he made that much in a month in the store. I think it was the chance of getting a look at the stamp that sold him, because he finally nodded and said, "Let me lock up."

He turned to the unpainted inner door of the store and shielded the lock from me with his body while he did something to it.

"Not much in there to appeal to your average downtown thief," he said when he was done. He sounded apologetic. "No trade-in value, but a lot of the things are valuable to me."

Did Tom Walton spend everything he had on stamps? That idea was strengthened when we went out to his car, parked in the alley behind the store, and drove off to the Iron Gate Inn on N Street. He drove a 1974 white Dodge Dart rusted through at the bottom of the doors and under the fenders. I think cars are one of humanity's most boring inventions, but even I noticed that this vehicle was due for retirement.

I was a regular at the restaurant and I knew the menu by heart. He insisted on studying it carefully, a fixed stare of concentration on his face. I had the impression that he was more accustomed to food that came out of a paper bag.

While he read the menu I had an opportunity for a closer look at him. I changed my original estimate of his age. His innocent face said early twenties, but his hair was thinning at the temples. (Later, when I referred to him to Jill Fahnestock as "the Walton kid" she stared at me and said, "Kid? He's thirty-two—three years older than you." "But he looks—I don't know—brand-new." "You mean *unused.* I know. There's more to Tom than meets the eye.")

There was quite a bit of him that did meet the eye. "I'm on a diet," he explained, when he was ready to order.

"I see." Not before time, but I could hardly tell him that. "How long have you been dieting?"

"This time?" He paused. "Four years, almost."

Then he went ahead, quite unself-consciously, to order and eat a vast meal of hummus, couscous, and beer. I couldn't complain, because he was also determined to earn his dinner. We talked about stamps, and only stamps. At first I made a feeble attempt to take notes but after a few minutes I concentrated on my own food. There was no way I would remember all that he said, and with him as my consultant I didn't need to.

Stamps are colored bits of paper that you lick and stick on letters, right?

Not to Tom Walton and a million other people. To the collectors, stamps are an obsession and an endless search. They spend their lives rummaging through dusty old collections, or bidding on large lots at auctions to get a single stamp, or writing letters all over the world for first-day covers. They have their own vocabulary—*double impressions* (where a sheet of stamps has been put through the press twice, and the second imprint is slightly off from the first one); *mint* (a stamp with its original gum undamaged and with an unblemished face); *inverted center* (when a stamp is made using two plates, and a sheet is accidentally reversed when it is passed through the second press, so the stamp's center is upside down relative to its frame); *tête-bêche* (where a plate has been made with one stamp upside down in the whole sheet of stamps).

They also have their own versions of the Holy Grail, stamps so rare and valuable that only the museums and superrich collectors can own them: the 1856 "One-Penny Magenta" stamp from British Guiana; the Cape of Good Hope "Triangle" from the 1850's; the 1843 Brazilian

"Bull's-Eye," first stamp issued in the western hemisphere; the tricol-ored Basel "Dove" issued in Switzerland in 1845; the 1847 Mauritius "Post Office" stamp.

And there are the anomalies, the stamps that are interesting because of some defect in their manufacture. Tom Walton owned a 1918 U.S. Airmail stamp, an example of an inverted center in which the plane in the stamp's center is flying upside-down. He told me it was very rare, with only one sheet of a hundred stamps ever reaching the public.

I don't know how much time he spent alone in that store of his but he was starved for company. He would probably have talked to me all evening, and to my surprise I was enjoying listening to him. But by the time we were onto baklava and a second cup of coffee my own preoccu-pations were beginning to take over.

"I'm sorry, Tom." I interrupted his description of the "$1.00 Trans-Mississippi" commemorative stamp, one of his favorites. "But I've got to pay the check and go now. I promised Mrs. Lockyer that I'd be over to see her this evening at her apartment."

He nodded. "Ready when you are, Rachel."

He seemed to assume that he was going with me. I hadn't intended it, but it made sense. If I were considering adding him to the payroll it was a near-certainty that Eleanor Lockyer would want to talk to him. (Though I was not sure that I wanted to expose him to *her*.)

The Lockyer apartment was out in yuppie-land on Massachusetts Avenue, far from any subway stop. Tom Walton's car received an in-credulous look from the guard at the main entrance, but when we told him who we were going to see he couldn't refuse to let us in. We parked between a Mercedes 560 and an Audi 5000. Tom carefully checked that all his car doors were locked.

As we went inside and entered the elevator I decided that the second cup of coffee had been a mistake. I have an incipient ulcer, and my stom-ach hurt. Then I decided that the coffee was not to blame. What was getting to me was the prospect of another meeting with Eleanor Lockyer.

She was on the telephone when the maid ushered us in, and she took her time in finishing the conversation. We were not invited to sit down. She was obviously preparing to go out, because she was wearing a long dress and a cape that my year's income would not have paid for. I intro-duced Tom Walton as someone who was helping me with the investigation. She gave him the briefest of glances with bored gray eyes, dismissed him as a nonentity, and waved her arm at the table.

"Jason's mail for the past two days. I haven't looked at most of it, but you probably want to open it all and see what's there."

"I'll do that," I said. Tom Walton began to edge his way over to the stack of letters and envelopes.

"Right. You've been working on this for four days now. I hope you have results. What have you found out?"

"Quite a bit. We're making good progress." The tone in her voice was so critical I felt obliged to overstate what I had done. "First, we can rule out any possibility of kidnapping. Wherever he went, his trip was planned. The woman who cleaned the apartment in Baltimore is sure that there are a couple of suitcases missing, along with his clothes and toilet articles. She also thinks there are some spaces in the bookcases, but she can't remember what books used to be there, though they were in the middle of a group of books about single-celled plants and animals. Second, he's almost certainly still somewhere in this country. His passport was in his study here. Third—the absolute clincher, in my opinion—he left his notes for the rest of the semester with his teaching assistant at the university. Fourth—"

"But *where* is he?" she interrupted.

"I don't know."

"And you call that *progress?* You're telling me he could be anywhere in fifty states, millions of square miles, and you've no idea where, or how to find him. That's not what I'm paying you for. What good does that do me?"

"It's part of the whole investigative process. We have to rule out certain possibilities before I can explore others. For instance, now that we know he wasn't abducted against his will—Mrs. Lockyer, I don't know an easy way to ask this; but is there any chance that Jason Lockyer might have had a girlfriend?"

She didn't laugh. She sneered. "Jason? Why not ask a sensible question? He has the sex drive of a lettuce. One woman in his life is too much for him."

You'd be too much for most people. But that's the sort of thing you think and don't say. Fortunately I didn't have to ask a "sensible question" because we were interrupted by a loud whistle from Tom Walton.

"Look at this letter!" he said. "Professor Lockyer is going to be awarded the Copley Medal of the Royal Society, for his work on bacterial DNA transfer. That's really great."

It was a breakthrough, of sorts. It proved that Tom Walton was interested in something other than postage stamps.

But it did nothing for Eleanor Lockyer. She changed the direction of her scorn. "That's just the sort of nonsense I've had to put up with for five years. Bacteria, and worms, and slimes. If anyone deserves a medal it's *me,* having to live with that sort of rubbish." The buzzer sounded. She looked at her watch, then at me. "I must say, I'm most disappointed and dismayed by your lack of progress. You have to do better or I'm certainly not going to keep on paying you for nothing. Get to work. Look at this apartment again, and go over that mail with a toothcomb. When you are finished here Maria will let you out. I have to go. General Shellstock's limousine is waiting downstairs and the general asked me to be on time."

She was turning to leave when Tom Walton said quietly, "Walter Shellstock, by any chance?"

"Yes. He's visiting Washington for a few days."

"Say hello."

"Hello? You mean from *you?*"

"Sure. Wally Shellstock's my godfather."

It was a pleasure to watch Eleanor Lockyer's reaction. Her bottom lip went down so far that I could see the receding gum-line on her lower teeth, and she said, *"You.* You're . . . But who . . . ?"

She had forgotten his name, or never registered it when I introduced them.

He realized her problem. "Well, in business I just use Tom Walton. But my full name is Thomas Walton Shellstock. Actually it's Thomas Walton Shellstock the Fourth, though I don't know why anyone would care about counting the numbers."

"The *Pennsylvania* Shellstock's?"

"That's right. Well, have fun with Wally." Tom turned back to the pile of letters, peering at each one and ignoring Eleanor.

I've never seen a woman so torn. The buzzer sounded again, this time more urgently. She turned toward the door, but then she hurried back and took Tom by the arm.

"Thomas, I'm having a small dinner party here next week. I'd love it if you could come."

"Send me an invitation. Rachel has my address."

"Of course. You and . . ." She turned to give me a look of frustration. It meant, I sure as hell don't want to have to invite *you,* you're the hired help—but I'm not sure what your relationship is to Thomas Walton Shellstock, and if you two are screwing I may have to include you just to get him.

"Both of you," she said at last. Tom didn't give her another look, and finally she went out.

"You'd really come to her dinner party?" I said. I had a lot of questions but that seemed like the most important one.

"What do you think? Saying 'send me an invitation' is a lot easier than saying no in person."

"What are the Pennsylvania Shellstock's? She almost dropped her teeth."

"Ah." He had finished looking at the stamps on the unopened letters, and now he was sitting idly at the table. " 'Old money, my d-dear,' " he said in a falsetto. " 'The only *real* kind of money.' That's what people like Mrs. Lockyer say—and that's why I don't use my full name. We happen to have rather a lot of it—money, I mean, no thanks to me. Isn't she revolting?"

"I wondered if it was just me. When I hear her talk about her husband it doesn't sound like she wants me to find him. It sounds like she wants me to prove he's *dead.*"

"I don't understand why they're married at all. You said he's in his sixties, she can't be more than forty."

"Forty-five, if she's a day," I said. Pure malice. "His first wife died—he's got grown-up kids, and contacting them is on my agenda. Eleanor knew a good thing when she saw one. No responsibilities, lots of money—so she grabbed him."

"No children in this marriage?"

"Perish the thought. Children, my dear, they're such a *nuisance.* And having them is so *messy.*"

He was laughing without making a sound. "And worse than that, my dear, I'm told it actually *hurts.* Rachel, it's none of my business but I think you have a problem."

"Mrs. Lockyer? Don't I know it."

"I wasn't thinking of that. From what you said it's quite obvious that Jason Lockyer disappeared because he wanted to disappear. If he intended his wife to know about it he'd have told her. So now you're trying to go against what he wanted, just to please her. Doesn't that give you fits?"

"Tom, she's my *client*."

"So drop her, my dear."

"Right. And find at the end of the month I can't pay the rent. I'm in a funny business, Tom. Some of my clients are people you'd cross the street to avoid meeting. And I won't even touch the worst cases, the bitter divorce settlements and the child abusers. But the nice, normal people of the world don't seem to have much need for detectives."

There was a conscience inside all that fat, because after a moment he shook his head and said, "I'm sorry. I shouldn't have said that, it's not my business."

"No, and it never will be. Know why, Tom? Because you're *rich*." I was angry but most of it was guilt. He was right, I shouldn't be hounding Jason Lockyer just to please Eleanor Lockyer. "You don't have the same pressures on you. I saw your face when I offered you three hundred and fifty dollars a day to work on this. A lousy three-fifty, you thought, that isn't worth bothering with. Why do you run that stamp store at all if you don't need money? Why don't you do something *important?*"

There must be a branch of etiquette that says you don't harangue near-strangers; but poor Tom Walton didn't feel like a stranger, so I unloaded on him.

After a few moments he sighed. "All right, all right. I'll help you look for Jason Lockyer. And why do I run the stamp store? I'll tell you, I do it to *avoid* conversations like this—with my own damned family. They're all overachievers, and they went on at me for years, telling me to go out and change the world—run for public office, or buy a position on the New York Stock Exchange, or win a Nobel Prize." His voice was becoming steadily louder. "I don't want to do *any* of those things. I want a nice, peaceful life, looking at interesting things. And no one else is willing to let me do that! That's one nice thing about stamps. The family accepts that I'm running a business, they stay away and the stamps don't *harass* you."

That was the moment when I began to revise my opinion of Tom Walton. I had neatly pegged him as a pleasant, shy, introverted, and slightly kooky young man, preferring stamps to people, silence to speeches, and solitude to most types of company. I didn't think he knew how to shout. Now I saw another side of him, stronger and more determined. Anyone who got between Tom and what he wanted was in for a tough time.

Maria had heard the noise from another room of the apartment—she could have heard it from *any* room, and maybe out in the street. She appeared at the door and politely asked us if we were ready to leave. We were. Both of us became subdued. Thomas Walton Shellstock (the Fourth) drove me back to my apartment on Connecticut Avenue. We didn't speak.

As he stopped in front of the building he said: "I hate all this, Rachel. Really hate it. I'm not interested in looking for Jason Lockyer, and if I see his wife ever again that will be too soon."

I reached over and switched off the ignition key. "I know how you must feel," I said. "But I hope you'll decide to stick with it. It would be easy for you to say to hell with it, and quit. I feel the same way myself, but you know I can't do that. For one thing I need the money, and for another I could get a complaint that will cost me my license. And I need your help on this—you can see I'm floundering. Please, Tom. Don't back out now."

It was unfair pressure, and I knew it. After a couple of silent moments Tom lifted his head to look up at the front of the building.

"Oh, hell," he said. "If you want to, bring that lousy golliwog stamp around to my store tomorrow morning."

(Looking back, I see this as the critical moment when I began to use Tom Walton's essential niceness to ease him out of his shell. And if it was also the first step in saving or destroying the world, that's another matter—I certainly didn't suspect it at the time.)

I opened the door and stepped out. "Thanks, Tom," I said. "You're a real nice guy and I won't forget this. See you about ten o'clock. Good night."

I walked away quickly. I wanted to be inside the lobby before he could tell me he had changed his mind.

I had taken the liberty of carrying Jason Lockyer's newly arrived mail away in my purse from the Lockyer apartment. After all, Eleanor had just about ordered me to take it away and study it.

After two coffees and that conversation with Tom Walton I knew it was going to be difficult to go to sleep (yes, I have a conscience, too). I didn't even try. I spread out the mail on the kitchen table and began to go through it piece by piece. About half-past eleven I had a break-through, courtesy of the U.S. Postal Service. It's rare to thank the USPS for slow service, but I was ready to do it.

Although the letters had all been delivered to Lockyer's apartment that morning or the day before, one of them had been *mailed* nearly three weeks earlier. It should have reached Jason Lockyer long before he left for parts unknown, but of course it hadn't.

It bore a first-class postage stamp and a near-illegible postmark. I could make out the date and the letters "CO"—Colorado—at the bottom, but the town name was impossible. The handwritten envelope was addressed to Professor Jason Lockyer. Inside was a second envelope, this time with nothing written on it—but there was a golliwog stamp in the upper right corner. And inside *that* was the following typed message:

I think it's time to give you another progress report, even though it's sooner than I said. Seven and Eight are running along so-so, nothing much different from what you heard about in my last report. But Nine—you'd never believe Nine if you didn't see it for yourself. It's still changing, and no one can estimate an end-point. The crew are supposed to go inside in another week. Marcia says we'll be in no danger and she wants us to stay there longer than usual. She's done something new on the DNA splicing, and she believes that Nine is moving to a totally different limit, one with a Strange Attractor we've never seen before. She thinks it may be the one we've been searching for all along. Me, I'm afraid it may be the ultimate boss system—the real Mega-Mother. Certainly the efficiency of energy utilization is fantastic—more than double any of the others, and still increasing.

I tell you frankly, I'm scared, but I'll have to go in there. No way out of it. You told me that if I ever wanted advice you'd give it. I think that's what we all need here, a new look without any publicity. Any chance you can arrange to come? I'll write again or telephone in the next few days to keep you up-to-date. Then maybe you can tell me it's all my imagination.

The one-page letter was unsigned and undated, but I had the date on the postmark. And I had the log of Jason Lockyer's incoming long-distance phone calls at the university and at each apartment. It should be straightforward to find out who had written the cryptic note.

By half-past one I had changed my ideas about that. The incoming log showed nothing from Colorado anywhere near the right dates. As a final act of desperation I at last went to the log of Jason Lockyer's outgoing calls, ones he had placed himself. I had looked at this log before, but he made so many calls to so many places that I had not been able to see anything significant.

Sweet success.

It jumped out at me in the first ten seconds of looking. Six days after this letter had been mailed, Lockyer had placed a series of four phone calls in one day to Nathrop, Colorado. One call had lasted for over forty minutes. I checked in my National Geographic atlas. Nathrop was a small town about seventy miles west of Colorado Springs. It lay on the Arkansas River with the Sawatch Range of the High Rockies rearing up to over fourteen thousand feet just to the west.

Nathrop, Colorado.

For the first time, I had a place to look for Jason Lockyer that was smaller than the continental United States.

Within two minutes I knew I would be going to Nathrop myself. Calling that telephone number was a tempting thought, but there was a danger that it might make Jason Lockyer run before I had a chance to talk to him face to face. The real question was, would I tell Eleanor Lockyer what I was doing? She was my client, so the natural answer was, yes, she had to know and approve. But now I had to face Tom's question: did I *want* to find Jason Lockyer for her when he didn't want to be found?

I went to bed. I spent the rest of the night tossing and turning in mixed feelings of satisfaction and uneasiness.

I was standing at the door of Tom's shop on 15th Street by eight-thirty. Nice district. I was propositioned twice, and would have been moved on, too, if I hadn't been able to show the cops my license.

Tom's white Dodge wheezed around the corner at nine o'clock. He saw me and waved before he turned to park in the alley behind the building. He was eating an Egg McMuffin. I'm not a breakfast person, but I wished I had one.

"Got the stamp?" he said as soon as he came out of the alley. He was wearing a tan sports coat and matching flannels, and a well-ironed white shirt. His hair was combed and he was so clean-shaven his skin had a scraped look.

"Better than that. I have two of them."

I explained while he was opening the front door of the store.

"Good," he said. "It's nice to have a spare. It means I won't have to be quite so c-careful with the first one. And if you want my opinion, you ought to find Jason Lockyer and hear his side of the story before you tell Eleanor Lockyer a damned thing."

He went straight past the counter, unlocked the inner door, and waved me through.

It was just as well that I had learned the previous night that Tom was from a wealthy family. Otherwise, the word that would have entered my head when I stepped through the beige-painted wooden door into the rear of the store would have been: *drugs*. Money had been spent here, lots of money, and in downtown D.C. big money says illegal drugs more often than you would believe. At the back of the store was a massive Mosler safe, the sort of thing you'd normally see in a top-secret security installation or a bank vault. There was a well-equipped optical table along one wall and a mass of computer gear along another. Tom explained to me that it was an Apollo image analysis workstation, with a digitizer and raster scanner as input devices.

"I can view a stamp or a marking ink with a dozen different visible wavelength filters," he said. "Or in ultraviolet or multiband infrared. We can do chemical tests, too, on a tiny corner, so small you'd never know we'd touched it. I have calipers that will measure to a micron or better, and the raster scanner will create a digital image for computer processing. I can do computer matching against all the standard papers and inks."

"And the safe?"

"Stamps. They're negotiable currency, of course, but that's not the point. The old and rare ones have a worth quite unrelated to their face value."

Just like Tom Walton.

He took the envelope containing the first golliwog stamp and placed it carefully on a light-table. Those fat fingers were surprisingly precise and delicate. As he placed a high-powered stereo lens in position and bent over it, he said: "Why are you rejecting the most obvious reason of all for Jason Lockyer running off—that he c-can't stand his wife? Seems to me he has an excellent reason, right there."

"If he just wanted to get away from her he wouldn't need to disappear. He had good legal advice before they married. They have a marriage contract, and if they split up he knows exactly how much it would cost him. He can afford it. All he would have to do is stay over in Baltimore and tell his lawyers to go ahead with the separation papers. If he were to die, that's another matter. She gets a lot more. I think that's one reason why Eleanor is willing to pay me to find out what happened. She wants that money so bad she can taste it."

I watched as Tom grunted in satisfaction and straightened up. He fed the second envelope carefully into a machine that looked like a horizontal toaster.

"The thousand dollar version of the old steam kettle," he said. "It takes the stamp off the cover with minimal damage to the mucilage. Here it comes." The stamp was appearing from the other side of the machine on a little porcelain tray. He removed it, placed it between two pieces of transparent film, and secured it in position on the scanner.

"There's one other reason why I'm sure Lockyer's not planning to stay away forever," I went on. "He didn't take any checkbooks, and he hasn't used any credit cards. What will he do when he runs out of money?"

"What about coupon clipping?" asked Tom. And then, when I looked puzzled, "I mean dividends. If he's like me he gets dividend checks all the time, and he can cash them easily. All he would have to do is change the mailing address for receipt of those, and he could live off them indefinitely."

"Damn. I never thought of that. I'll have to check it."

He closed the cover on the scanner, leaned back, and stared at me. "It's none of my business, but how did you get into this detective work? And how long have you been doing it?"

"Six years. Two years on my own, since my uncle died. It was really his business, and I used to help him out in the summers when I was still in school. When I graduated a job was hard to find. Tell an employer you have a double degree in English and psychology and it's like saying you have AIDS and leprosy."

"But why do you *stay* in it?"

"Well, I've got an investment. There's a hundred and fifty-eight dollar fee for the application for a D.C. license. And another sixteen-fifty for fingerprinting, and thirty for business cards. It adds up."

I was trying to tease him, but he was too smart and it didn't work.

"Do you make any money?" he asked.

He wasn't teasing at all, he was just making conversation while the scanner did its thing on the stamp. But unfortunately it *did* work. I've grown hypersensitive about what I do for a living. I broke up with my last boyfriend, Larry, over just this subject.

"I pay the rent," I snapped back at him. "And I bought your dinner last night. You say you're rich but I didn't see you itching to pick up the tab."

"I've been trained not to," he said quietly. "That's one of the things I was told at my mother's knee—everyone in the world will try to soak you for a loan or a f-free meal, as soon as they find out you're a Shellstock. I guess that's another reason why I'm Tom Walton. But I'll buy you dinner anytime you want me to, Rachel."

Which of course left me feeling like the ultimate jerk. I hadn't bought him dinner—the Lockyers had, since it would be on my expense account. And he knew that, yet he offered to buy me dinner out of his own pocket. I'd slapped him and he was offering the other cheek.

"Let me tell you about the golliwog stamp," he went on. I was quite ready to let him change the subject. "There's more to be measured, but a few things are obvious already. First, look at the perforations on the edge of the stamp. Even without a lens you can see that only the top and bottom are perforated, with the sides clean. That means this stamp is from a vertical coil—a roll of stamps rather than a sheet, with the stamps joined at top and bottom, not at the sides. And even without measuring I can tell you this is 'perf 12'—twelve perforations in twenty millimeters. Nothing unusual about any of this, though horizontal coils are more common. What's more interesting is the way the stamp was produced. Take a look."

He moved me to the light-table and showed me how to adjust the binocular lens to suit my eyes.

"See the pattern of lines across the stamp? That's called a *laid batonné* paper, a woven paper with heavier lines in a certain direction. And there's no watermark—that's a pretty sure sign that these stamps were never intended for use as commercial postage."

"So what's the point of them?"

"My guess is that they were made to identify a certain group of people—like a secret sign, or a password. Put one of these on the envelope, you see, and it proves you're one of the inside group. I've seen it done before, though this is an unusually well-executed design for that sort of thing. The choice of a golliwog supports my idea because it's not a symbol I'd ever expect to see on a commercial stamp. Now, look at the actual design of the golliwog."

I stared at it and waited for revelation.

"There are five main processes used in manufacturing stamps," he went on. "First, engraved *intaglio,* where a design is cut directly into the surface of the plate—that's been used for as long as stamps have been made. Second, letterpress, in which the design is a *cameo,* a pattern raised in relief above the surface of the plate. Third, *lithography,* which uses water and an oily ink drawn on a stone, or actually on a metal surface prepared to simulate stone. Fourth, *embossed,* where a die is used to give the stamp a raised surface. Fifth, *photogravure,* where the lines are photographed onto a film covering the plate, and then etched onto the surface as though they were an engraving. Clearly, what you are looking at there is a photogravure."

Clearly. To him, perhaps. "I'll believe you. But I don't see where that takes us." I was losing interest in stamps and itching to head off for Colorado. I didn't have the gall to tell him, though, not when he thought what he was doing was important.

"It takes us to a very definite place." All signs of stammer had gone from Tom's voice. "To Philadelphia. You see, there aren't all that many people who do the design work for stamps. And I'm ninety-five percent sure I recognize the designer of that one you're looking at. I know his style. He likes vertical coils, and he likes to do intaglio photogravure. His name is Raymond Sines, and if you want me to I'll call Ray right now."

Why hadn't he told me that to start with, instead of giving me the rigmarole about *intaglio* and *cameo?* Because he liked to talk about stamps, that's why.

I stopped pretending to look at the golliwog. "I'm not sure what talking to Raymond Sines would do for me. How well do you know him?"

He hesitated. I was learning. Hesitation in Tom Walton usually meant uneasiness.

"So-so. I've met Ray a few times informally, at the Collectors' Club in New York City. He's a pretty peculiar guy. Very smart, and a terrific artist and designer. But when he gets away from stamps he's a one-subject talker. He's a space nut, and a founder member of Ascend Forever—a group that designs space habitats."

"I don't see that taking us to Jason Lockyer. Do you realize that yesterday I had no leads and now I have two? And they go off in wildly different directions."

"Two's a lot better than zero. And I think you may need them both."

I saw his point. Nathrop showed a population of less than five hundred people, so if Lockyer was there I couldn't miss him; but it was also a wilderness area with hundreds of square miles of land and very few people. So if he *wasn't* in the town . . .

"I'm afraid you're right," I said. "It could be that whoever wrote the letter to Lockyer was just using the Nathrop post office mailbox and telephone. What do we do if we go there and find nothing?"

"We come back. Do you have the letter with you? If so, I'd like to see it for myself."

I handed it over and watched while he read it. "Make any sense to you?"

He shook his head. "Strange Attractor?"

"I know. I've never heard the phrase before."

"I have. I can tell you what it means at the Scientific American level. It's a math-physics thing, where you keep feeding the output of a system back in as a new input. Sometimes it converges to a steady state—an attractor; sometimes it goes wild, and ends up unstable or with total chaos; and sometimes it sort of wanders around a region—around a strange attractor. The type of behavior depends on some critical system variable, like flow rate or chemical concentration or temperature. It's obvious from this letter that the writer is involved in a set of experiments—but it's anybody's guess as to what field they're in. And *Mega-Mother?*" He placed the letter back on the light-table. "Maybe he's using 'Strange Attractor' to mean something different from what I've seen before. I don't think we're going to get much out of this."

"I'm not, that's for sure. And it's irrelevant. I'm trying to find Jason Lockyer, not solve puzzles. Useless or not, I guess I have to head for Colorado."

"Will you hold off for one day—so I can make a quick run up to Philly. Ray Sines has his own engraving shop there and I want to drop in on him."

"What do you think he can tell you?"

"If I knew, I wouldn't be going." Tom took a blank envelope over to the typewriter next to the safe and typed his own name on it. Then he removed the golliwog stamp from the scanner, placed a thin layer of gum on the back of it, and carefully stuck it on the envelope. Finally he placed the letter from Colorado inside it. "I'll call Ray now and tell him I'm interested in tracing works by an early American engraver. That's quite true, and he's bound to be interested. And during the meeting I want him to catch a look at this." He held up the envelope. "And we'll t-take it from there."

I had expected Eleanor Lockyer to quiz me about my proposed travel and give me a general hard time. Instead she was sweet and reasonable, and didn't ask me one question about where I was going, or why.

"Tell Thomas that the invitation is in the mail," she said. "It will be just a small, intimate group, no more than a dozen."

"I'll tell him." (I didn't.)

He wanted to drive to Philadelphia in the Dodge death trap. I talked him out of it by suggesting that if we went by train we could fly straight to Denver after our meeting with Sines. Tom seemed surprised that I wanted to go with him, but he didn't seem to mind.

"Just don't say too much about stamps or engraving," he said.

The least of my worries.

Ray Sines was younger than I had expected, a thin, red-faced man of about thirty who suffered premature baldness. He was attempting the disastrous trick of training the remaining strands of hair to a pattern that covered his whole head, and every couple of minutes he ran his hand in a circular motion around his scalp. The top of his head looked like a rotary shoe-polisher. His office, above an industrial warehouse, reminded me of Tom's store, dusty and shabby and somehow irrelevant to what went on there.

He showed pleasure and no surprise at our visit, and he and Tom went off at once into their polite sarabande of talk about Gibbons and Scott and Minkus catalogs, the location of the printing equipment of the legendary Jacob Perkins of Massachusetts, and the newly discovered stamps of the 1842 City Despatch Post of New York City. I sat on the edge of my chair, drank four cups of coffee that I would later regret, and itched for Tom to get to the real business.

After about an hour and a half I realized the dreadful truth: he wasn't going to do it. The envelope and the golliwog stamp were there in

Tom's case, standing by his leg—and it was going to stay there. He had had no trouble devising a theoretical plan to startle information out of Ray Sines, but when it came to the act he couldn't bring himself to begin.

Finally I reached down, hoisted the case, and placed it on Tom's lap. "The catalog. Don't you have a catalog in here that you want to show Mr. Sines?"

Tom glared at me, but he was stuck. He opened the case and peered inside. "I don't know if I remembered to bring it," he said. While Sines looked on he lifted out a layer of papers and placed them on the low table in front of us. On top was the envelope addressed to him, with its prominent golliwog stamp.

Sines stared at it and his face lit up. "I didn't know you were a member!" he said to Tom. Then he gave me a quick and nervous look.

"Yes," Tom started to say. "Both of us—"

"Member of what?" I rapped at Sines. If this were a secret organization any self-respecting member would check a stranger's credentials before admitting its existence.

For answer, Sines reached behind him and produced a whole roll of golliwog stamps. "My design," he said proudly. "I worked harder on this than on any commercial assignment. It's all right, you can talk to me. I was one of the first people that Marcia allowed in. When did you join?"

Tom looked at me beseechingly.

"I came in about four months ago," I said. "Tom's a recent acquisition, he joined just a month back."

"Terrific!" Sines leaned back in his chair and beamed at both of us. "If you haven't been out to the site already, there's a real treat in store for you."

I reached into my purse and waved our airline tickets at him. "We're on our way there now. Maybe you can tell us, what's the best way once we arrive at the airport?"

He frowned at me. "Isn't someone meeting you?"

We were moving onto tricky ground. I had an urge to get out quickly, but we needed information. "Everyone has their hands full," I said. "There seem to be problems with one of the systems—Seven, is it?"

"No, it's Nine." He relaxed again. "Yes, I hear it's still doing funny things. We'll get the right one eventually. Where are you flying to?"

"Denver."

"Pity. You should have flown to Colorado Springs. Either way, though, you'll have some pretty high driving ahead of you. Take Route 285 out of Denver until you meet Route 24 into Buena Vista. Go north from there and you should see the site on your left, up on the slopes of Mount Harvard."

"How far from Nathrop?" I asked.

"A few miles. But if you get there, you've gone the wrong way out of Buena Vista. Pretty good steak restaurant, though, if you do make the wrong turn." He frowned. "If you would like me to call ahead and try to arrange—"

"No. Please don't." I took Tom's arm and stood up. "We'd hate to make a nuisance of ourselves before we even arrive. And we'd better go now, our plane leaves in an hour and a half."

"You'll need a cab." He stood up, too. "I just wish I was going with you. Give me a call when you get back, tell me what you think of things out there. For me, it's the most exciting thing that's happened in my whole life."

He escorted us to the entrance of the building. "Ascend forever!" he said as we left, and raised his arm.

"Ascend forever!" I replied, but Tom said nothing. As soon as Sines was out of sight and sound he exploded at me. "I hate that sort of thing!"

"You think I enjoy it?" I had the caffeine shakes and I needed to go to the bathroom. "I know we lied to him, but what did you want me to do? Break down and explain to Sines that we went there to trick him?"

He didn't reply. But I suspected that it was not the lying that had him upset. It was me, pushing the attaché case at him, pushing him to do something alien to his temperament. He'd never believe me, but I was as upset about that as he was.

Denver's Stapleton Airport is at five thousand feet; our drive south and west took us steadily higher. Within the hour we were up over nine thousand, with snowcapped mountains filling the sky ahead. I had never been to Colorado before and the scenery bowled me over—magnificent country, like moving to a different planet after the rampant azaleas and dogwoods of May in Washington.

Tom was less impressed. He had been here before—"skiing in Vail and Aspen, while I tried to persuade the family that they weren't doing me any favors by sending me. I finally managed to break a leg, and that did it."

On the plane and again in the car we beat to death what we learned from Ray Sines, and what we knew or surmised about its relevance to Jason Lockyer's disappearance.

"Ascend Forever is in the middle of this," said Tom. "Or perhaps it's a subgroup of them. More likely that, because they're going through a procedure to keep it a big secret, and that's quite impossible with too many participants."

"A pretty childish procedure, don't you think? I haven't run across special stamps and secret symbols and hidden messages since I was in high school."

"You'd never make a Freemason. And I knew a bunch of people at Princeton who were still into private codes. Let's go on. They have some project—"

"—a group of projects. Remember Seven, Eight, and Nine. Which also means there's probably a One through Six—"

"—OK, at least nine projects, but they're probably all doing similar things. There is some sort of development activity associated with them and it's out in the Colorado mountains, west of Nathrop and Buena Vista. It's pretty big, visible from a fair distance. And it's in some sort of trouble—"

"—or part of it is. Remember, Seven and Eight are doing fine. It's Nine that's off, enough to want Jason Lockyer to come out and take a look at what's going on."

"And he's a famous biologist. But the projects have something to do with strange attractors. Not to mention the old Mega-Mother." Tom shrugged. "You're the detective. Can you put it together?"

"Not a clue. Unless Jason Lockyer has other talents, and the group is calling on those to help them."

Grasping at straws. We both knew it and after a while we dropped it in favor of general chat. We uncovered a total of three common acquaintances, not counting Jill Fahnestock, and we agreed that except for Jill we liked none of them. He found out, to his horror, that the purple mark on my left forearm was the scar of a bullet-wound, inflicted when a man I approached in a child custody case fired at me without warning. ("Cocaine," I said. "He was carrying eight ounces of it, nothing to do with child custody. I was just unlucky—or lucky, depending on your point of view.") I found out, with equal horror, that Tom carried no health insurance of any kind and did not propose to get any. ("Health insurance is for people who don't have money. Obviously, it costs more on average to buy insurance than it does to be sick—otherwise, how could insurance companies stay in business. Health insurance is a bourgeois concept, Rachel." That last sentence was to annoy me, but this time I handled it better.)

He ate when he was happy. So did I. The fact that he was forty pounds overweight while I was too thin to please anyone but a clothes designer was lost on neither of us.

Eventually we stopped talking and simply sat in companionable silence. Tom was one of the rare people whose presence you enjoy without speaking.

Buena Vista came finally into view, a town that couldn't be more than a couple of thousand people. For the past half hour we had scanned the mountains ahead of us for any anomalies, and seen nothing even though it was a glittering spring day and visibility was perfect.

I had been driving, because we were renting a Toyota Celica and since I was considering buying one I wanted to see how it handled. When we reached Buena Vista I stopped the car at what looked like a general purpose store on the main through street.

"You need to buy something?" said Tom.

"Information. Want to come in with me?"

The bored youth behind the counter knew instantly what I was talking about. "The Observatory, you mean," he said. "You can see it from the road, but you have to look hard. Take the road north and look for a gravel cutoff to the left. That goes all the way on up, you can't miss it." He stared at us. "You'll be working there?"

"No. Just visiting."

"Ah. They say they're making a spaceship up there, one that's going off to the end of the universe."

"I don't know about that. We'll see." I bought two cans of Coke and we left.

"So much for the big secret," Tom said when we were back in the car. "They're practically running guided tours."

"If you want to hide something, disguise it as something else that local people don't much care about—like an observatory."

Tom upended his can of Coke. He inhaled it more than drank it, in one long gulp. "What about the spaceship?"

"Safe enough. No one in their right mind would believe it."

We had a major decision to make as we drove up the winding gravel-covered road. Would we barrel on up to the entrance, or would we leave the car and play Indian Scout?

We discussed it for another minute, then compromised. A complex of buildings stood on the south-facing slope of the mountainside. We parked the car three-quarters of a mile away, where the top of the blue Toyota would barely be visible over the top of the final ridge. I led the way as we walked until we had a good view. The location was well above ten thousand feet, and three minutes walk up the slight incline left us gasping.

There were five major structures ahead. Three of them were large, hemispherical, geodesic domes, made of glass or plastic. Two of those were transparent, and we could see shadows inside where trees or shrubs seemed to be growing marked off by triangular support ribbing of painted metal or yellow plastic. The third dome was apparently of tinted material, and its wall panels gleamed dull orange-red. The three domes stood in roughly an equilateral triangle, each one sixty feet across, and at the center of that triangle were two more conventional buildings. They were white and square-sided, with the look of prefabricated or temporary structures. I counted seven cars parked outside the larger one.

A stiff breeze blew from the west, and even in the bright sunlight it was too cold to stand and watch for more than a few minutes. In that time no one appeared from any of the buildings or domes, nor was there evidence of activity within.

We went back to the car and sat inside. I put my hand on my stomach. The Coke had been a mistake. I had the jitters and a pain that ran from my solar plexus around the lower right-hand side of my ribs.

"What now?" said Tom. He looked like the detective, calm and confident. His question probably meant he had made up his own mind what we ought to do.

I burped, in as ladylike a way as I could manage. "If Jason Lockyer is inside one of those buildings it won't do us any good to sit here. And if Jason Lockyer's *not* inside, and he's a thousand or two thousand miles away, it still won't do us any good to sit here."

"My thoughts exactly." It was his turn to reach out and turn a car's ignition key. "Let's do it, Rachel. Let's go up there and take the golliwog by the horns."

I eased up the slope at a sedate twenty miles an hour, all my attention on the road. Halfway there, Tom said, "Hold on a minute. Is something wrong with my eyes?"

I stopped the car. It took a few moments, then I saw it, too. The orange-red dome had changed color to a darker, muddier tone, with rising streaks of deep purple within it. Tom and I looked at each other.

"We'll never find out from here," I said. I let in the clutch—badly—and we jerked forward again. We crept all the way up to the larger building and parked in the line of cars. I did an automatic inventory. A new Buick, two old Mustangs, a Camaro that had been in an accident and needed bodywork, two VW Rabbits, and an ancient Plymouth that made even Tom's car look fresh off the assembly line. The same sort of mix as I might expect to see in a Washington car park, but with a bit more Buy-American. The air was clear, the sunlight blinding, and there was not a sound to be heard. Living in the city you forget how quiet real quiet can be. We walked over to the building—aluminum-sided, I now saw—almost on tiptoe. My pulse rate was up in the hundreds, and I could feel it in my ears, the loudest sound in the world.

"Inside?" whispered Tom.

I nodded and he led the way. The front door was closed but not locked. It opened to a big lobby about twenty feet square, spotlessly clean and containing nothing but half a dozen metal-frame chairs. As we paused I heard a clatter of footsteps on the aluminum floor, and a man carrying a couple of thick notebooks came hurrying in. Tom and I froze.

"Well, thank Heaven," the new arrival said. "I didn't know anyone was coming out. We've been so shorthanded this last week I've been on continuous double shifts."

New York accent, California tan. He was no more than twenty-two or twenty-three, and he was wearing an all-white uniform like a medical orderly. The first impression was of a clean-cut, clean-living lad who should have been carrying an apple for his teacher along with his notebooks. A closer look added something different. He had a spaced-out glassy stare in his eyes, a look that I had seen before only among the ranks of the Moonies and the Hare Krishnas.

"First visit?" he said.

Tom and I nodded. I hope I looked as casual and at ease as he did.

"Great. You'll love it here. I'm Scott."

"Rachel," I said. As I took his outstretched hand the inside of my head made its own swirling list of mysteries: vanished professor—

golliwog stamp roll—observatory—spaceship—biology experiment—
strange attractor—religion—sanctuary—lunatic asylum.

What was I missing?

"I'll tell Marcia you're here." Scott had shaken hands with Tom and
was heading off along a passageway. "But let's settle you in first, and
then find something for you to do."

We followed him to a long room with a dozen beds and a shower and
toilet facility at the far end. "You'll sleep in here," Scott said. "Make
yourselves comfortable. I'll be back in five minutes."

I sat down shakily on one of the beds. Hard as a rock. "Prison? Military barracks? Hospital? Tom, we were crazy to come here."

"Don't you want to find Lockyer?" Tom shook his head. "Not
prison, not hospital. Boy Scouts, or the dorm in Vermont summer camp.
Kids away from home for a big adventure, mummy and daddy miles
away. But they've gone unisex."

"What *is* this place?"

"I don't know. Sounds like Marcia's the kingpin, whoever she is. Or
queenpin. Or camp counselor. Everyone defers to her, even Ray Sines."
He went across to the window and stood gazing out at it. "My imagination, or is it changing again?"

I followed his pointing finger. The third dome was now a mottled
and virulent green. A flowing column of darker color seemed to be rising steadily through the paint on the dome. Before we could discuss
what we were seeing Scott came hurrying back in.

"Right," he said. "A quick look around, then introductions will
have to wait until tonight. We'll need uniforms."

He led us to an array of tall lockers at the end of the room. While he
watched—no thoughts of privacy here—Tom and I took off our outer
garments and replaced them with aseptic-looking white uniforms identical to the one that Scott was wearing. Tom had a little trouble finding
one that fitted him; the members of Ascend Forever were presumably an
undernourished group.

When we were dressed to Scott's satisfaction he took us to the entrance hall—and back outside the building. Tom gave me a quick
glance. Why bother with sterile clothing if we were going to be outside?
Answer: sterility was not the point; uniformity was.

We marched to one of the three domes and peered in through the
transparent wall panels. I saw a sloping floor with a little fountain at the

upper end, close to where we were standing. A trickle of water ran across
the dome's interior and vanished at the other side. The rest of the floor
was covered with dusty-looking plants, growing halfheartedly in a
light-colored soil. The plants looked tired, and slightly wilted. In the
center of the floor stood the skeleton of a much smaller dome, with only
half its walls paneled, and within that structure three human figures
were bending over what looked like a computer console.

A telephone handset hung on the outside of the dome, and Scott
reached for it. "New arrivals," he said. "Any changes?"

The three figures inside straightened to stare out at us and waved a
greeting. "Welcome aboard." The voice on the phone was young,
friendly, and enthusiastic. "Nothing special happening here. We've
been trying to find out what's wiping out the legumes, but we don't
have an answer. Oxygen and nitrogen down a little bit more—still de-
creasing."

"Still trying changed illumination?"

"Just finished it. We're putting in a bit less power from the ceiling
lights, we're making it longer wavelength. We won't know how it
works for a while."

"No danger, though?"

"Not yet. No matter what, we'll have another couple of weeks before
we begin to worry. But it's a pain to see it go this way. Three weeks ago
we were pretty sure this one would make it."

"Maybe it will." Scott waved to the people inside. "We'll keep trying, too. Now that I have some help maybe I'll have time to run an
independent analysis."

He hung the handset back on its closed stand and pointed to the
panel next to it. "This is all new," he said. "And a real improvement.
We have dual controls now, inside and outside. Temperature and humidity and lighting levels in the dome can be controlled from this panel
here. When we started out, all the controls were inside and it was a real
nuisance. If there was no crew we had to send someone through the airlock whenever we wanted to vary the interior environmental conditions."

He started toward the middle of the complex. "Anyway, that's
Eight," he said as we walked. "Not going too good now. Seven is a lot
better."

"What happened to One through Six?" asked Tom.

"They went to stable end-forms, but they weren't ones that humans could live in. So we brought the crews back outside, closed down the operations, and reused the domes."

He didn't notice Tom's raised eyebrows, and went on, "But Nine's the interesting one! I'll warn you now, though, you won't see much of the inside of it from here. We've had to ship a TV camera to the interior, to supplement the audio descriptions, otherwise we'd be short of data. But we'll take a look through the panels, anyway."

We were closing on the strangest of the domes, and now I could see that its wall panels were neither painted nor made of opaque materials. They were coated on the inside. Scott went to a telephone set in the wall—in that respect this was identical to the other dome.

"Marcia?" he said. "New arrivals. How about clearing a patch, so we can take a look inside Nine?"

The coating of the wall panels was close in color to the way we had first seen it, an orange-red with a touch of brown. While we stood and watched, a circular cleared patch began to appear on the wall panel closest to us. Soon we could see a hand holding a plastic scraper.

"Tough coating," said a woman's voice. "A good deal tougher than yesterday."

The clear patch was finished and about a foot across. In the middle of that patch a frowning black face suddenly appeared. It was that of a woman, with protruding eyes and black straight hair that stuck out wildly in all directions.

We hadn't found Jason Lockyer; but we had found the inspiration for the caricature design of the golliwog stamp.

"New arrivals," said Scott again. The tone of his voice was quite different from the way it had been at the other dome. Now he was respectful and subdued, almost fearful.

This time there was no cheery wave. The golliwog face stared hard at me and Tom. "What chapter?" said a gruff voice through the handset.

We had no choice.

"Philadelphia," I said.

"Your names?"

"Rachel Banks and Tom Walton."

The way to the car was around the dome and then dead ahead. We could be in it in thirty seconds and driving down the mountain. On the other hand, Scott was acclimatized to ten thousand feet and we were not. I couldn't run more than fifty yards without stopping for breath, and overweight Tom was sure to be in worse shape. . . .

While those thoughts were running through my head the face on the other side of the panel had disappeared. We stood there for about thirty seconds, while my instinct to run became stronger and stronger. I was all ready to shout at Tom to make a break for it when Marcia's face appeared again at the panel. Already the wall was partly coated, and she had to use the scraper again to clear it.

"I've told all the chapters," she said. "I have to approve any new members *in advance* of joining—and certainly in advance of being sent here. We must check on you two. And while that's being done we can't afford any risks. Building Two, Scott. You're responsible for them."

There was no doubt who was in charge. And I had waited too long. I half-turned, and found that Marcia had used her brief absence to call for reinforcements. Four men were on their way over to the dome, all young and tanned and fit-looking.

Tom looked to me for direction. I shook my head. Marcia's check on us was going to show that we were not members of whatever group she led, we could be sure of that. But this was not the time or place to look for an escape. I suddenly realized something I should have been aware of minutes ago: the car keys were in my purse—and my purse was back at the lockers with the rest of my clothes. Thank God I hadn't told Tom to run for it. I would have felt like the world's prize idiot, sitting inside the car while our pursuers came closer and I explained to him that I had no way to start the engine.

We were escorted, very politely, to the second and smaller of the two white buildings. I noticed for the first time that it had no windows.

"This is just part of the standard procedure," said Scott. He was embarrassed. "I know everything will be all right. I'll check as soon as I can with the group leader in Philadelphia, and then I'll come and let you out. Help yourself to any food you want from the refrigerator."

The door was thick and made of braced aluminum. It closed behind us. And locked.

We were standing in a room with three beds, a kitchen, and one other door. Tom went across to it.

"Locked," he said after a moment. "But padlocked on *this* side. Where do you think it leads?"

"Not outside, that's for sure. Probably upstairs. It wouldn't help, though—there are no windows there, either." I went across to the refrigerator and found a carton of milk. I had savage heartburn and what I would have really liked was a Mylanta tablet, but they were also in my purse. I was proving to be quite a klutz of a detective.

Tom was still over at the door. "It's wood, not aluminum. And nowhere near as strong as the one that leads outside."

"Good. Can you break the damned thing open?"

"Break it!" He stared at me in horror. "Rachel, this is someone's private property."

"It sure as hell is. Tom, I know you were brought up to regard personal property as sacred. But we're in a fix. That bloody golliwog woman is all ready to serve us on the halfshell, and I don't give a shit about property. Break it." I was drinking from the carton—most unhygienic, but I was past caring. "Whatever they plan to do with us, I doubt if adding a broken door to the list of crimes will make much difference. Have fun. Smash away."

"Well, if you really think we have to." Tom was still hesitating. "All right, I'll do it. With luck I won't need to do any actual smashing."

He wandered over to the kitchen area of the room and found a blunt knife. The door's padlock was held in position by four wood screws. It took him only three or four minutes to remove all of them. He swung the door open and we found we were looking at the foot of a tightly spiraling staircase.

"We can't get out this way," I said. "But there's nothing better to do. Let's take a look."

He went up the stairs in front of me, clutching the central support pole. On the second floor we came to another door, this one unlocked.

Tom opened it. We were looking at a carbon copy of the room below, but with one important difference. At the table in the kitchen area sat a man with a loaf of bread and a lump of cheese—Edam, by the look of it—in front of him. Next to those stood a bottle of red wine, and the man facing us had a full glass in his hand and was sniffing at it thoughtfully. When the door opened he looked up in surprise.

I think I was more surprised than he was, though of course I had no right to be. I knew him from his picture. We were looking at Jason Lockyer.

The introductions and explanation of who we were and how we got there took a few minutes.

"And it seems we're all stuck here," I said.

"Well, there are worse places," said Lockyer. We had set a couple more chairs around the table and were all sitting there. "I ought to apologize, because of course this is all my fault. When I look back I can see I started the whole damned thing."

He was a small, neatly built man with a good-humored face and the faint residual of a Boston accent. The fact that he was locked up, with no idea what was likely to happen to him next, did nothing to ruin his appetite. His only complaint was the quality of the wine. ("California 'burgundy,' " he said. "It shouldn't be allowed to use the name. It's no excuse to say wine like this is cheap. It ought to be *free.*")

"Three years ago," he went on, "I was invited to give a talk to the local chapter of Ascend Forever in Baltimore. I had no idea what to say to them, until one of my best students—Marcia Seretto—who was also a member of the society, mentioned the society's interest in establishing stand-alone colonies out in space. That would imply a completely stable, totally recycling environment. After that it was obvious what I had to talk about.

"Most people know that one fully recycling environment, driven only by energy from the sun, already exists. That's the biosphere of the planet Earth. What I pointed out—and what got Marcia so excited that she almost had a fit—was the existence today of other biospheres. They were small, and they only supported life at the microbe level, but they were—and are—genuine miniature ecospheres, relying on nothing but solar energy to keep them going. The first ones were made by Clair Folsome in Hawaii in 1967, and they're still going."

"Small?" I asked. "How small?"

"You sound like Marcia. Small enough to fit in this wine bottle. The original self-sustaining ecospheres lived in one-liter containers."

"That's *small,*" said Tom.

"You also sound like Marcia. *Too* small, she said. But she asked me if it would be possible to design an ecosphere that was big enough for a few humans to live in—and live off, in the sense that it would provide them with food, water, and air—but not much bigger than a house. I told her I didn't see why not, and I even sketched out the way I would go about designing the mix of living organisms to do it. You need something that does photosynthesis, and you need saprophytes that help to decompose complex organic chemicals to simpler forms. But with an adequate energy supply there's no reason why an ecosphere to support humans has to be Earth-sized.

"Marcia graduated, and I thought she had taken a job somewhere on the West Coast. I didn't worry about her, because she was the most charismatic person I had ever met. She seemed able to talk the rest of the students into doing anything. It turned out that I was right but I had underestimated her. The next thing I knew, I had a letter from another one of my students. He wanted to know what end-forms were possible when you started an ecosphere with a given mix of organisms. The answer, of course, is that today's theories are inadequate. No one knows where you'll finish. But it was the first hint I had that something had gone on beyond my lecture. I sent him a reply, and a week later in my In-box at the university I found a letter with an odd stamp on it, like a caricature of a black-faced doll."

"A golliwog," I said.

"So I learned. I also realized that it looked a lot like Marcia. The letter said that I was the official founding father of the Habitat League. I've seen stuff like that before, silly student jokes. So it didn't worry me. But *then* I began to receive anonymous letters with the same stamp. And when I read those, I began to worry."

"We saw one," I said. "It was sent to you but the mails fouled up the delivery."

"The person who wrote them said that Marcia had set up her own organization within Ascend Forever, with its own chapters and its own sponsors for funding. She had organized a camp in Colorado—this one—and they were following my advice on setting up self-sustaining ecospheres that could be used as a model for space habitats. I replied to him, saying the Colorado mountains were not a bad site, but they weren't the best."

"Why not?"

"Simulated space environment," said Tom, before Lockyer could answer. "If you want to match the spectrum of solar radiation in low earth orbit, you should go as high as you can and as near the equator as you can, where the sunlight is less affected by the atmosphere. Somewhere in the Andes near Quito would be ideal."

"You're a member of the Habitat League?" Lockyer was worried.

"Never heard of them until today. But I've read about space colonies and habitats."

"Then you probably know that you have to do things a lot differently than they're done in the Earth's natural biosphere. For example, the carbon dioxide cycle on Earth, from atmosphere, through plants and animals, and back to the atmosphere, takes eight to ten years. In the ecospheres that I helped to design, that was down to a day or two. And that means other changes—major ones. And *that* means unpredictable behavior of the ecosphere, and no way to know the stable end conditions without trying them. Sometimes the whole ecosphere will damp down to a low level where only microbial life-forms can be supported. That happened in the first half dozen attempts out here. And there was always the possibility of a real anomaly, a thriving, stable ecosphere that seemed to be heading to an end-point equal in vigor to the Earth biosphere, but grossly different from it."

"Ecosphere Nine?" I said.

"You've got it. That one was first established four months ago, with its own initial mix of macro and micro life-forms. Almost from the beginning it began to show strange oscillatory behavior—cyclic patterns of development that weren't exactly repeating. It reminded me when I saw it of the life cycle and aggregation patterns of the amoebic slime molds, such as *Dictyostelium discoideum,* though you may be more reminded of the behavior of the Belousov-Zhabotinsky chemical reaction, or of the Oregonator and Brusselator systems. They all have limit cycles around stable attractor conditions."

He must have seen the expression on my face. "Well, let's just say that the behavior of Ecosphere Nine originally had some resemblance to phenomena in the literature. But it isn't in a stable limit cycle. The man who wrote to me was worried by that, because he was one of the people who would live in Nine's habitat. He called me and asked if I would make a trip out here and look at Nine, without telling anyone back home where I was going—he had promised to keep this secret, just as all the others had.

"I agreed, and I must say I was fascinated by the whole project. When I arrived here, ten days ago, I was greeted very warmly—almost embarrassingly warmly—by Marcia Seretto, and shown Nine with great pride. In her eagerness to show me how my ideas had been implemented it did not occur to her immediately to ask why I was here. Nine was doing wonderfully well as a possible space habitat, easily sustaining the three humans inside it. But I realized at once that it hadn't stabilized. And it has still not stabilized. It is *evolving,* and evolving fast. I have no idea of its end state, but I do know this: the life cycles in Ecosphere Nine are more efficient than those on Earth and that means they are biologically more *aggressive.* I pointed that out to Marcia, and five days ago I recommended action."

A door slammed downstairs and I heard a hubbub of voices.

"What did you recommend?" asked Tom. He ignored the downstairs noise.

"That the human occupants of Nine be removed from it at once. And that the whole ecosphere be sterilized. I appealed to the staff to support my views. But I didn't realize at the time how things are run here. Marcia controls everything, and I think she is insane. She violently opposed my suggestions, and to prove her point that there is no danger she herself went in to Ecosphere Nine. She is there now, together with the man who brought me out here. And she insisted that I be held here. No one will say for how long, or what will happen to me next."

There was a clatter of footsteps on the spiral staircase and Scott burst into the room followed by the other four who had brought us here. His face was pale, but he was obviously relieved when he saw all three of us quietly seated at the table.

"You lied," he said to me. "You have nothing to do with our Philadelphia chapter, or any other. You have to come with me. Marcia wants to talk to you. Both of you."

"What about me?" said Lockyer.

"She didn't say anything about seeing you."

"Well, I need to talk to her." He stood up. "Let's go."

"We're not supposed to take you."

"We won't go if Lockyer doesn't," I said quickly. "You'll have to drag us."

Scott and the others looked agonized. They weren't at all the types to approve of violence, but they had to follow orders.

"All right," said Scott at last. "All of you. Come on."

He led the three of us downstairs, with the others close behind. I expected to go back to the dome and peer in again through a cleared patch of wall panel, but instead we headed for the main building. I looked across at the dome. It was almost four in the afternoon and the sun was lower in the sky. The dome's internal lights must be on, for its panels were glowing now with a mottling of pale purples and greens.

When we had entered the main building earlier in the day it had seemed deserted. Now it swarmed with people. The entrance area had been equipped with a 48-inch TV projection screen, a TV camera, and about twenty chairs. Men and women were sitting on the chairs, staring silently at the screen. They were all in their early twenties and they all had the same squeaky-clean airhead look that we had first noticed in Scott.

As the main attraction we were led to chairs in the front row, and found ourselves staring up at the screen.

What we were looking at had to be the interior of Ecosphere Nine. There was a purple-green tinge to the air, as though it were filled with microscopic floating dust motes, and as the camera inside Nine panned across the interior I could see peculiar mushroom-shaped plants, three or four feet high, rising from the floor. And that floor was nothing like the soil we had seen in Ecosphere Eight. It was a fuzzy, wispy carpet of pale green and white, as though the whole area had been planted with alfalfa sprouts. As I watched, the carpet rippled and began to change color to a darker tone.

Lockyer grunted and leaned forward, but before the color change was complete the camera had zoomed in on three figures sitting on the floor near the far side of the dome. It focused still closer, so that only Marcia Seretto was in the field of view.

She must have been able to see exactly what was happening in the room we were in, because she at once pointed her finger at us. "I gave no instructions for *him* to be brought here," she said in a hoarse voice. The golliwog face was angry. "Can't you obey the simplest directive?"

"The other two refused to come without Professor Lockyer." Scott was close to groveling. "I thought the best thing to do was bring all three of them."

"I was the one who insisted on being here, Marcia," said Lockyer. He was not at all put out by her manner and he was studying her closely. "And I was quite right to do so. You have to get out of Nine—at once. Take a look at yourself, and listen to yourself. Look around you at the air. You're inhaling spores all the time, the air is full of them, and God knows what they'll do to you. And look at those fungi—if they are still fungi—like nothing you've ever seen before. The habitat is changing faster than ever."

She glared out of the screen at him. "Professor Lockyer, I respect you as a teacher, but on matters like this you don't know what you are talking about. I feel fine, the people in here with me feel fine. This is just what we have been looking for, a small habitat that will support humans and is perfect for use in space." She waved her arm. "Take a close look. We have more efficient energy utilization than we ever dreamed of, and that means we can make more compact living environments."

"Marcia, didn't you understand what I said?" Lockyer was not the type to raise his voice, but he spoke more slowly and clearly, as though to a small child. "You're not in a stable environment, as you seem to think. You are involved with a different attractor from any you've seen before, and everything in the ecosphere will be governed by it. You hear me? *The habitat is evolving.* And you form part of the habitat. If you remain there, neither I nor anyone else can predict what is going to happen. You have to get out—now."

She ignored him completely. "As for you two," she said to me and Tom. "I don't know why you came here and I don't much care. You represent a sheer nuisance and I'm not going to allow you to interfere with our work."

"So what are you going to do with us?" I asked.

"We don't owe you one thing. No one asked you two to come here, no one wanted you to come here. We'll decide if you leave and when you leave." Her protruding eyes bulged farther than ever and she rapped out: "What we're doing is more important than any individual. But I'll listen to you. If you can offer any reason why you shouldn't be held until we're ready to let you go, tell me now."

The force of personality, even through a TV link, was frightening. It made my nerves jangle and I could think of nothing at all to say. The surprise came from Tom.

"Professor Lockyer was your professor, wasn't he?" he said quietly. "The spiritual father of the Habitat League."

"What of it?"

"He provided you with the original idea for habitats, and the original designs for them. He's one of the world experts on microbial lifeforms, far more knowledgeable than anyone here. When he says it's dangerous in Nine, shouldn't you believe him?"

"I respect Professor Lockyer. But he has no experience with habitats of this size. And he's wrong about Nine." Marcia glared at us. "Anything else?"

When we did not speak she nodded and said, "Scott, take them back. All three of them. And then I want you here."

Within ten minutes we were back upstairs in the windowless build-

238 / GEORGIA ON MY MIND and other places

ing and sitting again at the same table. The thick outer door on the ground floor had been locked, and two women members of the project had been left outside as guards. They had a radio unit with them, and knowing Marcia's style it wouldn't have surprised me if the two of them were expected to watch us all night.

Lockyer picked up his wine glass, still half-full from our rapid departure. "At least we know where we are with Marcia."

"She's a maniac," I said. "How long does she intend to stay in that habitat?"

"Maybe months. Certainly weeks."

"Continuously?"

He nodded. "She has to. That's the whole point about the habitat being a complete ecosphere. She's part of it, and if she leaves she upsets the thermal and material balance. Also, anyone who goes in and out provides a disturbance of another type, too: they carry foreign organisms. Even if it's only bacteria or viruses, every new living entry destroys the totally sealed nature of the habitat."

I was listening with half an ear and trying to think of ways we might get away. But Tom came to full attention and grabbed my arm hard enough to hurt. "Are you saying what I think you are?" he said to Lockyer. "When Marcia Seretto comes out of Ecosystem Nine, she'll bring out with her anything that happens to be in there."

"Roughly speaking. Of course, I'm talking mainly at a microorganism level. She won't come out carrying plants and fungi."

"But you have no idea which part of the habitat is the 'aggressive' part. For all you know, when Marcia and the others step out of that habitat they'll be carrying with them the seeds of something that is more efficient and vigorous than the natural biosphere here on Earth. The damned thing could take over the whole planet. It'll be the Mega-Mother they talked about in that letter, wiping out the natural biosphere—and maybe we won't be able to live in it."

Lockyer put down his glass and frowned at the table. "I don't think so," he said at last. "The chances are, any ecosystem that works in the habitat won't be well-suited to control the Earth's biosphere. If it were, it should have occurred naturally during biological history."

Then he was silent for a much longer interval, and when he looked up his face was troubled. "But I am reminded of one thing. Marcia had an excellent understanding of recombinant DNA techniques. If she has been using them, to create tailored forms that provide efficient energy utilization and a more efficient ecosphere . . ."

"Then we'll all be in trouble when she comes out—and the longer she stays in there, the worse the odds." Tom jumped to his feet. "We can't risk wiping out Earth life, even if the chances are only one in a million that it will happen. We have to get the people out of Nine—and sterilize it."

"Sure. How do we get out of *here* for starters?" I said.

But Tom was already rushing down the spiral stairs. By the time I followed him he was hurtling toward the heavy outside door. He hit it at full speed, all two hundred and thirty pounds of him. It didn't cave in or fly open, but it certainly shivered on its hinges.

Tom hammered at it with both fists. "Open up!" he roared. "Open up!"

Only an idiot or a genius would expect jailers to respond to a command like that, but the Habitat League members were different—or maybe they were just used to obeying orders.

"What do you want?" said a nervous voice.

"We have to get out. There's a—a f-fire in here."

There was a scream of horror from the other side of the door, and a rattling of a key. Before the door could fully open Tom was pushing through. The two women were standing there, mouths gaping.

I tried to move past Tom. I knew what would happen next. He could never bring himself to hit a woman and he would just stand there. They had been foolish enough to let us out, but now they would either shout for help over the radio or run for the other building—and they were used to being at ten thousand feet. We would never keep up. It was up to me to stop them.

I had underestimated Tom. He reached out and grabbed the girls by the neck, one in each hand. While I watched in astonishment he banged their heads ruthlessly together and dropped the women half-stunned to the floor.

This was Tom, the gentlest of men! I stared at him in disbelief. I thought, *You've come a long way, baby.*

But he was off, blundering away in the semidarkness toward the dome that housed Ecosystem Nine. "Take care of them," he shouted over his shoulder. "I need five minutes."

They didn't need much taking care of. They were down in the dirt, flinching away when I bent toward them. I picked up the radio and swung it by its strap against the wall of the building. The case cracked open and the batteries flew out. When I bent over one of the women and grabbed her arm, she moaned in fear and wriggled away from me.

"Inside," I said. With Lockyer's help—he had finally sauntered downstairs and out of the building—I pushed them through the door, slammed it, and turned the key. Then I walked—slowly, I might need my wind in a minute or two—toward the main building. Tom had said he needed five minutes. If anything had been sent over the radio before I destroyed it, I wasn't sure I could guarantee him five seconds.

I sneaked closer in the gathering darkness with Lockyer just behind me. The door of the building remained closed, and there was no sign of activity there. I crept forward to look in the window. Three people sat quietly reading.

"The dome!" said Lockyer in an urgent whisper. Then he moved rapidly away from me.

I looked after him. The third dome, the one that housed Nine, was glowing bright pink in the night. The internal lighting level had been turned way up.

After one more glance at the main building—all still quiet there—I headed after Lockyer. If one of the project teams happened to be outside, they would surely be drawn to the bright dome. I could help Tom better there than I could anywhere else.

He was standing by the dome controls and trying to peer in through one of the wall panels. The telephone was in his hand, but he was not using it.

"Can't get any response," he said when he saw me. "I called inside, told Marcia to get the hell out of there while they could. But not a word back. Not one word."

I saw that the illumination level on the control panel had been turned to its maximum and the internal temperature was set at sterilization level—three hundred and twenty Celsius, hot enough to kill any organism that I knew about, hot enough even to destroy the Mega-Mother. The panel control knobs were broken off and lay on the floor.

"Tom, you'll kill them."

"I hope not. I warned them. I'm not going to stop. I won't stop until Ecosphere Nine is burned clean, and anyway I *can't* stop it—I buggered the controls here." He turned to Lockyer. "These people all respect you, they'll at least listen. Go back to the building where they have the TV, and see what's going on inside Nine. Tell them all that Marcia has to get out in the next ten minutes, otherwise she'll be cooked."

Lockyer didn't flap easily. He nodded and set off without a word. I stood around useless for a little while, and finally followed him. There was nothing to be done here and at least I could confirm what Lockyer said to the others.

The door was wide open when I got there and the building reception area was empty. Lockyer stood frozen in front of the big TV screen. It was still turned on, with the dome's camera set to provide a general view of the interior. The glare of lights at their maximum setting showed every detail.

Nine had changed again. No part of it resembled any Earth plant or animal that I could recognize. The floating spores were gone but the air was filled with tiny, wriggling threadworms, supported on gossamer strands attached to the walls and ceiling. The fuzzy carpet of green and white alfalfa sprouts had gone, too, passing through a color change and a riotous growth. The sprouts had formed long, wispy tendrils of purple-black, threading the whole interior and wriggling like a tangle of thin snakes across the floor and up the walls. They were connected to the squat mushroom plants, and small black spheres hung on them like beads on a necklace.

The increased lighting level seemed to be driving the whole eco-sphere to a frenzy of activity. A crystalline silver framework of lines and nodes was forming, linking all parts of the dome into a tetrahedral lat-tice. The habitat pulsed with energy. As I watched a new wave of black spheres began to inch their way toward the middle of the dome, where a great cluster of them sat on a lumpy structure near the dome's center.

It took me a few seconds to recognize that structure. It was formed of Marcia and her two companion crew members.

They sat quietly on the floor of the dome. Black spheres formed a dense layer over their bodies, and long tendrils of wriggling white grew from ears, mouths, and nostrils. Their skins had a wrinkled, withered look.

I grabbed at Lockyer's arm. "We have to get back to the dome," I exclaimed. "Turn off the heat. Marcia and the others are still inside and they're . . ."

They're still alive, I was going to say. But when I looked at them I could not believe it.

"No point now," said Lockyer in a hushed voice. "It's too late." And then, still capable of objective analysis, he added, "Drained. Drained and absorbed. They are on the way to becoming part of the ecosphere. It's evolving faster than ever, accepting everything. Look at the walls."

I saw that the dome's wall panels had an eroded, eaten look. Where the gossamer threads were attached, the hard panel material was being dissolved. In places the plastic support ribbing was almost eaten through. Given a little more time, Ecosphere Nine would break free of the dome's constraint and have access to the vast potential habitat of Earth.

But Nine would not be given time.

The internal temperature was rising rapidly. As we watched the support tendrils began to writhe and convulse. The silver network shivered. Black spheres were thrown free and rolled around on the floor, pulping delicate filaments beneath them. As the mushroom structures split open, ejecting a black fluid that spattered across the interior, it was easy to see the ecosphere as one great organism, sucking in more and more energy from the blazing lights and fighting desperately for survival while the temperature went up and up.

(There was a clatter of footsteps and two men and a woman came into the room. Lockyer and I hardly noticed them. They sensed that something final and terrible was happening and they joined us, staring in horror at the TV screen.)

Ecosphere Nine was losing its battle. The black spheres inflated and burst, throwing off puffs of vapor like popping corn as the internal temperature rose above boiling point. Gossamer threads shrivelled and fell to the floor, long tendrils writhed and withered. In the blistering heat the broken mushroom structures sagged and dwindled, sinking back to floor level.

Steam filled the interior, and in the final moments it was difficult to see; but I was watching when the last spheres fell away from Marcia and her companions, and the tendrils trailed limp from their open mouths. What remained was hardly recognizable as human beings. Their bodies were eaten away, corroded to show the staring white bones of chest and limbs.

And then, quite suddenly, it ended. Tendrils slowed and drooped, spheres lay on the floor like burst balloons. The silver lattice disappeared. Inside the dome, nothing moved but rising steam.

Lockyer felt his way toward one of the metal chairs and collapsed into it. The three camp members next to him clung to each other and wept.

I went outside and called to Tom. "Are you all right?"

"I'm fine but I can't see into the dome. What's happening?"

"It's over," I said. "It's dead. They're all dead."

And then I leaned over in the cold Colorado night, and vomited until I thought I was going to die, too.

I thought that was the end, but of course it was just the beginning.

No one could think of sleep that night. There seemed to be a thousand things to do: police to be informed, families told, the interior of the dome inspected, the bodies recovered.

But none of this could begin until the morning, and some of it would take much longer; the dome needed at least forty-eight hours to cool before anyone could go inside.

Tom, Jason Lockyer, and I went back to our former prison and sat at the table, talking and drinking wine. I didn't ask the vintage or the pedigree, and I didn't care what it would do to my stomach or my liver. I sluiced it down—we all did.

"Thank God it's over," I said, after several minutes of silence.

Lockyer sighed. "Back to the real world. Pity in some ways, I quite like it here. You've no idea how complimented a professor feels when his students appreciate him enough to take his teaching and actually *implement* it. I'll be sorry to leave."

Not a word about wife Eleanor, waiting with her claws out back in Washington.

"I don't think you should leave," said Tom. "In fact, I don't think any of us should leave. It would be irresponsible."

He was sitting with his shirtsleeves rolled up and his hands in a bowl of cold water. There were great bruises on them, from where he had hammered on the metal door, and his fingertips were bloody from tearing off the dome's control knobs.

"But there's nothing to do here now," I said. "With Marcia dead the group will break up."

"I hope not. I hope they will all stay here." Tom looked at Lockyer. "The job's not finished, is it?"

Lockyer shook his head. "I think I know what you mean and no, it's not finished. There is no self-contained ecosphere that can support a human population."

"Who cares?" My mind was boiling over with a hundred dreadful images from the interior of Habitat Nine. I couldn't get out of my head the thought of Marcia and the others, invaded by the organisms of the habitat. Had she realized what was happening to her in those final few minutes before her mind and body succumbed? I hoped not.

"If I have the choice," I went on, "I'll never look at an ecosphere again—never. Let the Ascend Forever people have their fun, but keep me out."

"That's the problem," said Tom. "We can't stay out. No one can. We destroyed Ecosphere Nine, but this group isn't the only one trying to create self-contained habitats. There must be a dozen others around the world."

"At least that," said Lockyer. "The Habitat League used to send me newsletters."

"Fine." I didn't like the expression on Tom's face—all the softness had gone from it. "Let them play. That doesn't mean *we* have to."

"I'm afraid it does," said Tom. "If the end-point for the biological forms of Ecosphere Nine is a stable attractor, it can arise from a whole variety of different starting conditions. So if people keep on experimenting, Nine can show up again. We were lucky. Nine didn't break free and come into contact with Biosphere One—the whole Earth—but it came close. If one did get free you couldn't sterilize the Earth the way we did with the chamber."

"But that seems like a case *against* fooling around any more with the ecospheres," I protested. "If more habitats are made here they'll add to the danger of a wild one getting loose."

Lockyer and Tom looked at each other. "She's right, of course," said Lockyer. "But so are you, Tom. We're damned if we do and we're damned if we don't. We have to keep working, so we'll understand ways that ecospheres can develop and learn how to handle dangerous forms."

"And we need to find a biosphere that people can live in in space," said Tom. "We're going to need it—if anything like Nine ever gets free on Earth."

That was two months ago. Tom, Jason Lockyer, and I went back to Washington, but only to clean up unfinished business that the three of us left behind. Then we returned to Colorado.

Amazingly, nearly half the staff of the project elected to stay on. They are a dedicated group, putting the project ahead of everything. Even before Marcia brainwashed them, they were all space fanatics. Thanks to them, the project picked up again with hardly a hitch. Ecospheres Ten, Eleven, and Twelve are already in operation. None of them looks particularly promising—and none looks anything like Nine.

Naturally, every aspect of ecosphere development is closely monitored. Jason Lockyer supervises every biological change and approves every technique used. It is hard to imagine how any group could be more careful.

And Tom runs the whole show—shy, introverted, overweight Tom Walton. But he is not the man I met in his stamp shop in Washington. He has lost thirty pounds, he doesn't stammer, he never mentions stamps. He does not have Marcia's domineering manner, but he makes up for that with his sense of urgency. And if he pushes others, he pushes himself harder. Like Ecosphere Nine, he is still changing, developing, evolving. He will become—I don't know what.

I'm not sure I like the new Tom Walton—the Tom I helped to shape—as well as the old one. Sometimes I feel that I, like Marcia, created my own monster, so that now under his leadership we must all become God, the Builder of Worlds.

And also, perhaps, their annihilator.

(It was Jason Lockyer, the calmest and most cerebral of our group, who recalled Robert Oppenheimer's quotation of Vishnu from the *Bhagavad Gita,* at the time of the testing of the first atomic bomb: "I am become Death, the Destroyer of Worlds.")

Which brings my thoughts, again and again, to Marcia. How much did she understand at the very end, as Nine took her for its own and the world around her faded? Surely she knew at least this much, that she had created a monster. But Nine was *her* monster, her baby, her private universe, her unique creation, and in some sense she must have loved it. Loved it so much that when logic said the ecosphere must be destroyed, she could not bring herself to do it. She must have somehow justified her actions. What did she say, what did she think, how did she *feel,* in those last minutes?

I hope that I will never know.

Afterword to "Destroyer of Worlds"

One April day in 1989 I was driving my car around Washington, D. C., when the radio played a piece by Debussy called "The Golliwog's Cakewalk." Instead of listening to the music I started to ponder the word, *Golliwog*. It conjured up a mental image of a fuzzy-haired black-face doll, something I recalled from childhood but had not seen for at least twenty years. It occurred to me that "The Golliwog's Something-or-other" (I was not sure of the missing word) would be an intriguing title for a story.

At the time I was for some obscure reason reading about the history of the postal services, so my mind filled in the last word of the title as "Stamp" or "Roll" or something else Post Officeish. I wrote the story and sold it to Gardner Dozois at *Asimov's* with the title "The Golliwog Roll." Only after it was sold did someone point out to us that, although in the United States the word "golliwog" has no particular weight, in England it carries definite and unpleasant racist overtones. We changed the title, I must admit a bit reluctantly on my part, and the story became "Destroyer of Worlds."

A couple of years later the story was published in the Ace collection, *Isaac Asimov's Earth,* and in due course I received a check. The stub of the check bore this simple message: "Charles Sheffield: Destroyer of Words." The money was nice. But why did Gardner have to tell the truth about me?

THE FIFTEENTH STATION OF THE CROSS

THE RULER OF the Earth should not look like this. Weak, emaciated, yellow-faced, lolling in a wheelchair. Puladi was aware of the contradiction. Eight billion people under his absolute control; and one body which refused to do the bidding of its owner's fierce will.

Puladi's internal defenses were crumbling at the same time as his external ones became more and more impregnable. He sat in a room whose outer structure justified every superlative: four hundred feet by four hundred feet, with a ceiling fifty feet high and a floor that shone glassy, empty, and impervious. The walls were plain, polished steel. Recessed fluorescents in the high ceiling illuminated every square inch with a harsh and uniform light.

At the room's exact center stood the metal box of the inner chamber; not small—it was forty feet across and ten feet high—but dwarfed by its surroundings. Anyone who entered the outer room must cross an unprotected sixty yards of featureless bare floor to the single and sealed inner entrance, controlled from within.

Puladi was frowning, in thought more than in anger. He watched through concealed cameras as a white-coated woman and a tall, gray-garbed man crossed the expanse of the outer chamber and approached the inner door.

Near their destination, they slowed. There was a muttered conversation between them, easily picked up by sensitive wall microphones. At last the man stepped reluctantly forward and rapped on the metal panel.

Puladi touched a button, one of scores that sat in the armrests of his padded chair. The views of the outer room vanished from the bank of screens on the wall in front of him. The door slid open.

The tall man entered, stooping and blinking as his eyes began to adjust from the outside glare to a dim-lit interior. He caught a glimpse in the background of the rear of the room, with its bed and medical station, its food and disposal system. Then his eyes were drawn to the slight figure before him, sitting in the wheeled chair and propped on a pile of soft cushions and water pillows.

"Dr. Salino, is it not?" Puladi's voice was weak, but full of a chilly authority. "I assume that you have the results."

"Yes, Excellency."

"No title. I do not use one. I am Puladi. The tests—what do they show?" And, when Salino shook his head but did not speak, "Sit down. I command it. And *talk*."

The tall man did not so much sit, as collapse back into a hard chair half a dozen feet from Puladi's own. He raised his hands to his face, and they were trembling. "Excellency—Puladi. There is bad news. The worst news. It is spreading. Again."

"I suspected as much. How long?"

The tall man shook his head again, but said nothing.

"Ernesto Salino. Look at me." Puladi's eyes were brown and glowing. It was said that no one could encounter those dark orbs without feeling fear. Salino looked, and at last Puladi nodded.

"Good. I asked a question: How long do I have? And before you answer, let me inform you of one thing. You have heard, I am sure, that people are afraid to give me bad news. It is true that I do not welcome it. Who does? But the fate of one who gives me such news is as nothing, compared to the fate of any man or woman who lies to me. So speak— and be assured that there will be no third asking of my question."

"You have about one month. Three at most." Salino's voice was faint and husky. "That is of course with regular transfusions, with everything that we know how to do."

"What about the research program?"

"I reviewed it this morning. Too slow, even with every resource poured into it. I think that in fifteen years, perhaps even in ten, there will be a successful treatment and cure. Horst Calvin believes that he is making real progress. But today—"

"Today, I have a month. Can you guarantee that?"

"No. Nor can any human. But it is our best estimate."

"*Our* estimate?"

"Mine. And Dr. Vissarion's."

"Who is, I assume, waiting outside to hear the result of this meeting. As your superior, did she order you to come in and tell me about the results and unfavorable prognosis, rather than doing it herself?"

"Sir—"

"*Did she?*"

"Yes, Puladi. She commanded it."

"Very good. You are learning to tell the truth." Puladi lifted his gaze away from the tall doctor, and seemed to speak into the air above his chair. "*Ekaterina Vissarion should have come in herself. That means she has not been doing her duty. I do not wish to see her again.*"

"Oh! P-P—"

"Not you, Salino." Puladi's piercing eyes returned to the other man. "The guards will not remove you. In fact, I will be seeing you frequently, since you have just become my senior physician. Administrator Kelb will provide you with a complete briefing on your duties, later today." He held out a wasted right arm. "Meanwhile, you will complete my treatment. And you will also return here at this time tomorrow. You must keep up my strength, because I have much work to do." As Salino stood up and nervously gripped the proffered arm, Puladi continued in a musing tone: "Fifteen years, you say. Fifteen years from now, Dr. Salino, do you really think there will be a cure?"

Salino nodded. "Yes, Puladi."

"Thank you. That is most interesting. Continue."

As the perfusion IV attached itself to his right arm, Puladi's left hand began to dance across the keys in the arm of the chair. Data bank linkages flickered on the forty screens that covered the wall in front of him. He seemed to be seeking something very specific. Directories with the titles "BREAKTHROUGH AREAS," "PRIORITIES," "CHRONIC ANOMALIES," "TEMPORAL RESEARCH," and "FUNDING STATUS" flashed into existence on five screens. As the cursors moved through them, other screens provided real-time images from half a dozen research laboratories. Puladi merged six files. A new directory, "CHRONOCLASTIC FLOW" suddenly popped up on all screens simultaneously. Puladi grunted. He became fully absorbed in reviewing its subdirectories.

Ernesto Salino breathed a prayer of thanks as he bent to his task. At last, with those eyes off him and Puladi focused elsewhere, he had some hope of performing competent medical work.

Twelve hours later, Rustum Belur sat facing Puladi. He was weary, nervous, and utterly bewildered. He had left the Calcutta lab tired after a long day's work, eaten a light dinner, and gone straight to bed. Two hours later he had been roused, forced to dress, and flown on a high-speed personal transport halfway around the world. Now he was meeting a man he had never in his life expected to encounter—the reclusive figure who ran the world.

And that man seemed to be dying. Puladi was terribly thin, jaundiced in complexion, and apparently too weak to move from his chair.

"Help you?" Belur said again. "Excellency—"

"Puladi," whispered the man standing behind him. It was Administrator Kelb, the burly, lion-faced man who had brought him into the room. "Puladi must be called only *Puladi*."

"Puladi, there must be some mistake. I cannot help you. I am not a physician—I am a *physicist*."

"I know what you are." Puladi seemed almost too frail to talk. "You are Professor Belur, of the Calcutta Institute for Advanced Studies. You are the originator of the theory of chronoclastic flows. You are also, according to the research data banks, the creator of a machine that can develop and exploit such flows. True, or false?"

"True. It is called the Chronoclast. But the machine—"

"Is now being brought here, from your laboratory. You have used it to transport objects, living and nonliving, through time. True, or false?"

"True. Small objects, and small creatures."

"But that is not, as I understand it, a basic limitation?"

"No. It is a function of available energy supply, and the chronoclastic rigidity coefficients—which determine how difficult it is to fracture time, locally. Puladi, I do not understand—"

"You will. When the Chronoclast arrives, you will give me a demonstration. Meanwhile, tell me this. Would it be possible to carry an individual, together possibly with a piece of medical equipment, through time; for, let us say, fifteen years?"

"A human being? Sir, we have never attempted anything so big. The risk, to that person—"

"Answer my question, if you please." Puladi's eyes seemed to glow with light and draw Belur into them.

The professor sank back in the chair. "A human, across fifteen years? We have never carried anything for more than two years—and nothing bigger than a few grams. The energy goes as the cube of the mass, and it is quadratic in the transport time. It might deplete the local chronic supply. And it would need huge power."

"Assume that the whole of the world's energy is available to you."

"Then it can probably be done." Belur was silent for a few seconds, and when he spoke again his voice was stronger. "I will be more definite. It can be done. There is only one possible complication. The chronoclastic viewer allows us to look to an exact moment of time, but in the time-transport process itself there is a slight uncertainty. You might find that you aim to carry something across two years exactly, but the Chronoclast will bring it from two years plus or minus a few hours."

"That is no problem. I have one other question. Can you identify a specific individual."

"Certainly, if you know what he or she looks like, and you can tell me *where* to look, and *when* to look. That is the whole purpose of the chronoclastic viewer—to see and specify just what is to be transported."

"So now I can answer your question, by telling you exactly how you must help me. Once we have provided an adequate energy supply for your equipment, I will give you sufficient information for you to identify an individual—almost certainly, it will be a physician, Dr. Horst Calvin. I will also give you the precise coordinates of his laboratory office. You will then operate your Chronoclast to bring him here, from a time fifteen years in the future, together with any necessary medical—"

"The *future*." Rustum Belur jerked upright.

"Correct. I assume that the Chronoclast operates as easily on the past or the future?"

"No! Bringing something from the future is *impossible*. The future is—" Belur waved his arms in the empty air around him "—the future is not *real*. It represents only *potentialities*, endless new possible branches every second. Only the *past* is real. Only the past is accessible to the Chronoclast. My reports make all that very clear. You don't know what you are talking about, if you suggest that something might be brought from the future."

Kelb, standing behind Rustum Belur, growled and grabbed the professor by the shoulders. "Puladi, I'll get him right out of here. The guards will take care of him."

"Not yet. Not quite yet. Belur, are you sure that your reports clearly indicated that the Chronoclast has access only to the past?"

"I swear it. On my life."

"On your life it will be. But I have been a careless reader. Or perhaps I have been guilty of wishful thinking. Leave him alone, Kelb. And sit down, Belur. When the equipment arrives, I still want to see that demonstration."

He lifted his arm, and stared at its veined skin and prominent bones. "And now I need time to think. Perhaps I will still want to use the Chronoclast. When high probability options vanish, it is time to consider long shots."

The prototype Chronoclast, fully assembled, had proved too big for the inner chamber. But Puladi would not allow it to be moved far away. It had been put together in the outer room, and sat as a dull jumble of gray and green that sprawled across fifty feet of floor. The transport chamber stood at its edge, a horizontal cylinder ten feet long and six feet high. Thick cables snaked to it from an augmented power supply.

Puladi, reclining in his wheeled chair, stared impatiently at the swirling, misted surface of the cylinder.

"How much longer?"

"I do not know." Rustum Belur sounded subdued and nervous. In the four days since his arrival he had learned that assistants of Puladi might be valued, but that did not mean they were not expendable. Two men had bungled the arrangements for delivery of the Chronoclast. They had sought to conceal the fact; and they had disappeared.

I do not wish to see him again, spoken by Puladi to the apparently empty air; and the named individual was seen no more.

Belur remembered Salino's advice: "Tell the truth. You may get away with one or two pieces of bad news; but a lie, never. And you should speak only when Puladi demands it."

"The flows must stabilize before the cocoon can be safely opened," Belur went on. "With small objects and short transport times, that takes only a few seconds. But with something this size, and over so long a period—it could be hours, or even days."

"Then wait here. Both of you. I have work to do." Puladi touched the keypad on the chair's arm, and it swiveled to carry him back to the inner chamber.

"Me, too, Puladi?" Salino, in his surprise, broke one of his own rules.

"Naturally. When it is safe to open the cocoon, you will both enter. You, Belur, will confirm the identification. And you, Salino, will check on the medical parameters. I do not expect that we will introduce to our time some source of old disease, but I want to be sure of that before I am exposed. Inform me when your work is complete, and I will return."

The gray cylinder remained misted for five hours. When the cloudy swirls dwindled and the surface cleared, Rustum Belur broke the seals with hands almost too nervous to function. He led the way in. Ernesto Salino followed, fingering his diagnostic palette like the beads of a rosary.

When they came out, an hour later, Belur was so close to collapse that he had to support himself on Salino's shoulder.

"I am a dead man," he said, over and over. "I am a dead man. A dead man. What can I do?"

"Tell the truth. You can do nothing else." Salino was worried about guilt by association. He believed that Belur was doomed, but for himself there was a faint gleam of hope. "Come on. Let's get it over with."

Puladi's calm, when he rolled his wheeled chair forward to peer inside the cylinder of the Chronoclast, was as terrifying as any rage. He took a long, thoughtful look at the brown-skinned unconscious figure lying naked within, and turned to Rustum Belur.

"You told me that you were absolutely sure of the identification."

"I thought that I was." Belur had passed beyond fear to resignation. "I checked scores of times. I fixed the right moment, the right place, the right background. I could not have made a mistake."

"And yet you bring me this." Puladi waved a dismissive hand. "Not a man, but a child. Not the hope of a miracle cure, but a fiasco."

"Puladi, I cannot explain it. In all my experiments with the Chronoclast, nothing like this has ever happened before. All I can suggest is that some new phenomenon presents itself when the transport time is very large. We went so far back—more than two thousand years—we were completely beyond all earlier experience. . . ."

"You are quite sure that this is the wrong one—that he is not much older than he looks? Salino?"

"No, Puladi. The man that we wanted was in his thirties. I estimate this one's age at fifteen."

"Not a child, then, or a man. A youth. But quite useless to me. You have failed, Belur."

Administrator Kelb had appeared from the inner chamber, and

Puladi turned to him and pointed at the cylinder of the Chronoclast. "Kelb, get rid of that lump of flesh in there. It is of no value."

"Yes, Puladi. And for the rest . . ." Kelb stared accusingly at Rustum Belur and Ernesto Salino.

"The youth may not be useless." Salino spoke rapidly, and wondered if he was being a fool as he did so. When Puladi was angry, no one should draw attention to himself. But now he had gone too far to pull back. As Puladi glared, he went on, "Just as you ordered, I checked his medical parameters. He is healthy, and he will recover consciousness in the next half hour—"

"He will be gone long before that," Kelb said softly. "I have my orders."

"—but the important thing is his *blood.*" Salino blundered on. "It is the same rare group as your own, Puladi, and it matches you far more closely at every physiological and chemical level than anything that we have available in the banks. If we used *him*—in direct coupling, vein to vein and with a very slow transfer rate—it would be much better than what I have been able to do."

It seemed at first as though Puladi had not been listening. He was eyeing Rustum Belur. "And you, Professor. If you failed to bring me what I needed, is there a future here for you? I think not." He stared up to the ceiling, while Rustum Belur wailed in hopeless fear.

And Puladi smiled, a skeletal show of teeth in the jaundiced face. "No future *here.* So you can return to Calcutta, Professor. Go to your institute, and tell them all of Puladi's great mercy. You failed me, but who knows? Perhaps I will find some future use for you, and for the Chronoclast."

Kelb grunted in surprise, while Belur gasped and fell to his knees. Puladi ignored both of them. He swiveled his chair to face Ernesto Salino. "You talk of blood transfer at a very slow rate. Hours?"

"Many hours. It is best done overnight."

"Very good. We will begin tomorrow." Puladi touched his armrest keypad, and the wheeled chair started for the inner chamber. "But I have no desire to converse with him," he said over his shoulder, "even if that were possible. Before you bring him to me, sedate him; and keep him sedated as long as he is with me."

At three in the morning, Puladi was wide awake. That was not unusual. Easy sleep was a rare prize, denied him since his youth. What was unusual was the feeling of uneasiness that possessed his mind, as he wandered around the world and checked its status through his remote mobile monitors.

The miniature cameras returned sounds and images from a thousand places, logical and illogical sites for possible dissent or insurrection: homes and bars and hotels and restaurants, freezing log cabins and tall tents and stifling squat mud huts, churches and chapels and synagogues, hospitals and prisons and asylums and refuge shelters, on and under land and sea, in the air and out in the vacuum of space.

Puladi performed this surveillance nightly, rarely visiting the same place twice, always alert for the tiny anomalies that spoke to him—and only to him—of civil unrest.

Everywhere was calm. Nowhere could he find anything unusual. Out of habit, he culled a couple of hundred troublesome cases, giving oral instructions to the guards as to who should be taken and where they could be found. Two hundred was nothing, compared with any night during a time of major purge. Yet his jaundiced skin still prickled with a sense of trouble. He checked the temperature of the room. It was exactly as usual; still the sweat ran down his neck, and was clammy on his face and hands. He could find no easy position on the piled cushions and pillows.

Maybe it was the effect of the change in medical treatment. Or maybe it was the simple presence of another person, even an unconscious one, in his sleeping quarters.

Puladi glanced at his own arm, following the narrow tube of the perfusion IV across to the bed mounted next to his wheeled chair. The other end of the IV was attached to a slim brown arm. The metered flow was invisible, but every second a drop of new blood was pumped across to enter Puladi's body.

He activated a ceiling light, and shone it on the face of the youth. The boy's nose was sharp, his lips thin. They were parted to show a gleam of white teeth. The eyelids flickered, even as Puladi watched, and there was the faint murmur of an exhalation through the open mouth.

The stimulus, surely, of the brighter light. The youth was soundly sedated, and he had not moved since the bed was wheeled in. But the face showed a peace that Puladi envied.

He dimmed the overhead light, turned off the bank of displays that covered the wall, and watched the sleeping face. When had he known such tranquillity, such content? He could not remember a time, ever.

He gazed, and brooded on the distant past. Finally, without knowing it, he fell asleep.

He was still sleeping, to Salino's amazement, when the doctor checked the telemetry signals from Puladi's body at eight the next morning.

Puladi *never* slept so late! Terrified, Salino reviewed all the monitored outputs.

They were fine—better than fine, almost unbelievable. Puladi had been losing weight steadily, fifty grams a day, for months, while his ion balances oscillated randomly and his liver chemistry moved farther and farther away from acceptable levels. Today he was a hundred grams heavier, and all his functions showed a slight but definite improvement.

It was the new blood, it had to be, so close in its properties to Puladi's own. The temptation to wake the ruler, to tell him the good news at once, was strong, but Salino knew better. Sleep, easy natural sleep, was better for Puladi than any medication.

The physician waited impatiently by the telemetry unit, until there were clear signs from Puladi's breathing and eye movement patterns that the ruler was waking. At that point he hurried to the inner chamber and rapped on the metal panel. It slid open. As he went in he said, "Puladi, I have good news—"

"You do not need to say it." Puladi smiled, close to laughing aloud. "I *feel* it. For the first time in years, I am hungry. What can I eat?"

"Anything that you like—in small amounts. Your stomach is not used to real meals." Salino was busy, unhooking the IV and checking the sleeping body on the bed. He glanced at the *in situ* monitors, and nodded his approval.

"He is all right?" Puladi asked. His smile had vanished, and he showed a hint of anxiety.

"He is fine—young, and strong, and healthy. You took only half a liter of his blood, in ten hours. It will be safe to repeat that, three days from now."

"When will he waken?"

"As soon as I provide the appropriate stimulant." Salino was preparing to wheel the bed out of the chamber. "I assume that you are willing to allow him to be awake, when he is not with you?"

"More than that." Puladi raised himself on his mound of cushions, and stared again at the face of the youth. "I've changed my mind about sedation. It's not much to my taste, to be connected to a human vegetable all through the night. Does he have intelligence?"

"Normal, so far as I can tell."

"Then next time, there will be no need to bring him here unconscious."

"But you will not be able to talk to each other. He was awake for a while yesterday, and no one understood a word that he said—naturally, he speaks only the crude babble of his time and place."

"That's exactly what language teaching machines are for. I'll instruct Kelb to make one available to you, something with a maximum modern vocabulary. I don't want you to fry his brain, but I do want him able to talk and listen, next time you bring him here."

"Very good." Salino pushed the bed in front of him, but at the door of the chamber he paused and glanced over his shoulder.

"Yes?"

"Puladi, it would be easy to lie to you."

"At your peril. What is it?"

"I do not want to give you false hopes. The new blood has produced a great improvement, but it will surely be only temporary. The prognosis is much the same."

"How long?"

"Maybe it has increased from one month, to four."

"Then keep working on it, Dr. Salino. For your sake as much as mine." And, when the other man stared at him in perplexity, "How many days do you think you will have left, when I am gone? Take a look at Kelb, at Mavermine, at Jaworsky, at any of the Administrators who can't wait for me to die. Someone will win in the battle for the succession. But whoever it is, do you think that you will become *his* physician, as you are mine? Or is it more likely that you will be snuffed out like a candle, as someone who was close to me?"

Puladi laughed. He was feeling too well to take anything very seriously—a dangerous mood, as he recognized. "Keep me, alive, doctor. I can get along without you. But you will not get along without me."

When the bed was wheeled in three days later, Puladi stared at it and turned on Salino.

"What the devil are you doing? I told you that this time he was not to be sedated."

"He is not sedated." Salino was pushing the wheeled bed, and he had no hands free. But he shrugged, to express his own amazement. "He is *asleep*. He fell asleep as I was bringing him here."

"Knowing that he was on his way to me? Incredible! Wake him up. At once."

But the slim figure on the bed was already stirring. He yawned hugely, to show the tip of a pink tongue and splendid, even teeth. He sat up and stared all around him.

Puladi saw that his eyes, open at last, were a clear and startling brown, with hints of amber at the inner edge of the irises. The expression on the face was different, too, the placidity of sleep exchanged for an alert confidence.

"Hook us up for the night, Salino," Puladi said, and to the young man on the bed next to him. "Can you understand me yet? Do you know who I am?"

"I can under-stand you." The reply was clear and quick, with only a slight hesitancy on the longest word. "You are Puladi."

"That's a good start. I'm also, so you don't have any doubts about it, the man who brought you here."

"You are the man who is stealing my blood."

Dr. Salino flinched. "I told you to show respect!"

"You also warned me not to lie. Which do you want?"

"I want—I mean, Puladi wants—I assume Puladi wants—"

Salino hesitated, while Puladi sighed and said, "Finish connecting us, doctor, and get out of here. Quickly. I know what Puladi wants, a lot better than you'll ever know." And to the youth sitting up on the bed, "I'm going to be working for much of the night. You will speak only when you are spoken to."

That earned Puladi a cocking of the head and a raising of dark eyebrows. But there was silence as Salino finished his work, made a final check that the remote telemetry system to his own lab was all in order, and at last obtained permission to leave.

"Take your cues from him," Puladi said, as Salino left the chamber. "His boss is gone, and *her* boss is gone, and the two before that are gone."

"Gone." The youth rolled his eyes. "You say *gone,* but you mean dead."

"Quite right. I do mean dead, although I never see it happen. I say the word, and the guards take care of the rest." Puladi glanced along the line of the IV, then switched his attention to the other's face. "You've only been here a short time, and I suppose you haven't learned. You should be afraid of me. You're not. Why aren't you afraid?"

"I was afraid, once, of . . . something. But not anymore. Not of you, not of anything."

"We can change that. Kelb and company were supposed to give you a background briefing along with the language. It looks like they didn't go far enough. How much do you know about me?"

"That you are Puladi, although that is perhaps not your original name. That you are thirty-nine years old. That you have killed many, many men and women. That you run the world, and have done so for eighteen years."

"Not quite. The world has its own power and energy. It runs itself. I *control* the world, which is a much more delicate business. But the rest is accurate. See those displays?" Puladi pointed a bony finger at the wall. "I can look at anything, anywhere, anytime, no matter how much people may imagine it is hidden. I have sensors that appear as a fly on the wall, a dog's eye, an open rose, the flame of a candle. And because I can see so much, anyone but a fool must assume that I can see everything. That is the secret of power: information, and the assumption by others of *complete* information."

"I think that you are boasting."

"Not at all." But Puladi realized, with a rush of self-awareness that he had not felt for years, that the youth on the bed was perhaps right. Certainly, he had been emphasizing his powers. Why did he have this odd need to show off, and to such a nonentity?

"Maybe I am boasting—a little. But everything that I have said is true."

The lad sniffed. "Then if you are so all-powerful, why are you afraid?"

Puladi laughed. If Kelb or Mavermine could hear that! "What makes you think that I am afraid? I don't *fear,* boy, I *am feared.* There's a huge difference. Watch me, now. I'm going to take us on a world tour."

He began to work the keypads in the arms of the chair, varying location and scale and point of view like a master organist. There was no way that the youth on the bed could possibly appreciate just how much skill went into manipulating the sensors, or to juggling among complex data banks; but there were views to offer that alone would be enough to astonish. Puladi swooped from salt mining on the shores of the Dead Sea, to telescopes on the highest peaks of the Karakoram range, to the dark abyssal Pacific trench where the semiorganic submersibles winnowed out high-grade metallic nodules.

Finally he moved to the orbiting monitors that were patiently scanning the surface, inch by inch. He used them to zoom in, so that the view showed the North American continent, narrowed to the central plains, then a sprawling city landscape, and at last to the gold spire on one great building.

"That's us." Puladi froze the display. "We're sitting inside that building, at this very moment. And if you want to see what's happening in any particular room, I can show you. Want to take a look?"

There was no reply. Puladi turned. He saw to his great annoyance that the youth on the bed was sound asleep. How dare he sleep, in the presence of Puladi?

But how young the boy looked, and how peaceful and relaxed. He had said that he was not afraid—and amazingly, he had been telling the truth. A terrified person could not sleep; Puladi knew that very well.

In that same moment he felt a great wave of weariness and tranquillity sweep through him, as though it had transferred instantly along the line of the IV. He yawned—once. The screens on the wall seemed to dance and flicker before his eyes.

Half a minute later he was gone, down into the deepest slumber of his adult life.

"I *think* I am fifteen," said the voice from the darkness. "But we do not—did not—think of years as you count them, and I cannot be sure."

Puladi grunted. The viewing screens were all turned off. He did not have the energy, or maybe it was the desire, to look at them. Three more days had passed, they were deep into the third treatment, and according to Dr. Salino he was physically stronger than he had been for years; but he knew, better than anyone, that the mind controlled the body. He did not feel worse, but he felt *different*. Diffuse, drifting, disembodied.

"Before I was brought here," the voice continued, "I did not know that there could be so many years. We were sure that the world must end, long before two full thousands of years had passed. But it did not. We were wrong about that; about many things."

Puladi touched the IV. He had become so used to it, he hardly knew that it was attached to his arm. The strongest link in the world connected him to that slender figure on the bed, unseen in the darkness: the link of blood. *Blood.* If one had to choose a single word to stand for the whole of human history, could there be a better one? Bloodlines, blood feuds, blood money, blood sports, blood oaths, blood ties. Royal blood. Blue blood. Hot blood. Bad blood. Written in blood.

"Do you?" said an insistent voice.

"Do I what?" While Puladi drifted far away, the other must have gone on talking.

"Remember. What you were like, when you yourself were fifteen years old."

Puladi sighed. "Yes, indeed. Like it was yesterday. Closer than yesterday."

"You were not—afraid?"

"Not the slightest bit. That was the year that I realized I had unique genius; the time when I discovered the data banks." Puladi sat up straighter, buoyed by memory. "It was bliss. Everything that I needed came to me so easily, it was as though I had already known it. While others plodded and staggered from one data level to another, I was a light-foot dancer, making great leaps that no one else had ever dreamed possible. By the time that I was sixteen, I could access *anything:* the most secret files, the most hidden code, the deepest data layers. No one else even suspected what I was doing. They were like blind people, in a world where I alone was sighted. And all the data banks were interlocked! I realized then that I could own everything. In another five years, I did."

"And it made you happy?"

"Of course. Whatever I wanted was mine—is mine."

"Except good health."

"I have not given up the hope of that. Though you were a great disappointment to me."

"My *blood?*"

Puladi decided that he must have said that word aloud, at some point in his musings. "Your blood is fine. But I did not bring you two thousand years and more, just for your blood. I thought I was bringing someone else, someone with the power to cure me."

"A healer. I understand." The youth was silent for a few moments, and when he spoke again his voice was wistful and reflective. "There was a time, just two of my years ago, when I thought that I might be a great healer. People told me that I had the gift, and I felt it move within me."

"What happened?"

"I saw a vision. I became afraid. I made a choice. But you, if you were healed, would you then hope to live forever?"

"Let's just say, for a long, long time."

"But you would live hated, for all those years. And who would want to live hated? Puladi, even your assistants do not love you, though they pretend love. They hate you, too. I can feel it in them."

"Of course they do. But they obey."

"But if they hate you, why don't they do something?"

"Carrion crows will not tear at living flesh. They await my death, when the time will come for them to fight among themselves."

"How can they rule, without your knowledge of the data banks?"

"Because they expect to inherit my monitoring and control system. World control would be impossible without it, but it becomes easy with it. The genius, you see, lies in setting up the system, far more than in operating it."

"When you die, I expect that I will die, too. They hate me also."

"A shrewd and accurate observation." Puladi smiled in the darkness. "They hate you, because they know that your visits here prolong my life."

"Administrator Kelb pretends otherwise. He suggests that I am brought here at night only for your sexual pleasures. Why do you permit such talk?"

"Kelb's time will come—soon. Anyway, in my condition perhaps I feel flattered. You would not understand that. You are too young to have had lovers."

The bed next to Puladi creaked, at some violent movement.

"That is not true! I am fifteen years old. I am a man, and I have had women—many, many women!—since I was thirteen."

"My apologies. Perhaps you would like a woman tomorrow? Or ten women, or a hundred, or a thousand? I am Puladi, and I own the world. Make your request. If it is not unreasonable, I will grant it."

There was silence from the bed. When it finally came, the voice sounded flat and empty. "Dr. Salino told me never to lie to you. But I did. I have not had lots of women. In truth, I have never had any woman, although most youths of my age have known them."

"There are lies and lies. Forget it. My offer still stands. Make your request. Do you want a hundred women?"

"No." There was a sigh. "I do not want even one. But I do have a request. I want to visit the laboratory of Professor Rustum Belur. I want to see the Chronoclast, the machine that brought me here."

Dr. Salino was in a difficult position. He dared not argue openly with Puladi, no matter how strongly he disagreed with him. All he could do was battle Kelb—who already resented and hated the physician, for his guaranteed round-the-clock access to his master.

Salino flourished the medical records at the Administrator. "It was working, and all the evidence suggested to me that it would continue to work. There had been minor recent abnormalities, but conditions were stable for the first time in more than a year. Why did you take the risk?"

"What risk?" Kelb was quite ready to argue Puladi's case for him.

"How do I know what risk?" Salino looked to Puladi for support, and found none. "Suppose that the boy becomes sick, because of the different food in India—too sick for us to continue treatment when he returns? Suppose that he is killed in a transportation accident? Suppose that his return is delayed? Didn't you consider all those possibilities?"

"Naturally." Kelb's leonine face was smug. "And after assessing all factors, it was Puladi's own decision that the boy should go to Calcutta. Are you questioning his wisdom?"

Yes. The fatal word was on the tip of Salino's tongue. But before he could say it and damn himself totally, Puladi finally spoke.

"Dr. Salino, all the risks that you mention are real, but they are risks to *me* more than to anyone. And most of them are already in the past. He has visited Belur's lab and seen the Chronoclast, and he is on his way back here. So now you wonder why I allowed him to do it—I can see the question in your face. The answer is simple: I was taking your advice. You told me that worry and stress change the chemical balance of the blood. Correct?"

"That is so."

"And the 'minor recent abnormalities' that you mentioned. They were in the blood being transferred to me. In its chemistry. True or false?"

"True."

"So would you like to know what was causing it? Near the end of the last treatment sessions, he told me that the desire to go back to his own time had been growing on him, to the point where it was an obsession. I agreed to let him visit Belur and the Chronoclast, for one simple reason: I wanted him to know that a return to his own time is absolutely impossible. I spoke to him a few hours ago. He is at last convinced. And he will be here tonight, in time for the next treatment. All right?"

Salino nodded, grudgingly satisfied.

He would have been amazed by Puladi's own unvoiced question to himself: Why had he *really* agreed to the visit to Calcutta? He did not know. And following that came the odd realization, of how much he was looking forward to the coming nighttime session.

Ten hours later, Puladi was questioning the wisdom of his decision. The visit to the Chronoclast had on the face of it achieved just what he wanted. And yet something else had happened. He could read it on the countenance of the youth who lay on the bed next to his wheelchair. There were smudges of exhaustion beneath the clear brown eyes, and the mouth was more tightly drawn than before.

A boy had gone to Calcutta, and a man had returned.

"Did you see Rustum Belur himself?"

"For a few minutes." The tense mouth relaxed to a quick smile. "Did you know, Puladi, that he admires you greatly? He described you as a kind and generous man."

"Then he is indeed a rarity. I spared his life, that is all. On an impulse. One man, among many. I do not know how many." Puladi realized that he truly did not. The purges and the culling had gone on for so long, day after day and year after year. "Would you believe millions? Maybe ten million?"

He was talking of matters about which he never talked; but the other did not seem shocked.

"No, I would not believe it." The brown eyes met Puladi's own, in a way that no man's had ever done. "I might believe fifty million. When you give an order to the guards, Kelb and Mavermine and Jaworsky compete in their zeal to make sure that it is carried out thoroughly. But you spared Belur, he said, when Kelb would cheerfully have destroyed him. And he said that you had every reason to have him killed. The Chronoclast was not working as he had promised. He knows the problem now."

Puladi felt a quiver of hope, and dismissed it at once as quite irrational. If Rustum Belur had found a way to access the future, the news would have come to him that same day. "What was wrong with the Chronoclast?"

"Nothing, in terms of its function. But he told you of a slight uncertainty in the transport time, which might give an hour or two of error over a couple of years. He did not know it at the time, but that error grows for longer intervals—what is the word for it—quadratically?"

"That sounds right."

"So the final error can be large."

"And to use the Chronoclast to *return* something or someone to the past—"

"—is quite impossible. Just as you said."

"You are disappointed."

"Yes."

"Do not be." Puladi's voice was gentle. "You see, even if it had been possible, I could never let you go. You are my lifeline."

"I know. But I thought, if you were dead . . ." He turned his head away, and closed his eyes.

Puladi turned away also, to stare at the bank of displays. *If I were dead, you would soon be dead, too. I may be your tormentor, but I am also your protector. Kelb dare not touch you, or anyone, as long as I am alive.*

And after that?

It was something he seldom considered, but maybe it was time to think about it. He recalled one of their late night exchanges:

"I was hoping for a miracle cure."

"And if you had found it, what then? No one lives forever."

"No. But maybe thirty years more, instead of a few months . . ."

"One month, or thirty years. There is no difference. It is *how* you live, not *how long* you live, that matters."

Words of wisdom. From a child.

And now, again, tonight. One dead, or fifty million. It is not *how many* you kill, but *that* you kill.

And he had done it all to preserve—what?

The screens in front of Puladi were restlessly active. All the displays were under his control. When he did not give direct instructions they would operate from preexisting programs, scanning for high-activity areas and recording anything that the algorithms considered significant. They were designed to report every doubtful case, leaving it to Puladi himself to evaluate later the need for action. More often than not he rejected their suggestions as unnecessary.

Would Kelb, or Mavermine, or Jaworsky, operate with as much restraint when he was gone? They did not understand the natural dynamics of human activities. If his successor took every report at face value, the world would turn into a sea of blood. And they would not even know how to destroy the system. He had protected against that very danger, so that he alone could disable it.

Puladi was roused by a whimper from the bed next to him. His companion had fallen asleep. He was dreaming. His dark head shook from side to side, and he was mouthing, "No, no, no."

Puladi gathered the long IV tube in one hand and reached across. He took warm brown fingers in his and pressed them gently. The contact sent an electric surge through his whole body.

"Wake up. Everything's all right. Come on, wake up, you are having a nightmare, that's all."

It took a few seconds until the brown eyes opened, and Puladi heard a quivering sigh.

"Oh. I am here."

"You are here. You are safe."

"I was dreaming. It was happening again. I was afraid."

"There is no need for fear. Tell me about it. If you can."

"It was the dream again, the one that I hoped was over forever." He sat up, rubbing at his throat. "It came first when I was twelve years old. I was walking along a little valley between two hills, by the side of a river, through cedars and poplars and ash trees. The stream branched into two parts. The left side went past a little house, and a farmyard, and growing crops. A family was working in the fields, a man and a wife and five sons. And I knew I was that man, bent down with age and toil.

"But the right branch of the stream rose up toward the hills. I saw a crowd of people on the hillside, calling to me. They shouted that I was their champion, that I would rule the whole world, that I was so strong I could defeat Death itself. I started their way, and they began throwing flowers on the ground, and cheering, and laughing. But when I drew close to them, the stream turned from water to blood. The sun vanished from the sky. Pain came from nowhere, all through my body. I fell to the ground; and I saw grinning Death, standing over me.

"That was the dream. For a full year it tortured me, over and over.

Until finally, one night, I made a great effort. In my dream I closed my eyes and put my hands over my ears. I did not see the flowers or hear the cheers. I managed to turn around, and struggled back to where the stream divided. I went the other way, up the left-hand branch to the quiet little farm. I stayed there. I became the old man, happy with his wife and his children.

"And I woke. I never had that dream again. Until tonight. Then it came—but this time *you* were standing at the division in the stream, telling me that I must not take the peaceful branch. I must follow the other path, through pain and darkness, to fight Death himself."

Puladi was still holding that slender brown hand. He patted it reassuringly. "Dreams are dreams, nothing more. I'd hate to tell you my own nightmares. You are safe here. There is no reason at all to be afraid."

"But you are here. And you are afraid."

"To die? Everyone is afraid to die."

"I do not mean that. You are afraid of the world."

"Never." But Puladi found the clear brown eyes boring into his. "Never. Why do you say such a thing?"

"I talked with Rustum Belur. He could not understand why you spared his life, when it was so easy for you to allow Kelb to take him away and have him killed."

"Maybe I have killed enough."

"True. And why? Because if they were alive, you would fear what they might do. You did not kill Rustum Belur, only because you had no reason to fear him. He could do nothing to harm you."

"Nonsense!" But Puladi could not meet those eyes any longer. He stared up at the displays. His free hand, without any thought on his part, began to tap at the keypad in the armrest of his wheeled chair. The screens came to life again.

This time it was not hidden meeting places, or furtive clusters of people on street corners, or two heads together in a dimly lit bar or quiet coffeehouse. This time Puladi had unconsciously sent his sensors high and far, seeking out the beautiful and the spectacular.

The screens filled, one by one: a sunlit South American waterfall, Cherun-Meru, dropping three thousand feet amid a mist of droplets and rainbow light; a towering thunderhead, black over the Java Sea, with lightning flickering through its turbulent base. Glittering Antarctic icebergs, calving away from the Ross Ice Shelf; whales, by the score and by the hundred, sounding and surfacing on their Pacific journey from pole to pole; dunes, hundreds of feet high, singing and murmuring their *mingsha* song to the Taklamakan Desert as the sands cooled and shifted with the setting sun; termite mounds, dotting an arid African plain like an army of ten-foot soldiers frozen in place and cased in brown cement; the taiga of the north, stunted junipers and pines, with the midnight sun hovering on the horizon.

While those scenes flashed into place, a quiet voice at Puladi's side spoke to him, or maybe to itself. "But since there is still fear, even here, even for someone who controls the whole world, then there can be fear anywhere. You are right, Puladi. It is wrong that I was so afraid. I must go back. I must take the road through pain and darkness. I must fight Death itself. And maybe I will triumph."

Puladi had needed the displays to calm his own thoughts. Now as he watched and listened, an idea flashed through his brain like jagged lightning.

"No. If I am afraid, it is not for me alone. It is for this. Think what may come after me. The jackals are already gathered, waiting for my death." Puladi gestured at the wall displays. "Look at Earth, so various, so beautiful. When I am gone, what will happen to it? I have organized the world and forced it to peace. At my death it will fall to chaos."

"Is chaos different from freedom? I think not. I must go back."

The impossibility of that statement no longer mattered to Puladi. He writhed in his padded chair. "No. I need you. *Earth* needs you. Never before have I found anyone that I would trust as my successor. You are not like Kelb and the others, here for what they hope to gain. You would be a force for good. Stay, become my adopted son—and rule the world, as your dream foretold. It will all be yours."

This time it was the thin brown hand that reached out, and gripped Puladi's.

"You tempt me, but it is not to be. I must go back."

"Back in time? You *cannot.*" Puladi said what he no longer believed. "It is physically impossible. Rustum Belur told you so."

"Perhaps. But speak the truth, Puladi. *You* do not think that it is impossible. You think that I can do it."

"No. I do not think you can do it." The touch of the thin hand had turned Puladi's insides to bubbling lava, and suddenly he was filled with an overwhelming knowledge. "I do not *think* you can go back, I *know* you can." He gripped hard, fingers quivering. "But if you must go, heal me first. Please, before you leave."

There was a creak from the bed, and the clear brown eyes were inches from Puladi's face. Hands gripped both of his.

"That is not necessary. You are already healed. All that remains is the fear. Before the night has ended, that too will disappear."

"Do not leave me. Please."

"I must. But we will meet again . . . if you choose. That I promise." He was standing up, moving away. "It is farewell, Puladi, but it need not be goodbye."

The alarm sounded, and Salino came awake in one great spasm of nerves.

Puladi's monitors! One hour ago they had all shown normal life signs. Now they were jumping all over the screens, out of control, values beyond any range that he had ever seen before. No man could live long with those vital functions.

He scurried across the long space between the inner and outer chambers at a speed dangerously close to triggering the automatic protection system.

The chamber door was open! He ran inside.

Puladi was sitting in his wheeled chair. The IV hung uselessly from his arm. He lolled back like a soft dummy. But he was busy. He was engaged on some intricate manipulation of the keypads in his chair. While Salino watched, a bank of directories appeared, then flickered away one by one in a strange nested chain reaction.

"Puladi—what happened to you? What are you doing?" Salino stared around the room. "Where is he?"

"One question at a time." Puladi's dry voice was the faintest whisper. His face was gray and rigid, only the eyes holding life. "Answer number one: I am dying. Number two: I am dismantling the world control system. Number three: he has gone, back where he came from. And I advise you to go somewhere, too, Dr. Salino, while there is still time. I estimate that you have maybe one half hour, before Kelb and friends arrive here."

"I have done nothing to harm them."

Puladi keyed in a new sequence. Five more screens flickered and died. "You are close to me; that is enough. They will certainly kill you."

"You are my patient. I cannot leave."

"I am your patient no longer. I rely on other hands than yours. Go, doctor. I command it."

Salino hesitated, nodded, turned, and ran for the door. On its threshold he spun around and came back to the chair.

"Puladi, let me take you with me! I can hide you. I can save you from them."

The chin in the gray mask was setting to its final rigid position. Puladi's words could barely be understood.

"You are a good man, Salino. But it is not necessary to save me. I am saved. Go now, and save yourself."

The final screens were blinking out as Salino ran. One by one they showed a brief scatter-plot of color, then turned to uniform gray. One picture popped back into existence for a few seconds, a calm wilderness of primeval forest. It revealed no evidence of human activity, no sign even of human existence.

Then it too streaked and flickered on the screen. A moment later it was gone. The overhead lights faded. Only the murmur of a laboring life-support system disturbed the room's silence.

Puladi waited. It was dark, he was alone, and his face was too set to show any expression. No one would ever know that he wanted to smile.

Afterword to "The Fifteenth Station of the Cross"

On April 5th, 1992, I was spending a Sunday afternoon as I love to, loafing and reading and talking. I picked up a Harlan Ellison collection, *Deathbird Stories,* and read a story in it called "Corpse." I found it quite baffling. I passed it along to the person at the other end of the couch, who read it in turn, shook her head, and asked me, "What does it mean?"

I said, "I don't know—but look at this bit."

And I pointed out a couple of sentences in the middle, that read, ". . . the years from twelve to thirty during which nothing was heard of Jesus of Nazareth. They are known as the 'lost' years of Jesus."

"I know exactly where Jesus was, and what he was doing," I said.

I still had to write it out, which took me until the following Sunday; but at that very moment I had this story.

TRAPALANDA

JOHN KENYON MARTINDALE seldom did things the usual way. Until a first-class return air ticket and a check for $10,000 arrived at my home in Lausanne I did not know he existed. The enclosed note said only: "For consulting services of Klaus Jacobi in New York, June 6th–7th." It was typed on his letterhead and initialed, JKM. The check was drawn on the Riggs Bank of Washington, D.C. The tickets were for Geneva–New York on June 5th, with an open return.

I did not need work. I did not need money. I had no particular interest in New York, and a transatlantic telephone call to John Kenyon Martindale revealed only that he was out of town until June 5th. Why would I bother with him? It is easy to forget what killed the cat.

The limousine that met me at Kennedy Airport drove to a stone mansion on the East River, with a garden that went right down to the water's edge. An old woman with the nose, chin, and hairy moles of a storybook witch opened the door. She took me upstairs to the fourth floor, while my baggage disappeared under the house with the limousine. The mansion was amazingly quiet. The elevator made no noise at all, and when we stepped out of it the deeply carpeted floors of the corridor were matched by walls thick with oriental tapestries. I was not used to so much silence. When I was ushered into a long, shadowed conservatory filled with flowering plants and found myself in the presence of a man and woman, I wanted to shout. Instead I stared.

Shirley Martindale was a brunette, with black hair, thick eyebrows, and a flawless, creamy skin. She was no more than five feet three, but full-figured and strongly built. In normal company she would have been a center of attention; with John Kenyon Martindale present, she was ignored.

He was of medium height and slender build, with a wide, smiling mouth. His hair was thin and wheat-colored, combed straight back from his face. Any other expression he might have had was invisible. From an inch below his eyes to two inches above them, a flat, black shield extended across his whole face. Within that curved strip of darkness colored shadows moved, little darting points and glints of light that flared red and green and electric blue. They were hypnotic, moving in patterns that could be followed but never quite predicted, and they drew and held the attention. They were so striking that it took me a few moments to realize that John Kenyon Martindale must be blind.

He did not act like a person without sight. When I came into the room he at once came forward and confidently shook my hand. His grip was firm, and surprisingly strong for so slight a man.

"A long trip," he said, when the introductions were complete. "May I offer a little refreshment?"

Although the witch was still standing in the room, waiting, he mixed the drinks himself, cracking ice, selecting bottles, and pouring the correct measures slowly but without error. When he handed a glass to me and smilingly said "There! How's that?", I glanced at Shirley Martindale and replied, "It's fine; but before we start the toasts I'd like to learn what we are toasting. Why am I here?"

"No messing about, eh? You are very direct. Very Swiss—even though you are not one." He turned his head to his wife, and the little lights twinkled behind the black mask. "What did I tell you, Shirley? This is the man." And then to me. "You are here to make a million dollars. Is that enough reason?"

"No. Mr. Martindale, it is not. It was not money that brought me here. I have enough money."

"Then perhaps you are here to become a Swiss citizen. Is that a better offer?"

"Yes. If you can pay in advance." Already I had an idea what John Martindale wanted of me. I am not psychic, but I can read and see. The inner wall of the conservatory was papered with maps of South America.

"Let us say, I will pay half in advance. You will receive five hundred thousand dollars in your account before we leave. The remainder, and the Swiss citizenship papers, will be waiting when we return from Patagonia."

"We? Who are 'we'?"

"You and I. Other guides if you need them. We will be going through difficult country, though I understand that you know it better than anyone."

I looked at Shirley Martindale, and she shook her head decisively. "Not me, Klaus. Not for one million dollars, not for ten million dollars. This is all John's baby."

"Then my answer must be no." I sipped the best pisco sour I had tasted since I was last in Peru, and wondered where he had learned the technique. "Mr. Martindale, I retired four years ago to Switzerland. Since then I have not set foot in Argentina, even though I still carry those citizenship papers. If you want someone to lead you through the *echter Rand* of Patagonia, there must now be a dozen others more qualified than I. But that is beside the point. Even when I was in my best condition, even when I was so young and cocky that I thought nothing could kill me or touch me—even then I would have refused to lead a blind man to the high places that you display on your walls. With your wife's presence and her assistance to you for personal matters, it might barely be possible. Without her—have you any idea at all what conditions are like there?"

"Better than most people." He leaned forward. "Mr. Jacobi, let us perform a little test. Take something from your pocket, and hold it up in front of you. Something that should be completely unfamiliar to me."

I hate games, and this smacked of one; but there was something infinitely persuasive about that thin, smiling man. What did I have in my pocket? I reached in, felt my wallet, and slipped out a photograph. I did not look at it, and I was not sure myself what I had selected. I held it between thumb and forefinger, a few feet away from Martindale's intent face.

"Hold it very steady," he said. Then, while the points of light twinkled and shivered, "It is a picture, a photograph of a woman. It is your assistant, Helga Korein. Correct?"

I turned it to me. It was a portrait of Helga, smiling into the camera. "You apparently know far more about me than I know of you. However, you are not quite correct. It is a picture of my wife, Helga Jacobi. I married her four years ago, when I retired. You are not blind?"

"Legally, I am completely blind and have been since my twenty-second year, when I was foolish enough to drive a racing car into a retaining wall." Martindale tapped the black shield. "Without this, I can see nothing. With it, I am neither blind nor seeing. I receive charge-coupled diode inputs directly to my optic nerves, and I interpret them. I see neither at the wavelengths nor with the resolution provided by the human eye, nor is what I reconstruct anything like the images that I remember from the time before I became blind; but I see. On another occasion I will be happy to tell you all that I know about the technology. What you need to know tonight is that I will be able to pull my own weight on any journey. I can give you that assurance. And now I ask again: will you do it?"

It was, of course, curiosity that killed the cat. Martindale had given me almost no information as to where he wanted to go, or when, or why. But something was driving John Martindale, and I wanted to hear what it was.

I nodded my head, convinced now that he would see my movement. "We certainly need to talk in detail; but for the moment let us use that fine old legal phrase, and say there is agreement in principle."

There is agreement in principle. With that sentence, I destroyed my life.

Shirley Martindale came to my room that night. I was not surprised. John Martindale's surrogate vision was a miracle of technology, but it had certain limitations. The device could not resolve the fleeting look in a woman's eye, or the millimeter jut to a lower lip. I had caught the signal in the first minute.

We did not speak until it was done and we were lying side by side in my bed. I knew it was not finished. She had not relaxed against me. I waited. "There is more than he told you," she said at last.

I nodded. "There is always more. But he was quite right about that place. I have felt it myself, many times."

As South America narrows from the great equatorial swell of the Amazon Basin, the land becomes colder and more broken. The great spine of the Andean cordillera loses height as one travels south. Ranges that tower to twenty-three thousand feet in the tropics dwindle to a modest twelve thousand. The land is shared between Argentina and Chile, and along their border, beginning with the chill depths of Lago Buenos Aires (sixty miles long, ten miles wide; bigger than anything in

Switzerland), a great chain of mountain lakes straddles the frontier, all the way south to Tierra del Fuego and the flowering Chilean city of Punta Arenas.

For fourteen years, the Argentina-Chile borderland between latitude 46 and 50 South had been my home, roughly from Lago Buenos Aires to Lago Argentina. It had become closer to me than any human, closer even than Helga. The east side of the Andes in this region is a bitter, parched desert, where gale-force winds blow incessantly three hundred and sixty days of the year. They come from the snowbound slopes of the mountains, freezing whatever they touch. I knew the country and I loved it, but Helga had persuaded me that it was not a land to which a man could retire. The buffeting wind was an endless drain, too much for old blood. Better, she said, to leave in early middle age, when a life elsewhere could still be shaped.

When the time came for us to board the aircraft that would take me away to Buenos Aires and then to Europe, I wanted to throw away my ticket. I am not a sentimental man, but only Helga's presence allowed me to leave the Kingdom of the Winds.

Now John Martindale was tempting me to return there, with more than money. At one end of his conservatory-study stood a massive globe, about six feet across. Presumably it dated from the time before he had acquired his artificial eyes, because it differed from all other globes I had ever seen in one important respect; namely, it was a relief globe. Oceans were all smooth surface, while mountain ranges of the world stood out from the surface of the flattened sphere. The degree of relief had been exaggerated, but everything was in proportion. Himalayan and Karakoram ranges projected a few tenths of an inch more than the Rockies and the Andes, and they in turn were a little higher than the Alps or the volcanic ranges of Indonesia.

When my drink was finished Martindale had walked me across to that globe. He ran his finger down the backbone of the Americas, following the continuous mountain chains from their beginning in Alaska, through the American Rockies, through Central America, and on to the rising Andes and northern Chile. When he finally came to Patagonia his fingers slowed and stopped.

"Here," he said. "It begins here."

His fingertip was resting on an area very familiar to me. It was right on the Argentina-Chile border, with another of the cold mountain lakes at the center of it. I knew the lake as Lago Pueyrredon, but as usual with bodies of water that straddle the border there was a different name—Lago Cochrane—in use on the Chilean side. The little town of Paso Roballo, where I had spent a dozen nights in a dozen years, lay just to the northeast.

If I closed my eyes I could see the whole landscape that lay beneath his finger. To the east it was dry and dusty, sustaining only thornbush and tough grasses on the dark surface of old volcanic flows; westward were the tall flowering grasses and the thicketed forests of redwood, cypress, and Antarctic beech. Even in the springtime of late November there would be snow on the higher ground, with snow-fed lake waters lying black as jet under a Prussian-blue sky.

I could see all this, but it seemed impossible that John Martindale could do so. His blind skull must hold a different vision.

"What begins here?" I asked, and wondered again how much he could receive through those arrays of inorganic crystal.

"The anomalies. This region has weather patterns that defy all logic and all models."

"I agree with that, from personal experience. That area has the most curious pattern of winds of any place in the world." It had been a long flight and a long day, and by this time I was feeling a little weary. I was ready to defer discussion of the weather until tomorrow, and I wanted time to reflect on our "agreement in principle." I continued, "However, I do not see why those winds should interest you."

"I am a meteorologist. Now wait a moment." His sensor array must have caught something of my expression. "Do not jump to a wrong conclusion. Mine is a perfect profession for a blind man. Who can see the weather? I was ten times as sensitive as a sighted person to winds, to warmth, to changes in humidity and barometric pressure. What I could not see was cloud formations, and those are consequences rather than causes. I could deduce their appearance from other variables. Eight years ago I began to develop my own computer models of weather patterns, analyzing the interaction of snow, winds, and topography. Five years ago I believed that my method was completely general, and completely accurate. Then I studied the Andean system; and in one area—only one—it failed." He tapped the globe. "Here. Here there are winds with no sustaining source of energy. I can define a circulation pattern and locate a vortex, but I cannot account for its existence."

"The area you show is known locally as the Kingdom of the Winds."

"I know. I want to go there."

And so did I.

When he spoke I felt a great longing to return, to see again the *altiplano* of the eastern Andean slopes and hear the banshee music of the western wind. It was all behind me. I had sworn to myself that Argentina existed only in my past, that the Patagonian spell was broken forever. John Martindale was giving me a million dollars and Swiss citizenship, but more than that he was giving me an *excuse*. For four years I had been unconsciously searching for one.

I held out my glass. "I think, Mr. Martindale, that I would like another drink."

Or two. Or three.

Shirley Martindale was moving by my side now, running her hand restlessly along my arm. "There is more. He wants to understand the winds, but there is more. He hopes to find Trapalanda."

She did not ask me if I had heard of it. No one who spends more than a week in central Patagonia can be ignorant of Trapalanda. For three hundred years, explorers have searched for the "City of the Caesars," *Trapalanda*, the Patagonian version of El Dorado. Rumor and speculation said that Trapalanda would be found at about 47 degrees South, at the same latitude as Paso Roballo. Its fabled treasure-houses of gold and gemstones had drawn hundreds of men to their death in the high Andes. People did not come back, and say, "I sought Trapalanda, and I failed to find it." They did not come back at all. I was an exception.

"I am disappointed," I said. "I had thought your husband to be a wiser man."

"What do you mean?"

"Everyone wants to find Trapalanda. Four years of my life went into the search for it, and I had the best equipment and the best knowledge. I told your husband that there were a dozen better guides, but I was lying. I know that country better than any man alive. He is certain to fail."

"He believes that he has special knowledge. And you are going to do it. You are going to take him there. For Trapalanda."

She knew better than I. Until she spoke, I did not know what I would do. But she was right. Forget the "agreement in principle." I would go.

"You want me to do it, don't you?" I said. "But I do not understand *your* reasons. You are married to a very wealthy man. He seems to have as much money as he can ever spend."

"John is curious, always curious. He is like a little boy. He is not doing this for money. He does not care about money."

She had not answered my implied question. I had never asked for John Kenyon Martindale's motives, I had been looking for *her* reasons why he should go. Then it occurred to me that her presence, here in my bed, told me all I needed to know. He would go to the Kingdom of the Winds. If he found what he was looking for, it would bring enormous wealth. Should he fail to return, Shirley Martindale would be a free and very wealthy widow.

"Sex with your husband is not good?" I asked.

"What do you think? I am here, am I not?" Then she relented. "It is worse than not good, it is terrible. It is as bad with him as it is exciting with you. John is a gentle, thoughtful man, but I need someone who takes me and does not ask or explain. You are a strong man, and I suspect that you are a cold, selfish man. Since we have been together, you have not once spoken my name, or said a single word of affection. You do not feel it is necessary to pretend to commitments. And you are sexist. I noticed John's reaction when you said, 'I married Helga.' He would always say it differently, perhaps 'Shirley and I got married.' " Her hands moved from my arm, and were touching me more intimately. She sighed. "I do not mind your attitude. What John finds hard to stand, I *need.* You saw what you did to me here, without one word. You make me shiver."

I turned to bring our bodies into full contact. "And John?" I said. "Why did he marry you?" There was no need to ask why she had married him.

"What do you think," she said. "Was it my wit, my looks, my charm? Give me your hand." She gently moved my fingers along her face and breasts. "It was five years ago. John was still blind. We met, and when we said good night he felt my cheek." Her voice was bitter. "He married me for my pelt."

The texture was astonishing. I could feel no roughness, no blemish, not even the most delicate of hairs. Shirley Martindale had the warm, flawless skin of a six-month-old baby. It was growing warm under my touch.

Before we began she raised herself high above me, propping herself on straight arms. "Helga. What is she like? I cannot imagine her."

"You will see," I said. "Tomorrow I will telephone Lausanne and tell her to come to New York. She will go with us to Trapalanda."

Trapalanda. Had I said that? I was very tired, I had meant to say Patagonia.

I reached up to touch her breasts. "No talk now," I said. "No more talk." Her eyes were as black as jet, as dark as mountain lakes. I dived into their depths.

Shirley Martindale did not meet Helga; not in New York, not anywhere, not ever. John Kenyon Martindale made his position clear to me the next morning as we walked together around the seventh floor library. "I won't allow her to stay in this house," he said. "It's not for my sake or yours, and certainly not for Shirley's. It is for her sake. I know how Shirley would treat her."

He did not seem at all annoyed, but I stared at the blind black mask and revised my ideas about how much he could see with his CCDs and fiber optic bundles.

"Did she tell you last night why I am going to Patagonia?" he asked, as he picked out a book and placed it in the hopper of an iron potbellied stove with electronic aspirations.

I hesitated, and told the truth. "She said you were seeking Trapalanda."

He laughed. "I wanted to go to Patagonia. The easiest way to do it without an argument from Shirley was to hold out a fifty billion dollar bait. The odd thing, though, is that she is quite right. I am seeking Trapalanda." And he laughed again, more heartily than anything he had said would justify.

The black machine in front of us made a little purr of contentment, and a pleasant woman's voice began to read aloud. It was a mathematics text on the foundations of geometry. I had noticed that although Martindale described himself as a meteorologist, four-fifths of the books in the library were mathematics and theoretical physics. There were too many things about John Martindale that were not what they seemed.

"Shirley's voice," he said, while we stood by the machine and listened to a mystifying definition of the intrinsic curvature of a surface. "And a very pleasant voice, don't you think, to have whispering sweet epsilons in your ear? I borrowed it for use with this optical character recognition equipment, before I got my eyes."

"I didn't think there was a machine in the world that could do that."

"Oh, yes." He switched it off, and Shirley halted in midword. "This isn't even state-of-the-art anymore. It was, when it was made, and it cost the earth. Next year it will be an antique, and they'll give this much capability out in cereal packets. Come on, let's go and join Shirley for a prelunch aperitif."

If John Martindale were angry with me or with his wife, he concealed it well. I realized that the mask extended well beyond the black casing.

Five days later we flew to Argentina. When Martindale mentioned his idea of being in the Kingdom of the Winds in time for the winter solstice, season of the anomaly's strongest showing, I dropped any thoughts of a trip back to Lausanne. I arranged for Helga to pack what I needed and meet us in Buenos Aires. She would wait at Ezeiza Airport without going into the city proper, and we would fly farther south at once. Even if our travels went well, we would need luck as well as efficiency to have a week near Paso Roballo before solstice.

It amused me to see Martindale searching for Helga in the airport arrival lounge as we walked off the plane. He had seen her photograph, and I had assured him that she would be there. He could not find her. Within seconds, long before it was possible to see her features, I had picked her out. She was staring down at a book on her lap. Every fifteen seconds her head lifted for a rapid radarlike scan of the passenger lounge, and returned to the page. Martindale did not notice her until we were at her side.

I introduced them. Helga nodded but did not speak. She stood up and led the way. She had rented a four-seater plane on open charter, and in her usual efficient way she had arranged for our luggage to be transferred to it.

Customs clearance, you ask? Let us be realistic. The Customs Office in Argentina is no more corrupt than that of, say, Bolivia or Ecuador; that is quite sufficient. Should John Martindale be successful in divining the legendary treasures of Trapalanda, plenty of hands would help to remove them illegally from the country.

Helga led the way through the airport. She was apparently not what he had expected of my wife, and I could see him studying her closely. Helga stood no more than five feet two, to my six-two, and her thin body was not quite straight. Her left shoulder dipped a bit, and she favored her left leg a trifle as she walked.

Since I was the only one with a pilot's license I sat forward in the copilot's chair, next to Owen Davies. I had used Owen before as a by-the-day hired pilot. He knew the Kingdom of the Winds, and he respected it. He would not take risks. In spite of his name he was Argentina born—one of the many Welshmen who found almost any job preferable to their parents' Argentinean sheep-farming. Martindale and Helga sat behind us, side-by-side in the back, as we flew to Comodoro Rivadavia on the Atlantic coast. It was the last real airfield we would see for a while unless we dipped across the Chilean border to Cochrane. I preferred not to try that. In the old days, you risked a few machine-gun bullets from frontier posts. Today it is likely to be a surface-to-air missile.

We would complete our supplies in Comodoro Rivadavia, then use dry dirt airstrips the rest of the way. The provisions were supposed to be waiting for us. While Helga and Owen were checking to make sure that the delivery included everything we had ordered, Martindale came up to my side.

"Does she never talk?" he said. "Or is it just my lack of charm?" He did not sound annoyed, merely puzzled.

"Give her time." I looked to see what Owen and Helga were doing. They were pointing at three open chests of supplies, and Owen was becoming rather loud.

"You noticed how Helga walks, and how she holds her left arm?"

The black shield dipped down and up, making me suddenly curious as to what lay behind it. "I even tried to hint at a question in that direction," he said. "Quite properly she ignored it."

"She was not born that way. When Helga walked into my office nine years ago, I assumed that I was looking at some congenital condition. She said nothing, nor did I. I was looking for an assistant, someone who was as interested in the high border country as I was, and Helga fitted. She was only twenty-one years old and still green, but I could tell she was intelligent and trainable."

"Biddable," said Martindale. "Sorry, go on."

"You have to be fit to wander around in freezing temperatures at ten thousand feet," I said. "As part of Helga's condition of employment, she had to take a full physical. She didn't want to. She agreed only when she saw that the job depended on it. She was in excellent shape and passed easily; but the doctor—quite improperly—allowed me to look at her X rays."

Were the eyebrows raised, behind that obsidian visor? Martindale cocked his head to the right, a small gesture of inquiry. Helga and Owen Davies were walking our way.

"She was put together like a jigsaw puzzle. Almost every bone in her arms and legs showed marks of fracture and healing. Her ribs, too. When she was small she had been what these enlightened times call 'abused.' Tortured. As a very small child, Helga learned to keep quiet. The best thing she could hope for was to be ignored. You saw already how invisible she can be."

"I have never heard you angry before," he said. "You sound like her father, not her husband." His tone was calm, but something new hid behind that mask. "And is that," he continued, "why in New York—"

He was interrupted. "Tomorrow," said Owen from behind him. "He says he'll have the rest then. I believe him. I told him he's a fat idle bastard, and if we weren't on our way by noon I'd personally kick the shit out of him."

Martindale nodded at me. Conversation closed. We headed into town for Alberto McShane's bar and the uncertain pleasures of nightlife in Comodoro Rivadavia. Martindale didn't give up. All the way there he talked quietly to Helga. He may have received ten words in return.

It had been five years. Alberto McShane didn't blink when we walked in. He took my order without comment, but when Helga walked past him he reached out his good arm and gave her a big hug. She smiled like the sun. She was home. She had hung around the *Guanaco* bar since she was twelve years old, an oil brat brought here in the boom years. When her parents left, she stayed. She hid among the beer barrels in McShane's cellar until the plane took off. Then she could relax for the first time in her life. Poverty and hard work were luxuries after what she had been through.

The decor of the bar hadn't changed since last time. The bottle of dirty black oil (the first one pumped at Comodoro Rivadavia, if you believe McShane) hung over the bar, and the same stuffed guanaco and rhea stood beside it. McShane's pet armadillo, or its grandson, ambled among the tables looking for beer heeltaps.

I knew our search plans, but Helga and Owen Davies needed briefing. Martindale took Owen's 1:1,000,000 scale ONC's, with their emendations and local detail in Owen's careful hand, added to them the 1:250,000 color photomaps that had been made for him in the United States, and spread the collection out to cover the whole table.

"From here, to here," he said. His fingers tapped the map near Laguna del Sello, then moved south and west until they reached Lago Belgrano.

Owen studied them for a few moments. "All on this side of the border," he said. "That's good. What do you want to do there?"

"I want to land. Here, and here, and here." Martindale indicated seven points, on a roughly north-south line.

Owen Davies squinted down, assessing each location. "Lago Gio, Paso Roballo, Lago Posadas. Know 'em all. Tough landing at two, and that last point is in the middle of the Perito Moreno National Park; but we can find a place." He looked up, not at Martindale but at me. "You're not in the true high country, though. You're twenty miles too far east. What do you want to do when you get there?"

"I want to get out, and look west," said Martindale. "After that, I'll tell you where we have to go."

Owen Davies said nothing more, but when we were at the bar picking up more drinks he gave me a shrug. *Too far east,* it said. *You're not in the high country. You won't find Trapalanda there, where he's proposing to land. What's the story?*

Owen was an honest man and a great pilot who had made his own failed attempt at Trapalanda (sometimes I thought that was true of everyone who lived below 46 degrees South). He found it hard to believe that anyone could succeed where he had not, but he couldn't resist the lure.

"He knows something he's not telling us," I said. "He's keeping information to himself. Wouldn't you?"

Owen nodded. Barrels of star rubies and tons of platinum and gold bars shone in his dark Welsh eyes.

When we returned to the table John Martindale had made his breakthrough. Helga was talking and bubbling with laughter. "How did you *do* that," she was saying. "He's untouchable. What did you *do* to him?" McShane's armadillo was sitting on top of the table, chewing happily at a piece of apple. Martindale was rubbing the ruffle of horny plates behind its neck, and the armadillo was pushing itself against his hand.

"He thinks I'm one of them." Martindale touched the black screen across his eyes. "See? We've both got plates. I'm just one of the family." His face turned up to me. I read the satisfaction behind the mask. *And should I do to your wife, Klaus, what you did to mine?* it said. *It would be no more than justice.*

Those were not Martindale's thoughts. I realized that. They were mine. And that was the moment when my liking for John Kenyon Martindale began to tilt toward resentment.

At ground level, the western winds skim off the Andean slopes at seventy knots or more. At nine thousand feet, they blow at less then thirty. Owen was an economy-minded pilot. He flew west at ten thousand until we were at the preferred landing point, then dropped us to the ground in three sickening sideslips.

He had his landing already planned. Most of Patagonia is built of great level slabs, rising like terraces from the high coastal cliffs on the Atlantic Ocean to the Andean heights in the west. The exception was in the area we were exploring. Volcanic eruptions there have pushed great layers of basalt out onto the surface. The ground is cracked and irregular, and scarred by the scouring of endless winds. It takes special skill to land a plane when the wind speed exceeds the landing airspeed, and Owen Davies had it. We showed an airspeed of over a hundred knots when we touched down, light as a dust mote, and rolled to a perfect landing. "Good enough," said Owen.

He had brought us down on a flat strip of dark lava, at three o'clock in the afternoon. The sun hung low on the northwest horizon, and we stepped out into the teeth of a cold and dust-filled gale. The wind beat and tugged and pushed our bodies, trying to blow us back to the Atlantic. Owen, Helga, and I wore goggles and helmets against the driving clouds of grit and sand.

Martindale was bareheaded. He planted a GPS transponder on the ground to confirm our exact position, and faced west. With his head tilted upward and his straw-colored hair blowing wild, he made an adjustment to the side of his visor, then nodded. "It is there," he said. "I knew it must be."

We looked, and saw nothing. "What is there?" said Helga.

"I'll tell you in a moment. Note these down. I'm going to read off heights and headings." Martindale looked at the sun and the compass. He began to turn slowly from north to south. Every fifteen degrees he stopped, stared at the featureless sky, and read off a list of numbers. When he was finished he nodded to Owen. "All right. We can do the next one now."

"You mean that's *it? The whole thing?* All you're going to do is stand there?" Owen is many good things, but he is not diplomatic.

"That's it—for the moment." Martindale led the way back to the aircraft.

I could not follow. Not at once. I had lifted my goggles and was peering with wind-teared eyes to the west. The land there fell upward to the dark-blue twilight sky. It was the surge of the Andes, less than twenty miles away, rolling up in long, snowcapped breakers. I walked across the tufts of bunchgrass and reached out a hand to steady myself on an isolated ten-foot beech tree. Wind-shaped and stunted it stood, trunk and branches curved to the east, hiding its head from the deadly western wind. It was the only one within sight.

This was my Patagonia, the true, the terrible.

I felt a gentle touch on my arm. Helga stood there, waiting. I patted her hand in reply, and she instinctively recoiled. Together we followed Martindale and Davies back to the aircraft.

"I found what I was looking for," Martindale said, when we were all safely inside. The gale buffeted and rocked the craft, resenting our presence. "It's no secret now. When the winds approach the Andes from the Chilean side, they shed all the moisture they have picked up over the Pacific; and they accelerate. The energy balance equation is the same everywhere in the world. It depends on terrain, moisture, heating, and atmospheric layers. The same equation everywhere—except that *here*, in the Kingdom of the Winds, something goes wrong. The winds pick up so much speed that they are thermodynamically impossible. There is a mechanism at work, pumping energy into the moving air. I knew it before I left New York City; and I knew what it must be. There had to be a long, horizontal line-vortex, running north to south and transmitting energy to the western wind. But that too was impossible. First, then, I had to confirm that the vortex existed." He nodded vigorously. "It does. With my vision sensors I can see the patterns of compression and rarefaction. In other words, I can see direct evidence of the vortex. With half a dozen more readings, I will pinpoint the exact origin of its energy source."

"But what's all that got to do with finding . . ." Owen trailed off and looked at me guiltily. I had told him what Martindale was after, but I had also cautioned him never to mention it.

"With finding Trapalanda?" finished Martindale. "Why, it has everything to do with it. There must be one site, a specific place where the generator exists to power the vortex line. Find that, and we will have found Trapalanda."

Like God, Duty, or Paradise, Trapalanda means different things to different people. I could see from the expression on Owen's face that a line-vortex power generator was not *his* Trapalanda, no matter what it meant to Martindale.

I had allowed six days; it took three. On the evening of June 17th, we sat around the tiny table in the aircraft's rear cabin. There would be no flying tomorrow, and Owen had produced a bottle of *usquebaugh australis;* "southern whiskey," the worst drink in the world.

"On foot," John Martindale was saying. "Now it has to be on foot— and just in case, one of us will stay at the camp in radio contact."

"Helga," I said. She and Martindale shook heads in unison. "Suppose you have to carry somebody out?" she said. "I can't do that. It must be you or Owen."

At least she was taking this seriously, which Owen Davies was not. He had watched with increasing disgust while Martindale made atmospheric observations at seven sites. Afterward he came to me secretly. "We're working for a madman," he said. "We'll find no treasure. I'd almost rather work for Diego."

Diego Luria—"Mad Diego"—believed that the location of Trapalanda could be found by a correct interpretation of the Gospel According to Saint John. He had made five expeditions to the *altiplano,* four of them with Owen as pilot. It was harder on Owen than you might think, since Diego sometimes said that human sacrifice would be needed before Trapalanda could be discovered. They had found nothing; but they had come back, and that in itself was no mean feat.

Martindale had done his own exact triangulation, and pinpointed a place on the map. He had calculated UTM coordinates accurate to within twenty meters. They were not promising. When we flew as close as possible to his chosen location we found that we were looking at a point halfway up a steep rock face, where a set of broken waterfalls cascaded down a near-vertical cliff.

"I am sure," he said, in reply to my implied question. "The data-fit residuals are too small to leave any doubt." He tapped the map, and looked out of the aircraft window at the distant rock face. "Tomorrow. You, and Helga, and I will go. You, Owen, you stay here and monitor our transmission frequency. If we are off the air for more than twelve hours, come and get us."

He was taking this *too* seriously. Before the light faded I went outside again and trained my binoculars on the rock face. According to Martindale, at that location was a power generator that could modify the flow of winds along two hundred and fifty miles of mountain range. I saw nothing but the blown white spray of falls and cataracts, and a gray highland fox picking its way easily up the vertical rock face.

"Trust me." Martindale had appeared suddenly at my side. "I can *see* those wind patterns when I set my sensors to function at the right wavelengths. What's your problem?"

"Size." I turned to him. "Can you make your sensors provide telescopic images?"

"Up to three inch effective aperture."

"Then take a look up there. You're predicting that we'll find a machine which produces tremendous power—"

"Many gigawatts."

"—more power than a whole power station. And there is nothing there, nothing to see. That's impossible."

"Not at all." The sun was crawling along the northern horizon. The thin daylight lasted for only eight hours, and already it was fading. John Kenyon Martindale peered off westward and shook his head. He tapped his black visor. "You've had a good look at this," he said. "Suppose I had wanted to buy something that could do what this does, say, five years ago. Do you know what it would have weighed?"

"*Weighed?*" I shook my head.

"At least a ton. And ten years ago, it would have been impossible to build, no matter how big you allowed it to be. In another ten years, this assembly will fit easily inside a prosthetic eye. The way is toward miniaturization, higher energy densities, more compact design. I expect the generator to be small." He suddenly turned again to look right into my face. "I have a question for you, and it is an unforgivably personal one. Have you ever consummated your marriage with Helga?"

He had anticipated my lunge at him, and he backed away rapidly. "Do not misunderstand me," he said. "Helga's extreme aversion to physical contact is obvious. If it is total, there are New York specialists who can probably help her. I have influence there."

I looked down at my hands as they held the binoculars. They were trembling. "It is—total," I said.

"You knew that—and yet you married her. Why?"

"Why did you marry *your* wife, knowing you would be cuckolded?" I was lashing out, not expecting an answer.

"Did she tell you it was for her skin?" His voice was weary, and he was turning away as he spoke. "I'm sure she did. Well, I will tell you. I married Shirley—because she wanted me to."

Then I was standing alone in the deepening darkness. Shirley Martindale had warned me, back in New York. He was like a child, curious about everything. Including me, including Helga, including me and Helga.

Damn you, John Martindale. I looked at the bare hillside, and prayed that Trapalanda would somehow swallow him whole. Then I would never again have to endure that insidious, probing voice, asking the unanswerable.

The plane had landed on the only level piece of ground in miles. Our destination was a mile and a half away, but it was across some formidable territory. We would have to descend a steep scree, cross a quarter mile of boulders until we came to a fast-moving stream, and follow that watercourse upward, until we were in the middle of the waterfalls themselves.

The plain of boulders showed the translucent sheen of a thin ice coating. The journey could not be done in poor light. We would wait until morning, and leave promptly at ten.

Helga and I went to bed early, leaving Martindale with his calculations and Owen Davies with his *usquebaugh australis.* At a pinch the aircraft would sleep four, but Helga and I slept outside in a small reinforced tent brought along for the purpose. The floor area was five feet by seven. We had pitched the tent in the lee of the aircraft, where the howl of the wind was muted. I listened to Helga's breathing, and knew after half an hour that she was still awake.

"Think we'll find anything?" I said softly.

"I don't know." And then, after maybe one minute. "It's not that. It's you, Klaus."

"I've never been better."

"That's the problem. I've seen you, these last few days. You love it here. I should never have taken you away."

"I'm not complaining."

"That's part of the problem, too. You never complain. I wish you would." I heard her turn to face me in the dark, and for one second I imagined a hand was reaching out toward me. It was an illusion. She went on, "When I said I wanted to leave Patagonia and live in Europe, you agreed without an argument. But your heart has always been here."

"Oh, well, I don't know . . ." The lie stuck in my throat.

"And there's something else. I wasn't going to tell you, because I was afraid that you would misunderstand. But I will tell you. John Martindale tried to touch me."

I stirred, began to sit up, and felt the rough canvas against my forehead. Outside, the wind gave a sudden scream around the tent. "You mean he tried to—to—"

"No. He reached out, and tried to touch the back of my hand. That was all. I don't know why he did it, but I think it was just curiosity. He watches everything, and he has been watching us. I pulled my hand away before he got near. But it made me think of you. I have not been a wife to you, Klaus. You've done your best, and I've tried my hardest but it hasn't improved at all. Be honest with yourself, you know it hasn't. So if you want to stay here when this work is finished . . ."

I hated to hear her sound so confused and lost. "Let's not discuss it now," I said.

In other words, I can't bear to talk about it.

We had tried so hard at first, with Helga gritting her teeth at every gentle touch. When I finally realized that the sweat on her forehead and the quiver in her thin limbs was a hundred percent fear and zero percent arousal, I stopped trying. After that we had been happy—or at least, I had. I had not been faithful physically, but I could explain that well enough. And then, with this trip and the arrival on the scene of John Kenyon Martindale, the whole relationship between Helga and me felt threatened. And I did not know why.

"We ought to get as much sleep as we can tonight," I said, after another twenty seconds or so. "Tomorrow will be a tough day."

She said nothing, but she remained awake for a long, long time. And so, of course, did I.

The first quarter mile was easy, a walk down a gently sloping incline of weathered basalt. Owen Davies had watched us leave with an odd mixture of disdain and greed on his face. We were not going to find anything, he was quite sure of that—but on the other hand, if by some miracle we *did,* and he was not there to see it . . .

We carried minimal packs. I thought it would be no more than a two-hour trek to our target point, and we had no intention of being away overnight.

When we came to the field of boulders I revised my estimate. Every square millimeter of surface was coated with the thinnest and most treacherous layer of clear ice. In principle its presence was impossible. With an atmosphere of this temperature and dryness, that ice should have sublimed away.

We picked our way carefully across, concentrating on balance far more than progress. The wind buffeted us, always at the worst moments. It took another hour and a half before we were at the bottom of the waterfalls and could see how to tackle the rock face. It didn't look too bad. There were enough cracks and ledges to make the climb fairly easy.

"That's the spot," said Martindale. "Right in there."

We followed his pointing finger. About seventy feet above our heads one of the bigger waterfalls came cascading its way out from the cliff for a thirty-foot vertical drop.

"The waterfall?" said Helga. Her tone of voice said more than her words. *That's supposed to be a generator of two hundred and fifty miles of gale-force winds?* she was saying. *Tell me another one.*

"Behind it." Martindale was walking along the base of the cliff, looking for a likely point where he could begin the climb. "The coordinates are actually *inside* the cliff. Which means we have to look *behind* the waterfall. And that means we have to come at it from the side."

We had brought rock-climbing gear with us. We did not need it. Martindale found a diagonal groove that ran at an angle of thirty degrees up the side of the cliff, and after following it to a vertical chimney, we found another slanting ledge running the other way. Two more changes of route, neither difficult, and we were on a ledge about two feet wide that ran up to and right behind our waterfall.

Two feet is a lot less when you are seventy feet up and walking a rock ledge slippery with water. Even here, the winds plucked restlessly at our clothes. We roped ourselves together, Martindale leading, and inched our way forward. When we were a few feet from the waterfall Martindale lengthened the rope between him and me, and went on alone behind the cascading water.

"It's all right." He had to shout to be heard above the crash of water. "It gets easier. The ledge gets wider. It runs into a cave in the face of the cliff. Come on."

We were carrying powerful electric flashlights, and we needed them. Once we were in behind the screen of water, the light paled and dwindled. We shone the lights toward the back of the cave. We were standing on a flat area, maybe ten feet wide and twelve feet deep. So much for Owen's dream of endless caverns of treasure; so much for my dreams, too, though they had been a lot less grandiose than his.

Standing about nine feet in from the edge of the ledge stood a dark blue cylinder, maybe four feet long and as thick as a man's thigh. It was smooth-surfaced and uniform, with no sign of controls or markings on its surface. I heard Martindale grunt in satisfaction.

"Bingo," he said. "That's it."

"The whole thing?"

"Certainly. Remember what I said last night, about advanced technology making this smaller? There's the source of the line-vortex—the power unit for the whole Kingdom of the Winds." He took two steps toward it, and as he did so Helga cried out, "Look out!"

The blank wall at the back of the cave had suddenly changed. Instead of damp gray stone, a rectangle of striated darkness had formed, maybe seven feet high and five feet wide.

Martindale laughed in triumph, and turned back to us. "Don't move for the moment. But don't worry, this is exactly what I hoped we might find. I suspected something like this when I first saw that anomaly. The winds are just an accidental by-product—like an eddy. The equipment here must be a little bit off in its tuning. But it's still working, no doubt about that. Feel the inertial dragging?"

I could feel something, a weak but persistent force drawing me toward the dark rectangle. I leaned backward to counteract it and looked more closely at the opening. As my eyes adjusted I realized that it was not true darkness there. Faint blue lines of luminescence started in from the edges of the aperture and flew rapidly toward a vanishing point at the center. There they disappeared, while new blue threads came into being at the outside.

"Where did the opening come from?" said Helga. "It wasn't there when we came in."

"No. It's a portal. I'm sure it only switches on when it senses the right object within range." Martindale took another couple of steps forward. Now he was standing at the very edge of the aperture, staring through at something invisible to me.

"What is it?" I said. In spite of Martindale's words I too had taken a couple of steps closer, and so had Helga.

"A portal—a gate to some other part of the universe, built around a gravitational line singularity." He laughed, and his voice sounded half an octave lower in pitch. "Somebody left it here for us humans, and it leads to the stars. You wanted Trapalanda? This is it—the most priceless discovery in the history of the human race."

He took one more step forward. His moving leg stretched out forever in front of him, lengthening and lengthening. When his foot came down, the leg looked fifty yards long and it dwindled away to the tiny, distant speck of his foot. He lifted his back foot from the ground, and as he leaned forward his whole body rippled and distorted, stretching away from me. Now he looked his usual self—but he was a hundred yards away, carried with one stride along a tunnel that ran as far as the eye could follow.

Martindale turned, and reached out his hand. A long arm zoomed back toward us, still attached to that distant body, and a normal-sized right hand appeared out of the aperture.

"Come on." The voice was lower again in tone, and strangely slowed. "Both of you. Don't you want to see the rest of the universe? Here's the best chance that you will ever have."

Helga and I took another step forward, staring in to the very edge of the opening. Martindale reached out his left hand too, and it hurtled toward us, growing rapidly, until it was there to be taken and held. I took another step, and I was within the portal itself. I felt normal, but I was aware of that force again, tugging us harder toward the tunnel. Suddenly I was gripped by an irrational and irresistible fear. I had to get away. I turned to move back from the aperture, and found myself looking at Helga. She was thirty yards away, drastically diminished, standing in front of a tiny wall of falling water.

One more step would have taken me outside again to safety, clear of the aperture and its persistent, tugging field. But as I was poised to take that step, Helga acted. She closed her eyes and took a long, trembling step forward. I could see her mouth moving, almost as though in prayer. And then the action I could not believe: she leaned forward to grasp convulsively at John Martindale's outstretched hand.

I heard her gasp, and saw her shiver. Then she was taking another step forward. And another.

"Helga!" I changed my direction and blundered after her along that endless tunnel. "This way. I'll get us out."

"No." She had taken another shivering step, and she was still clutching Martindale's hand. "No, Klaus." Her voice was breathless. "He's right. This is the biggest adventure ever. It's worth everything."

"Don't be afraid,' said a hollow, booming voice. It was Martindale, and now all I could see of him was a shimmering silhouette. The man had been replaced by a sparkling outline. "Come on, Klaus. It's almost here."

The tugging force was stronger, pulling on every cell of my body. I looked at Helga, a shining outline now like John Martindale. They were dwindling, vanishing. They were gone. I wearily turned around and tried to walk back the way we had come. Tons of weight hung on me, wreathed themselves around every limb. I was trying to drag the whole world up an endless hill. I forced my legs to take one small step, then another. It was impossible to see if I was making progress. I was surrounded by that roaring silent pattern of rushing blue lines, all going in the opposite direction from me, every one doing its best to drag me back.

I inched along. Finally I could see the white of the waterfall ahead. It was growing in size, but at the same time it was losing definition. My eyes ached. By the time I took the final step and fell on my face on the stone floor of the cave, the waterfall was no more than a milky haze and a sound of rushing water.

Owen Davies saved my life, what there is of it. I did my part to help him. I wanted to live when I woke up, and weak as I was, and half-blind, I managed to crawl down that steep rock face. I was dragging myself over the icy boulders when he found me. My clothes were shredding, falling off my body, and I was shivering and weeping from cold and fear. He wrapped me in his own jacket and helped me back to the aircraft.

Then he went off to look for John Martindale and Helga. He never came back. I do not know to this day if he found and entered the portal, or if he came to grief somewhere on the way.

I spent two days in the aircraft, knowing that I was too sick and my eyes were too bad to dream of flying anywhere. My front teeth had all gone, and I ate porridge or biscuits soaked in tea. Three more days, and I began to realize that if I did not fly myself, I was not going anywhere. On the seventh day I managed a faltering, incompetent takeoff and flew northeast, peering at the instruments with my newly purblind eyes. I made a crash landing at Comodoro Rivadavia, was dragged from the wreckage, and flown to a hospital in Bahía Blanca. They did what they could for me, which was not too much. By that time I was beginning to have some faint idea what had happened to my body, and as soon as the hospital was willing to release me I took a flight to Buenos Aires, and went on at once to Geneva's Lakeside Hospital. They removed the cataracts from my eyes. Three weeks later I could see again without that filmy mist over everything.

Before I left the hospital I insisted on a complete physical. Thanks to John Martindale's half-million dollar deposit, money was not going to be a problem. The doctor who went over the results with me was about thirty years old, a Viennese Jew who had been practicing for only a couple of years. He looked oddly similar to one of my cousins at that age. "Well, Mr. Jacobi," he said (after a quick look at his dossier to make sure of my name), "there are no organic abnormalities, no cardiovascular problems, only slight circulation problems. You have some osteoarthritis in your hips and your knees. I'm delighted to be able to tell you that you are in excellent overall health for your age."

"If you didn't know," I said, "how old would you think I am?"

He looked again at his crib sheet, but found no help there. I had deliberately left out my age at the place where the hospital entry form required it. "Well," he said. He was going to humor me. "Seventy-six?"

"Spot on," I said.

I had the feeling that he had knocked a couple of years off his estimate, just to make me feel good. So let's say my biological age was seventy-eight or seventy-nine. When I flew with John Martindale to Buenos Aires, I had been one month short of my forty-fourth birthday.

At that point I flew to New York, and went to John Kenyon Martindale's house. I met with Shirley—briefly. She did not recognize me, and I did not try to identify myself. I gave my name as Owen Davies. In John's absence, I said, I was interested in contacting some of the mathematician friends that he had told me I would like to meet. Could she remember the names of any of them, so I could call them even before John came back? She looked bored, but she came back with a telephone book and produced three names. One was in San Francisco, one was in Boston, and the third was here in New York, at the Courant Institute.

He was in his middle twenties, a fit-looking curly haired man with bright blue eyes and a big smile. The thing that astonished him about my visit, I think, was not the subject matter. It was the fact that I made the visit. He found it astonishing that a spavined antique like me would come to his office to ask about this sort of topic in theoretical physics.

"What you are suggesting is not just *permitted* in today's view of space and time, Mr. Davies," he said. "It's absolutely *required.* You can't do something to *space*—such as making an instantaneous link between two places, as you have been suggesting—without at the same time having profound effects on *time.* Space and time are really a single entity. Distances and elapsed times are intimately related, like two sides of the same coin."

"And the line-vortex generator?" I said. I had told him far less about this, mainly because all I knew of it had been told to us by John Martindale.

"Well, if the generator in some sense approximated an infinitely long, rapidly rotating cylinder, then yes. General relativity insists that very peculiar things would happen there. There could be global causality violations—'before' and 'after' getting confused, cause and effect becoming mixed up, that sort of thing. God knows what time and space look like near the line singularity itself. But don't misunderstand me. Before any of these things could happen, you would have to be dealing with a huge system, something many times as massive as the sun."

I resisted the urge to tell him he was wrong. Apparently he did not accept John Martindale's unshakable confidence in the idea that with better technology came increase in capability *and* decrease in size. I stood up and leaned on my cane. My left hip was a little dodgy and became tired if I walked too far. "You've been very helpful."

"Not at all." He stood up, too, and said, "Actually, I'm going to be giving a lecture at the institute on these subjects in a couple of weeks. If you'd like to come . . ."

I noted down the time and place, but I knew I would not be there. It was three months to the day since John Martindale, Helga, and I had climbed the rock face and walked behind the waterfall. Time—my time—was short. I had to head south again.

The flight to Argentina was uneventful. Comodoro Rivadavia was the same as always. Now I am sitting in Alberto McShane's bar, drinking one last beer (all that my digestion today will permit) and waiting for the pilot. McShane did not recognize me, but the armadillo did. It trundled to my table, and sat looking up at me. *Where's my friend John Martindale,* it was saying.

Where indeed? I will tell you soon. The plane is ready. We are going to Trapalanda.

It will take all my strength, but I think I can do it. I have added equipment that will help me to cross that icy field of boulders and ascend the rock face. It is September. The weather will be warmer, and the going easier. If I close my eyes I can see the portal now, behind the waterfall, its black depths and shimmering blue streaks rushing away toward the vanishing point.

Thirty-five years. That is what the portal owes me. It sucked them out of my body as I struggled back against the gravity gradient. Maybe it is impossible to get them back. I don't know. My young mathematician friend insisted that time is infinitely fluid, with no more constraints on movement through it than there are on travel through space. I don't know, but I want my thirty-five years. If I die in the attempt, I will be losing little.

I am terrified of that open gate, with its alien twisting of the world's geometry. I am more afraid of it than I have ever been of anything. Last time I failed, and I could not go through it. But I will go through it now.

This time I have something more than Martindale's scientific curiosity to drive me on. It is not thoughts of danger or death that fill my mind as I sit here. I have that final image of Helga, reaching out and taking John Martindale's hand in hers. Reaching out, to grasp his hand, voluntarily. I love Helga, I am sure of that, but I cannot make sense of my other emotions; fear, jealousy, resentment, hope, excitement. She was *touching* him. Did she do it because she wanted to go through the portal, wanted it so much that every fear was insignificant? Or had she, after thirty years, finally found someone whom she could touch without cringing and loathing?

The pilot has arrived. My glass is empty. Tomorrow I will know.

Afterword to "Trapalanda"

John Kenyon Martindale is a major character in this story. John Kenyon Martindale *Sanderson* is my father-in-law, Sandy, the father of my late wife, Sarah ("Georgia on My Mind" is really about Sarah). Sandy lives in Walton-on-Thames, near London. He is eighty-eight years old, and eats, drinks, walks, and laughs like someone half his age. He is what I want to be at that age. He has been reading science fiction since the 1920s, he hung around with the Bloomsbury set, and he knew H. G. Wells. (Irrelevant side note: Wells was very popular with women, even though he was not handsome and had a funny voice. Sandy asked a couple of ladies why they found Wells so attractive. They said, "He has a really interesting smell.")

Anyway, this story was written for Sandy, even though it was not dedicated to him. Unfortunately, when he read it he didn't like it. He thought that the narrator had a diseased mind. I didn't tell him it was really me.

Ah, well. He loved "Beyond the Golden Road." I'll have to settle for that.

Obsolete Skill

I HAD BEEN a lifelong agnostic. So when the hammer blow to the chest came at three o'clock on Friday afternoon, I knew it was the end of everything.

I had just enough time to put the pan back on the stove, curse my own stupidity—those pains in the left arm and chest were clear enough signs of heart trouble, but who likes to visit doctors?—then I was falling toward the floor and the lights were going out. Goodbye, world.

It was a big surprise to drift back to consciousness and find that the world was apparently still there. CPR? But then who could have saved me? I had been alone in the house, with the alarm system on and no visitors expected. It occurred to me that I didn't merely feel pleased to be alive, like any man who has survived a massive heart attack; I felt *good*. Weak and feeble, sure—but healthy, if you can imagine that combination.

Without opening my eyes I groped automatically for my glasses.

"What do you want?" said a disembodied man's voice a few feet away from me.

"Spectacles." My eyelids seemed to weigh a ton each.

"They are unnecessary."

That *was* enough to make me blink my eyes open. I was staring straight up at a blue-painted ceiling, glowing all over with a soft internal lighting. Every detail was visible, down to a little spider-web of sensors over in the corner, and a raft of things like glowing pink buttons right over me. The area that I could see without turning my head held a clutter of other miniaturized electronics, doing I knew not what. Fine lines of violet light crisscrossed the whole field of view.

"Try to relax," said the voice. "The instruments are monitoring your isotonic responses, and four of them show high readings. Don't be frightened, there is no danger."

That was bad—I was supposed to understand something about self-control. I lay back and closed my eyes again.

I must not fear. Fear is the death. Fear is the little-death that brings obliteration. (Not, it's not my own prescription—but it works. I've never been too proud to borrow.)

"How long has it been?" I said after a few more seconds.

There was a gasping intake of breath from the man next to me. "You know what has happened? Already?"

"I can make a good guess. I died; and now I'm not dead anymore. So somebody took me, and either they transferred my consciousness to a new body, or they froze me, cured me, and woke me up again. I'd guess the second, because it still feels like my own body. Which was it?" I opened my eyes and turned my head, to look at the slightly built man who sat at my bedside.

"Not quite either." He was staring at me in a puzzled way. "You were frozen, as you say. But the body was given certain desirable modifications before you were allowed to regain consciousness." He leaned forward. "We have revived many who were cryogenically preserved, but never one who has at once realized what has happened. How did you *know?*"

"Did you ever read my stories?" I looked at his smooth face—yellowish complexion, epicanthic fold on the eyes, black hair. "I guess you didn't. I've written that scenario a dozen times."

I sat up. As I'd thought, I was as weak as a cup of tea in a Scots' boardinghouse. "Now you can answer one for me. *How long?*"

"Since you—died?"

I nodded.

"One hundred and ninety-seven and a half years."

Jesus. No wonder I felt rested. And weak. I was two hundred and eighty years old. "Nearly two centuries. And my works are still read?"

"Not exactly." He hesitated. "Reading is no longer necessary. However, certain of your works are still *studied.*"

Better than nothing. Looking at him more closely with my new twenty-twenty eyes I noticed an odd thing about his speech. The words seemed to lag a little behind his facial expressions. That had its own implications. "Studied—but not in English," I said. "When did the language die out?"

"It did not." He smiled at me, trying to be nice. "There are still many who speak it. But as you might guess from my appearance it is not my native tongue. My name is Chen, and my native language is a variation of Mandarin Chinese. But of course, most of the editions of your works that have survived are in Japanese."

Of course. Japanese. "And you—you are hooked up to a computer that makes the actual translation from your language to English?"

"That is correct." He saw my satisfied smile. "Again—you wrote of this?"

"A score of times." I tried to swing my legs over the edge of the bed, but I was too weak to make it. Go steady—I suspected I had plenty of time to regain my strength.

"Let's get down to the nitty-gritty," I said. "I'm here, I'm alive, and I never gave any instructions to be put into cryogenic storage. I made a lot of money, but I spent a lot, too. It must have taken a bundle to keep me down at liquid helium temperatures for two centuries. So what the hell is going on? I'm not complaining, but why aren't I a couple of hundred years dead?"

"It was a plan prepared by a group of your admirers—special admirers, the people who were known as *fans*. They argued that if anyone should be preserved for the future, you should, because you had a unique knowledge of your own times, and a special feeling for times to come. Having thought so much about possible futures, you would be less disturbed by any real future. Without telling you, they arranged for the collection of funds over the years at every one of their meetings—conventions—and placed it into an interest-bearing account pending your demise. When that occurred, you were transferred to the cryogenic vaults and prepared for storage."

No sinus headache, no postnasal drip. No buzzing in the left ear. I shrugged my shoulders, and there was no arthritic twinge from my left side. Somebody had done a good job on me.

"Thanks, fans. I don't know I deserve it, considering what I've said about you over the years. What comes next?"

"First, it is necessary that you recuperate and gain strength. That will take a few days. You will stay here for that period, since we do not wish you to experience too much cultural shock."

He frowned, and leaned forward to stare at me. I felt sure there were a dozen sensors peering out through his almond eyes. "Are you feeling all right?" he said.

"Just fine."

"I wondered, because you seem almost *too* calm. To arrive here, far in your future, and to know suddenly that all your friends and fellow-writers are dead . . . it must be most upsetting."

"Chen, I was *old*. Hell, most of my friends and the writers that I knew well were already dead before I died." *(And I was glad to see most of 'em go, the two-faced bastards.)*

He nodded thoughtfully, and his face again went blank for a split second. "I do not have your reference system to work with. But of course, in your day eighty-two years *was* old. Very well. When you are fully recovered from the awakening, we have a number of people who would like to talk to you—historians, and students of twentieth-century literature. The authorship of many works from your time is left in doubt, particularly because of the translation change, to and from the Japanese. The original titles have often been lost." He paused, as though listening inside his head for a second. "It is not easy to identify your output, even with the best references. For example, were you the author of a work named *Tales of New Space?*"

"Sure was."

"*Spaceship Troopers?*"

"Right."

"And *The Nine Worlds Saga?*"

"Yup."

"*The Nude Sun?* And *Timeskip?*"

"Sure."

"How about *Nine Princes in Aspic?*"

I shook my head. "Not me. Try farther along the alphabet." God, I felt good. "Listen, these people who want to talk to me—didn't your records tell you that I wouldn't do interviews?"

"They do show that—but there is some contradiction. One of your biographies—"

"How many of them are there?"

"Ten." He paused at my grunt. "You are surprised?"

"I'd hoped for more. But carry on."

"The interviews. You did give interviews. One of your biographies states quite unambiguously that on a visit to Rome you agreed to meet with a certain important person there who was a keen reader of your works. Is that not true?"

"It's true enough. But I always thought of that particular meeting as an *audience* with me more than an interview. I don't do interviews. Can't they ask somebody else?" A thought struck me. "Hey, just how many other writers from my time were frozen—I mean, *science fiction* writers." (The only sort that were worth diddly-squat.)

"Only two."

"Then who was the other? Surely not that boring old windbag—"

"No."

Big relief—and a stir of excitement, too. He named the only woman science fiction writer I'd ever felt really attracted to. Sure, it made sense, her fans would have done the same for her as mine did for me. Let's hope she died young.

"She was of course born quite a few years later than you," Chen went on. "But the scholars of today know that she had read your works, and they assert that her books very clearly draw in some ways from you. There is a part of you in her."

But not the part of me I'd like. One problem with this renovated body, it had the hormones flowing as I'd not felt them flow in thirty years. "I feel flattered," I said. "Perhaps she and I can meet when I am fully recovered."

"It can be arranged, though there are subtle questions to be asked of her—the social conventions have changed much since your day. A meeting cannot be assured." Chen sat up a little straighter. "You will probably also be wondering what your role will be in this 'brave new world' to which you have awakened."

"Naturally." As a matter of fact, up to that point I hadn't given it a thought. I was going to be a *writer,* wasn't I? What else was there to do?

"Then I am afraid that I bring you bad news. When you were frozen, your admirers did it with the full confidence that your abilities would find unique recognition here in the future. You were widely regarded as one of the most learned men of your time, a person whose knowledge seemed almost boundless, in many diverse fields. Some suggested that you knew more than any other living human."

Some suggested! Was Chen trying to get me irritated? "They were just being kind to me," I said modestly.

"Be that as it may, your admirers had unfortunately badly mis-judged the future." Chen leaned forward, an earnest expression on his unlined face. "You see, sir, there has been a change in the world, and it is one that will shock you. *Knowledge*—that which you possess in such full measure—is no longer useful. Knowledge has become an obsolete skill."

Was he crazy? There was no way, in a world that could revive a fro-zen corpse and bring it back to life and health, that knowledge could become obsolete. The whole technological society must depend on it. And the room I was in was a miracle of technology.

"I don't understand you," I said. "How can knowledge lose its value?"

"I will show you. Is there a subject on which you would say you are particularly expert?"

You must be kidding. "There are several."

"Then name one."

"Oh—let's say, European history. Or botany. Or communications theory. Or organ music. Or the Roman Empire. Want more?"

"Very good. That is enough. Now, ask me a question—any difficult question of fact—that relates to one of those fields."

He didn't seem to be joking. I thought for a second. "All right, I'll bite. Who was leading the French Army when it surrendered at Sedan in the Franco-Prussian war? And when did it happen?"

He sat there looking half-witted for maybe half a second, then said, "MacMahon, on September 1st, 1870, at four-fifteen P.M."

Once I had seen it happen, I knew exactly what must be going on. Little Chen was hooked up through some high-rate electronic link with a bunch of data banks, and he had access to them directly by thinking the right sequence. It meant he had immediate access to whole librar-ies—perhaps to all the libraries in today's world. Well, I could play that game, too, once I knew how to hook in.

"You don't mean knowledge is obsolete," I said. "You mean you've replaced the need for one sort of knowledge with another. People just have to learn how to use the new sort—they need to know how to gain access to the data banks."

Again, he seemed astonished at my response.

"I wrote that story, too," I went on, before he could speak. "About implants for data access and direct mind-to-mind communication. Back in the late 70's. It didn't make much of a stir—but I noticed a lot of other people using the same idea in the next few years."

"You do not appreciate the problem," he said. "It is true, we all have access to the data banks, and you will not be denied that access. But what is involved is no simple matter of exchanging one kind of *fact* for another, as you seem to think. It is a question of structure and approach. Remember, many hundreds of people have been frozen and reawakened since the technique was perfected. We have done our best to train each of them in the use of the mental data banks—without success. I will leave you to work on this, but already I am sure of the outcome. Some banks you will learn to enter without a problem. But the general *technique* that stands behind it . . . well, I wish you luck."

He meant it, too. But I didn't share his worries for a moment. In sixty years of writing science fiction, I had picked up a working knowledge of a hundred different fields. Lots of them were supposedly difficult except for the "specially trained." I'd learned to recognize that for what it was: territorial imperative, an attempt to keep out anybody who hadn't paid for the formal training and the official carrying card of the profession. It was nonsense. I had picked up what I needed from scratch, on my own, without anyone around to guide me.

It was an article of faith. There wasn't a branch of know-how I couldn't acquire, or a system I couldn't master, as easily as breathing.

I shrugged. "Let me try it. Maybe I'll be lucky."

"Maybe." His tone denied the possibility.

"If I don't make it, what then? Euthanasia? The junkyard?"

Chen looked more than uncomfortable—he was horrified. "No! How can you make such a suggestion. We will arrange a pleasant life for you, along with all the others who have been reawakened. We will provide special living quarters, and excellent contentment drugs—stronger than we have for ourselves. You will be perfectly happy."

Sure. *Walk this way, and don't worry about the slight smell of gas.*

Or maybe he *was* quite sincere. A two-hundred-year nap leaves you waking up kind of crotchety.

"Here is the way that you will interact with our system," he said. He handed a little flat oblong across to me. "Naturally, if it turns out by some lucky chance that you *can* master full access to the data banks, we will arrange for your own implant and code signal. But it is best to begin like this. Anything else you want can be obtained by pressing this orange place on the side of the calling device."

He left, after promising to arrange for delivery of my personal belongings. Apparently, like the pharoahs, I had been sealed in the vault with at least a few possessions to comfort me when I awoke in the afterlife. Whoever made that decision understood human psychology. I found I was really looking forward to putting on some of my old convention finery—the diamond stickpin, the gold nugget cuff links, the African red-gold ring, and the silver pocket watch with its hand-worked chain. The final Worldcon may have been centuries ago, but as far as I was concerned it had happened last week.

Time for the fun stuff later. I sat down at the terminal Chen had given me, and went to work.

Do you know the rotten part of all this? It turned out that Chen was quite right. I'd have bet money against him, but he was spot-on correct in his prediction. Every single item of information known to the human race was in those banks, waiting for me to call it out. All I needed to know were the correct access codes—the series of digital strings and pointers, leading the inquiry from one data bank to the next.

Simple, you say? That's what I thought. Then it turned out that there was a hidden symmetry and structure to the systems of lists and markers, a natural hierarchy that made recall simple and fast. Without an understanding of that underlying form, access to the banks was marginally possible, but it took ages and it was unreliable.

I could not, try as I might, grasp that structure. I worked at it until I was cursing myself and bursting with frustration. It did no good. I got nowhere. I could find my way into certain data banks, almost at random, but I couldn't work the system as it was supposed to be worked.

After twelve hours, I recalled a melancholy fact about the human brain. If a person does not learn to speak by a certain age, that person will *never* speak properly—no matter how long and hard he tries. The data bank system seemed to be like that. You acquired the understanding by a certain age, or you were forever on the outside, peering in.

I tried all night long. By morning I had a lot more general facts about the world I was in, but no success with the *system*.

What was this new world like? I could perceive it only dimly, though maybe that would change with more exposure. I did not even try to understand how it derived from the world I knew. As I've said many times, history doesn't know how to plot worth a damn. If you look at the events that lead up to a major change in the world, they're too improbably for any rational person to accept. The human race goes rolling and staggering on into the future, with no more idea of the path than a drunken duchess.

Some things were clear. We had the solar system, twenty billion humans spread across the face of it and running things the way they wanted to. We had the stars, too. That was nice. I'd missed badly on one thing there. I had assumed that when everyone was linked into the central data banks, they wouldn't want to go too far from home because the light-speed limit would make them lose contact with almost everything they knew. Plausible—but the light-speed limit had been one of the first things to go. Hell, if I'd hung on for a few more years I'd have seen it myself.

But still no aliens on the scene. And no signals from anyone out there, to show we're not the only game in town. Lots of good science fiction went down the tubes on that one.

When Chen called back I was pretty tired. He hadn't told me what the limits of my modified body would be, but I thought I might as well find out for myself. After twenty-four hours without sleep (or alcohol; the food supply system refused to give it to me) I felt as though I could use a twenty-minute nap. No more than that.

He called before he came, sending me a message through the terminal. I guess anybody who was wired into the system would get it direct, brain-to-brain, but I couldn't qualify.

"Is there anything that I can bring you?" he said. "Anything you need?"

"Not a thing. Come on over."

He disconnected. If he were curious to know what progress I had made, he didn't show it.

My old convention outfit had been delivered while I was working on the terminal. It had been superbly preserved. I put on the formal clothes, the ruffed shirt, the scarlet sash, the black patent leather shoes. Then the cuff-links, the ring, and diamond stickpin. Finally I lay down for that twenty-minute nap before Chen arrived. I wanted to be fresh and alert.

When he came into the room I was carefully winding my fob watch. So far as I am concerned, wrist watches and digital watches are two backward steps of the human race. There's no sound on earth more satisfying than the ticking of a decent-sized pocket watch, and no weight that hefts more naturally and comfortably in the hand.

Chen stared at the watch on its long golden chain. "A *clockwork* watch? Worked by a spring?"

"That's right. If I'm obsolete, I might as well have obsolete technology to match."

I set the time on it, closed the case, and lifted it up by its long chain. "All done," I said. "Now I can face the future." *And try a few obsolete skills.*

Chen was watching me with an expression of pity. He seemed like a really nice guy. No doubt about it, the human race had come a long way in two hundred years. Somewhere on that winding road to tomorrow, the viciousness and insensitivity had disappeared—maybe because it's hard to ignore how others are feeling when you have mind-to-mind contact.

Whatever had made the difference to the way people felt, Chen was pretty miserable when he sat down across from me. I didn't need to tell him that I couldn't crack the data banks the way that he could. He *knew.* Hundreds of others had tried and failed.

I nodded at him. "You were quite right. I can *learn* the pointers and the lists. But I can't get the hang of *manipulating* them efficiently."

He nodded. "I was convinced that would prove to be the case. You are ready, then, to join the others who were revived? I know that you will have a pleasant and tranquil life."

"I'm not *quite* ready for that yet." I leaned back a little in my chair. This took concentration. I had read about it a dozen times, and I knew exactly how it was done; but this was only the second time I had tried it.

"You know, Chen," I went on, "when you've lived as long as I have, and read as much as I have, and done as many things as I've done, you find it hard to accept the idea that one of those things somehow wouldn't prove useful. Even today, in a world that's so different from the one that I knew, you think there must be *something* you know or do that will have value. I can't get that idea out of my mind. Most of my skills are obsolete today, but isn't there some little talent or piece of know-how that might still have value? I had an experience not too different from that, fifty—make that two hundred and fifty, I guess—years ago, when I was on a trip to Mexico. I'd been staying in this little town, where the only safe thing to drink was the beer. And I didn't really know where my next meal was coming from . . ."

He humored me, allowing me to wind on through my slow and soft-spoken tale. I didn't hurry. I didn't once raise my voice. He listened patiently. He must have thought that it was the least the new age could do for the old, giving me a hearing before they dumped me into the old folks' home and forgot about us.

All the time I talked I was sitting with my eyes fixed on his, casually holding that old silver watch on its chain of gold links, and swinging it back and forth in front of him.

Five minutes, and his mouth was open. Ten minutes, and his eyes were glassy. He was gone. I put the watch back into my pocket. Interesting, what you pick up in a misspent lifetime.

"Stand up, Chen."

He rose to his feet and looked quietly down at me.

"Very good," I said. "Now, Chen, I want to know the names of the parents of the Emperor Claudius, of the Roman Empire."

A split-second pause. "Drusus; and Antonia."

"Right. And what were the names of the operas that Mozart composed in 1781 and 1782?"

"Idomoneo, and *Die Entführung aus dem Serail."* He stumbled over the words.

"Good enough. Now we want something a little more complicated. But don't begin at once. Wait until I say the word 'Idomoneo.' All right?" I put my hand on his shoulder in a friendly fashion. "First, Chen, we are going to need the entry points into the data banks that control world communications, transportation, and food supply. We particularly need to locate the major nodes, the places that permit complete system control. Understand?"

He nodded.

"Good. And while you are at it, Chen, I want you to link me through to the place where the *other* science fiction writer is living. I'll need to visit her and talk to her. We have a lot of plans to make. But first, though, you'll bring all that food, transportation, and communication data up for display on my screen. *Idomoneo."*

It took him a minute or two this time. I stayed calm. We were in no particular rush, and we had to do it right. I leaned back, swung my watch on its chain, and wondered about those ten biographies of me.

Had any of them been *really* honest—honest enough to say that I was an ornery son of a bitch? Probably not.

Chen was nodding his head at last, and the data I wanted came flowing out onto the screen. All the solar system critical nodes were identified, every nexus from Vulcan to the Oort Cloud. I put Chen into a deeper sleep while I settled down to study them. After a few minutes I touched the first key, one that began to take over surreptitious control of the food supply lines.

Control. That was the key word. Some concepts and skills never become obsolete. I looked again at Chen. From the glaze on him he was under deeper hypnosis than anyone I had ever seen. He was my man. One down, twenty billion to go.

Ten lousy biographies? I'd change that, one way or another.

Afterword to "Obsolete Skill"

If you have money to spare and no expectation of needing it during your lifetime, you can arrange to have your body frozen at liquid nitrogen temperatures when you die. You will then be kept in cold storage for as long as your estate can pay for it, or until someone in the future decides to revive you. For rather less money, you can have just your head frozen, although I rather consider this to be false economy. As Woody Allen says when his brain is going to be removed, "Not my brain, it's my second favorite organ." (See "The Feynman Saltation.")

However, regardless of the preferred body parts there is a bigger snag to the freezing bet. Most people today have nothing special to offer to future generations. Why should someone a century from now choose to revive you, even assuming that the disease that killed you can be cured?

In my opinion, the only group worth waking—surprise, surprise— is people who have spent much of their lives thinking about the future, and, by their writings, even *defining* the future; namely, science fiction authors. Once I reached that conclusion, this story wrote itself.

The narrator of this tale is a sneaky, cunning character with a very high opinion of himself. I have several times been asked who it is *really*. Is it Heinlein, or Pohl, or Niven, or Brin, or me? My answer is, it is *every* SF writer, and I am certainly not sexist enough to limit that statement to males.

GEORGIA ON MY MIND

I FIRST TANGLED with digital computers late in 1958. That may sound like the Dark Ages, but we considered ourselves infinitely more advanced than our predecessors of a decade earlier, when programming was done mostly by sticking plugs into plug-boards and a card-sequenced programmable calculator was considered the height of sophistication.

Even so, 1958 was still early enough that the argument between analog and digital computers had not yet been settled, decisively, in favor of the digital. And the first computer that I programmed was, by anyone's standards, a brute.

It was called DEUCE, which stood for Digital Electronic Universal Computing Engine, and it was, reasonably enough to cardplayers, the next thing after the ACE (for Automatic Computing Engine), developed by the National Physical Laboratory at Teddington. Unlike ACE, DEUCE was a commercial machine; and some idea of its possible shortcomings is provided by one of the designers' comments about ACE itself: "If we had known that it was going to be developed commercially, we would have finished it."

DEUCE was big enough to walk inside. The engineers would do that, tapping at suspect vacuum tubes with a screwdriver when the whole beast was proving balky. Which was often. Machine errors were as common a cause of trouble as programming errors; and programming errors were dreadfully frequent, because we were working at a level so close to basic machine logic that it is hard to imagine it today.

I was about to say that the computer had no compilers or assemblers, but that is not strictly true. There was a floating-point compiler known as ALPHACODE, but it ran a thousand times slower than a machine code program and no one with any self-respect ever used it. We programmed in absolute, to make the best possible use of the machine's 402 words of high-speed (mercury delay line) memory, and its 8,192 words of back-up (rotating drum) memory. Anything needing more than that had to use punched cards as intermediate storage, with the programmer standing by to shovel them from the output hopper back into the input hopper.

When I add that binary-to-decimal conversion routines were usually avoided because they wasted space, that all instructions were defined in binary, that programmers therefore had to be very familiar with the binary representation of numbers, that we did our own card punching with hand (not electric) punches, and that the machine itself, for some reason that still remains obscure to me, worked with binary numbers whose most significant digit was on the *right*, rather than on the left—so that 13, for example, became 1011, rather than the usual 1101—well, by this time the general flavor of DEUCE programming ought to be coming through.

Now, I mention these things not because they are interesting (to the few) or because they are dull (to the many) but to make the point that anyone programming DEUCE in those far-off days was an individual not to be taken lightly. We at least thought so, though I suspect that to higher management we were all harebrained children who did incomprehensible things, many of them in the middle of the night (when debug time was more easily to be had).

A few years later more computers became available, the diaspora inevitably took place, and we all went off to other interesting places. Some found their way to university professorships, some into commerce, and many to foreign parts. But we did tend to keep in touch, because those early days had generated a special feeling.

One of the most interesting characters was Bill Rigley. He was a tall, dashing, wavy-haired fellow who wore English tweeds and spoke with the open "a" sound that to most Americans indicates a Boston origin. But Bill was a New Zealander, who had seen at firsthand things like the Great Barrier Reef that the rest of us had barely heard of. He didn't talk much about his home and family, but he must have pined for them, because after a few years in Europe and America he went back to take a faculty position in the Department of Mathematics (and later the Computer Science Department, when one was finally created) at the University of Auckland.

Auckland is on the North Island, a bit less remote than the bleaker South Island, but a long way from the East Coast of the United States, where I had put down my own roots. Even so, Bill and I kept in close contact, because our scientific interests were very similar. We saw each other every few years in Stanford, or London, or wherever else our paths intersected, and we knew each other at the deep level where few people touch. It was Bill who helped me to mourn when my wife died, and I in turn knew (but never talked about) the dark secret that had scarred Bill's own life. No matter how long we had been separated, our conversations when we met picked up as though they had never left off.

Bill's interests were encyclopedic, and he had a special fondness for scientific history. So it was no surprise that when he went back to New Zealand he would wander around there, examining its contribution to world science. What was a surprise to me was a letter from him a few months ago, stating that in a farmhouse near Dunedin, toward the south end of the South Island, he had come across some bits and pieces of Charles Babbage's Analytical Engine.

Even back in the late 1950's, we had known all about Babbage. There was at the time only one decent book about digital computers, Bowden's *Faster Than Thought,* but its first chapter talked all about that eccentric but formidable Englishman, with his hatred of street musicians and his low opinion of the Royal Society (existing only to hold dinners, he said, at which they gave each other medals). Despite these odd views, Babbage was still our patron saint. For starting in 1834 and continuing for the rest of his life, he tried—unsuccessfully—to build the world's first programmable digital computer. He understood the principles perfectly well, but he was thwarted because he had to work with mechanical parts. Can you imagine a computer built of cogs and toothed cylinders and gears and springs and levers?

Babbage could. And he might have triumphed even over the inadequacy of the available technology, but for one fatal problem: he kept thinking of improvements. As soon as a design was half assembled, he would want to tear it apart and start using the bits to build something better. At the time of Babbage's death in 1871, his wonderful Analytical Engine was still a dream. The bits and pieces were carted off to London's Kensington Science Museum, where they remain today.

Given our early exposure to Babbage, my reaction to Bill Rigley's letter was pure skepticism. It was understandable that Bill would *want* to find evidence of parts of the Analytical Engine somewhere on his home stamping ground; but his claim to have done so was surely self-delusion.

I wrote back, suggesting this in as tactful a way as I could; and received in prompt reply not recantation, but the most extraordinary package of documents I had ever seen in my life (I should say, to that point; there were stranger to come).

The first was a letter from Bill, explaining in his usual blunt way that the machinery he had found had survived on the South Island of New Zealand because "we don't chuck good stuff away, the way you lot do." He also pointed out, through dozens of examples, that in the nineteenth century there was much more contact between Britain and its antipodes than I had ever dreamed. A visit to Australia and New Zealand was common among educated persons, a kind of expanded version of the European Grand Tour. Charles Darwin was of course a visitor, on the *Beagle,* but so also were scores of less well-known scientists, world travelers, and gentlemen of the leisured class. Two of Charles Babbage's own sons were there in the 1850's.

The second item in the package was a batch of photographs of the machinery that Bill had found. It looked to me like what it was, a bunch of toothed cylinders and gears and wheels. They certainly resembled parts of the Analytical Engine, or the earlier Difference Machine, although I could not see how they might fit together.

Neither the letter nor the photographs were persuasive. Rather the opposite. I started to write in my mind the letter that said as much, but I hesitated for one reason: many historians of science know a lot more history than science, and few are trained computer specialists. But Bill was the other way round, the computer expert who happened to be fascinated by scientific history. It would be awfully hard to fool him— unless he chose to fool himself.

So I had another difficult letter to write. But I was spared the trouble, for what I could not dismiss or misunderstand was the third item in the package. It was a copy of a programming manual, handwritten, for the Babbage Analytical Engine. It was dated July 7, 1854. Bill said that he had the original in his possession. He also told me that I was the only person who knew of his discovery, and he asked me to keep it to myself.

And here, to explain my astonishment, I have to dip again into computer history. Not merely to the late 1950's, where we started, but all the way to 1840. In that year an Italian mathematician, Luigi Federico Menabrea, heard Babbage talk in Turin about the new machine that he was building. After more explanations by letter from Babbage, Menabrea wrote a paper on the Analytical Engine, in French, which was published in 1842. And late that year Ada Lovelace (Lord Byron's daughter; Lady Augusta Ada Byron Lovelace, to give her complete name) translated Menabrea's memoir, and added her own lengthy notes. Those notes formed the world's first software manual; Ada Lovelace described how to program the Analytical Engine, including the tricky techniques of recursion, looping, and branching.

So, twelve years before 1854, a programming manual for the Analytical Engine existed; and one could argue that what Bill had found in New Zealand was no more than a copy of the one written in 1842 by Ada Lovelace.

But there were problems. The document that Bill sent me went far beyond the 1842 notes. It tackled the difficult topics of indirect addressing, relocatable programs, and subroutines, and it offered a new language for programming the Analytical Engine—what amounted to a primitive assembler.

Ada Lovelace just might have entertained such advanced ideas, and written such a manual. It is possible that she had the talent, although all signs of her own mathematical notebooks have been lost. But she died in 1852, and there was no evidence in any of her surviving works that she ever blazed the astonishing trail defined in the document that I received from Bill. Furthermore, the manual bore on its first page the author's initials, L.D. Ada Lovelace for her published work had used her own initials, A.A.L.

I read the manual, over and over, particularly the final section. It contained a sample program, for the computation of the volume of an irregular solid by numerical integration—and it included a page of *output,* the printed results of the program.

At that point I recognized only three possibilities. FIrst, that someone in the past few years had carefully planted a deliberate forgery down near Dunedin, and led Bill Rigley to "discover" it. Second, that Bill himself was involved in attempting an elaborate hoax, for reasons I could not fathom.

I had problems with both those explanations. Bill was perhaps the most cautious, thorough, and conservative researcher that I had ever met. He was painstaking to a fault, and he did not fool easily. He was also the last man in the world to think that devising a hoax could be in any way amusing.

Which left the third possibility. Someone in New Zealand had built a version of the Analytical Engine, made it work, and taken it well beyond the place where Charles Babbage had left off.

I call that the third possibility, but it seemed at the time much more like the third *impossibility*. No wonder that Bill had asked for secrecy. He didn't want to become the laughingstock of the computer historians.

Nor did I. I took a step that was unusual in my relationship with Bill: I picked up the phone and called him in New Zealand.

"Well, what do you think?" he said, as soon as he recognized my voice on the line.

"I'm afraid to think at all. How much checking have you done?"

"I sent paper samples to five places, one in Japan, two in Europe, and two in the United States. The dates they assign to the paper and the ink range from 1840 to 1875, with 1850 as the average. The machinery that I found had been protected by wrapping in sacking soaked in linseed oil. Dates for that ranged from 1830 to 1880." There was a pause at the other end of the line. "There's more. Things I didn't have until two weeks ago."

"Tell me."

"I'd rather not. Not like this." There was another, longer silence. "You *are* coming out, aren't you?"

"Why do you think I'm on the telephone? Where should I fly to?"

"Christchurch. South Island. We'll be going farther south, past Dunedin. Bring warm clothes. It's winter here."

"I know. I'll call as soon as I have my arrival time."

And that was the beginning.

The wavy mop of fair hair had turned to gray, and Bill Rigley now favored a pepper-and-salt beard which with his weather-beaten face turned him into an approximation of the Ancient Mariner. But nothing else had changed, except perhaps for the strange tension in his eyes.

We didn't shake hands when he met me at Christchurch airport, or exchange one word of conventional greeting. Bill just said, as soon as we were within speaking range, "If this wasn't happening to me, I'd insist it couldn't happen to anybody," and led me to his car.

Bill was South Island born, so the long drive from Christchurch to Dunedin was home territory to him. I, in that odd but pleasant daze that comes after long air travel—after you deplane, and before the jetlag hits you—stared out at the scenery from what I thought of as the driver's seat (they still drive on the left, like the British).

We were crossing the flat Canterbury Plains, on a straight road across a level and empty expanse of muddy fields. It was almost three months after harvest—wheat or barley, from the look of the stubble— and there was nothing much to see until at Timaru we came to the coast road, with dull gray sea to the left and empty brown coastal plain on the right. I had visited South Island once before, but that had been a light-ning trip, little more than a tour of Christchurch. Now for the first time I began to appreciate Bill's grumbling about "overcrowded" Auckland on the North Island. We saw cars and people, but in terms of what I was used to it was a thin sprinkle of both. It was late afternoon, and as we drove farther south it became colder and began to rain. The sea faded from view behind a curtain of fog and drizzle.

We had been chatting about nothing from the time we climbed into the car. It was talk designed to avoid talking, and we both knew it. But at last Bill, after a few seconds in which the only sounds were the engine and the *whump-whump-whump* of windshield wipers, said: "I'm glad to have you here. There's been times in the past few weeks when I've seri-ously wondered if I was going off my head. What I want to do is this. Tomorrow morning, after you've had a good sleep, I'm going to show you *everything,* just as I found it. Most of it just *where* I found it. And then I want you to tell me what *you* think is going on."

I nodded. "What's the population of New Zealand?"

Without turning my head, I saw Bill's quick glance. "Total? Four million, tops."

"And what was it in 1850?"

"That's a hell of a good question. I don't know if anyone can really tell you. I'd say, a couple of hundred thousand. But the vast majority of those were native Maori. I know where you're going, and I agree totally. There's no way that anyone could have built a version of the Analytical Engine in New Zealand in the middle of the last century. The manufac-turing industry just didn't exist here. The final assembly could be done, but the subunits would have to be built and shipped in big chunks from Europe."

"From Babbage?"

"Absolutely not. He was still alive in 1854. He didn't die until 1871, and if he had learned that a version of the Analytical Engine was being built *anywhere,* he'd have talked about it nonstop all over Europe."

"But if it wasn't Babbage—"

"Then who was it? I know. Be patient for a few more hours. Don't try to think it through until you've rested, and had a chance to see the whole thing for yourself."

He was right. I had been traveling nonstop around the clock, and my brain was going on strike. I pulled my overcoat collar up around my ears, and sagged lower in my seat. In the past few days I had absorbed as much information about Babbage and the Analytical Engine as my head could handle. Now I needed to let it sort itself out, along with what Bill was going to show me. Then we would see if I could come up with a more plausible explanation for what he had found.

As I drifted into half-consciousness, I flashed on to the biggest puzzle of all. Until that moment I had been telling myself, subconsciously, that Bill was just plain wrong. It was my way of avoiding the logical consequences of his being *right.* But suppose he *were* right. Then the biggest puzzle was not the appearance of an Analytical Engine, with its advanced programming tools, in New Zealand. It was the *disappearance* of those things, from the face of the Earth.

Where the devil had they gone?

Our destination was a farmhouse about fifteen miles south of Dunedin. I didn't see much of it when we arrived, because it was raining and pitch-black and I was three-quarters asleep. If I had any thoughts at all as I was shown to a small, narrow room and collapsed into bed, it was that in the morning, bright and early, Bill would show me everything and my perplexity would end.

It didn't work out that way. For one thing, I overslept and felt terrible when I got up. I had forgotten what a long, sleepless journey can do to your system. For the past five years I had done less and less traveling, and I was getting soft. For another thing, the rain had changed to sleet during the night and was driving down in freezing gusts. The wind was blowing briskly from the east, in off the sea. Bill and I sat at the battered wooden table in the farm kitchen, while Mrs. Trevelyan pushed bacon, eggs, homemade sausage, bread, and hot sweet tea into me until I showed signs of life. She was a spry, red-cheeked lady in her middle sixties, and if she was surprised that Bill had finally brought someone else with him to explore Little House, she hid it well.

"Well, then," she said, when I was stuffed. "If you're stepping up the hill you'll be needing a mac. Jim put the one on when he went out, but we have plenty of spares."

Jim Trevelyan was apparently off somewhere tending the farm animals, and had been since dawn. Bill grinned sadistically at the look on my face. "You don't want a little rain to stop work, do you?"

I wanted to go back to bed. But I hadn't come ten thousand miles to lie around. The "step up the hill" to Little House turned out to be about half a mile, through squelching mud covered with a thin layer of sour turf.

"How did you ever find this place?" I asked Bill.

"By asking and looking. I've been into a thousand like this before, and found nothing."

We were approaching a solidly built square house made out of mortared limestone blocks. It had a weathered look, but the slate roof and chimney were intact. To me it did not seem much smaller than the main farmhouse.

"It's not called 'Little House' because it's *small*," Bill explained. "It's Little House because that's where the little ones are supposed to live when they first marry. You're seeing a twentieth century tragedy here. Jim and Annie Trevelyan are fourth generation farmers. They have five children. Every one went off to college, and not a one has come back to live in Little House and wait their turn to run the farm. Jim and Annie hang on at Big House, waiting and hoping."

As we went inside, the heavy wooden door was snug-fitting and moved easily on oiled hinges.

"Jim Trevelyan keeps the place up, and I think they're glad to have me here to give it a lived-in feel," said Bill. "I suspect that they both think I'm mad as a hatter, but they never say a word. Hold tight to this, while I get myself organized."

He had been carrying a square box lantern. When he passed it to me I was astonished by the weight—and he had carried it for half a mile.

"Batteries, mostly," Bill explained. "Little House has oil lamps, but of course there's no electricity. After a year or two wandering around out-of-the-way places I decided there was no point in driving two hundred miles to look at something if you can't see it when you get there. I can recharge this from the car if we have to."

As Bill closed the door the sound of the wind dropped to nothing. We went through a washhouse to a kitchen furnished with solid wooden chairs, table, and dresser. The room was freezing cold, and I looked longingly at the scuttle of coal and the dry kindling standing by the fireplace.

"Go ahead," said Bill, "while I sort us out here. Keep your coat on, though—you can sit and toast yourself later."

He lit two big oil lamps that stood on the table, while I placed layers of rolled paper, sticks, and small pieces of coal in the grate. It was thirty years since I had built a coal fire, but it's not much of an art. In a couple of minutes I could stand up, keep one eye on the fire to make sure it was catching properly, and take a much better look at the room. There were no rugs, but over by the door leading through to the bedrooms was a long strip of coconut matting. Bill rolled it back, to reveal a square wooden trapdoor. He slipped his belt through the iron ring and lifted, grunting with effort until the trap finally came free and turned upward on brass hinges.

"Storage space," he said. "Now we'll need the lantern. Turn it on, and pass it down to me."

He lowered himself into the darkness, but not far. His chest and head still showed when he was standing on the lower surface. I switched on the electric lantern and handed it down to Bill.

"Just a second," I said. I went across to the fireplace, added half a dozen larger lumps of coal, then hurried back to the trapdoor. Bill had already disappeared when I lowered myself into the opening.

The storage space was no more than waist high, with a hard dirt floor. I followed the lantern light to where a wooden section at the far end was raised a few inches off the ground on thick beams. On that raised floor stood three big tea-chests. The lantern threw a steady, powerful light on them.

"I told you you'd see just what I saw," said Bill. "These have all been out and examined, of course, but everything is very much the way it was when I found it. All right, hardware first."

He carefully lifted the lid off the right-hand tea-chest. It was half full of old sacks. Bill lifted one, unfolded it, and handed me the contents. I was holding a solid metal cylinder, lightly oiled and apparently made of brass. The digits from 0 through 9 ran around its upper part, and at the lower end was a cogwheel of slightly greater size.

I examined it carefully, taking my time. "It could be," I said. "It's certainly the way the pictures look."

I didn't need to tell him which pictures. He knew that I had thought of little but Charles Babbage and his Analytical Engines for the past few weeks, just as he had.

"I don't think it was made in England," said Bill. "I've been all over it with a lens, and I can't see a manufacturer's mark. My guess is that it was made in France."

"Any particular reason?"

"The numerals. Same style as some of the best French clockmakers—see, I've been working, too." He took the cylinder and wrapped it again, with infinite care, in the oiled sacking.

I stared all around us, from the dirt floor to the dusty rafters. "This isn't the best place for valuable property."

"It's done all right for a hundred and forty years. I don't think you can say as much of most other places." There was something else, that Bill did not need to say. This was a perfect place for valuable property— so long as no one thought that it had any value.

"There's nowhere near enough pieces here to make an Analytical Engine, of course," he went on. "These must have just been spares. I've taken a few of them to Auckland. I don't have the original of the programming manual here, either. That's back in Auckland, too, locked up in a safe at the university. I brought a copy, if we need it."

"So did I." We grinned at each other. Underneath my calm I was almost too excited to speak, and I could tell that he felt the same. "Any clue as to who 'L.D.' might be, on the title page?"

"Not a glimmer." The lid was back on the first tea-chest and Bill was removing the cover of the second. "But I've got another L.D. mystery for you. That's next."

He was wearing thin gloves and opening, very carefully, a folder of stained cardboard, tied with a ribbon like a legal brief. When it was untied he laid it on the lid of the third chest.

"I'd rather you didn't touch this at all," he said. "It may be pretty fragile. Let me know whenever you want to see the next sheet. And here's a lens."

They were drawings. One to a sheet, Indian ink on fine white paper, and done with a fine-nibbed pen. And they had nothing whatsoever to do with Charles Babbage, programming manuals, or Analytical Engines. What they did have, so small that first I had to peer, then use the lens, was a tiny, neat "L.D." at the upper right-hand corner of each sheet.

They were drawings of *animals,* the sort of multilegged, random animals that you find scuttling around in tidal pools, or hidden away in rotting tree bark. Or rather, as I realized when I examined them more closely, the sheets in the folder were drawings of *one* animal, seen from top, bottom, and all sides.

"Well?" said Bill expectantly.

But I was back to my examination of the tiny artist's mark. "It's not the same, is it. That's a different 'L.D.' from the software manual."

"You're a lot sharper than I am," said Bill. "I had to look fifty times before I saw that. But I agree completely, the 'L' is different, and so is the 'D.' What about the animal?"

"I've never seen anything like it. Beautiful drawings, but I'm no zoologist. You ought to photograph these, and take them to your biology department."

"I did. You don't know Ray Weddle, but he's a top man. He says they have to be just drawings, made up things, because there's nothing like them, and there never has been." He was carefully retying the folder, and placing it back in the chest. "I've got photographs of these with me, too, but I wanted you to see the originals, exactly as I first saw them. We'll come back to these, but meanwhile: next exhibit."

He was into the third tea-chest, removing more wrapped pieces of machinery, then a thick layer of straw. And now his hands were trembling. I hated to think how Bill must have sweated and agonized over this, before telling anyone. The urge to publish such a discovery had to be overwhelming; but the fear of being derided as part of the scientific lunatic fringe had to be just as strong.

If what he had produced so far was complex and mystifying, what came next was almost laughably simple—if it were genuine. Bill was lifting, with a good deal of effort, a bar, about six inches by two inches by three. It gleamed hypnotically in the light of the lantern.

"It is, you know," he said, in answer to my shocked expression. "Twenty-four carat gold, solid. There are thirteen more of them."

"But the Trevelyans, and the people who farmed here before that—"

"Never bothered to look. These were stowed at the bottom of a chest, underneath bits of the Analytical Engine and old sacks. I guess nobody ever got past the top layer until I came along." He smiled at me. "Tempted? If I were twenty years younger, I'd take the money and run."

"How much?"

"What's gold worth these days, U.S. currency?"

"God knows. Maybe three hundred and fifty dollars an ounce?"

"You're the calculating boy wonder, not me. So you do the arithmetic. Fourteen bars, each one weighs twenty-five pounds—I'm using avoirdupois, not troy, even though it's gold."

"One point nine-six million. Say two million dollars, in round numbers. How long has it been here?"

"Who knows? But since it was *under* the parts of the Analytical Engine, I'd say it's been there as long as the rest."

"And who owns it?"

"If you asked the government, I bet they'd say that they do. If you ask me, it's whoever found it. Me. And now maybe me and thee." He grinned, diabolical in the lantern light. "Ready for the next exhibit?"

I wasn't. "For somebody to bring a fortune in gold here, and just *leave* it . . ."

Underneath his raincoat, Bill was wearing an old sports jacket and jeans. He owned, to my knowledge, three suits, none less than ten years old. His vices were beer, travel to museums, and about four cigars a year. I could not see him as the Two Million Dollar Man, and I didn't believe he could see himself that way. His next words confirmed it.

"So far as I'm concerned," he said, "this all belongs to the Trevelyans. But I'll have to explain to them that gold may be the least valuable thing here." He was back into the second tea-chest, the one that held the drawings, and his hands were trembling again.

"These are what I *really* wanted you to see," he went on, in a husky voice. "I've not had the chance to have them dated yet, but my bet is that they're all genuine. You can touch them, but be gentle."

He was holding three slim volumes, as large as accounting ledgers. Each one was about twenty inches by ten, and bound in a shiny black material like thin, sandpapery leather. I took the top one when he held it out, and opened it.

I saw neat tables of numbers, column after column of them. They were definitely not the product of any Analytical Engine, because they were handwritten and had occasional crossings-out and corrections.

I flipped on through the pages. Numbers. Nothing else, no notes, no signature. Dates on each page. They were all in October 1855. The handwriting was that of the programming manual.

The second book had no dates at all. It was a series of exquisitely detailed machine drawings, with elaborately interlocking cogs and gears. There was writing, in the form of terse explanatory notes and dimensions, but it was in an unfamiliar hand.

"I'll save you the effort," said Bill as I reached for the lens. "These are definitely not by L.D. They are exact copies of some of Babbage's own plans for his calculating engines. I'll show you other reproductions if you like, back in Auckland, but you'll notice that these aren't *photographs*. I don't know what copying process was used. My bet is that all these things were placed here at the same time—whenever that was."

I wouldn't take Bill's word for it. After all, I had come to New Zealand to provide an independent check on his ideas. But five minutes were enough to make me agree, for the moment, with what he was saying.

"I'd like to take this and the other books up to the kitchen," I said, as I handed the second ledger back to him. "I want to have a really good look at them."

"Of course." Bill nodded. "That's exactly what I expected. I told the Trevelyans that we might be here in Little House for up to a week. We can cook for ourselves, or Annie says she'd be more than happy to expect us at mealtimes. I think she likes the company."

I wasn't so sure of that. I'm not an elitist, but my own guess was that the conversation between Bill and me in the next few days was likely to be incomprehensible to Annie Trevelyan or almost anyone else.

I held out my hand for the third book. This was all handwritten, without a single drawing. It appeared to be a series of letters, running on one after the other, with the ledger turned sideways to provide a writing area ten inches across and twenty deep. There were no paragraphs within the letters. The writing was beautiful and uniform, by a different hand than had penned the numerical tables of the first book, and an exact half-inch space separated the end of one letter from the beginning of the next.

The first was dated 12 October, 1850. It began:

My dear J.G., The native people continue to be as friendly and as kind in nature as one could wish, though they, alas, cling to their paganism. As our ability to understand them increases, we learn that their dispersion is far wider than we at first suspected. I formerly mentioned the northern islands, ranging from Taheete to Rarotonga. However, it appears that there has been a southern spread of the Maori people also, to lands far from here. I wonder if they may extend their settlements all the way to the great Southern Continent, explored by James Cook and more recently by Captain Ross. I am myself contemplating a journey to a more southerly island, with native assistance. Truly, a whole life's work is awaiting us. We both feel that, despite the absence of well-loved friends such as yourself, Europe and finance is "a world well lost." Louisa has recovered completely from the ailment that so worried me two years ago, and I must believe that the main reason for that improvement is a strengthening of spirit. She has begun her scientific work again, more productively, I believe, than ever before. My own efforts in the biological sciences prove ever more fascinating. When you write again tell us, I beg you, not of the transitory social or political events of London, but of the progress of science. It is in this area that L. and I are most starved of new knowledge. With affection, and with the assurance that we think of you and talk of you constantly, L.D.

The next letter was dated 14 December, 1850. Two months after the first. Was that time enough for a letter to reach England, and a reply to return? The initials at the end were again L.D.

I turned to the back of the volume. The final twenty pages or so were blank, and in the last few entries the beautiful regular handwriting had degenerated to a more hasty scribble. The latest date that I saw was October 1855.

Bill was watching me intently. "Just the one book of letters?" I said.

He nodded. "But it doesn't mean they stopped. Only that we don't have them."

"If they didn't stop, why leave the last pages blank? Let's go back upstairs. With the books."

I wanted to read every letter, and examine every page. But if I tried to do it in the chilly crawl space beneath the kitchen, I would have pneumonia before I finished. Already I was beginning to shiver.

"First impressions?" asked Bill, as he set the three ledgers carefully on the table and went back to close the trapdoor and replace the coconut matting. "I know you haven't had a chance to read, but I can't wait to hear what you're thinking."

I pulled a couple of the chairs over close to the fireplace. The coal fire was blazing, and the chill was already off the air in the room.

"There are *two* L.D.'s," I said. "Husband and wife?"

"Agreed. Or maybe brother and sister."

"One of them—the woman—wrote the programming manual for the Analytical Engine. The other one, the man—if it is a man, and we can't be sure of that—did the animal drawings, and he wrote letters. He kept fair copies of what he sent off to Europe, in that third ledger. No sign of the replies, I suppose?"

"You've now seen everything that I've seen." Bill leaned forward and held chilled hands out to the fire. "I knew there were two, from the letters. But I didn't make the division of labor right away, the way you did. I bet you're right, though. Anything else?"

"Give me a chance. I need to *read.*" I took the third book, the one of letters, from the table and returned with it to the fireside. "But they sound like missionaries."

"Missionaries, and scientists. The old nineteenth century mixture." Bill watched me reading for two minutes, then his urge to be up and doing something—or interrupt me with more questions—took over. His desire to talk was burning him up, while at the same time he didn't want to stop me from working.

"I'm going back to Big House," he said abruptly. "Shall I tell Annie we'll be there for a late lunch?"

I thought of the old farmhouse, generation after generation of life and children. Now there were just the two old folks, and the empty future. I nodded. "If I try to talk about this to them, make me stop."

"I will. If I can. And if I don't start doing it myself." He buttoned his raincoat, and paused in the doorway. "About the gold. I considered telling Jim and Annie when I first found it, because I'm sure that legally they have the best claim to it. But I'd hate for their kids to come hurrying home for all the wrong reasons. I'd appreciate your advice on timing. I hate to play God."

"So you want me to. Tell me one thing. What reason could there be for somebody to come down here to South Island in the 1850's, *in secret,* and never tell a soul what they were doing? That's what we are assuming."

"I'm tempted to say, maybe they found pieces of an Analytical Engine, one that had been left untouched here for a century and a half. But that gets a shade too recursive for my taste. And they did say what they were doing. Read the letters."

And then he was gone, and I was sitting alone in front of the warm fire. I stewed comfortably in wet pants and shoes, and read. Soon the words and the heat carried me away a hundred and forty years into the past, working my way systematically through the book's entries.

Most of the letters concerned religious or business matters, and went to friends in England, France, and Ireland. Each person was identified only by initials. It became obvious that the female L.D. had kept up her own active correspondence, not recorded in this ledger, and casual references to the spending of large sums of money made Bill's discovery of the gold bars much less surprising. The L.D.'s, whoever they were, had great wealth in Europe. They had not traveled to New Zealand because of financial problems back home.

But not all the correspondence was of mundane matters back in England. Scattered in among the normal chat to friends were the surprises, as sudden and as unpredictable as lightning from a clear sky. The first of them was a short note, dated January 1851:

Dear J.G., L. has heard via A.v.H. that C.B. now despairs of completing his grand design. In his own words, "There is no chance of the machine ever being executed during my own life and I am even doubtful of how to dispose of the drawings after its termination." This is a great tragedy, and L. is beside herself at the possible loss. Can we do anything about this? If it should happen to be no more than a matter of money . . .

And then, more than two years later, in April 1853:

Dear J.G., Many thanks for the shipped materials, but apparently there was rough weather on the journey, and inadequate packing, and three of the cylinders arrived with one or more broken teeth. I am enclosing identification for these items. It is possible that repair can be done here, although our few skilled workmen are a far cry from the machinists of Bologna or Paris. However, you would do me a great favor if you could determine whether this shipment was in fact insured, as we requested. Yours etc. L.D.

Cylinders, with toothed gearwheels. It was the first hint of the Analytical Engine, but certainly not the last. I could deduce, from other letters to J.G., that three or four earlier shipments had been made to New Zealand in 1852, although apparently these had all survived the journey in good condition.

In the interests of brevity, L.D. in copying the letters had made numerous abbreviations; w. did service for both "which" and "with," "for" was shortened to f., and so on. Most of the time it did not hinder comprehension at all, and reconstruction of the original was easy; but I cursed when people were reduced to initials. It was impossible to expand those back to discover their identity. A.v.H. was probably the great world traveler and writer, Alexander von Humboldt, whose fingerprint appears all across the natural science of Europe in the first half of the last century; and C.B. ought surely to be Charles Babbage. But who the devil was J.G.? Was it a man, or could it be a woman?

About a third of the way through the book, I learned that it was not just copies of letters sent to Europe. It probably began that way, but at some point L.D. started to use it also as a private diary. So by February 1854, after a gap of almost four months, I came across this entry:

22 February. Home at last, and thanks be to God that L. did not accompany me, for the seas to the south are more fierce than I ever dreamed, although the natives on the crew make nothing of them. They laugh in the teeth of the gale, and leap from ship to dinghy with impunity, in the highest sea. However, the prospect of a similar voyage during the winter months would deter the boldest soul, and defies my own imagination.

L. has made the most remarkable progress in her researches since my departure. She now believes that the design of the great engine is susceptible of considerable improvement, and that it could become capable of much more variation and power than even A.L. suspected. The latter, dear lady, struggles to escape the grasp of her tyrannical mother, but scarce seems destined to succeed. At her request, L. keeps her silence, and allows no word of her own efforts to be fed back to England. Were this work to become known, however, I feel sure that many throughout Europe would be astounded by such an effort—so ambitious, so noble, and carried through, in its entirety, by a woman!

So the news of Ada Lovelace's tragic death, in 1852, had apparently not been received in New Zealand. I wondered, and read on:

Meanwhile, what of the success of my own efforts? It has been modest at best. We sailed to the island, named Rormaurma by the natives, which my charts show as Macwherry or Macquarie. It is a great spear of land, fifteen miles long but very narrow, and abundantly supplied with penguins and other seabirds. However, of the "cold-loving people" that the natives had described to me, if I have interpreted their language correctly, there was no sign, nor did we find any of the artifacts, which the natives insist these people are able to make for speech and for motion across the water. It is important that the reason for their veneration of these supposedly "superior men" be understood fully by me, before the way of our Lord can be explained to and accepted by the natives.

On my first time through the book I skimmed the second half of the letter. I was more interested in the "remarkable progress" that L.D. was reporting. It was only later that I went back and pondered that last paragraph for a long time.

The letters offered an irregular and infuriating series of snapshots of the work that Louisa was performing. Apparently she was busy with other things, too, and could only squeeze in research when conscience permitted. But by early 1855, L.D. was able to write, in a letter to the same unknown correspondent:

Dear J.G., It is finished, and it is working!. And truth to tell, no one is more surprised than I. I imagine you now, shaking your head when you read those words, and I cannot deny what you told me, long ago, that our clever dear is the brains of the family—a thesis I will never again attempt to dispute.

It is finished, and it is working! I was reading that first sentence again, with a shiver in my spine, when the door opened. I looked up in annoyance. Then I realized that the room was chilly, the fire was almost out, and when I glanced at my watch it was almost three o'clock.

It was Bill. "Done reading?" he asked, with an urgency that made me sure he would not like my answer.

"I've got about ten pages to go on the letters. But I haven't even glanced at the tables and the drawings." I stood up, stiffly, and used the tongs to add half a dozen pieces of coal to the fire. "If you want to talk now, I'm game."

The internal struggle was obvious on his face, but after a few seconds he shook his head. "No. It might point you down the same mental path that I took, without either of us trying to do that. We both know how natural it is for us to prompt one another. I'll wait. Let's go on down to Big House. Annie told me to come and get you, and by the time we get there she'll have tea on the table."

My stomach growled at the thought. "What about these?"

"Leave them just where they are. You can pick up where you left off, and everything's safe enough here." But I noticed that after Bill said that, he carefully pulled the fireguard around the fender, so there was no possibility of stray sparks.

The weather outside had cleared, and the walk down the hill was just what I needed. We were at latitude 46 degrees South, it was close to the middle of winter, and already the sun was sloping down to the hills in the west. The wind still blew, hard and cold. If I took a beeline south, there was no land between me and the "great Southern Continent" that

L.D. had written about. Head east or west, and I would find only open water until I came to Chile and Argentina. No wonder the winds blew so strongly. They had an unbroken run around half the world to pick up speed.

Mrs. Trevelyan's "tea" was a farmer's tea, the main cooked meal of the day. Jim Trevelyan was already sitting, knife and fork in hand, when we arrived. He was a man in his early seventies, but thin, wiry, and alert. His only real sign of age was his deafness, which he handled by leaning forward with his hand cupped around his right ear, while he stared with an intense expression at any speaker.

The main course was squab pie, a thick crusted delicacy made with mutton, onions, apples, and cloves. I found it absolutely delicious, and delighted Annie Trevelyan by eating three helpings. Jim Trevelyan served us a homemade dark beer. He said little, but nodded his approval when Bill and I did as well with the drink as with the food.

After the third tankard I was drifting off into a pleasant dream state. I didn't feel like talking, and fortunately I didn't need to. I did my part by imitating Jim Trevelyan, listening to Annie as she told us about Big House and about her family, and nodding at the right places.

When the plates were cleared away she dragged out an old suitcase, full of photographs. She knew every person, and how each was related to each, across four generations. About halfway through the pile she stopped and glanced up self-consciously at me and Bill. "I must be boring you."

"Not a bit," I said. She wasn't, because her enthusiasm for the past was so great. In her own way she was as much a historian as Bill or me.

"Go on, please," added Bill. "It's really very interesting."

"All right." She blushed. "I get carried away, you know. But it's so good to have *youngsters* in the house again."

Bill caught my eye. Youngsters? Us? His grizzled beard, and my receding hairline. But Annie was moving on, backward into the past. We went all the way to the time of the first Trevelyan, and the building of Big House itself. At the very bottom of the case sat two framed pictures.

"And now you've got me," Annie said, laughing. "I don't know a thing about these two, though they're probably the oldest things here."

She passed them across the table for our inspection, giving one to each of us. Mine was a painting, not a photograph. It was of a plump man with a full beard and clear gray eyes. He held a churchwarden pipe in one hand, and he patted the head of a dog with the other. There was no hint as to who he might be.

Bill had taken the other, and was still staring at it. I held out my hand. Finally, after a long pause, he passed it across.

It was another painting. The man was in half-profile, as though torn between looking at the painter and the woman. He was dark-haired, and wore a long, drooping mustache. She stood by his side, a bouquet of flowers in her hands and her chin slightly lifted in what could have been an expression of resolution or defiance. Her eyes gazed straight out of the picture, into me and through my heart. Across the bottom, just above the frame, were four words in black ink: "Luke and Louisa Derwent."

I could not speak. It was Bill who broke the silence. "How do you come to have these two, if they're not family?"

His voice was gruff and wavering, but Annie did not seem to notice. "Didn't I ever tell you? The first Trevelyan built Big House, but there were others here before that. They lived in Little House—it was built first, years and years back, I'm not sure when. These pictures have to be from that family, near as I can tell."

Bill turned to glance at me. His mouth was hanging half-open, but at last he managed to close it and say, "Did you—I mean, are there *other* things? Things here, I mean, things that used to be in Little House."

Annie shook her head. "There used to be, but Granddad, Jim's dad, one day not long after we were married he did a big clear out. He didn't bother with the things you've been finding, because none of us ever used the crawl space under the kitchen. And I saved those two, because I like pictures. But everything else went."

She must have seen Bill and me subside in our chairs, because she shook her head and said, "Now then, I've been talking my fool head off, and never given you any afters. It's apple pie and cheese."

As she rose from her place and went to the pantry, and Jim Trevelyan followed her out of the kitchen, Bill turned to me.

"Can you believe it, I never thought to *ask?* I mean, I did ask Jim Trevelyan about things that used to be in Little House, and he said his father threw everything out but what's there now. But I left it at that. I never asked Annie."

"No harm done. We know now, don't we? Luke Derwent, he's the artist. And his wife, Louisa, she's the mathematician and engineer."

"And the *programmer*—a century before computer programming was supposed to exist." Bill stopped. We were not supposed to be discussing this until I had examined the rest of the materials. But we were saved from more talk by the return of Jim Trevelyan. He was holding a huge book, the size of a small suitcase, with a black embossed cover and brass-bound corners.

"I told you Dad chucked everything," he said. "And he did, near enough, threw it out or burned it. But he were a religious man, and he knew better than to destroy a Bible." He dropped it on the table, with a thump that shook the solid wood. "This come from Little House. If you want to take a look at it, even take it on back there with you, you're very welcome."

I pulled the book across to me and unhooked the thick metal clasp that held it shut. I knew, from the way that some of the pages did not lie fully closed at their edges, that there must be inserts. The room went silent, as I nervously leafed through to find them.

The disappointment that followed left me as hollow as though I had eaten nothing all day. There were inserts, sure enough: dried wildflowers, gathered long, long ago, and pressed between the pages of the Bible. I examined every one, and riffled through the rest of the book to make sure nothing else lay between the pages. At last I took a deep breath and pushed the Bible away from me.

Bill reached out and pulled it in front of him. "There's one other possibility," he said. "If their family happened to be anything like mine . . ."

He turned to the very last page of the Bible. The flyleaf was of thick, yellowed paper. On it, in faded multicolored inks, a careful hand had traced the Derwent family tree.

Apple pie and cheese were forgotten, while Bill and I, with the willing assistance of Jim and Annie Trevelyan, examined every name of the generations shown, and made a more readable copy as we went.

At the time it finally seemed like more disappointment. Not one of us recognized a single name, except for those of Luke and Louisa Derwent, and those we already knew. The one fact added by the family tree was that they were half brother and sister, with a common father. There were no dates, and Luke and Louisa were the last generation shown.

Bill and I admitted that we were at a dead end. Annie served a belated dessert, and after it the two of us wrapped the two pictures in waterproof covers (though it was not raining) and headed back up the hill to Little House, promising Annie that we would certainly be back for breakfast.

We were walking in silence, until halfway up the hill Bill said suddenly, "I'm sorry. I saw it, too, the resemblance to Eileen. I knew it would hit you. But I couldn't do anything about it."

"It was the expression, more than anything," I said. "That tilt to the chin, and the look in her eyes. But it was just coincidence, they're not really alike. That sort of thing is bound to happen."

"Hard on you, though."

"I'm fine."

"Great." Bill's voice showed his relief. "I wasn't going to say anything, but I had to be sure you were all right."

"I'm fine."

Fine, except that no more than a month ago a well-meaning friend of many years had asked me, "Do you think of Eileen as the love of your life?"

And my heart had dropped through a hole in the middle of my chest, and lodged like a cold rock in the pit of my belly.

When we reached Little House I pleaded residual travel fatigue and went straight to bed. With so much of Jim Trevelyan's powerful home brew inside me, my sleep should have been deep and dreamless. But the dead, once roused, do not lie still so easily.

Images of Eileen and the happy past rose before me, to mingle and merge with the Derwent picture. Even in sleep, I felt a terrible sadness. And the old impotence came back, telling me that I been unable to change in any way the only event in my life that really mattered.

With my head still half a world away in a different time zone, I woke long before dawn. The fire, well damped by Bill before he went to bed, was still glowing under the ash, and a handful of firewood and more coal was all it needed to bring it back to full life.

Bill was still asleep when I turned on the two oil lamps, pulled the three books within easy reach, and settled down to read. I was determined to be in a position to talk to him by the time we went down to Big House for breakfast, but it was harder than I expected. Yesterday I had been overtired, now I had to go back and reread some of the letters before I was ready to press on.

I had been in the spring of 1855, with some sort of Analytical Engine finished and working. But now, when I was desperate to hear more details, Luke Derwent frustrated me. He vanished for four months from the ledger, and returned at last not to report on Louisa's doings, but brimming over with wonder at his own doings.

21 September, 1855. Glory to Almighty God, and let me pray that I never again have doubts. L. and I have wondered, so many times, about our decision to come here. We have never regretted it, but we have asked if it was done for selfish reasons. Now, at last, it is clear that we are fulfilling a higher purpose.

Yesterday I returned from my latest journey to Macquarie Island. They were there! The "cold-loving people," just as my native friends assured me. In truth, they find the weather of the island too warm in all but the southern winter months of May to August, and were almost ready to depart again when our ship made landfall. For they are migrant visitors, and spend the bulk of the year in a more remote location.

The natives term them "people," and I must do the same, for although they do not hold the remotest outward aspect of humans, they are without doubt intelligent. They are able to speak to the natives, with the aid of a box that they carry from place to place. They possess amazing tools, able to fabricate the necessities of life with great speed. According to my native translators, although they have their more permanent base elsewhere in this hemisphere, they come originally from "far, far off." This to the Maori natives means from far across the seas, although I am less sure of this conclusion. And they have wonderful powers in medical matters. The Maori natives swear that one of their own number, so close to death from gangrenous wounds that death was no more than a day away, was brought to full recovery within hours. Another woman was held, frozen but alive, for a whole winter, until she could be treated and restored to health by the wonderful medical treatment brought from their permanent home by the "cold-loving people" (for whom in truth it is now incumbent upon me to find a better name). I should add that they are friendly, and readily humored me in my desire to make detailed drawings of their form. They asked me through my Maori interpreter to speak English, and assured me that upon my next visit they would be able to talk to me in my own language.

All this is fascinating. But it pales to nothing beside the one central question: Do these beings possess immortal souls? We are in no position to make a final decision on such a matter, but L. and I agree that in our actions we must assume that the answer is yes. For if we are in a position to bring to Christ even one of these beings who would otherwise have died unblessed, then it is our clear duty to do so.

It was a digression from the whole subject of the Analytical Engine, one so odd that I sat and stared at the page for a long time. And the next entry, with its great outburst of emotion, seemed to take me even farther afield.

Dear J.G., I have the worst news in the world. How can I tell you this— L.'s old disease is returned, and, alas, much worse than before. She said nothing to me, but yesterday I discovered bright blood on her handkerchief, and such evidence she could not deny. At my insistence she has visited a physician, and the prognosis is desperate indeed. She is amazingly calm about the future, but I cannot remain so sanguine. Pray for her, my dear friend, as I pray constantly.

The letter was dated 25 September, just a few days after his return from his travels. Immediately following, as though Luke could not contain his thoughts, the diary ran on:

Louisa insists what I cannot believe: that her disease is no more than God's just punishment, paid for the sin of both of us. Her calm and courage are beyond belief. She is delighted that I remain well, and she seems resigned to the prospect of her death as I can never be resigned. But what can I do? What? I cannot sit idly, and watch her slow decline. Except that it will not be slow. Six months, no more.

His travels among the colony of the "cold-loving people" were forgotten. The Analytical Engine was of no interest to him. But that brief diary entry told me a great deal. I pulled out the picture of Luke and Louisa Derwent, and was staring at it when Bill emerged rumple-haired from the bedroom.

This time, I was the one desperate to talk. "I know! I know why they came all the way to New Zealand."

He stared, at me and at the picture I was holding. "How can you?"

"We ought to have seen it last night. Remember the family tree in the Bible? It showed they're half brother and half sister. And *this.*" I held the painting out toward him.

He rubbed his eyes, and peered at it. "I saw. What about it?"

"Bill, it's a *wedding picture.* See the bouquet, and the ring on her finger? They couldn't possibly have married back in England, the scandal would have been too great. But here, where nobody knew them, they could make a fresh start and live as man and wife."

He was glancing across to the open ledger, and nodding. "Damn it, you're right. It explains everything. Their sin, he said. You got to that?"

"I was just there."

"Then you're almost at the end. Read the last few pages, then let's head down to Big House for breakfast. We can talk on the way."

He turned and disappeared back into the bedroom. I riffled through the ledger. As he said, I was close to the place where the entries gave way to blank pages.

There was just one more letter, to the same far-off friend. It was dated 6 October, 1855, and it was calm, even clinical.

Dear J.G., L. and I will in a few days be embarking upon a long journey to a distant island, where dwell a certain pagan native people; these are the Heteromorphs (to employ L.'s preferred term for them, since they are very different in appearance from other men, although apparently sharing our rational powers). To these beings we greatly wish to carry the blessings of Our Lord, Jesus Christ. It will be a dangerous voyage. Therefore, if you hear nothing from us within four years, please dispose of our estate according to my earlier instructions. I hope that this is not my last letter to you; however, should that prove to be the case, be assured that we talk of you constantly, and you are always in our thoughts. In the shared love of our Savior, L.D.

It was followed by the scribbled personal notes.

I may be able to deceive Louisa, and the world, but I do not deceive myself. God forgive me, when I confess that the conversion of the Heteromorphs is not my main goal. For while the message of Christ might wait until they return to their winter base on Macquarie Island, other matters cannot wait. My poor Louisa. Six months, at most. Already she is weakening, and the hectic blush sits on her cheek. Next May would be too late. I must take Louisa now, and pray that the Maori report of powerful Heteromorph medical skills is not mere fable.

We will carry with us the word of Christ. Louisa is filled with confidence that this is enough for every purpose, while I, rank apostate, am possessed by doubts. Suppose that they remain, rejecting divine truth, a nation of traders? I know exactly what I want from them. But what do I have to offer in return?

Perhaps this is truly a miracle of God's bounty. For I can provide what no man has ever seen before, a marvel for this and every age: Louisa's great Engine, which, in insensate mechanic operation, appears to mimic the thought of rational, breathing beings. This, surely, must be of inestimable value and interest, to any beings, no matter how advanced.

Then came a final entry, the writing of a man in frantic haste.

Louisa has at last completed the transformations of the information that I received from the Heteromorphs. We finally have the precise destination, and leave tomorrow on the morning tide. We are amply provisioned, and our native crew is ready and far more confident than I. Like Rabelais, "Je m'en vais chercher un grand peut-être." *God grant that I find it.*

I go to seek a great perhaps. I shivered, stood up, and went through to the bedroom, where Bill was pulling on a sweater.

"The Analytical Engine. They took it with them when they left."

"I agree." His expression was a strange blend of satisfaction and frustration. "But now tell me this. *Where did they go?*"

"I can't answer that."

"We have to. Take a look at this." Bill headed past me to the kitchen, his arms still halfway into the sleeves. He picked up the folder of drawings that we had brought from the crawl space. "You've hardly glanced at these, but I've spent as much time on them as on the letters. Here."

He passed me a pen-and-ink drawing that showed one of the creatures seen from the front. There was an abundance of spindly legs—I counted fourteen, plus four thin, whiskery antennae—and what I took to be two pairs of eyes on delicate protruding eyestalks.

Those were the obvious features. What took the closer second look were the little pouches on each side of the body, not part of the animal and apparently strapped in position. Held in four of the legs was a straight object with numbers marked along its length.

"That's a scale bar," said Bill, when I touched a finger to it. "If it's accurate, and I've no reason to think Luke Derwent would have drawn it wrong, his 'Heteromorphs' were about three feet tall."

"And those side pouches are for tools."

"Tools, food, communications equipment—they could be anything. See, now, why I told you I thought for the past couple of weeks I was going mad? To have this hanging in front of me, and have no idea how to handle it."

"That place he mentioned. Macquarie Island?"

"Real enough. About seven hundred miles south and west of here. But I can promise you, there's nothing there relating to this. It's too small, and it's been visited too often. Anything like the Heteromorphs would have been reported, over and over. And it's not where Derwent said he was going. He was heading somewhere else, to their more permanent base. Wherever that was." Bill's eyes were gleaming, and his mouth was quivering. He had been living with this for too long, and now he was walking the edge. "What are we going to *do?*"

"We're heading down to Big House, so Annie can feed us. And we're going to talk this through." I took his arm. "Come on."

The cold morning air cut into us as soon as we stepped outside the door. As I had hoped, it braced Bill and brought him down.

"Maybe we've gone as far as we can go," he said, in a quieter voice. "Maybe we ought to go public with everything, and just tell the world what we've found."

"We could. But it wouldn't work."

"Why not?"

"Because when you get right down to it, we haven't found *anything*. Bill, if it hadn't been you who sent me that letter and package of stuff, do you know what I would have said?"

"Yeah. Here's another damned kook."

"Or a fraud. I realized something else when I was reading those letters. If Jim and Annie Trevelyan had found everything in the crawl space, and shipped it to Christchurch, it would have been plausible. You can tell in a minute they know nothing about Babbage, or computers, or programming. But if you wanted two people who could have engineered a big fat hoax, you'd have to go a long way to find someone better qualified than the two of us. People would say, ah, they're computer nuts, and they're science history nuts, and they planned a fake to fool everybody."

"But we didn't!"

"Who knows that, Bill, other than me and you? We have nothing to *show*. What do we do, stand up and say, oh, yes, there really was an Analytical Engine, but it was taken away to show to these aliens? And unfortunately we don't know where they are, either."

Bill sighed. "Right on. We'd be better off saying it was stolen by fairies."

We had reached Big House. When we went inside, Annie Trevelyan took one look at our faces and said, "Ay, you've had bad news then." And as we sat down at the table and she began to serve hotcakes and sausage, "Well, no matter what it is, remember this: you are both young, and you've got your health. Whatever it is, it's not the end of the world."

It only seemed like it. But I think we both realized that Annie Trevelyan was smarter than both of us.

"I'll say it again," said Bill, after a moment or two. "What do we do now?"

"We have breakfast, and then we go back to Little House, and we go over *everything,* together. Maybe we're missing something."

"Yeah. So far, it's a month of my life." But Bill was starting to dig in to a pile of beef sausage, and that was a good sign. He and I are both normally what Annie called "good eaters," and others, less kind, would call gluttons.

She fed us until we refused another morsel of food, then ushered us out. "Go and get on with it," she said cheerfully. "You'll sort it out. I know you will."

It was good to have the confidence of at least one person in the world. Stuffed with food, we trudged back up the hill. I felt good, and optimistic. But I think that was because the materials were so new to me. Bill must have stared at them already until his eyes popped out.

Up at Little House once more, the real work started. We went over the letters and diary again, page by page, date by date, phrase by phrase. Nothing new there, although now that we had seen it once, we could see the evidence again and again of the brother-sister/husband-wife ambivalence.

The drawings came next. The Heteromorphs were so alien in appearance that we were often guessing as to the function of organs or the small objects that on close inspection appeared to be slung around their bodies or held in one of the numerous claws, but at the end of our analysis we had seen nothing to change our opinions, or add to our knowledge.

We were left with one more item: the ledger of tables of numbers, written in the hand of Louisa Derwent. Bill opened it at random and we stared at the page in silence.

"It's dated October 1855, like all the others," I said at last. "That's when they left."

"Right. And Luke wrote 'Louisa has completed the necessary calculations.' " Bill was scowling down at a list of numbers, accusing it of failing to reveal to us its secrets. "Necessary for what?"

I leaned over his shoulder. There were twenty-odd entries in the table, each a two or three digit number. "Nothing obvious. But it's reasonable to assume that this has something to do with the journey, because of the date. What else would Louisa have been working on in the last few weeks?"

"It doesn't look anything like a navigation guide. But it could be intermediate results. Worksheets." Bill went back to the first page of the ledger, and the first table. "These could be distances to places they would reach on the way."

"They could. Or they could be times, or weights, or angles, or a hundred other things. Even if they are distances, we have no idea what *units* they are in. They could be miles, or nautical miles, or kilometers, or anything."

It sounds as though I was offering destructive criticism, but Bill knew better. Each of us had to play devil's advocate, cross-checking the other every step of the way, if we were to avoid sloppy thinking and unwarranted assumptions.

"I'll accept all that," he said calmly. "We may have to try and abandon a dozen hypotheses before we're done. But let's start making them, and see where they lead. There's one main assumption, though, that we'll *have* to make: these tables were somehow used by Luke and Louisa Derwent to decide how to reach the Heteromorphs. Let's take it from there, and let's not lose sight of the only goal we have: we want to find the location of the Heteromorph base."

He didn't need to spell out to me the implications. If we could find the base, maybe the Analytical Engine would still be there. And I didn't need to spell out to him the other, overwhelming probability: chances were, the Derwents had perished on the journey, and their long-dead bodies lay somewhere on the ocean floor.

We began to work on the tables, proposing and rejecting interpretations for each one. The work was tedious, time-consuming, and full of blind alleys, but we did not consider giving up. From our point of view, progress of sorts was being made as long as we could think of and test new working assumptions. Real failure came only if we ran out of ideas.

We stopped for just two things: sleep, and meals at Big House. I think it was the walk up and down the hill, and the hours spent with Jim and Annie Trevelyan, that kept us relatively sane and balanced.

Five days fled by. We did not have a solution; the information in the ledger was not enough for that. But we finally, about noon on the sixth day, had a problem.

A *mathematical* problem. We had managed, with a frighteningly long list of assumptions and a great deal of work, to reduce our thoughts and calculations to a very unpleasant-looking nonlinear optimization. If it possessed a global maximum, and could be solved for that maximum, it might yield, at least in principle, the location on Earth whose probability of being a destination for the Derwents was maximized.

Lots of "ifs." But worse than that, having come this far neither Bill nor I could see a systematic approach to finding a solution. Trial-and-error, even with the fastest computer, would take the rest of our lives. We had been hoping that modern computing skills and vastly increased raw computational power could somehow compensate for all the extra information that Louisa Derwent had available to her and we were lacking. So far, the contest wasn't even close.

We finally admitted that, and sat in the kitchen staring at each other.

"Where's the nearest phone?" I asked.

"Dunedin, probably. Why?"

"We've gone as far as we can alone. Now we need expert help."

"I hate to agree with you." Bill stood up. "But I have to. We're out of our depth. We need the best numerical analyst we can find."

"That's who I'm going to call."

"But what will you tell him? What do we tell *anyone?*"

"Bits and pieces. As little as I can get away with." I was pulling on my coat, and picking up the results of our labors. "For the moment, they'll have to trust us."

"They'll have to be as crazy as we are," he said.

The good news was that the people we needed tended to be just that. Bill followed me out.

We didn't stop at Dunedin. We went all the way to Christchurch, where Bill could hitch a free ride on the university phone system.

We found a quiet room, and I called Stanford's computer science department. I had an old extension, but I reached the man I wanted after a couple of hops—I was a little surprised at that, because as a peripatetic and sociable bachelor he was as often as not in some other continent.

"Where are you?" Gene said, as soon as he knew who was on the line.

That may sound like an odd opening for a conversation with someone you have not spoken to for a year, but usually when one of us called the other, it meant that we were within dinner-eating distance. Then we would have a meal together, discuss life, death, and mathematics, and go our separate ways oddly comforted.

"I'm in Christchurch. Christchurch, New Zealand."

"Right." There was a barely perceptible pause at the other end of the line, then he said, "Well, you've got my attention. Are you all right?"

"I'm fine. But I need an algorithm."

I sketched out the nature of the problem, and after I was finished he said, "It sounds a bit like an underdetermined version of the Traveling Salesman problem, where you have incomplete information about the nodes."

"That's pretty much what we decided. We know a number of distances, and we know that some of the locations and the endpoint have to be on land. Also, the land boundaries place other constraints on the paths that can be taken. Trouble is, we've no idea how to solve the whole thing."

"This is really great," Gene said—and meant it. I could almost hear him rubbing his hands at the prospect of a neat new problem. "The way you describe it, it's definitely non-polynomial unless you can provide more information. I don't know how to solve it, either, but I do have ideas. You have to give me *all* the details."

"I was planning to. This was just to get you started thinking. I'll be on a midnight flight out of here, and I'll land at San Francisco about eight in the morning, your time. I can be at your place by eleven-thirty. I'll have the written details."

"That urgent?"

"It feels that way. Maybe you can talk me out of it over dinner."

After I rang off, Bill Rigley gave me a worried shake of his head. "Are you sure you know what you're doing? You'll have to tell him quite a bit."

"Less than you think. Gene will help, I promise." I had just realized what I *was* doing. I was cashing intellectual chips that I had been collecting for a quarter of a century.

"Come on," I said. "Let's go over everything one more time. Then I have to get out of here."

The final division of labor had been an easy one to perform. Bill had to go back to Little House, and make absolutely sure that we had not missed one scrap of information that might help us. I must head for the United States, and try to crack our computational problem. Bill's preliminary estimate, of 2,000 hours on a Cray Y-MP, was not encouraging.

I arrived in San Francisco one hour behind schedule, jet-lagged to the gills. But I made up for lost time on the way to Palo Alto, and was sitting in the living room of Gene's house on Constanza by midday.

True to form, he had not waited for my arrival. He had already been in touch with half a dozen people scattered around the United States and Canada to see if there was anything new and exciting in the problem area we were working. I gave him a restricted version of the story of Louisa Derwent and the vanished Analytical Engine, omitting all suggestion of aliens, and then showed him my copy of our analyses and the raw data from which we had drawn it. While he started work on that, I borrowed his telephone and wearily tackled the next phase.

Gene would give us an algorithm, I was sure of that, and it would be the best that today's numerical analysis could provide. But even with that best, I was convinced that we would face a most formidable computational problem.

I did not wait to learn just how formidable. Assuming that Bill and I were right, there would be other certainties. We would need a digital database of the whole world, or at least the southern hemisphere, with the land/sea boundaries defined. This time my phone call gave a less satisfactory answer. The Defense Mapping Agency might have what I needed, but it was almost certainly not generally available. My friend (with a guarantee of anonymity) promised to do some digging, and either finagle me a loaner data set or point me to the best commercial sources.

I had one more call to make, to Marvin Minsky at the MIT Media Lab. I looked at the clock as I dialed. One forty-five. On the East Coast it was approaching quitting time for the day. Personally, I felt long past quitting time.

I was lucky again. He came to the phone sounding slightly surprised. We knew each other, but not all that well—not the way that I knew Bill or Gene.

"Do you still have a good working relationship with Thinking Machines Corporation?" I asked.

"Yes." If a declarative word can also be a question, that was it.

"And Danny Hillis is still Chief Scientist, right?"

"He is."

"Good. Do you remember in Pasadena a few years ago you introduced us?"

"At the Voyager Neptune flyby. I remember it very well." Now his voice sounded more and more puzzled. No wonder. I was tired beyond belief, and struggling to stop my thoughts spinning off into non-sequiturs.

"I think I'm going to need a couple of hundred hours of time," I said, "on the fastest Connection Machine there is."

"You're talking to the wrong person."

"I may need some high priority access." I continued as though I had not heard him. "Do you have a few minutes while I tell you *why* I need it?"

"It's your nickel." Now the voice sounded a little bit skeptical, but I could tell he was intrigued.

"This has to be done in person. Maybe tomorrow morning?"

"Friday? Hold on a moment."

"Anywhere you like," I said, while a muttered conversation took place at the other end of the line. "It won't take long. Did you say tomorrow is *Friday?*"

I seemed to have lost a day somewhere. But that didn't matter. By tomorrow afternoon I would be ready and able to sleep for the whole weekend.

Everything had been rushing along, faster and faster, toward an inevitable conclusion. And at that point, just where Bill and I wanted the speed to be at a maximum, events slowed to a crawl.

In retrospect, the change of pace was only in our minds. By any normal standards, progress was spectacularly fast.

For example, Gene produced an algorithm in less than a week. He still wanted to do final polishing, especially to make it optimal for parallel processing, but there was no point in waiting before programming began. Bill had by this time flown in from New Zealand, and we were both up in Massachusetts. In ten days we had a working program and the geographic database was on-line.

Our first Connection Machine run was performed that same evening. It was a success, if by "success" you mean by that it did not bomb. But it failed to produce a well-defined maximum of any kind.

So then the tedious time began. The input parameters that we judged to be uncertain had to be run over their full permitted ranges, in every possible variation. Naturally, we had set up the program to perform that parametric variation automatically, and to proceed to the next case whenever the form of solution was not satisfactory. And just as naturally, we could hardly bear to leave the computer. We wanted to see the results of each run, to be there when—or if—the result we wanted finally popped out.

For four whole days, nothing emerged that was even encouraging. Any computed maxima were hopelessly broad and unacceptably poorly defined. We went on haunting the machine room, disappearing only for naps and hurried meals. It resembled the time of our youth, when hands-on program debugging was the only sort known. In the late night hours I felt a strange confluence of computer generations. Here we were, working as we had worked many years ago, but now we were employing today's most advanced machine in a strange quest for its own earliest ancestor.

We must have been a terrible nuisance to the operators, as we brooded over input and fretted over output, but no one said an unkind word. They must have sensed, from vague rumors, or from the more direct evidence of our behavior, that something very important to us was involved in these computations. They encouraged us to eat and rest; and it seemed almost inevitable that when at last the result that Bill and I had been waiting for so long emerged from the electronic blizzard of activity within the Connection Machine, neither of us would be there to see it.

The call came at eight-thirty in the morning. We had left an hour earlier, and were eating a weary breakfast in the Royal Sonesta Motel, not far from the installation.

"I have something I think you should see," said the hesitant voice of the shift operator. He had watched us sit dejected over a thousand outputs, and he was reluctant now to raise our hopes. "One of the runs shows a sharp peak. Really narrow and tight."

They had deduced what we were looking for. "We're on our way," said Bill. Breakfast was left half-eaten—a rare event for either of us—and in the car neither of us could think of anything to say.

The run results were everything that the operator had suggested. The two-dimensional probability density function was a set of beautiful concentric ellipses, surrounding a single land location. We could have checked coordinates with the geographic database, but we were in too much of a hurry. Bill had lugged a Times Atlas with him all the way from Auckland, and parked it in the computer room. Now he riffled through it, seeking the latitude and longitude defined by the run output.

"My God!" he said after a few seconds. "It's South Georgia."

After my first bizarre reaction—South Georgia! How could the Derwents have undertaken a journey to so preposterous a destination, in the southeastern United States?—I saw where Bill's finger lay.

South Georgia *Island*. I had hardly heard of it, but it was a lonely smear of land in the far south of the Atlantic Ocean.

Bill, of course, knew a good deal about the place. I have noticed this odd fact before, people who live *south* of the equator seem to know far more about the geography of their hemisphere than we do about ours. Bill's explanation, that there is a lot less southern land to know about, is true but not completely convincing.

It did not matter, however, because within forty-eight hours I too knew almost all there was to know about South Georgia. It was not very much. The Holy Grail that Bill and I had been seeking so hard was a desolate island, about a hundred miles long and twenty miles wide. The highest mountains were substantial, rising almost to ten thousand feet, and their fall to the sea was a dreadful chaos of rocks and glaciers. It would not be fair to say that the interior held nothing of interest, because no one had ever bothered to explore it.

South Georgia had enjoyed its brief moment of glory at the end of the last century, when it had been a base for Antarctic whalers, and even then only the coastal area had been inhabited. In 1916, Shackleton and a handful of his men made a desperate and successful crossing of the island's mountains, to obtain help for the rest of his stranded trans-Antarctic expedition. The next interior crossing was not until 1955, by a British survey team.

That is the end of South Georgia history. Whaling was the only industry. With its decline, the towns of Husvik and Grytviken dwindled and died. The island returned to its former role, as an outpost beyond civilization.

None of these facts was the reason, though, for Bill Rigley's shocked "My God!" when his finger came to rest on South Georgia. He was amazed by the *location*. The island lies in the Atlantic Ocean, at 54 degrees South. It is six thousand miles away from New Zealand, or from the Heteromorph winter outpost on Macquarie Island.

And those are no ordinary six thousand miles, of mild winds and easy trade routes.

"Look at the choice Derwent had to make," said Bill. "Either he went *west,* south of Africa and the Cape of Good Hope. That's the long way, nine or ten thousand miles, and all the way against the prevailing winds. Or he could sail *east.* That way would be shorter, maybe six thousand miles, and mostly with the winds. But he would have to go across the South Pacific, and then through the Drake Passage between Cape Horn and the Antarctic Peninsula."

His words meant more to me after I had done some reading. The southern seas of the Roaring Forties cause no shivers today, but a hundred years ago they were a legend to all sailing men, a region of cruel storms, monstrous waves, and deadly winds. They were worst of all in the Drake Passage, but that wild easterly route had been Luke Derwent's choice. It was quicker, and he was a man for whom time was running out.

While I did my reading, Bill was making travel plans.

Were we going to South Georgia? Of course we were, although any rational process in my brain told me, more strongly than ever, that we would find nothing there. Luke and Louisa Derwent never reached the island. They had died, as so many others had died, in attempting that terrible southern passage below Cape Horn.

There was surely nothing to be found. We knew that. But still we drained our savings, and Bill completed our travel plans. We would fly to Buenos Aires, then on to the Falkland Islands. After that came the final eight hundred miles to South Georgia, by boat, carrying the tiny two-person survey aircraft whose final assembly must be done on the island itself.

Already we knew the terrain of South Georgia as well as anyone had ever known it. I had ordered a couple of SPOT satellite images of the island, good cloud-free pictures with ten meter resolution. I went over them again and again, marking anomalies that we wanted to investigate.

Bill did the same. But at that point, oddly enough, our individual agendas diverged. His objective was the Analytical Engine, which had dominated his life for the past few months. He had written out, in full, the sequence of events that led to his discoveries in New Zealand, and to our activities afterward. He described the location and nature of all the materials at Little House. He sent copies of everything, dated, signed, and sealed, to the library of his own university, to the British Museum, to the Library of Congress, and to the Reed Collection of rare books and manuscripts in the Dunedin Public Library. The discovery of the Analytical Engine—or of any part of it—somewhere on South Georgia Island would validate and render undeniable everything in the written record.

And I? I wanted to find evidence of Louisa Derwent's Analytical Engine, and even more so of the Heteromorphs. But beyond that, my thoughts turned again and again to Luke Derwent, in his search for the "great perhaps."

He had told Louisa that their journey was undertaken to bring Christianity to the cold-loving people; but I knew better. Deep in his heart he had another, more selfish motive. He cared less about the conversion of the Heteromorphs than about access to their great medical powers. Why else would he carry with him, for trading purposes, Louisa's wondrous construct, the "marvel for this and every age"—a clanking mechanical computer, to beings who possessed machines small and powerful enough to serve as portable language translators.

I understood Luke Derwent completely, in those final days before he sailed east. The love of his life was dying, and he was desperate. Would he, for a chance to save her, have risked death on the wild southern ocean? Would he have sacrificed himself, his whole crew, and his own immortal soul, for the one-in-a-thousand chance of restoring her to health? Would *anyone* take such a risk?

I can answer that. Anyone would take the risk, and count himself blessed by the gods to be given the opportunity.

I want to find the Analytical Engine on South Georgia, and I want to find the Heteromorphs. But more than either of those, I want to find evidence that Luke Derwent *succeeded* in his final, reckless gamble. I want him to have beaten the odds. I want to find Louisa Derwent, frozen but alive in the still glaciers of the island, awaiting her resurrection and restoration to health.

I have a chance to test the kindness of reality. For in just two days, Bill and I fly south and seek our evidence, our own "great perhaps." Then I will know.

But now, at the last moment, when we are all prepared, events have taken a more complex turn. And I am not sure if what is happening will help us, or hinder us.

Back in Christchurch, Bill had worried about what I would tell people when we looked for help in the States. I told him that I would say as little as we could get away with, and I kept my word. No one was given more than a small part of the whole story, and the main groups involved were separated by the width of the continent.

But we were dealing with some of the world's smartest people. And today, physical distance means nothing. People talk constantly across the computer nets. Somewhere, in the swirling depths of GEnie, or across the invisible web of an Ethernet, a critical connection was made. And then the inevitable cross-talk began.

Bill learned of this almost by accident, discussing with a travel agent the flights to Buenos Aires. Since then I have followed it systematically.

We are not the only people heading for South Georgia Island. I know of at least three other groups, and I will bet that there are more.

Half the MIT Artificial Intelligence Laboratory seems to be flying south. So is a substantial fraction of the Stanford Computer Science Department, with additions from Lawrence Berkeley and Lawrence Livermore. And from southern California, predictably, comes an active group centered on Los Angeles. Niven, Pournelle, Forward, Benford, and Brin cannot be reached. A number of JPL staff members are mysteriously missing. Certain other scientists and writers from all over the country do not return telephone calls.

What are they all doing? It is not difficult to guess. We are talking about individuals with endless curiosity, and lots of disposable income. Knowing their style, I would not be surprised if the *Queen Mary* were refurbished in her home at Long Beach, and headed south.

Except that they, like everyone else, will be in a hurry, and go by air. No one wants to miss the party. These are the people, remember, who did not hesitate to fly to Pasadena for the Voyager close flybys of the outer planets, or to Hawaii and Mexico to see a total solar eclipse. Can you imagine them missing a chance to be in on the discovery of the century, of any century? Not only to *observe* it, but maybe to become part of the discovery process itself. They will converge on South Georgia in their dozens—their scores—their hundreds, with their powerful laptop computers and GPS terminals and their private planes and advanced sensing equipment.

Logic must tell them, as it tells me, that they will find absolutely nothing. Luke and Louisa Derwent are a century dead, deep beneath the icy waters of the Drake Passage. With them, if the machine ever existed, lie the rusting remnants of Louisa's Analytical Engine. The Heteromorphs, if they were ever on South Georgia Island, are long gone.

I know all that. So does Bill. But win or lose, Bill and I are going. So are all the others.

And win or lose, I know one other thing. After we, and our converging, energetic, curious, ingenious, sympathetic horde, are finished, South Georgia will never be the same.

This is for Garry Tee—who is a Professor of Computer Science at the University of Auckland;

—who is a mathematician, computer specialist, and historian of science;

—who discovered parts of Babbage's Difference Machine in Dunedin, New Zealand;

—who programmed the DEUCE *computer in the late 1950s, and has been a colleague and friend since that time;*

—who is no more Bill Rigley than I am the narrator of this story.

Charles Sheffield, December 31, 1991.

Afterword to "Georgia on My Mind"

This is the way that stories *really* get written. In December, 1991, I had lunch in New York with Stan Schmidt and Tina Lee of *Analog* magazine. Stan said he could use a good novelette about 10,000 words long. Since I had eaten lunch at his expense, I more or less promised him one and even gave him a title, "Georgia on My Mind." Then I had to write the story.

It came out as a strange mixture of autobiography and fiction. I felt when writing as though I was inventing very little. Almost every name is that of a real person. "Gene" in the story is Professor Gene Golub of Stanford, an old friend and for my money the world's best numerical analyst. Marvin Minsky is probably the world's top authority on Artificial Intelligence. Danny Hillis is Chief Scientist of Thinking Machines Corporation and the designer of the Connection Machine, and I was indeed introduced to him by Marvin Minsky in Pasadena at the Neptune flyby, just as the story says. "Bill Wrigley" is Garry Tee, who discovered bits of Babbage's Difference Machine in Dunedin, New Zealand; however, his physical appearance in the story matches that of another mathematician, Charles Broyden. The sf writers in the story are of course all real. DEUCE was an early and intractable digital computer, dear to the hearts of anyone who programmed it. Although the narrator of the story is not the same as its author, the two in this case are too close for comfort.

I finished the story on December 31st, 1991. It came out as 17,000 words, not 10,000. On the strength of that, I could claim that Stan Schmidt still owes me 7/10 of a lunch. On the other hand, since the story won the 1993 Nebula Award for Best Novelette, maybe I owe him one.

That is where this Afterword was supposed to end, but I have to say one other thing. Writing parts of this story caused me much personal pain and misery, what Kipling refers to as "the joy of an old wound waking." It is a depressing thought that internal bleeding may be the price of an honest story.